A MATTER OF CONSCIENCE

A MATTER OF CONSCIENCE

Rosemarie E. Bishop

To order additional copies of this book, contact:
Xlibris Corporation
1-888-7-XLIBRIS
www.Xlibris.com
Orders@Xlibris.com

CONTENTS

PART III

This book is dedicated to the men in my life.
My husband, Christopher,
My father, Steve,
My brother, David,
My father-in-law, Ray,
My nephew, Chris,
My godson, Nicholas,
and those who are with me in spirit;
My grandfather, Joe,
and my godfather, Uncle Bob.

ACKNOWLEDGMENTS

I would like to thank all those who guided my literary endeavors in some way. They include Cynthia Sterling at Lee Shore Literary Agency who led me to a series of three, Kathryn Williamson who started as a mentor, but quickly became a heart felt friend, and Patrick Porter, my high school Creative Writing teacher who taught me to study every sentence I write to be sure it says what I intend for it to say. I wish to thank my mother, Elaine Mandy, who was the first to edit this work, and who has always supported and encouraged my literary experiments with a portion of love for language and a lot of love for me. I wish to thank my father, Steve Mandy, for his eternal pride in all my artistic works and his heart full of love that helped me go further than I thought I could. I would like to thank Michelle and Ron Grucela for their friendship and for loaning me their Little People In the Woods to help build my web sites. Most of all, I wish to thank my husband, Christopher, for the home and the life that has allowed my spirit to soar, and the love that has kept me flying.

Realize the strength in the silence,
Feel the power in stillness,
Accept the wisdom in simplicity,
And you will find yourself.

PROLOGUE

November 25, 1997

Samuel walked across the frozen ground behind his house at the base of the Great Pyrenees mountains in France. He looked up at the half moon and noticed the clouds that drifted past, barely touching its shiny edge. He sighed. It was beautiful.

Diana was inside packing for their trip to the states. She had been excited for weeks. She loved America, the night life, the money, the people. Most of all, they both felt an attachment to a country that didn't exist when they had first met. They knew when the continent was founded and they had watched its development. Among all the countries involved, America grew to be their favorite. Diana had often asked if they might buy a home there as well, but Samuel always found a good reason why they should not. He couldn't bring himself to tell her the truth because he was certain it would mean the end of their relationship. How many centuries had it been? Almost six? And he still didn't know how he was ever going to tell Diana about her brother. Christian was the real reason for this trip, but Diana had no idea. She'd been so preoccupied with her travel plans that she never picked up his few stray thoughts. But Samuel had his own plans.

He knew when Christian moved to America in 1679, and he had deliberately kept Diana from finding out he was even alive. He'd done a good job. It had actually been quite easy since he and Christian hadn't spoken to each other since their argument over Diana in 1412. That was only two years after Samuel had saved his life by giving him immortal status as a vampire. Ah, he remembered it well.

Then, a year and a half ago he and Christian had occasion to catch up with each other. When Samuel had told Christian about Diana he was furious, as expected, but it didn't last long. Christian quickly settled down, excited at the chance to see her after all the time that had passed. Now that he'd told Christian, it was just a matter of time until Diana would find out. Christian had been very patient, so far. After all, they were eternal. But Christian had warned him that he would only wait so long. If Samuel didn't tell her, then Christian would. Samuel looked at the lights of the little town of Mirande off in the distance and sighed. So now it was Diana's turn to learn his secret and Samuel was scared to death.

He looked toward the house. He could see her walk past the bedroom window every few seconds with clothes in her hands. This time it was her pink, mohair sweater he'd bought for her on their last trip. He smiled. They weren't leaving for another week, and they were going to England first. But she was getting ready. He shook his head as he watched her clasp her palms together and look around the room. What was he going to do if he lost her because of the huge secret he'd kept? His heart seemed to roll over in his chest at the very thought. Why hadn't he just told her the truth as soon as she became immortal? He could have. Deep down he knew he should have.

Diana waved to him through the window, smiling like a little girl. He waved back and blew her a kiss. His heart hurt. She turned around to continue packing and he headed for the garden to sit down. How am I going to do this? he thought. When he reached the garden he sat on the concrete bench that allowed him to face the water fountain of the goddess Venus. It was a symbol of his and Diana's eternal love. His heart broke. He leaned forward, rested his head in his hands, and let his mind go blank.

PART I

"There's a time for everyone, if they'd only learn.
Every twist of the kaleidoscope moves us all in turn."

—Elton John

CHAPTER 1

December 5, 1997

The sun had not fully set when Christian Desmonde awoke, but his old friend, Samuel LaFleur, had recently taught him to tolerate more of it than he'd previously been able to and he took full advantage now. He reached toward the other side of the bed. Empty. Roni was already at work. Christian had spent many centuries by himself, but since he'd moved in with Veronica March it was different. There was a level of comfort in waking up alone knowing she would be home soon.

He stretched, got out of bed, and headed for the shower, a human need that he enjoyed more as a luxury than a necessity. There was a feeling of comfort that engulfed him when he was surrounded by the warm, liquid pressure. And it was one of the few instances when he was able to experience an extreme temperature difference. It made him feel more human. When he was done, he wrapped himself in the burgundy robe Roni had given him, and headed for the back deck, followed by their cats, Melvin and Sammi.

It was autumn, Roni's favorite time of year, but the weather was unseasonably warm. The sun was nearly finished setting amidst the oranges, russets, and reds that surrounded it in the late fall sky. Soon it would be engulfed in hues of deep blue and Christian would be able to feed quickly before Roni arrived home from work. For now, he would enjoy the little bit of sun that was left.

Christian reminisced a bit as he stood in the comfortable autumn air. He could not remember a time when his life had been better. Not since his mortal years and even those were too vague now to view in comparison. There was only one thing that still bothered him occasionally. He was a vampire and Roni, whom he loved more than all the world, was not. He had tried to understand her stubborn insistence in remaining mortal. He wanted so much to know they would always be together, like Samuel and Diana. But it seemed that Roni was sticking to her guns no matter what, and although Christian was frustrated by her decision, he couldn't help but admire her for her strength. It was difficult enough to keep and maintain a happy relationship. It was harder still to do the same for a relationship between a mortal and a vampire. In fact, it seemed impossible, but he knew it was their devotion to each other that made it possible. Roni's love for him was so intense it overwhelmed him. She had sacrificed so much, including her time in the sunlight in order to spend her life with him in his nights. He wondered how much that sacrifice might effect her health, but Roni repeatedly assured him that she enjoyed enough of the sun for her well-being, and asked him many times not to worry about such unimportant details.

Christian shook his head as he walked across the deck. He leaned on the railing and looked out through the woods that covered so much of their back yard. He thought back to a year and a half ago when Roni bought this house and asked him to move in with her. At first he'd chosen to wait because of a previous failed relationship. But even then he was already in love with Roni and knew it was inevitable. The relationship he'd had before her failed because of hatred. The woman he had loved, or thought he loved, was a vampire, but one who had taken his emptiness and his love and twisted them to meet her own needs. When he finally saw her selfishness he realized that she only wanted to be with him until he'd taught her all he could of a vampire's special talents. There was no love involved from her.

Christian pushed those thoughts out of his mind and sat down on the deck rail. He looked at the angel statues in the garden and shifted his thoughts back to Roni. She'd been so tired lately. The interior decorating business she ran from home in the evenings had been a major adjustment in her life so she could live on Christian's solar schedule, but it was taking a toll on her. She kept telling him she was fine, but he knew how hard she was pushing herself. He felt it with his vampire instincts and his heart that belonged only to her. She was driven and his blood would give her unending stamina, but she continued to insist she could do it herself.

Christian turned and walked back into the house with Roni still on his mind. He loved her more than the sunshine he had longed for centuries to see, more than the family he'd left so long ago, more than his own existence. And in loving her so completely he'd do anything to protect her, make her happy, and make her life easier. He'd do anything she asked of him. Anything. That included her frustrating request to remain mortal even though it meant he had to watch her suffer the human condition and eventually death, while his heart broke for her.

Christian shook off the sobering thoughts as he quickly checked the cat's food supply before returning to the bedroom to dress. He would feed alone tonight. He wanted to get it over with as quickly as possible and be home before Roni arrived. His friend, Samuel LaFleur, would not be accompanying him this time. He had gone back to Europe a month ago to take care of some personal business that was long over due.

When he was dressed, Christian walked the countrified roads of Norfolk, Massachusetts, and found himself missing Samuel's company more and more. Part of his friend's trip would take him home to his beloved France where he and Christian had first met. This time, however, there was a specific purpose for the trip home. Samuel was to finally tell Christian's sister, Diana, that her brother was still alive. Christian could imagine what the outcome would be. It had already been a year and a half since he'd found out about her and he'd been more than patient in giving Samuel the chance to tell her himself. He remembered how angry he had been with his old friend after learning that Samuel, his maker, had also turned Diana into one of their kind. It had happened in 1412AD! That was a mere two years after Christian himself had been changed, and only months after he'd left his home because of his growing shame at what he'd become. But he was partly to blame. He was so disgusted by his new existence he hadn't wanted his family to know the truth. He swore Samuel to secrecy, then left home. Christian found it hard to believe his sister had willingly accepted the change, even asked for it because her love for Samuel was supposedly so great. He would only believe it when he heard it from Diana's own lips. Assuming, of course, that Diana believed him when Samuel tried to convince her to go to the United States to see her brother whom she thought was dead. He imagined she'd probably be angry once she knew Samuel had kept Christian's existence a secret for the past five hundred eighty-six years. Once Diana was changed Samuel should have let her and Christian know about each other. It would have been the smarter thing to do, but he hadn't. Because of that, Samuel had caused himself a huge problem.

Christian chuckled to himself as he looked up into the clear night sky. "Ahhh, but you have to love him," he said out loud, remembering Diana's wild temper.

The air was turning cooler and damper with each passing minute, but Christian hardly felt the difference. He could feel the moisture clinging to his clothes, but the temperature change had little effect on him. He was hungry and growing hungrier by the minute. He needed to feed soon. He also needed to get home before Roni knew he was away. She was very perceptive and knew him well. She would realize immediately where he was.

Christian did his best to keep this side of his existence, the necessities for his survival, as far from Roni as possible. The reality of it was ugly, shameful, and embarrassing. The gruesome details had no place in her life. He was thankful, however, for the realistic way she approached the subject when it did wiggle its way out from the dark veil of secrecy behind which he performed the vampire's rites of longevity. Roni was no stranger to the only way

Christian could survive in the unique physical form he'd acquired so unexpectedly. For that unconditional acceptance, he loved her even more.

Voices.

He heard voices from a short distance away. Maybe only a mile or so, but to him that was a distance he could close in a matter of seconds.

In an instant, Christian was floating behind a young couple. He moved above them so he could watch from the air in silence as he hovered ten feet over their heads.

They walked along the side of the road. He knew one of them would be left alone soon enough. It was inevitable.

"I hate it when we have to go home," the girl said in a teenager's innocent, whiny voice.

The boy kissed her hair. "Someday we'll be going home together," he said. "Then we'll never have to be apart."

Christian was moved by the young lovers' sincerity. His own teenage years had been nothing like that. Endless days in the hot sun spent watching over the workers in the fields while they fertilized, harvested, planted anew, and on and on. The vineyard took its toll on his entire family and robbed his siblings of their younger years. There was no childhood in those days.

But times were different now.

Especially in America.

"Good night, Donny," the girl said while her arms hung loosely around the boy's shoulders.

"That's right," Donny said. He ran his hand along her back. "Good night, never good-bye."

He lowered his head to reach hers and they kissed a deeply passionate, high school kiss that lingered from the fear of being separated even long enough to get a good night's sleep. Christian was touched by the sentiment they shared to never say good-bye. He made it a point to remember that.

"I love you, Debbie." The boy sounded as if he'd breathed the words rather than spoken them.

"I love you too, Donny." The girl opened the door and walked into the house, then turned around and leaned out for one last kiss before giving in to her curfew. She stood in the doorway and watched as Donny walked across the porch and down the stairs to the sidewalk where he turned and blew her a kiss. She pretended to catch it and place it over her heart before sending one back to him.

Christian was touched by their sincerity, but saddened by the future that would shake them into reality. Such a serious display of emotions from babies. His five hundred years to their fifteen or sixteen, there was no comparison. These kids had no idea how serious life would get. Yet, for the moment, this teenage romance was the most important thing in all of creation to them. He envied them their naivete almost as much as he pitied them for the awakening they would face as they grew older, and most likely, apart.

Christian floated above the teenage boy as he walked down the quiet, country road. When they were near a wooded area that was almost completely pitch dark Christian sensed the boy's fear as well as his efforts to convince himself not to be afraid. He felt the thoughts emanate strongly from the boy's mind as he did his best to ignore the darkness, and the noises coming from places he couldn't see.

Christian floated down behind the teenager and began to walk on the ground so the boy could hear his footsteps. Donny stopped walking and cocked his head to listen. At that moment, Christian reached out and pinched the back of his neck, cutting off the brain's oxygen supply for only a second. That second was all it took for the teenager to completely lose consciousness.

Christian quickly went to work. He carried the boy deep into the woods where he could drink his fill in peace and quiet.

Ah, the blood of the young, he thought as he fed. There's truly nothing like it.

If Samuel had been with him, they would have taken both of the kids for nourishment even before they had reached the girl's house. They would've drank their fill and then deposited them together at one or the other's home leaving them to wake up in scandal or in secret, but either way, in a heap of trouble. And they would've laughed between themselves for the predicament in which they had put the young lovers, regretting only that they wouldn't be there to witness the chaos.

When Christian was fully sated he began to fly the teenager home to safety. It was easy to quickly learn every detail about the mortals on whom he fed. The life force in their blood connected Christian directly to their souls. Their memories. Their secrets. Sometimes the experience was quite frightening. Other times, enlightening. But always unpredictable.

When Christian was at the boy's home, he found the bedroom windows were closed, but unlocked. That made it easy for him to enter the young man's room and deposit him safely in his own bed. The boy would awaken feeling weak and achy in the morning, but his parents would probably decide it had been a twenty-four hour bug when their son was suddenly feeling better later that day.

Christian left the boy's house the same way he'd entered. He flew home like the wind in order to freshen up, start a fire in the fireplace, and be waiting when Roni got home. He felt wonderful; strong and energetic.

As he reached their house, Roni was pulling her Tracker into the driveway. Christian dropped out of the air and finished the jaunt home on his feet, walking up the driveway right behind her.

Roni slipped out of the vehicle and held on to the door for support as she reached in and dragged the many cumbersome, paper bags from the car and placed them on the ground. "Let me help you, Sweetheart." Christian quickened his pace to her side and took the bags from her.

"Oh, thank you," Roni said, a little out of breath. "Those Brandisons really wore me out tonight. They keep changing their minds. They fight about everything, and waste so much time. Maybe I should've been a marriage counselor instead of an interior decorator," she said, giving Christian a wink. She closed the car door, then repositioned her purse over her shoulder. "I spend more time playing 'domestic referee' than I do going over color schemes with them."

"Well, you're home now," Christian said. He leaned down and kissed her warmly on the lips, hoping she wouldn't taste his latest meal. "Let's get these things inside for you."

"Feeding?" Roni mused as she led him up the driveway and into the house.

Christian looked at her, trying to hide his alarm, but the serious look on her face wavered slightly, and he knew she was simply guessing. He had always done his best to keep this distasteful side of his existence from her.

"Or were you just out for an evening stroll?" she asked.

He smiled. "Both," he said honestly. He put her things on the kitchen table, then took her in his arms and held her close to him. "Why do you work?" he asked, burying his face in her shoulder-length, blonde hair. He loved the way the golden strands just reached the top of her shoulders. "You know you don't have to. Why do you push yourself like you do?"

"I enjoy what I do," Roni said, sounding defensive. "Besides, you know I don't want to be a sponge off your family's hard earned money. This is a partnership. Remember?"

"I remember everything you tell me," Christian said. He loosened his hold on her so they could look at each other. Her sparkling blue-grey eyes melted his heart. "I just don't agree with a lot of it. You make life so much harder than it has to be."

"If you weren't a vampire, your life would be just as hard, Christian." Roni sat down at the table and emptied the bags. She then began to organize the contents in neat piles according to what belonged where. Papers had their own place as did samples of fabric, color charts, and paint swatches.

"The fact is I am a vampire and because of it, neither one of our lives has to be hard," he said. "Maybe this was the plan, Roni. Maybe, God planned it this way."

"For what?" Roni asked. She began repacking her bags, keeping like items together.

"Maybe, so you wouldn't have to work so hard," he said. "Maybe, He wanted you to be able to relax more, so He sent me to you."

She stopped what she was doing and looked up at him. "Like a gift?"

"Something like that."

She stared at him for a few seconds, then gave him a mischievous smile. "Maybe it's a test." She raised her eyebrows and made ghostly gestures with her hands as if to mock him.

"Stop it, Roni!" He was hurt by her ridicule. "You're the one who taught me to trust Him. Don't mock me for doing it." Christian turned around and walked into the living room. He began to stack logs in the fireplace, sulking to himself as he worked. He was sincere when he thought that maybe he was a gift to Roni. He wanted to be a gift to her. He wanted to be anything and everything that was important to her.

"I'm sorry, Sweetie." Roni approached him from behind and put her arms around his shoulders. "I wasn't mocking you. I just don't think it's right to take the easy way out of something if it isn't really ethical. You know?"

Christian shrugged. "I guess."

"I love you, Christian," she sighed. "Let's not talk about me working too hard, or living off your family's money, or anything like that, alright?"

Christian didn't say a word, but he turned around slowly and held her close to him. She would know the subject was dropped for the time being. She'd know because he did everything she asked, even at his own expense. "Why don't you go get comfortable while I finish with the fire?" Christian said gently. "I'll have it roaring for us when you get back."

Roni turned and headed for the bedroom, but Christian suddenly stopped her. "Did you have anything to eat?"

"No," she said over her shoulder. "I didn't have any time."

"What would you like?" Christian called to her. He was fully prepared to cook Duck L'Orange' if she had a taste for it, even though the smell of cooking flesh would make him ill.

"Nothing."

He ignored her answer. "What would you like?" he asked, again. He lit the long wooden match and touched it to the old, dried pine cones that he had put in the fireplace. Almost immediately the house filled with the scent of fresh pine trees.

Roni walked back in the room, pulling her blue sweatshirt on over her head. "I'm not hungry," she said, straightening the hem of her shirt. "But I'm thirsty." She smoothed her hair as he headed into the kitchen.

Christian sat back on his heels and watched the pine cones burn. Flames spread to the logs placed carefully around them. The scent of fresh pine grew stronger as the sap that was stuck to the cones began to melt away, then burn.

He suspected Roni was sneaking something to eat while she was in the kitchen. She didn't like to eat in front of him because she was afraid it made them both glaringly aware of the differences between them. But Christian believed such an act only punctuated their differences that would otherwise have been overshadowed by familiarity if both of them went about their normal, functional routines. Once a person becomes accustomed to something, they no longer notice it quite as much as they did at first. For Roni and Christian, such familiarity would eventually blur their differences, even merge them to some extent. But Roni didn't see it that way.

Christian was still staring at the fire when Roni walked back through the room on her way to the bathroom. His vampire instincts told him she had not eaten while she was in the kitchen. Worried, he went to the refrigerator and took out a bottle of Sangria and a crock of Cheddar/Bleu cheese spread. He then emptied three partially empty boxes of crackers that he found in the cupboard and prepared a plate with Roni's favorite cheese dip in the middle surrounded by all of the different kinds of crackers. He set the plate on the table while he located two wine glasses and a butter knife with which to spread the cheese. Then, carefully balancing it all, he set a place on the floor in front of the fire and relaxed while he waited for Roni. He had to guard the snack plate from the cats who wanted nothing more than to dive head first into the crock of cheese. He had trained Melvin to sit and wait patiently for his treats, but Sammi was bold as well as cute, cuddly, and affectionate. Christian could not get mad at her. He had learned very early that the one thing she loved almost as much as food was attention. So he held her on her back in the crook of his arm like a baby until Roni was finished washing. It served the purpose.

Click. Whir.

"What the hell?" Christian turned toward the noise.

Roni began to laugh, camera in hand. "I couldn't resist," she said. She sat down beside him and immediately dipped a cracker into the cheese. "You looked adorable with Sammi lying in your arms like that."

"Very funny!" Christian said, gently placing the cat on the floor beside him.

He opened the Sangria, filled the two glasses, then handed one to Roni. "It's good for the blood," he said with a mischievous smile.

"I'll bet it is." Roni took a sip, then sat back.

Christian stared at his glass, marveling at the way the flames brought life to the liquid. "What do you think is happening with Samuel?" he asked.

Roni shook her head. "I don't know," she said. "You miss him, don't you?"

"Yes, I do," he said. "I wish I hadn't lost so much time with him. I should never have left France the way I did back then. I was jealous over him and Diana, and ashamed of what he'd turned me into. Look at all the time I lost because of my stubbornness and pride."

Christian sipped his wine, then looked into the fire. His eyes never blinked as he watched the logs burn and the flames roar up the brick tunnel into the cold autumn air outside. Staring into the fire was an easy way to clear his head so he could concentrate on reaching Samuel telepathically. He'd been trying to contact his friend for the past few days, but to no avail.

Roni watched him in silence while she petted Melvin who had crawled onto her lap.

Christian shook his head, and looked at the floor. "Nothing," he said. "I can't read his thoughts and I can't seem to get a message to him. It's frustrating. I don't know what he's up to or when he's coming back."

"Oh, Honey." Roni leaned into him, snuggling under his arm. Melvin, who rolled to the floor in the process, waited patiently until she was settled before reclaiming his place in her lap. "I'm sure everything will be all right," she said. "Diana will be thrilled to know you're alive just like you were thrilled to know she was alive." Roni reached over to spread cheese on another cracker, then split it and gave half to Melvin.

"If you remember," Christian said, "I was furious with him. If my very life hadn't been in danger a year and a half ago, he would never have come forward to tell me about Diana. It's true that he was gallant to come to my rescue the way he did, but he was cowardly and selfish to have avoided me and kept such a secret for five centuries just to try to 'have his cake and eat it too' with my sister."

"Maybe, he was," Roni said. "But in the larger scheme of things, it has turned out all right. I'm sure your sister will calm down once she has a chance to think about it. And if she's angry with Sam, then I think she has every right to be. It won't last, though." She wrapped her arms around his waist and closed her eyes.

"Then why is he taking so long to tell her?" Christian asked.

"Why don't you tell her yourself?" Roni looked at him and smiled.

Christian sighed and shook his head. "It's not my place."

"Then you'll have to be patient," she said. "Samuel's nervous. It's understandable. He's in a pickle, but I don't think it's as serious as you two make it out to be. You're her brother. That's the bottom line."

Christian nodded. "I guess you're right," he said, then deliberately tried to relax. "Tired?" he asked her. He sat up and began to caress the tension from her shoulders.

"No." She sighed. "Content."

"That's nice," Christian said. He dipped a cracker in the cheese, and fed it to her triggering her taste buds again in the process. She sat up and began to munch in earnest, sharing her meal with both cats until every last cracker was gone and the cats sat together bathing themselves on the floor in the middle of the room.

"What shall we do this evening?" Christian asked. "The sky's the limit. No traffic to fight, no lines to stand in."

"And blissful quiet everywhere," Roni said. "Maybe, after the fire dies down, we could fly over to that little pub up the road that's open late on Friday nights. It should be fun."

"Are you up to it?" he asked.

"Believe it or not, I am." She looked at him and smiled. "The Brandisons didn't wear me out that much."

"Great!" Christian kissed her on the forehead. "It's a date, then."

CHAPTER 2

December 6, 1997

Roni checked the time. It was three o'clock in the afternoon and she was lying down for the third time that day, trying very hard to ignore the telephone. The answering machine should pick up the call. She needed to figure out what was keeping her awake. She and Christian had a wonderful time at the pub last night. They had played darts for two hours until the place was ready to close. By that time she was yawning profusely and true slumber seemed only a breath away. But once they were home, she couldn't fall asleep. She would doze off for awhile, then be wide awake, again. She had walked around the house, sat with the cats, laid down, got up again, worked on room designs for the Brandisons, and simply sat thinking. But no matter what she did, sleep eluded her.

"Agghhhh! I'm not supposed to sleep at all today," she complained to Melvin, who lay dreaming at her feet. She listened while the answering machine played its greeting. But then the message began.

"Christian! Are you there? Pick up the phone. It's me. Samuel."

Roni sat bolt upright. She had to get the phone before the answering machine cut off the call. She could not ignore this one. She ran to the kitchen and grabbed the receiver. "Hello!" she yelled.

"Roni?"

"Yes, Sam. Where are you?"

"We're in England," he said. "Is Christian there?"

Roni looked at her watch. "What time is it in England?" A

momentary hesitation on the other end of the line told Roni she had made her point.

"Oh, boy," Samuel said. "I'm sorry I woke you. These time changes still confuse me."

Roni chuckled softly. She couldn't really be angry at Samuel. It wasn't his fault that she was still awake. "It's alright, Sam," she said. "Can he call you when he wakes up?"

"No," Samuel said. "But you can give him a message for me, if you would."

"Of course, I will."

"Tell him that Diana and I are coming to see you two for the Christmas season," Samuel said. "In fact, we should be leaving from here in just a few days."

"That's wonderful," she said. "So, you told Diana everything and she isn't angry? How did she take it?"

Samuel did not answer. His silence gave Roni a nervous premonition. "Sam, are you still there?" She hoped she was wrong, but she knew enough about Samuel to know better.

"I'm here," he said.

"Well," Roni said. "Did you tell Diana about Christian or didn't you? Is she all right with it?" She was desperate to hear the answer she knew Christian would want.

Again, Samuel did not reply and she knew her instincts were right.

"You didn't tell her! You coward!" she said. "What does she think you're coming to the states for?"

"Just a trip."

Roni began to tap her nails on the table. "Just a trip?" she asked. "I don't believe the way you do things. Don't you think you should tell her first?"

"No, I don't," he said. "I don't want to lose her. Roni, you don't know how angry she can get."

Roni's anger turned to compassion when she heard the fear in Samuel's voice. "You shouldn't be afraid of someone you love, Sam. That's all she can do is get mad."

"I'm not afraid of her," he said. "I'm afraid to lose her. There's a difference. Even if she only went away to cool off for a while, I still couldn't stand it. We have eternity, Roni. A little while is quite a bit different for us than it would be for you."

"That's not the point, Sam." Roni shook her head in disbelief. "You're really something. Well, give me the details then. When are you going to be here?"

"We're arriving in Boston on the thirteenth and we'll be staying through to the first week of January. We'll be staying at the Bostonian Hotel in Cambridge."

"That's all the way in the city!" Roni was hurt to think they would stay in a hotel rather than with her and Christian. "It's over twenty miles away. Change your plans and stay with us."

"I can't," Samuel said. "Diana doesn't know anything about you two."

"Well then, it might be a good way to break it to her," Roni said. "Or at least pick a hotel closer to us."

"We'll see what happens when we get there, but for now the plans can stay as they are." Samuel's tone was decisive. "Let Christian know, will you?"

"Good enough, Sam," Roni said. "I'll tell him. And you'd better think of a way to tell Diana that her brother is still alive. You don't want to give her a heart attack from the shock of seeing him without some kind of warning."

Samuel chuckled. "She's a vampire, Roni. She cannot have a heart attack."

Roni felt silly and smiled to herself. "Sorry."

"Forget it," Samuel said. "Just tell Christian I'll try to call again before the thirteenth. 'Til then, Au Revoir."

"Bye, Sam." Roni felt disheartened as she hung up the phone. There was no way she'd be able to sleep now. She knew Christian would be angry with Samuel once she told him what was happening. "What am I going to do?" she said aloud. She fiddled with the flowers on the table and tapped on the vase while she tried to stay calm. She should just tell him, but he was going to be angry.

She walked to the dining room window that overlooked the backyard and the woods beyond. The snow was coming down in soft flurries that floated slowly to the ground. It had a calm, hypnotic effect. She stood in the window and allowed visions of Christian's first meeting with Diana to roam freely through her head. What would it be like to see someone after five hundred years? What would it be like just to live that long?

Sammi wove her furry body gently through Roni's ankles and purred so loud it brought Roni out of her daydreams. She stooped down to pet her. "There's never a dull moment with Christian, is there?" she said to the cat.

Roni stood up and walked to the refrigerator. "Come on," she said. "A little snack should do us all some good." She poured a saucer of milk for the felines and a small glass for herself that she warmed in the microwave the way her grandmother used to do on the stove when she was a little girl. Roni needed sleep and she was willing to try anything.

She finished drinking her milk, then headed for the bedroom to try, once more, to doze off for the day.

She lay on her back and began to use the same breathing techniques she used in meditation as a means to relax her body and calm her mind.

She inhaled slowly to the count of four, held her breath a second, then released it to the count of three. She continued in this fashion concentrating on the flow of blood through her veins beginning with her feet and working her way up and through all of her limbs. Finally, she could feel the full course of her blood throughout her body. It gave the illusion of floating in mid-air.

Once her body was fully relaxed and her breathing slowed to a comfortable pace, Roni began to let her mind wander as if she were watching her thoughts play in front of her eyes like a movie. She imagined Samuel with Diana by his side packing their bags and planning their trip to America.

She pictured the first meeting after five hundred years between brother and sister.

She relived the Brandison's fight over which shade of green would look best in the dining room and felt her own agitation at their incessant bickering as if she were there watching it again.

She saw herself telling Christian about Samuel's trip. Then she recalled the visit with her dear friend, Father Larry Donnelly, on the day when he and Christian had first met. For some reason, that was her strongest thought. She had asked Father Larry to bless her new house two weeks ago. She remembered how nervous Christian had been about meeting Father Larry that day.

Roni noticed how Christian stared out the window as if he were deep in thought. "What's the matter, Honey?"

Christian didn't move. He continued to look out at the backyard. "I suppose I'm nervous about meeting the good Father," he said.

Roni stood beside him, then put her arm around his waist and smiled. "I know you are," she said. "But there's really nothing to worry about. I don't see how he could know you're a vampire unless you were to tell him yourself."

Christian turned to face her. "It's not that," he said. "This man is like family to you. You mean a lot to each other. I wouldn't want to disappoint either of you." He turned back toward the window. "Maybe it would be best if I went out for awhile."

Roni gently rubbed Christian's back and sighed. "Don't be silly." she said. "Father Larry likes everybody."

At that moment the doorbell rang. Christian flashed Roni a look of alarm as she went to answer it.

"Just be yourself and relax," she said over her shoulder. When she opened the front door Father Larry stood smiling at her with the Santa Claus twinkle in his blue eyes that had come to be his trademark.

"Hello, Father!" Roni hugged the priest, then motioned for him to come in.

"Hello, child," Father Larry said. "How've you been?" He stepped into the foyer and held Roni an arm's length away while he looked her in the eyes. He crooked his head sideways. "You look tired," he said. "You've been putting in those long hours with your business, haven't you? You know you have to relax, child."

Roni smiled. "It is mine," she said. "Someone's got to keep it up."

"Well, well." Father Larry stepped further into the room. "Except for that, you are simply glowing with joy." He turned his attention to Christian. "Is this the gentleman who put the sparkle in your eyes?"

Roni thought she caught a suspicious tone in his question. "Yes, I suppose he is," she said, smiling at Christian. "Father Larry, this is Christian Desmonde."

Both men reached out to shake each other's hand. Roni could have sworn she saw Father Larry twitch when he felt Christian's touch, but she did her best to dismiss it. "Christian," she continued, "this is Father Larry."

The two men stared at each other for a few seconds while they exchanged the usual greetings. There seemed to be more transpiring than just a simple introduction. Roni hadn't been concerned at all about the priest meeting the vampire. She had grown so accustomed to Christian and Samuel that she didn't think much about their true natures anymore. But now, it occurred to her that she probably should have given it a little more thought.

Father Larry smiled. "Will this house blessing be alright with you, Christian?" He looked embarrassed. "I mean, are you comfortable being around this sort of thing?"

Roni was stunned.

"Yes, Father." Christian nodded. "It will be fine."

Father Larry was still smiling when he gently broke the handshake, and stepped away from them. "Let's get on with it then." He removed a small bottle of blessed water from his right pocket and began to walk through the house from room to room. He prayed and sprinkled holy water in each one. Roni and Christian followed behind him and watched in silence. When he reached the entrance to the bedroom, he paused and looked at Christian.

A troubled expression crossed his face. Roni wondered for the second time if she'd done the right thing by not telling Father Larry all there was to know about Christian. She glanced at Christian for some sign of assurance and caught the slight nod that he gave the priest. Had some psychic understanding passed between them?

"It's alright," Christian said. "Go ahead."

Father Larry was obviously uncomfortable. He shook his head as if to dismiss whatever dark thoughts had entered his mind and walked through the doorway into the bedroom. He blessed the room and proceeded to the basement where Christian and Roni had been working to redecorate an area that would eventually be a recreation room. Father Larry blessed the half finished space and was done.

"I've laid out some goodies upstairs," Roni said. "Can you visit for awhile?"

Father Larry glanced at Christian. "If you like."

"We'd both enjoy that." Christian touched the priest lightly on his back and gestured for him to walk up the stairs.

When they were all on the main floor, Roni headed for the kitchen while Father Larry and Christian went into the living room. "What would you prefer, Father?" she asked. "Tea or coffee?"

"Oh, I've always preferred coffee," he said with a smile, "but Cora insists that tea is better for me." Father Larry took a seat on the plush, taupe sofa, then turned to Christian. "Cora takes care of everything at the rectory. Sort of a chief cook and bottle washer, but she keeps us all in line and healthy."

Roni couldn't help but laugh at the priest's description of the woman who had taken care of him for close to twenty years.

She left the men to themselves, and began to prepare a small selection of herbal tea bags on a plate for Father Larry and herself. This way she could eliminate the chance he might ask Christian what his preference was in order to be a polite house guest. Roni was certain Father Larry already had some questions about Christian, anyway. Better not to give him more to think about. Christian neither ate nor drank regular food, except for an occasional glass of wine. Mortal food was extremely disagreeable to his internal workings. Trying to explain that was not the way she wanted Father Larry to be told about Christian being a vampire.

She prepared an evening snack in the kitchen, while the two men sat in the next room in ominous silence. She carried a tray of vegetables and dip out to the coffee table in front of Father Larry. He dug right in, dipping a piece of cauliflower only moments after the tray was set down.

"Have some," he said to Christian.

Christian shook his head and put a hand on his stomach.

"Upset stomach, eh?" Father Larry asked, chewing heartily on his morsel.

"Something like that," Christian said.

Father Larry seemed to study him, then smiled. "So, Christian," he said, "what is it you do for a living?"

Roni got the feeling Father Larry was only being casually polite, but she was relieved to see a conversation begin to develop between them.

While the priest waited for an answer from Christian he stared at his face. Roni worried if he could see the pinkish glow in the other man's eyes. She looked at Christian herself to be sure it wasn't too obvious, but it was. His eyes appeared blood shot. She hoped Father Larry would attribute it to a lack of sleep.

"At the moment," Christian said, "not too much, short of supporting Roni as much as possible with her business. I do what I can to help her."

Father Larry flashed Roni a look that said, "free-loader." Christian did not seem to have noticed the visual exchange between them. Roni was thankful for that.

"Don't you find it difficult keeping up with her unusual hours?" Father Larry asked.

Christian cast him a knowing look. The hint of a smile curled up one corner of his mouth as he took his time responding to the priest's subtle question. "Not at all," he said. "I got used to it in no time."

"Hmmm. What did you do before you met her?" His line of questioning was beginning to sound like a verbal test.

Christian sat back comfortably in the corner of the matching love seat and returned the priest's inquisitive stare. "I travelled," he said. "I toured the United States for quite a number of years."

"If you don't mind my asking, where did you ever get the money? To travel, I mean." Father Larry did his best to smile, but Roni did not miss the slight quiver in his lower lip.

"For generations my family owned and operated a huge vineyard in France," Christian said. "I ran it for ten years until my brothers learned enough of the business to take over. My share of the profits from the investments have set me up quite nicely." Christian sat as natural as could be, and waited for the priest to respond. He seemed to be curiously entertained with the entire conversation.

Father Larry chuckled. "That explains the accent," he said. "Sounds like an interesting way to grow up."

Christian nodded and smiled, but never took his eyes off the priest. "It was." He shifted his weight in the chair, then leaned his chin against his hand. "What about you, Father? Have you enjoyed your vocation as a priest?"

Father Larry looked surprised, but he nodded, then rolled back in his seat. "It has been rewarding," he said. "Everything in life has its ups and downs, you know. Even the priesthood is not ideal."

Christian moved his head sideways and raised his eyebrows. "Oh? I've always envisioned it as being the perfect life, closer to heaven than the rest of us. But I suppose you have the same health concerns, financial problems, that sort of thing."

"More than that," Father Larry said. "We see the news, read the papers. We know what goes on out there."

"Oh, but it doesn't effect you," Christian said. "You may hear about it, but you're somewhat protected, are you not?"

Father Larry smiled and shook his head. "I have often thought we see worse than the rest of the world would believe."

"How's that?"

"Many of us, not all of us mind you, but many of us encounter evil on a fierce level." Father Larry studied Christian's face, then looked at Roni.

"Father Larry has been involved in many exorcisms," Roni said to Christian.

"Not many," Father Larry said. "But a few."

"That must have been fascinating."

Roni's stomach began to churn. Did Father Larry know how close he was getting to the truth about Christian with this subject? She looked at Christian, but he was intent on his discussion.

"It was at first," Father Larry said. "But it's also been quite frightening. There are forces at work that most people believe are only found in the movies, but I've seen much of it for myself."

"I'd love to hear about what you've seen," Christian said.

Roni looked from him to Father Larry. "He probably doesn't want to relive those experiences," she said.

Father Larry turned to her. "Don't worry, child. This doesn't bother me as much as you might think." He looked at Christian and smiled. "I've been called to homes that were believed to be haunted many times."

"And were they?"

"Sometimes, yes. And other times it turned out to be someone's over active imagination." Father Larry patted himself on the belly and looked down. "The frightening cases are the ones where spiritual possession seems to have occurred. Those are always nasty, involving a very powerful evil presence." He shook his head as if to clear a bad thought. "No priest I know looks forward to those."

Christian nodded, still staring at the priest. "Interesting."

Father Larry looked up at him. "It is," he said. He leaned over and dipped another cauliflower. "I've learned so much from those experiences."

"Such as?"

He looked at Christian again, then eased himself back into a comfortable position. "I've learned not to be so surprised when

I'm faced with a situation that is, how shall I say this, out of the ordinary." He smiled at Christian, but said nothing more.

What next? Roni thought. It wasn't like Father Larry to play verbal charades with anyone, yet that was exactly what he was doing now. Her throat tightened, and butterflies moved up and down her windpipe as a myriad of thoughts ran through her mind. She knew she had to leave the room. "If you'll both excuse me." She pointed toward the kitchen and started to walk away. "I'll get the tea now."

Both men were silent in the next room as Roni filled the teapot and gathered the snack trays from the kitchen. The silence added to her sense of foreboding, and she could feel the tension from the living room. She took the teapot out to them and set it on the coffee table. She glanced at Father Larry and noticed how his mouth seemed to be in the throes of forming words, but no sound came out.

She quickly returned to the kitchen and gathered up the tray of cups, tea bags, and crackers. Just as she prepared herself to carry all that was left of their tiny meal into the living room she heard what she feared the most.

"Are you . . . a . . . vampire?" Father Larry asked.

In the living room, there was silence. Around the corner in the kitchen, however, Roni dropped both trays that she was carrying, and stood like a statue afraid to move. She was sure Father Larry would feel uncomfortable now that he knew she had heard the question. He might even feel embarrassed to have asked it. She didn't want that either, but she was too dumfounded to say a word of comfort, and too stunned to move.

Christian, handled the matter in his usual calm, refined manner. "Yes," he said. "I am. Now if you'll excuse me for just a minute, I believe I'm needed elsewhere."

Roni could only imagine Father Larry's reaction.

Christian entered the kitchen. He looked at the tea bags and crackers from one tray mixed with the pieces of broken china from the other laying all over the floor. He began to pick up the mess while Roni stood there.

Christian looked up at her. "Are you alright?"

She barely heard him. Instead she listened to Father Larry's footsteps as he slowly approached. He walked into the room, knelt down, and began to help Christian separate the tea bags from the shards of china on the floor. Roni stared at the two men working together to clean the mess from the kitchen floor. It was as if nothing unusual had just happened.

"I'm so sorry," Father Larry said. "I didn't mean to startle you." He looked up at Roni. "I didn't think you could hear us."

"I wasn't listening," she said. "I just heard you. I . . ." She tried gesturing with her hands to show how she had walked through the room and around the corner, but finally gave up when she realized an explanation wasn't needed. They had stopped cleaning the floor and looked at her. It brought her to her senses. "I'll take care of this," she said, moving her hands as if to push them away.

"It's almost done," Christian said. He picked up the last of the fallen tea bags and placed it on the tray with the rest of them.

"Well then, I'll wipe up the floor." Roni wet an old rag from the drawer by the oven and turned to look at the two men as if she had never seen them before. "Go! Go, sit down," she said. "I'll do this."

Both men stood up simultaneously.

Christian leaned toward her and kissed her on the cheek. "Call me if you need me," he said.

The warmth Roni felt in her heart at that moment calmed her. She knew no matter how the rest of the evening went, it wouldn't change a thing in her relationship with either of them. If they were meant to get along, they would.

Christian went into the living room, but Father Larry stayed behind. The look on his face set her mind completely at ease. His smile was full of warmth and sincerity.

"You're not angry?" she asked.

Father Larry chuckled. "No child," he said. "We make our

own choices. He seems nice enough."

Roni was baffled.

"Don't look so surprised," he said. "Things are not always as they seem, don't you know." He touched her shoulder gently, then turned and went back to the living room.

CHAPTER 3

December 6, 1997

Diana and Samuel walked the streets of London hand in hand. It was night and the city still bustled with activity, but they had no trouble blending in. In the distance, the lights of Big Ben were lit up like a beacon to the tourists. It was most impressive decorated in the colors of the season, red and green. Diana turned to Samuel and pouted. "Why are we wasting time in England?" she asked him. "We've been here countless times. You know the climate depresses me."

Samuel loved London. He adored the old architecture, gothic and ornate in detail. Large stone structures with black wrought iron trim, balconies and oriels that gave the outside walls a depth similar to what he'd known in France. It suited his tastes perfectly because it was comfortable. But Diana seemed to enjoy the more modern lines that were found in America. "And just where would you rather be, mon cheri?" He knew how much she loved the night life in the states, but he was in no hurry to get there this time. "Back in France, perhaps?" He flashed her a mischievous smile.

Diana stopped walking and slapped him playfully on the shoulder. "Why do you tease me? You know how I hate that."

Samuel reached for her and wrapped his arms around her waist. He pulled her toward him and looked at her with half-closed eyes. "Because I love the abuse." He bent down and briefly touched his lips to hers. "Because you're everything to me."

"Even after five hundred years together?" she asked.

He looked at her. His stare bored through to her soul. "Even after five hundred years together," he said.

Diana looked down at his chest and ran her index finger along the lapel of his coat. "Don't you ever regret changing me?"

Samuel held her tighter. "Never," he said. "My only fear, mon amour, is that you will see the day when you regret having allowed me to change you."

Diana flashed him an angry look, then backed away. "Impossible," she said. "How can you doubt my loyalty? My love for you? I'm insulted."

"Ah, the mortal spirit that has never changed," he said, smiling. "I admire that. I've known many mortals who have entered our world. Many lose something through the change. But not you, my Diana. You still have the energy and spirit you had from the day I met you."

Diana looked away. "I told you, I would never change," she said. "And I haven't"

He felt the serious edge in her demeanor grow sad and he became concerned. "What is it?" he asked. "What depresses you now?" He saw the pink tears flow down her cheeks. "I didn't mean to upset you with my insecure concerns." He wiped a single tear from her cheek, then touched her chin and gently nudged her head up so she had to look at him. "Diana, my love. Tell me."

She shook her head, then looked into his eyes. "Christian," she said. "I still miss him. Why can't I accept it? It's been so long."

His pulse began to race and he tried to hide his growing alarm. There was never a reason for him to be concerned about her love or loyalty for him as long as she didn't know about his connection to her brother. But she was Christian's little sister, younger by four years. How would she feel to find out that he was the one who had changed them both.

He took her in his arms to comfort her. "I know you miss him."

"If only he'd been alive when you and I met," she said, sniffling. "He might be with us now." She looked at him. "I wish

Christian could have seen all that I've seen. He would have been amazed at the changes that have taken place in this world."

Samuel caressed her hair and tried hard not to think about the truth. It was too easy for Diana to read his thoughts even by accident. Telepathically, she was very strong. "That he would," he said to her.

Diana looked at him and frowned. "You didn't even know my brother," she said. "How would you know what Christian would enjoy?"

"Ah, mon cheri." Samuel tried to keep his voice sounding calm. "After all you've told me about him, it's apparent that he would enjoy what you and I have enjoyed. I feel like I know him through you."

She smiled and placed a kiss on his chin. "I'm sure you do," she said. "I suppose I talk about him too much even after all this time has passed. It's just that his death was so horrible. How it must have felt to be killed in that ridiculous fight, then carried off and eaten by wild animals. What if he wasn't dead when they reached him? Oh, it's just too horrible. You'd think I'd have accepted it after five centuries, but I haven't. Maybe if I'd been able to see it happen for myself it would've been different. But I guess it never seemed real to me."

Samuel was quiet as they walked. He rubbed her back, but said nothing.

"I think about him so often," she said. "Sometimes I talk to him in my mind so he knows he was never forgotten."

"Oh, I'm sure he knows." Samuel was being more realistic than he hoped she'd ever know. It took all his strength to keep the thoughts out of his head that would give away the only secret he'd ever kept from her. The truth was that he had changed Christian that very night. Wild animals were never a part of it. *Oh, what have I done?* he thought to himself.

"What do you mean?" Diana asked.

Samuel was surprised when he realized a stray thought had reached her. He had no idea how he would tell her that Christian never wanted her to know what he had become. It was not a little white lie, but a huge black one that had stood the test of time because of the wedge she alone had unknowingly driven between her brother and her lover.

"I was wondering what I might have done to make you unhappy," Samuel said. "We were having such a fun time, and then you were sad. I'm so sorry for whatever I did to remind you of your brother."

Diana stroked his cheek and smiled at him. "It's not your fault, silly one," she said. "You know I get melancholy every so often. I should apologize to you. I wish I could stop myself from feeling this way, but it just seems to happen."

"Well," Samuel said, "I'll bet you that every time you feel this way it's because some part of you knows your brother is thinking about you."

Diana looked at him, her eyes sparkled. "You're right," she said, smiling. "Why haven't I ever realized it before? I must feel him thinking about me and it makes me miss him."

Samuel was relieved to see her in better spirits. "Now I'm sorry I never thought of it either." He was certain she actually did pick up some residual pieces of Christian's memories of her. It was another reason why he'd kept them so far apart all these years.

"Let's go to America tonight," Diana said. "We haven't been there for so long. Let's just pack up and leave."

Samuel shook his head and smiled. "It's only another week, Cherie," he said. "Surely, you can wait that long."

"Yes," Diana said. "But I'm so happy right now I want to celebrate. But not here. I want to celebrate in America. I love the excitement there. Let's go."

Samuel looked into her big, brown eyes, and felt his insides melt like butter in the hot sun. At any other time they would have packed up and been on their way already. All she ever had to do was ask and it was hers.

But not this time. Samuel knew the sooner they reached America, the sooner she'd meet Christian. Once that happened she'd learn the truth of Samuel's deception, and her love for him would die. He did not look forward to the heartache he would feel for all eternity if she left him. Never had he loved anyone or anything the way he loved Diana. Having known that feeling, he would never survive without it.

"Why are you being so impossible about this?" she asked, squinting her eyes at him. "You never put off going to America before."

The look on her face showed her growing anger peppered with a touch of suspicion. He knew he had to do something to calm her down before she started the silent treatment that would drive him insane. He touched her cheek and gave her a serious look. "Because I have a surprise for you there." That certainly was true. "And it won't be ready until we get there in another week." Just a little lie this time, but his conscience made it clear how the guilt in him had grown.

"Really?" Diana seemed interested the way a child becomes interested in opening presents once they see the colorful wrappings with all the ribbons and bows. She smiled and gave him a sideways glance. "Is it for Christmas?"

He stroked her cheek again, then turned to continue walking. "Something like that," he said. "You'll have to be patient and see."

"I don't have any patience," Diana said, laughing. "You know that!" She raced past him, then turned around and began to walk backward up the street facing him while she tried to pry the secret of her surprise from him.

The evening fog surrounded them. Diana hopped, turned, and walked face forward then backward, her hair spinning wildly with every movement, while the fog clouded around her covering parts of her body so that she seemed to disappear then reappear over and over. It gave him a strange premonition of how close he was getting to losing her forever. He watched her and enjoyed every minute of her delight, but he also felt guilty that the kind of surprise she expected was not nearly the kind of surprise that awaited her.

After a few minutes Diana seemed to give up on the game. She started to walk by his side once again. "Where in America are we going this time?"

"Boston."

"Massachusetts? As in New England?"

"That's the one."

"What's in Boston?"

"Well, you're going to have to wait and see, now. Aren't you?"

"You might give me a hint," Diana said, wrapping both her arms around one of his. She leaned her head on his shoulder letting her long, brown hair fall down his back.

He kissed her on top of her head and smiled. "Nice try, Di," he teased.

"Oh, you!" She continued to walk with him, still attached to his arm. He knew she was disappointed, but he was relieved the subject was dropped for the moment. He began to wonder if there might be some way he could soften the blow and lessen the chances that Diana would be as hurt and angry as he expected her to be when she finally saw Christian. Her temper had the capacity to be as volatile as her daily demeanor was innocent, even though Diana was not so innocent after all that life as a vampire had shown her. That contrast was one of the most captivating things about her.

"Are you hungry?" he asked.

"I could take it or leave it tonight," she said.

She's just like her brother, he thought as the twinge of guilt stabbed him through his heart yet again.

"In that case," Samuel said, "why don't we go shopping? What do you need?"

She pushed her hair behind her ear and looked down. "I have everything I need," she said.

He smiled. "What do you want, then?"

She thought for a moment. "Oh, I don't know."

"Jewelry? Clothing? What do you think, Diana?"

"I suppose I should pick up a few extra sweaters before we get to America. Maybe a couple pairs of jeans, too," she said. "It's going to be cold there on the east coast."

Samuel couldn't help but laugh. "You don't feel the cold, anyway," he said. He knew she would never have enough blue jeans or sweaters. They'd been her style from the day they become fashionable. "How about Bennetton?" he suggested. "It's two doors up from here."

"Perfect," she said. "That's one of my favorite stores."

They walked to the end of the block where the entrance to the store was located. Diana tried one of the doors, but it was locked. "They're closed," she said, a tone of mock concern in her voice.

Samuel flashed a mischievous smile toward her and chuckled. "I guess you know what that means," he said. Without hesitation, he shifted the molecular structure of his body in order to vaporize so he could easily waft under the door. Diana was right behind him. They had done this many times in different countries, but it was still an adventure to them.

Once they were inside the store, they drifted out of sight of the security cameras and quickly allowed their bodies to solidify. They covered the lens' with articles of clothing without being captured on film, then turned to each other and smiled.

"Good thing there are no sensors to deal with," Samuel said.

Diana nodded, but wasted no time inspecting the clothes. Almost immediately she found four bulky, warm sweaters that Samuel knew would be going with them. "Try them on," he said. "Make sure they fit before we leave here."

She looked at him and rolled her eyes. "I know what you're up to," she said. "They're huge and we both know they're going to fit just fine." She turned and headed for the jeans and chinos.

Samuel watched from behind the racks of lingerie as Diana rummaged through the casual slacks. He heard her mumble under her breath, "Free show . . . what a pervert . . . I'm not giving him a free show . . . ," but she giggled softly as she said it.

He smiled. "I heard that, you know."

Diana was moving toward the jeans rack. "I know you did,

Honey," she said without turning around. "And get away from there. Go look at some clothes for yourself while we're here. Leave the women's things alone."

But Samuel transported himself to her side in an instant and surprised her. It was one of the tricks that still caught her off guard. "I'd much rather look for things I'd like to see you in," he said softly in her ear. He held a lavender satin and lace teddy before her. "Try it on for me, Diana."

She giggled. "Then we'll have to take it with us, Sam," she said. Her voice had an edge of agitation that Samuel chose to ignore. "I'll never wear it for real so put it back."

Samuel did not move. Instead, he began to massage her back and shoulders while he breathed his hot, passionate breath down her neck. Diana could be a tough one when she was aggravated, but Samuel knew how to calm her. Even as she spoke he could feel her body's involuntary reaction to his nearness, and to the feel of his caresses. He felt her lean slightly into him as she stopped speaking and he knew she was his once more.

He laid the teddy over the top of the rack of jeans and wrapped his other arm firmly around her waist. His hand that was now empty came around to touch her cheek as he planted light butterfly kisses up and down her neck, and across her throat to the other side.

Diana moaned softly as she closed her eyes for a moment and swayed, dropping the sweaters she'd been holding on the floor beside her. Both of her arms wound themselves around Samuel's shoulders. He felt her let go of her emotions, allowing her senses to fly free within her.

He knew no words were necessary. He felt his energy level start to rise. The particles of life that made up his body began to vibrate at a faster than normal rate. He looked at Diana and saw through her to the clothes that hung beyond where she stood. Her entire essence showed itself in hues of blue and rose. He moved closer to her so their auras could merge. His heightened awareness and finely honed senses made love-making an all-powerful experience as he shuddered with the first blending of their souls. He felt her surround him and fill him at the same time. He experienced her body as if it were his, her thoughts and feelings as if they too belonged to him. He found her pains of the past and her worries of the future in the shadowed pockets of slow movement within her. He knew her memories even in past lives and everything she had seen. He became her and felt the love she had for him. Nothing was hidden.

But Samuel had never been able to allow Diana the same un-bridled access to his soul. He maintained the barrier around his memories of Christian and the guilt it caused, but let everything else go to her. Even with that one dark spot in him, he revelled in the experience much like any mortal man revels in the sexual expe-rience of the physical. But there was one huge difference. He and Diana had combined their molecules so as to literally become one in a way that no two mortals could ever be. He experienced the physical sensations she felt to his nearness. He felt her truest emo-tions of contentment and love as if they were his own. He knew which parts of her body desired his touch at the exact moment her desire was born. And he knew which parts of her soul should be caressed and precisely how.

But when Diana tried to become him so she would know him in the same way her frustration left him cold. She didn't under-stand not being able to care for the part of him he kept hidden and he suffered every bit of her discontent. He concentrated all the more on filling her soul with his devotion in order to distract her from his past. When they reached their highest spiritual and physi-cal peaks together, their spirits cried out in joyous freedom while their bodies trembled in physical rapture. Their experience was on a different plane of reality and their satisfaction lasted for hours.

Afterward, they lay together on the floor of Bennetton's among the fallen sweaters and racks of clothes. Their bodies still prickly from the molecules settling back into place. Samuel held her to his side and relished her nearness. "Oh, how I love you, Diana."

She moved closer toward him and laid her head on his chest.

"And I am eternally yours," she whispered. "Here or in the other realm. It doesn't matter."

He said nothing, but lay with her wishing she could say the same after his secret was out in the open. She was drained now. It was the only time he could think freely without worrying if she would know what was on his mind.

After a few minutes, he sat up slowly, lifting Diana with him. "Let's finish your shopping and call it a night," he said. "We should've made love at the hotel, then relaxed together."

Diana gathered together the sweaters she had dropped, and stood up. "Well, it was your idea, Sam," she teased.

"I just couldn't help myself," he said. "I've been drawn to you from the very beginning, and I'll be drawn to you for all of eternity." He kissed her gently on the forehead, took a step backward, then waved his arm out as if to clear a path before her.

"Go to it!" he said. "The store is yours, mon amour."

Diana spent an hour making the rest of her selections. She ended up with two pairs of jeans and three pairs of loose, casual slacks.

Together, she and Samuel removed the price tags from each item of clothing and added them up to reach the final purchase amount. They placed the tickets in a neat pile near the cash register with the correct amount of money. Samuel wrote a quick note of thanks to the store manager for the use of the store after hours with a reassurance that they did not take anything else that was not accounted for in the price tags.

Diana read the note he wrote, then put it back on the counter and sighed. "I miss the days when tailors and dressmakers were at a person's beck and call," she said.

Samuel nodded. "So do I," he said. "Those were the days when they took pride in their work. There've been so many changes I would have preferred not to take place."

Diana began to fold each article of clothing and neatly place them in a bag from the store. "I agree," she said. "But, then again, if it weren't for retail stores with all their ready-made clothing, these items wouldn't be so accessible for us."

"That's true, too," Samuel said. "I guess there's good and bad sides to everything."

Diana shrugged. "I've always said that." She placed the bags on the floor by the counter and looked around the store. "We'd better uncover the cameras and go."

Samuel nodded. He picked up one of the bags and handed her the other one. They both vaporized, then went to uncover the cameras before heading to the door to exit the same way they'd entered.

In no time at all they were walking down the foggy streets of London on the way back to their hotel.

"Look! The sun." Diana said. "How beautiful! I hope we'll figure out how to watch it for an entire day sometime."

Samuel smiled and shook his head. "I'm satisfied with the little I can see." He looked around at the misty atmosphere. "I enjoy London."

They were approaching the entrance to their hotel. Samuel stopped and pulled her to him. "I am still thankful that I found you," he said.

Diana put her arms around his neck, the bag of clothes hanging down his back. "So, there's no chance we could leave for America tonight, is there?"

Samuel laughed and shook his head. "Diana, you are persistent. But honestly, no. There's no point in going until we're scheduled to go." Samuel checked her reaction to be sure she understood and would not continue to push the issue. He was relieved when she smiled. "After all," he said, "America isn't going anywhere and neither are we so why not just wait? Anticipation always makes the 'getting' more enjoyable, don't you think?."

Diana looked up at him, her head tilted. "You're a tease," she said, her eyes glistening in the dawn light.

"And you love me for it." He kissed her forehead, then took her hand and led her into the hotel.

CHAPTER 4

December 6, 1997

Christian opened his eyes and looked at the clock on the night stand. It was five thirty in the afternoon. The sun had begun to set, but Roni was still sound asleep beside him. He got out of bed and went downstairs to finish panelling the rec room, but an hour later there was still no sound from upstairs to let him know Roni had awaken. The antique table clock on the work bench showed that it was going on seven o'clock in the evening. It wasn't like her to sleep this late.

He took a break and went back up to check on her. He peeked in the bedroom and saw that she was still sleeping. His first inclination was to wake her, but he decided to wait a little longer. He sat next to her on the bed and tried to sense what was wrong. She felt more tired than she normally did, but that was all he was able to pick up. He hoped she wasn't getting sick, but he didn't sense that. He wondered if turning her days into nights both for his sake, and for her job, was finally taking its toll by destroying her biological clock, but that was hard to tell. Some mortals are their best at night. All he knew for sure was that more was going on with her than even he could know. For a mortal, she was good at masking her feelings. He ran his fingers through his hair and looked around the room. Melvin lay curled up beside Roni's feet. Christian reached over to pet him on the head and the cat purred softly in response, pushing his forehead into Christian's hand, but he would not leave his self-appointed position at Roni's side.

"I know, she's your favorite," Christian said. The cat looked at him, swished his tail from side to side, then rested his head on Roni's foot. "You've always been loyal to her," Christian said. "Like me. Good boy. You stay put."

He bent down to kiss Roni on the forehead. "I love you," he whispered into her ear. He sat back and looked at her for a moment, then stood up and quietly left the room.

He went to the kitchen and poured himself a glass of port wine. Sammi brushed against his leg and he looked down to see her staring up at him. "You thirsty, too?" he asked her. He poured a small bowl of milk for both cats knowing full well she would drink it all before Melvin knew it was there, but Melvin wasn't going anywhere until Roni woke up. That alone told him something was wrong. But what?

He went into the living room and sat down to look out the window at the few snowflakes that were finally making a gentle appearance. For some reason, Father Larry popped into his head. It hadn't been that long ago when the short, round priest came to bless the house. Christian had been most impressed with his brilliant heart, and how easily he seemed to accept him, but he'd also felt sorry for the awkward position the priest was in that day.

Christian had wanted to meet and get to know him for Roni's sake, but deep down it was also important to do so for himself. He'd never been friends with a holy man. He thought it might give him the final closure to his dwindling sense of guilt over being a vampire if he could mean something to a man like Father Larry.

Christian shook his head and took another sip of wine. He thought Roni would visit Father Larry shortly after that to be sure he was comfortable with Christian, but she hadn't even mentioned it. It could've been because Roni worked too hard, and just couldn't find the time. It might also have been that she simply lost track of the days.

Sammi jumped up beside him and purred loud enough to be heard in the basement while she waited for some attention. He stroked her head and laughed to himself. "What do you think she'd do if I went to see Father Larry for her?" he asked the fluffy, white cat. "Do you think she'd be angry with me?" Sammi continued to purr in contentment, obviously happy to be getting the attention of her favorite person.

Christian stopped petting her, then stood up and walked to the sliding glass door by the kitchen table. *The truth of the matter is,* he thought, *I want to see Father Larry for myself, not for Roni.* Father Larry seemed to like him the day they met and Christian had not been able to get him off his mind. He'd never spoken with a priest like he had that day. *Why,* he asked himself silently, but he knew the answer and it was simple.

Until Christian met Roni he'd believed he was evil because he was a vampire. But worse was the way he was forced to feed off the living blood of human beings around him. The fact that he hadn't asked to be a vampire never seemed relevant enough to make a difference. But Roni helped him see he had a soul that was essentially good because he was good. She had shown him that God looked at what was in your heart, first and at your deeds, second.

Christian hoped she was right. He had never killed a human being. "That must count for something," he said aloud to himself. He fed as seldom as he could get away with because he didn't want to take life itself for granted. It was precious. It was something to be respected and cherished. He could not take advantage of the lives that fed him, simply because his own life would never end.

But if it weren't for Roni, his survival would mean as little to him now as it had before he'd met her. He lived for her because she had given him back the quality of life he knew when he was mortal. If only he could convince her to spend eternity with him so he could share all he'd seen with her and all that was to come. But he respected her free will and loved her enough to accept how she chose to use it.

He shook his head. He couldn't think about it anymore. He didn't want to. Instead, he turned his concentration to the snowflakes that fell a little faster than they had a half hour ago. The grass slowly turned white, then melted into green again as the snow was quickly absorbed by the warmer ground. Would Roni listen to Father Larry if he were to suggest such a thing? It didn't matter. He wasn't one to use people in such a manner.

He finished his wine, then placed the glass on the table. He bent down to pick up the cat who looked like the snowflakes piling up outside and carried her with him into the kitchen. He wanted to leave Roni a note so she wouldn't be alarmed when she finally woke and found him gone. He grabbed a pen and pad of paper from the cupboard and wrote,

> "My Love, I've gone to visit a mutual friend. I don't expect
> to be long, but if I am, please don't worry.
> > I love you always,
> > Your Christian"

He left the note on the table, then carried the cat into the bedroom. He wanted to check on Roni once more before he left. She was laying on her side, but still sound asleep. He placed the cat on the bed beside her. "Help Melvin take care of her," he instructed Sammi, then continued to pet her until she laid down. He kissed Roni gently on the lips and felt her warmth. How cold his kiss must feel to her when she's awake. Like the frozen flowers in her garden that are still so beautiful. That thought gave him an idea. He quickly vaporized and wafted outside. He snapped a rose half way down its stem and took it in to Roni where he placed it on her pillow so she would think of him first when she awoke.

Then, he left.

Father Larry finished saying the seven thirty evening mass at St. Joseph's. He waited for everyone to leave, then began to straighten up for Father O'Manley who would be handling the next mass at nine o'clock.

When he was finished, he walked through his beloved church and thought of everyone he knew and loved. He prayed for all of them as he did each evening, while he strolled up and down the long aisles, his soft, rubber soles barely making a sound on the marble floor. When he reached the nativity scene that was on display in front of the side altar, he stopped. The straw had been ruffled where the parishioners had removed some to take home. He straightened it up, redistributing the straw evenly to fill in the holes. As he did so, he heard the door from the main entrance move open slowly, then close softly with a 'whoosh' as the snowy breeze outside sucked it shut. He turned to see who had come in. He was alone at the moment and knew one could never be too careful. The unexpectedness of this visit, however, took him by such surprise that he had no time to do anything but allow his brain to register the inescapable fact that he was really seeing who he thought he was seeing.

Christian stood in the archway of the entrance to the main part of the church, directly down the aisle from the altar, facing the throne of the King of Kings and possibly the Lord God Himself, for all Father Larry knew just then. He stared, dumbfounded, and briefly wondered if this visit was a sacrilege. But he reminded himself that God's home was open to all who chose to visit. He hoped that included a vampire.

Father Larry took a step toward Christian, but was stopped dead in his tracks when he saw the stately form genuflect and bless himself. Once again, Father Larry was so surprised, he couldn't think clear enough to move.

Christian stood up and began to walk swiftly toward him. He created an image out of the old Dracula movies with his unbuttoned cashmere coat billowing out to the sides as if it were a cape. Father Larry's heart was beating so fast from the ghastly vision before him, he hoped he wasn't going to have a heart attack. By the time Christian stepped into the light nearest the manger scene and stopped, Father Larry was holding the rail in an attempt to get control of himself.

Christian extended his hand and smiled. "I can see from your expression that I caught you off guard. I didn't mean to frighten you," he said. "I simply came to visit, if that's alright."

Father Larry moved his arm forward as if he were forcing it to do something it did not want to do. He and Christian shook hands, but he was still unnerved, sweat dripping down the sides of his face. "You certainly did catch me off guard," he said. "You just looked so . . . so . . . gothic."

Christian held his vision, but was silent.

"Your coat." Father Larry gestured with his hands to show how Christian's coat looked like a cape.

Christian looked down at himself and laughed. "I suppose I was quite a sight," he said. "Roni bought this for me about a month ago, but it wasn't appropriate to wear until now."

Father Larry nodded, happy to have found common ground between them. "Speaking of Veronica," he said, "how is she? I confess, I've been expecting a visit from her." He looked directly into the vampire's eyes. "Is she alright, Christian?"

Christian looked away, then turned back. "Right now, she's sleeping," he said. "She doesn't know I'm here."

Father Larry nodded once. He thought he understood why Christian would not have told her, but he needed confirmation. "What brings you here?" he asked.

Christian said nothing at first. He looked around the church as if he hadn't heard the question, but his line of sight came back to rest on Father Larry. "Because Roni hadn't come to see you yet so I thought I'd do it for her," he said. He turned away from the priest, and walked to the front of the nativity where he stood and seemed to study it.

Father Larry followed him. "Do you like it?"

Christian did not take his eyes off the scene. "Very much, actually,"

"Do you know what it all means?"

Christian turned slowly to look at him, then smiled. "Yes," he said, "I know all about Jesus."

Father Larry looked down, embarrassed. "Good," he said. "I'm very proud of this manger scene. I create it myself every year. I pour my heart and soul into this project." He reached out and placed his hand on the miniature barn. "From the blessed straw that covers the ground of the stable to the huge star that hangs above the entire scene, I leave a piece of myself in this little place."

Christian nodded. "The star is quite large."

"Just as it was the night Jesus was born," Father Larry replied. "It draws your attention to this small display the same way the real star guided the Wise Men, the Kings, and all those who followed it to the birthplace of our Lord, that night."

Christian nodded as he continued to examine the pieces of the nativity.

"The church is open to all visitors at this time of year," Father Larry went on in order to avoid the uncomfortable silence that seemed imminent. "We want to encourage everyone to come here to visit the newborn King just as people did the night He was born. The straw is blessed. It's our gift to the parishioners as well as the public. We encourage them all to take a piece or two with them to carry throughout the year."

"What happens to the straw that's left?" Christian asked.

"It's burned," Father Larry answered. "As is proper." He watched Christian begin to reach toward the straw. He removed two pieces from the table, then turned to look at him.

"Take it with you," Father Larry said. "It's there for anyone who wants it. Just as our Lord is there for whomever wants Him."

Christian nodded, then placed the straw gently in his pocket. "Roni told me you're an understanding man."

"That reminds me," Father Larry said. "Is something wrong with her, Christian? You seemed upset a minute ago when I asked you how she was?"

Christian shook his head and looked away. "I don't know. She was still in bed when I left."

"Maybe she had trouble sleeping," Father Larry said. "She's probably just catching up." He was growing more and more curious about this man, a vampire who obviously loved Roni very much, but who also acknowledged the power of God when he entered the church. Now he stood almost mesmerized by the scene depicting the birth of the Christ child. This was not what Father Larry would have expected of a vampire, assuming he ever thought he'd meet one at all. It baffled him.

"I suppose," Christian said. "In any event, I left her a note so she wouldn't worry, but I didn't say I was coming here." He looked at Father Larry. "I thought I'd see how this visit went first."

Father Larry nodded and motioned to the nearest pew. "Would you like to sit down and talk?" he asked. "Or would you be more comfortable in the rectory?"

"I'm not going to burn up and turn to dust like you've been led to believe," Christian said, smiling. "Right here will be fine."

"I'm sorry," the priest said, embarrassed again. "I didn't realize you knew what I was thinking. I didn't mean to insult you or anything."

Christian chuckled. "I'm not insulted," he said. "How many vampires have you actually known in your time?"

Another shock wave went through the old priest's body when he heard Christian openly claim his nature. He felt his pulse start to race again. "None," he said.

"I've never really known a priest, either. Not even in my mortal years," Christian said. "So I guess we're pretty much on an even keel here." Christian took a seat in the pew and turned to face Father Larry from a lower, less threatening eye level.

Father Larry sat down beside him. "How did you know the proper way to act in a church?" he asked. "That surprised me more than the thing with the coat."

"I was raised according to Roman Catholic beliefs and traditions," Christian said. "My mother was very strict about that with all of us, even my father." He smiled. "She taught us prayers and told us stories about Christ that were passed on to her." He looked away. "After this happened to me I followed the development of the Church as an outsider looking in. At first I didn't think I'd be welcome in the Church. I believed that God had abandoned me because of the change I'd gone through. But the Church had become quite," Christian paused and looked at Father Larry, "forgive me for saying so, but in the fifteenth century the Church had become so corrupt I eventually felt comfortable within its walls."

Father Larry looked at him wide-eyed. "Do you mean to say that you attended mass back then?"

Christian didn't answer right away. He seemed to think about it for a few seconds, then he shook his head. "Not exactly," he said.

"Then what did you mean, you felt comfortable in the church?"

Christian looked at him, an angry glare in his eyes. "I hid there when it was necessary. No one ever looked for a vampire in a church."

Father Larry nodded once. "Oh," he said. The look on Christian's face made him want to run, but he chose to put himself in God's hands instead.

"Something gnawed at me, though." Christian looked at the altar. "I started to think that if I could feel comfortable within the tainted walls of the Church, then something was very wrong with the whole picture. Only evil should feel comfortable with evil. Then in 1517 the Reformation began and it only made me feel like the devil himself."

Father Larry turned to face Christian directly. "How so? I don't think I understand."

"The Catholics themselves had turned away from their own Church because of its corruption," Christian said. "It was no wonder I felt comfortable there." He looked down at his hands that were clenched in his lap. "To me, it was proof of the dreadful being I had become."

Father Larry looked at him and sighed. "Yes," he said. "The Church certainly experienced some difficult growing pains."

Christian nodded. "When the Counter-Reformation started and the Church got rid of the riff-raff, I felt like even more of an outcast," he said. "Nothing made sense. How could a religion change so much? How could the spiritual leaders make so many mistakes?"

"They were human," Father Larry said.

Christian looked at him. "So was I, once. But what I'd become would never change. I didn't have the luxury to fix things like that. I wandered throughout Europe on something of a mission I called 'Self-destruction of the soul.'" He turned to face straight ahead as if he were too ashamed to face the priest. His hands fidgeted in his lap. "You see, I believed my soul had died when my body was changed. I thought I was walking through life just a shell of a man. I believed a lot of things, and everything that was happening around me seemed to strengthen those beliefs."

Father Larry heard a mixture of sarcasm and sincerity in Christian's voice that seemed to emphasize the confusion he must have felt during those early years of his vampirism. "I've seen mortals go through similar crises in their lives when they wander so far from God they deliberately live the evil lives of the devils they think they're doomed to spend eternity with." Father Larry put a hand on Christian's shoulder. "It's actually a very human reaction." He dropped his arm so Christian wouldn't feel uncomfortable.

Christian nodded and took a deep breath. "After nearly a century of living this way I came to the States," he said. "I continued to be the same monster here that I had been overseas." He hesitated, then turned toward Father Larry. "But you know," he said. "I felt awful for everything I'd ever done wrong. And it never made sense to me why I still had a conscience if I was so evil. I never felt that way in here." He pointed to his chest. "It was more in my mind. I felt like I was pretending to be something I'm not. But I couldn't stop being a vampire, so I wondered how I could stop doing evil things. It seemed to me that vampirism and evil went hand-in-hand." He looked away.

"And now?" Father Larry asked. He wondered what evil Christian might have done, but in truth, he really didn't want to know.

"Now, I still wonder about some things. But I learned to separate the physical part of being a vampire from the moral characteristic of being evil. I learned to accept myself as I am. I'm a vampire through no choice of my own, but I'm not an evil person because of it. Roni made me see my life a lot different. She just accepts things at face value sometimes. Looking at my own life through her helped me realize a lot of things." Christian looked up at the crucifix on the altar for a few seconds before he continued. "I know I still have a soul and I know God doesn't abandon any of us."

Father Larry nodded and studied Christian's profile. "What is it that you still wonder about then?"

Christian looked away from the altar, down at the back of the seat in front of him, then at his lap. "I wonder why Roni doesn't want to join me on this side. I don't know that I could handle it when her mortality is over." He caught a sob in his throat that nearly made him choke. "I can understand the thought of drinking blood is unappealing, to say the least. I remember how I felt about it at first. But there are other ways to handle that."

Father Larry realized his suspicions had been correct after all. Christian's visit was not for Roni as much as it was for Christian himself. "Will it change her, Christian?"

"Honestly, Father, I don't know for sure. I have seen it change others once they realized how the possibilities are endless once you're on this side. But I can't see that happening to her. It would keep her healthy. It would keep us together."

Father Larry waited while Christian sat in silence. He had a thousand questions running through his mind when they had started to talk, but now all he wanted to do was help Christian in any way he could.

"I know it would change her physically," Christian said. "But if you're worried about her becoming a monster, don't." He shrugged. "She's outright refused, so it doesn't really matter."

Father Larry couldn't help but let out a sigh of relief as he watched Christian stare at the seat in front of them. He thought he saw a tear fall on his hand. "How old are you?" he asked.

Christian looked at him curiously with an awkward, sideways glance before turning his head to face the priest. "That's an odd question," he said. "What does my age have to do with it?"

"Isn't that the point, Christian?" Father Larry said. "You've been on this earth for quite a long time, and my guess would be that you've spent most of it alone."

"OK." Christian shrugged.

"Well, it seems to me that you've fallen in love with Veronica after such an incredibly long time by yourself and now, you don't ever want to be alone again. Am I right?" He hoped he wasn't overstepping his bounds with this man he was just getting to know.

Christian frowned. "Well, of course you're right." he answered. "What fool would feel any different?"

Father Larry laid a hand on Christian's shoulder once again. "Calm yourself," he said. "It's understandable that you would want to take this love with you through the rest of your years, maybe through eternity. No one would ever find fault with that. But you know that man's eternity is with the Lord in His kingdom and we cannot turn our backs on that. I'm sure Veronica is considering this as part of her decision."

"So, she says."

"Well, what if something were to happen to you, say, a few hundred years from now? Would Veronica be left to walk the earth alone like you have? Would you really want that for her?" Father Larry could hardly believe he was having this conversation. It was too normal to be real.

"No, I wouldn't wish that on her," Christian said. "But mortal years are too short. There's just not enough time for anything. There's too much to do and see."

"And many others feel that they've lived a full life after only seventy years," Father Larry said.

Christian shrugged. "So, it's relative."

Father Larry shook his head. "Nothing in life is cut and dry like so many of us would like it to be," he said. "God gave us rules to live by, but even His rules are, somewhat, open for interpretation depending on the century, the language of the times, restrictions. There are so many variables that it's hard to know what's right sometimes."

"Then how do you know?" Christian asked.

Father Larry smiled. "That's what the conscience is for," he said. "God gave us the greatest gift there is. The gift of free will.

Part of that gift is choosing how to use it. All of our choices are made accordingly. Have you ever heard the saying, 'Let your conscience be your guide?' Your conscience is a piece of God that is always with us and everyone's behaves differently. Roni is only following hers."

Christian's silence made Father Larry uncomfortable. He wished he could read Christian's thoughts.

"A friend of mine that I hadn't seen in years told me that my little sister is one of us by choice," Christian said.

Father Larry wasn't sure how to react. "Oh?"

"I haven't seen her since the day I was changed," Christian closed his eyes and shook his head. "I didn't even know she was still alive until this old friend and I were reunited."

Father Larry felt awful for him. "Does she know about you?"

"No."

"How was that possible?"

Christian looked at him. "The one who changed her is the same who changed me."

Father Larry wasn't sure what he was getting at. He waited.

"He kept us apart all this time because he knew how close we were in our mortal years," Christian said. "When he changed me I made him swear not to tell my family. He let them believe I was carried off by wild animals."

Father Larry leaned back a little and frowned. "Do you mean to tell me your family knew this other vampire?"

Christian held up a hand as if to calm the priest. "Yes, but they didn't know his true nature. Only my sister was told because she fell in love with him."

"I don't understand," Father Larry said. "Why didn't he tell her the truth about you then?"

"Hmm," Christian said with a sarcastic smile. "Because he was afraid she'd leave him when she found out how he lied to her."

"Not after he explained how you asked him to," Father Larry said.

"That's true," Christian said. "It was so close to the time it happened to me that I know she would've understood. But now it's been centuries. I don't think you can justify a lie that's gone on so long."

Father Larry shook his head. "I don't think so either." He looked at Christian. "Does she know now?"

Christian frowned.

"You're kidding," Father Larry said. "When does he plan to tell her?"

Christian shrugged his shoulders.

"Alright, so why did this person finally tell you about her?"

"Samuel, that's his name," Christian said. "He helped me out of a jam not too long ago. It was a relationship gone bad with another vampire who tried to kill me. After all this time, Samuel showed up to help me. It became a sort of reunion. That's when he told me. He said it was her choice, but I didn't believe him. I told him I'd only believe it once I heard it from her own lips. But the more I thought about it the more it started to make sense that it would be true because her love was so strong for him." Christian turned to look at the people who had begun to straggle in for the next mass.

"So, you became jealous?" Father Larry asked. "Maybe wondered if Veronica didn't love you enough if she wasn't willing to join you, as it were?"

"Something like that." Christian turned back toward the priest. "My sister and my friend have so much ahead of them, so much to look forward to and they've already been together such a long time."

"I can't even begin to imagine," Father Larry said. "I wish I could."

Christian turned to him sharply. "Would you like to be immortal, Father?"

Father Larry was caught off guard and suddenly frightened. He looked at the vampire expecting to see the fangs of Bela Lugosi coming at him, but Christian sat calmly waiting for an answer. "I will be," he said. "When I'm with God, I will be."

Christian's face became one of defeat and his expression fell.

"That's exactly how Roni is looking at it," he said. "Why didn't Diana look at it that way?"

"Christian," Father Larry said. "I feel sorry for the beating your heart is taking over this. I've been in love myself. But the bottom line is simple. Each of us has to do what we can honestly answer for with a clear conscience. There is no rationalizing with God because He knows what's in your heart. All of your intentions have to be good and clean and all of your motives have to be as well. I'm sure your sister made her decision with no doubts. Right now, though, Veronica can't. She may never be able to."

A tear fell on to Christian's pant leg. Father Larry saw it and watched it soak into the fabric leaving only a small dark dot.

No, definitely not what I would've expected from a vampire, he thought, then remembered Christian could read his thoughts.

"It's alright," Christian said. "Maybe she'll change her mind someday."

"Maybe," Father Larry agreed.

"What do you think?" Christian asked, still looking down at his lap.

"I think you should enjoy all of your time together," he said. "I think you should stop carrying this burden with you and be thankful you found her at all. And I think you should accept whatever happens as God's will for you both." Father Larry wasn't sure how far he could go giving Christian advice, but he couldn't stop now. "He does everything for His own reasons. After meeting you, I have to admit that I need to rethink some of my own positions on a few things."

Father Larry stood up and patted Christian on the back as he looked around to see the church filling up. "The next mass will be starting soon," he said. "Stay if you like, but I thought you should know."

Christian stood. "No," he said. "I've been gone long enough. I'd better head home in case Roni woke up."

They walked to the back of the church together.

"What should I tell her about the friend I went to visit?" Christian asked him.

Father Larry looked at him and gave him a warm smile. "Tell her the truth, Christian," he said. "This truth won't hurt her."

The two men shook hands, then Christian turned and walked out of the church.

Father Larry watched him go, then remembered he hadn't thanked him for the visit. He opened the door to catch him before he left, but didn't see him anywhere. He looked around for cars that were leaving the parking lot, but only saw three of them entering all of whom he recognized.

"Hmm." Father Larry looked for Christian once more before heading back inside the church. *That was fast,* he thought to himself. *Maybe he flies, too.*

CHAPTER 5

December 6, 1997

Roni sat up with a start, causing Sammie, who had been sleeping on her chest, to fall to the floor. "Silly cat," she mumbled, feeling groggy. She leaned over to check the digital alarm clock on the night stand. "Eight thirty!" She jumped out of bed and haphazardly put on her robe. "I had an appointment at seven!" She turned on the light next to the bed and immediately saw the rose Christian had left on her pillow. She reached over and picked it up. It was thawed and wilted, and it left a water mark, but she didn't care. It warmed her heart to see it.

She walked out of the bedroom and down the hall. "Christian?" she called. "Why didn't you . . ." She stopped when she found his note on the kitchen table. She read it, then quickly checked the answering machine. There was a message from Janet Brandison cancelling her parents' appointment that evening because something had come up. Roni breathed a sigh of relief and went into the kitchen to start brewing a pot of tea. When the water was boiled and the tea bags were in the pot, she went to the window and admired the beauty of the season while both cats wound themselves around her ankles. The snow outside was coming down fast. It had already piled up on the grass enough to completely hide every blade. It was beautiful in its glistening, white silence as it covered everything in sight.

She wondered where Christian had gone. The only friend she knew of besides Samuel was a man Christian visited every so often on Nantucket Island, but that was so seldom Roni hardly ever thought of him. *That couldn't be where he went,* she thought to herself. *He's not a mutual friend.*

The smell of fully brewed tea caught her attention. She turned and went back into the kitchen to pour herself a cup, then sat down at the window in the living room to savor it while she continued to watch the snow fall. Melvin jumped up on her lap the minute she was settled on the sofa. She tucked her legs under herself so she could sit sideways and watch the weather from the window behind her. It felt good to relax. She needed time to herself, from her business that drained her because even though she knew when she'd done too much, she wasn't always smart enough to stop.

"Where did he go, Mel?" she asked the fifteen pound cat who nuzzled her nose to nose. He purred softly in response, then curled up by her knees. "Who's the mutual friend whose name he couldn't write down?" She stroked the cat along his back. "I don't know anyone as old as him except Samuel." She knew he had numerous acquaintances, some of which he might not want her to meet. That was understandable and she accepted it.

"No one you wouldn't approve of," Christian whispered as soft as a cloud into her ear. She felt his arms surround her from behind with their comforting warmth. She leaned back against him neither startled nor surprised that he was suddenly in the room. She was used to it.

"Mmmmm," she moaned. "I'm glad you're home."

Christian smiled. "Are you?" he asked. "You look perfectly happy with your hot cup of tea and your little body guard by your side." He reached over and petted the aloof tabby who reacted as if he had been rudely disturbed.

"I am," Roni said. "But everything gets better when you're with me." She turned around and kissed him gently on the lips, then sat back and looked out the window. She assumed he knew what was on her mind since he could easily read her thoughts so she waited for him to tell her where he'd gone.

"It's really coming down out there," he said. "Samuel would love this weather."

"Oh! That reminds me!" Roni sat up quickly and turned to face him. "He called. He's bringing Diana to the States with him for Christmas."

Christian's face lit up, his eyes sparkling at the sound of his sister's name. "When did he call? Where was he that he called while we were asleep?"

"Earlier this afternoon," Roni said. "I hadn't been able to sleep all day, so I was awake for the call. It just worked out that he messed up his time zones, again, when he phoned us."

Christian shook his head and smiled. "You'd think after all this time he'd be a pro at it. Why is it so difficult for him to understand?"

Roni couldn't help but chuckle. "It's probably not important to him," she said. "He knows where the sun is. That's what matters."

Christian nodded. "I guess. But why did you pick up the phone? That's what answering machines are for, Roni. I suppose that explains why you were so tired, though."

"Not just because of Samuel," she said. "I just couldn't sleep. But as it turned out, it's a good thing I got the phone."

"Why's that?"

Roni turned around and leaned her back into Christian again before she spoke. She knew there was no gentle way to tell him about the call, so she just said it. "He hasn't told your sister about you yet."

"What?" Christian's yell frightened both cats who jumped off the sofa and ran down the hall. "What do you mean 'He hasn't told my sister about me yet?'"

"Just what I said." She turned around to look at him. "Diana thinks they're just on a holiday vacation or something. He didn't tell her everything."

Christian shook his head and stared out the window. "My God," he said. "What could he be thinking?"

"The only thing I could get from our conversation is that he's so afraid of her reaction to the news that he seems to be putting it off until it's inevitable," Roni said. "Maybe it has to be out of his hands completely."

"You mean maybe someone else should tell her?"

"That's one possibility," Roni said. "I don't think he has the guts."

"Then why is he bringing her at all?" he asked. "And letting us know."

"That's what I mean," she said. "I really think he wants her to know once and for all, but I also think it has to happen on its own somehow."

"Well, it sure is one helluva burden to carry after all this time," he said, running his fingers through his hair. "Can you imagine holding in a secret like that?"

"No, I can't," Roni said. "Not for me, anyway. But Samuel? It fits. What I can't understand is how he can be so strong in every other way imaginable, but he can't handle taking care of this. He sounded petrified on the phone."

"That figures," Christian said. "But what is he afraid of, really?"

"He's afraid of making her angry with him," she said. "I suppose he has good reason to expect her to be."

"I'd say." Christian nodded. "She's going to be even more pissed off when she finds out that he didn't do anything to prepare her for the shock."

Roni looked at him, her head cocked sideways. "What could he do to prepare her?"

"Drop a few hints, maybe." He looked away. "I don't know. Ask her what she thought of the possibility that I might still be alive. I'm sure if he took the time to think about it he'd find a way."

Roni nodded. "Besides, what's the difference if he tells her now or a hundred years from now? It's been so long already, another century won't matter. He's digging himself a grave." She saw him frown and realized what she said. "So to speak."

"Thank you," Christian said. The sarcasm in his voice was obvious.

They sat in silence for a few moments. Then Christian leaned back and laid his head against the palm of his hand. He looked deflated. "So, now what do we do?"

"Well, I guess all we can do is let Samuel bury himself. You'll be glad to see Diana, of course, and the rest will just have to take care of itself." Roni was speaking practically, but in her heart she wanted to pound some sense into that friend of his. "Let's just wait and see what happens. Maybe she'll surprise him and take it just fine."

Christian's laugh was apprehensive. "Not if she's the same Diana I remember," he said. "That's one bird whose feathers you don't want to ruffle. Not ever. She's little, but she's tough."

Roni leaned back onto him for the third time. "Oh, well," she said. "If nothing else, this ought to be a very memorable Christmas."

Christian wrapped his arms around her and rested his chin on the top of her head. "That it will," he said. "Oh, by the way. I went to visit Father Larry tonight."

Immediately, Roni's body tensed up and her heart began to beat faster. She waited for him to tell her about it, but he said nothing. "How is he?" she asked.

"He seems well."

Roni nodded. "Oh, that's good." Part of her wanted to know why he went to visit Father Larry, but another part of her didn't want to know anything about it. She didn't know what she was afraid of, but she knew the idea of the two of them together made her uncomfortable right down to the churning that had started in her stomach.

"What's the matter?" Christian asked.

She turned to look at him. "What, exactly, made you go see

him tonight?" She couldn't hide the mix of anger and anxiety from her voice, but she didn't try very hard, either.

Christian kissed the side of her neck as if to soften the tension in her. "Well, at first, I thought I was doing you a favor since you hadn't gone to see him yourself in quite a while." He kissed her again softly on her ear, then on the side of her head. "Then, I realized that I wanted to meet him myself without you there to run interference for us. I wanted to see if we would get along."

"And, did you?"

He nodded. "Fabulously. I think we were both a little nervous at first, but it went well. The church is still standing, and aside from a temporary surge in his blood pressure, Father Larry is no worse for the wear."

Roni knew he was making light of the meeting so she wouldn't worry. "So, he didn't ask you a zillion stupid questions?"

Christian shook his head.

"One or two, maybe?"

"Nope."

"He didn't offer any advice on how to end your eternal existence so you could go to heaven and be with God like you're supposed to?" she asked.

"Nope," Christian said. "In fact, he seemed to feel that God's plans are, shall we say, open to interpretation."

She frowned. "Oh, really." Sarcasm was creeping back into her voice, but she was slowly gaining a playful understanding of his visit. "Well, I'm glad you two got along." She shrugged slightly as if to dismiss the subject, then snuggled closer against him, and sighed.

"Don't you want to know what we talked about?" he asked.

"No." It was her turn to make him wonder.

"Not even the least bit curious?"

"No."

"Why not?"

"It's none of my business," she said.

Christian turned her around to face him. "Sure it is," he said.

He sounded hurt. "If you'd gone to see him yourself after he blessed this house, I don't think I would've gone. But you didn't, so I went in your place."

"For what?"

"To make sure he was OK." Christian hesitated a moment. "You know. With me being what I am."

Now that Roni knew his true motives for going her heart melted. To think he loved her so much he'd try to be friends with Father Larry for her sake. "Christian," Roni said, "I'm not embarrassed by or concerned with your vampirism. I love you because of how you make me feel about me." She pointed to her chest for emphasis. "You make me a better person because your love is so strong. And you're so open with it that I know it's always there no matter what. When the rest of the world has treated me lousy all day I know I can walk right into your arms and never worry that they won't be open. You're my solace, my shelter. You keep me sane." She gently took his face in her hands and looked deep into his eyes. "Do you understand what I mean?"

Christian stared at her. His eyes held a look of wonder. "Your strength and confidence amaze me," he said. He put his hands over hers and held them a second. Then he took her in his arms again and laid his head on her shoulder. "I know exactly what you mean."

"That's why I never went to see Father Larry," she said. "I didn't have to."

"He said he'd been expecting you."

Roni backed out of his embrace and took his hands in her own, caressing them with her fingertips. "Maybe he was," she said. "But he knew how I felt about you the minute he walked through the door. Sure, I wanted the two of you to get along, but if you hadn't it certainly would not have changed anything between us. And it would not have changed anything between Father Larry and me, either. I know the kind of man he is, accepting and open-minded. He's a wonderful human being and one helluva priest. No matter what, he would always be there for me." She looked down at Christian's hands. "The bottom line is, if I'd gone rushing to see him it would've looked like I was ashamed of something and had to get his approval in order to make it right. But the truth is, Honey, whether Father Larry was alright with the reality of vampires or not, it wouldn't have made any difference with how I feel for you. So, what was the point?"

"Because you wanted to make sure he wasn't shaken up by meeting me?" he asked.

Roni looked up at him. "Did he look that badly shaken up to you when he left here?"

Christian nodded. "A little, maybe. But who wouldn't be?"

"Exactly," Roni said. "Do you feel better now that you went to see him?"

"As a matter of fact, I do," Christian said. "I feel a ton better."

"Why?"

He seemed to think a minute. "I don't know exactly," he said. "Maybe because he's a priest, but he didn't condemn me or judge me like I expected him to."

"Did you really need his approval in order to justify your existence, Christian?" she asked. "Isn't my love for you enough?"

He was thoughtful for a moment, but didn't say anything.

Roni realized he still lived in the shadows of embarrassment that being a vampire had caused. "When will you be able to approve of yourself without justification from anywhere?"

"I guess I saw him as being one step closer to God," Christian said. "I think it's God's approval that I'm really looking for."

"Oh, Honey." Roni ran the backs of her fingers along the side of his cheek. "God is love. That's not just a bumper sticker on the back of somebody's rusty, old car. It's the truth. Without God's presence there can be no love in our lives. The simple fact that you're able to love and to be loved is proof of God's presence in your life."

"OK," Christian said, "that's His presence you're talking about. I'm talking about getting His approval."

"Alright. Then look at it this way." She leaned back and put her arm across the top of the sofa. "Do you think God would hang out with Satan?" she asked. "That's quite a verbal picture, don't you think?"

Christian laughed, then kissed her on the forehead. "I get the idea," he said. "I see what you're getting at and it makes sense." He turned around and placed his arm across hers. "How do you know so much about God?"

"From Father Larry," she said. At that moment both cats jumped up on the sofa and made it very clear they wanted to get in on the attention.

"I'll go see him if you think I need to," Roni said. She playfully pushed him down on the sofa. "Father Larry does mean an awful lot to me. Maybe I was a little nervous about going to visit."

"No, I don't think you need to, now." Christian reached for her and playfully pulled her down on top of him.

Sammi immediately began to walk up Roni's back to get to Christian. He grabbed the cat with one hand and placed her upside down beside him on the sofa so he could rub her belly. The fluffy, white cat purred delightedly.

"Never-the-less," Roni said, laying her head on Christian's chest. "I'll go see him in a week or so. After he's had a chance to digest today's visit from you. I wouldn't want him to think I forgot about him because of you or anything." She watched Christian scratch Sammi under the chin.

"I'm sure he'll appreciate it," Christian said.

Roni got up from the sofa and headed for the kitchen. "I'm going for another cup of tea. Can I get you anything?" It was a habit of politeness that caused her to ask this question. She realized her error too late.

"I von to zuck yur blod," Christian mimicked from the living room.

"Port?" Roni asked, shaking the wine bottle for him to see.

"Sure. Then you."

"Oh?" Roni acted coquettish as she re-entered the living room with her tea and Christian's wine. "Just what did you have in mind?"

Christian took his glass of wine from her, sipped it, then placed it on the end table. He guided her to his lap where he wrapped both arms around her and held her close.

"Someone to watch the snow fall with," he said.

"And then?"

"Someone to watch it melt with?"

Roni punched him lightly on the shoulder causing her tea to spill a few drops on his shirt.

Christian ran a fingertip along her arm and looked at her with half closed eyes. "We'll see what happens," he said.

"I love you, Christian."

"And I, you," he said. "More than you could ever know."

She turned to look at him, but was taken aback when she saw a conflict of emotions on his face. "Diana?" she asked.

Christian looked away. "Yes," he said. "I'm sorry."

"Everything will be alright," Roni said. "It might be a little more complicated because of Samuel's fears, but it will all work out in the end. Things always work themselves out somehow."

Christian looked away and said nothing.

"Believe me," she said. She was doing her best to believe it herself.

Christian nodded, then pulled her tight to him once more as if she were the security blanket of a child. "I do believe you," he said. "But even more, I believe in you."

Roni smiled and did her best to hide the secret fear that her words of encouragement might be nothing more than that, mere words.

CHAPTER 6

December 9, 1997

The shuttle plane ride from Boston to Nantucket Island had been a bit rougher than the previous times when Father Larry had gone to visit Jesse Nestarius. It wasn't until a little after two o'clock when his feet felt solid ground that he was able to relax and look around. The sky looked a little suspicious and he dreaded the thought of getting caught in a snow storm. It was that time of the year.

Father Larry breathed in the salty island air and tried to settle down so he could work on finding a ride to Jesse's house on the northern shore. It had been many months since the two old friends had seen each other, maybe even a year. He couldn't remember exactly, time seemed to fly by so quickly the older he got. He did recall, however, that it had been a strange visit. It was the only time Jesse had ever come to Father Larry requesting an entire mass to be said for intentions he did not divulge.

Rarely did Father Larry say an additional mass by request. His health barely allowed him the strength to carry out the work he was bound to do, or the number of masses he was required to say each day. But when Jesse had asked the priest for this favor, Father Larry made the sacrifice and obliged his dear friend. Jesse never did explain the strange request, and Father Larry never asked.

While the priest stood near the parking lot of the Nantucket Municipal Airport, a taxi cab pulled up a few feet away. Father Larry watched as the driver got out of the vehicle and stretched his limbs while looking at the gray clouds that were beginning to roll in. He noticed the driver's worn khakis that were covered with paint stains, and the cracked workboots on his feet, yet when he turned toward him he saw the gold chain around his neck with a crucifix hanging from it. He was obviously not materialistic, abut he was proud of his faith. Father Larry liked that.

"Are you available?" he asked the elderly cab driver.

"Sure am," the driver replied. "Here, gimme." He lifted the priest's small bag and placed it in the trunk of the cab. "Can't be too careful these days, y'know," he joked.

"I suppose," Father Larry answered haphazardly as he got into the back seat of the vehicle.

The driver got in behind the steering wheel and turned around. "Where to?" he asked.

Father Larry thought a moment. I know he gave me the address, he thought to himself. "I'm not sure of the exact address," he told the driver. "But I can get us there."

"Good enough for me," the man replied, putting the cab in gear.

In past visits, Jesse knew ahead of time when Father Larry was coming to see him, and they had met at the airport. However, Jesse was not expecting Father Larry this time. This visit had been planned at the last minute out of a desperate need to confide in someone. Father Larry could not go to the Monsignor or the Bishop with this problem, but he knew Jesse to be calm and level-headed about everything. Most of all, it was Jesse's overall open-mindedness Father Larry needed right now. Especially when he explained what caused him to show up at his friend's door unannounced.

Had he been on the mainland at that moment, Father Larry would have turned around and gone home, embarrassed that he had thought to impose on a friend this way. But he wasn't on the mainland. In fact, Father Larry had gone through so much trouble to get the time away from the church and his duties in order to take this trip that it left him no choice but to see it through.

"Looks like we got a snow storm movin' in," the cab driver remarked.

Father Larry looked out the back seat window. Indeed, the dark, grey clouds seemed to be rolling in fast. "Yes, it does," he said. A gust of wind shook the taxi as if it were a toy. "What's in the forecast for today?" he asked.

"Don't know," the driver said. "I didn't catch it. Where did you say we were headed?"

"Turn right here," Father Larry told him. "Then another right at the first stop sign you see." The wind howled outside the cab making him thankful to have the shelter of the small, metal vehicle to break the striking cold that waited just outside the doors.

After nearly an hour of driving roads that were slippery in patches and guessing which turn came next, the cab finally pulled up about twenty yards from the back of Jesse's house.

"Never knew anyone lived out this way," the driver said. "Always thought it was wilderness and beaches." He scratched his head, and stared at the house as if he were seeing a lawn of red grass. "Amazing," he said. "Lived here all my life and never knew."

Father Larry thought nothing of the cab driver's ignorance concerning this side of the island. Jesse had told him how isolated he really was. Father Larry paid the man and got out of the car. He took four steps toward the house before the cab driver called him back.

"Don't forget your bag!" the driver yelled. He ran around to the trunk, opened it, and hurriedly handed the bag to the priest.

"Thank you," Father Larry said. "I don't know where my head was at."

"Don't mention it."

The cab driver waved as he pulled away, leaving the priest to stand alone, a small man against the background of snow and trees and Jesse's house.

It was cold on the island. Much colder than it was on the mainland when he left. Father Larry noticed how the snowplows had piled snow up everywhere along the main streets in town, but at this part of the island the snow stayed where it fell until it melted in the Spring. He remembered Jesse telling him how no one plowed or shoveled here because hardly anyone lived out this way. The few who did stocked up for the winter to avoid having to venture out, so the snow was never really in anyone's way.

Now that he was here Father Larry wondered about Jesse living in such isolation. He supposed Jesse stocked up on supplies for the winter like everyone else, but it was the fact that Jesse lived alone, that really bothered the priest. Father Larry wasn't sure how healthy that could be for anyone. However, considering that Jesse never showed any visible signs of aging, Father Larry decided there must be something to the solitary life. He was reminded of Dick Clark who was now in his seventies, but did not look a day over thirty five. Now, there was a man who lived anything but a solitary life and still managed to appear ageless. Then there was Sister Mary Rosalie at St. Joseph's Convent who was nearing eighty years old while maintaining a youthful appearance and a spirit that knew no bounds. Nope. Calendar years had nothing to do with aging.

Father Larry began his trek through Jesse's backyard and prepared to spring his rude, unannounced surprise on this man who had meant so much to him over the years.

"Ah, well," the priest mumbled, a visible breath of condensed air pouring from his mouth. "I'm here now." He walked through the four inches of snow along a row of trees and primrose bushes in order not to spoil the solid white of the yard. The foliage blocked most of the gusty wind making his trek through the expansive yard more bearable. He had a creepy feeling that Jesse might not even be at home. Then what would he do without access to a phone so he could call a cab if he needed one?

He wondered how far he'd have to walk to get to the nearest neighbor to use their phone.

He wondered how far away the nearest neighbor might actually be.

Father Larry approached the front of the house and walked up the steps onto the porch. He leaned over to knock on the door without disturbing the sparkling white floor of snow on the wooden boards at his feet. It just didn't seem right, somehow. It was bad enough that he was feeling more and more like an intruder. He didn't have to mess up the man's beautiful white landscape as well.

After a few relatively short seconds, Jesse appeared at the door causing the misplaced priest to release a huge, audible sigh of relief only to be followed by an equally large intake of breath when Jesse opened the solid, wood door and stood alone on the other side of the paned storm door.

"Jesse?" Father Larry asked.

He was a tall man, a little over six feet, with long hair that always seemed blonder in the summer months and brown in the winter. The fact that it was past his shoulders never seemed to strike the priest as much as it did now. Jesse had also grown a bit of a mustache since their last visit, and it looked as if he was in the beginning stages of growing a beard, as well. Either that or it was simply a day's worth of 'shadow.'

Father Larry had rarely seen this man in such an informal light, but he had never come to visit unexpectedly before, either. Once again, the aging priest found himself second guessing his need to make this visit, feeling more the intruder than the friend. He only hoped Jesse would understand.

"Larry!" Jesse said, smiling. "What on earth has brought you here?" Jesse opened the storm door and stepped onto the porch in his bare feet, putting the first marks in the undisturbed snow. He wore nothing more than a deep blue, full-length caftan, but he hardly seemed to feel the bite in the air as he put his arm around the priest's shoulders and guided him into the house. "Come in, come in," he said. "Sit down. I'll make us something to warm the insides. Then you can tell me what brought you all the way out here."

Jesse took Father Larry's coat and gently placed it on the coat rack in the kitchen. He put a kettle of water to boil on the old stove, then entered the sitting room where Father Larry had already tried to make himself comfortable. He sat on the worn sofa right next to the priest and studied his face for a second or two. "What is it?" he asked.

Father Larry suddenly felt as though his mind had been drained of all thoughts. He had no idea where to begin. "I'm sorry for dropping in on you like this," he said, stammering over his words. "I just needed to talk about something, and I couldn't think of anyone else who would be open-minded enough to listen without having me committed. I really need some down-to-earth insight on this one, Jesse." The priest looked at him, almost begging him to understand and be the right person to talk to, knowing all the time that there was no one else.

"You know I'm always here for you, Larry," Jesse said. His informal way of addressing the priest always made Father Larry feel at home. "You know you never have to question that. Nor do you need to worry about dropping in unannounced. I don't have a phone." He smiled. "How else would you have reached me?"

"True enough," Father Larry said. "I can't tell you how much I appreciate it."

"Forget about it," Jesse said, raising his hand to wave the thought away. "Now tell me what's wrong. Just come right out and say it. We'll deal with it from there. Together."

Father Larry sat in silence for a long while, with no idea how to say everything that had been running through his mind since Christian came to visit him at church the previous Saturday evening.

"Larry?" Jesse said, placing a hand on the priest's arm.

Father Larry looked at him. "I'm sorry," he said. He looked around the room trying to decide where to start. Then he settled his gaze on Jesse again. "I think . . .," he said, just as the kettle began to whistle.

Jesse stood up slowly motioning to the priest to follow him as he headed toward the next room. "Come join me in the kitchen if you'd like," he said. "Maybe you'll be more comfortable in there while I make our drinks."

Father Larry stood up. "I'm comfortable with you," he said, following Jesse. "It's the subject that I'm having trouble with."

The two men entered the kitchen. It was a warm, inviting room with windows on two adjacent walls that gave it a light, airy atmosphere. The fixtures were all very old, but that only added to the room's appeal. Father Larry sat at the yellow, metal table, while Jesse went to the stove and poured the steaming water from the kettle into the two mugs that already sat on the counter.

"What are we drinking?" Father Larry asked. He was stalling the conversation he knew they needed to have.

"Hot Toddies," Jesse answered. He held up a fifth of whisky and a plate of lemon wedges. "To warm you up, dry you out, and relax you completely."

Father Larry shifted in his seat and chuckled. "Well, that'll definitely do all of the above." He turned to look out the window and watched the surf roll up on the shore as far as the snow line allowed. It looked to him as if halves of two different pictures had been pasted together like a before and after scene. One side was 'before' the snow melted and the other was 'after' the snow melted.

"Takes some getting used to, doesn't it?" Jesse said. "Sand and snow together, I mean."

Father Larry did not turn from the window. "It sure does."

"When you see the ocean you expect it to be tropical," Jesse said, placing two plain, white mugs on the table. Both were steaming, the aroma was soothing and sweet. "Snow just doesn't fit into the picture at all."

"I don't think I've ever been here in the winter," Father Larry said. "I would have remembered a vision like this."

"No," Jesse said, "I don't believe you have."

Father Larry sat in silence while Jesse took a seat beside him.

"So tell me," Jesse said gently. "What's on your mind, Larry?"

"I met a vampire," Father Larry said, trying to keep his voice soft and steady. He continued to stare out the window at the winter ocean, but he said nothing more. He couldn't. He had surprised himself by saying it so quick. But he could feel Jesse studying him, and he waited for his reaction. He concentrated on the waves that crashed far out from the shore, then quickly glided up over the sand before ending in a frozen foam at the snow line. He'd said it. Now he could only wait. He was deeply troubled over Christian, but would Jesse understand?

"Did the two of you get along?" Jesse asked.

The question caught Father Larry completely off guard. He looked away from the window slowly and shifted his gaze to Jesse who sat patiently, waiting for an answer.

"You're not surprised?" the priest asked.

Jesse sipped his tea. "Not at all," he said, waving his mug toward the priest. "Drink your tea. It'll calm you."

Father Larry did as he was instructed before he continued to speak. He had no idea how to proceed with the conversation, and Jesse's reaction troubled him. "I said, I met a vampire," Father Larry repeated.

"I heard you," Jesse said. "Tell me about him. What kind of man was he? Where did you meet him?"

Father Larry moaned inwardly. "This isn't helping me at all. I came to talk to you because you always seem to understand things that are out of the ordinary, but it's backfiring."

Jesse smiled warmly. "What did you expect?"

"I think I expected you to talk me out of believing in vampires," Father Larry answered. "Maybe I expected you to be rational and make me understand how impossible it was for me to have met such a being. Instead, I'm beginning to wonder if maybe I'm not alone in my insanity."

Jesse laughed, then sipped his tea. "Oh, Larry," he said, shaking his head. "Nothing is impossible."

Father Larry turned to look out the window. He was discouraged. "I think we've both been too solitary."

Jesse leaned forward and smiled. "It's because of our solitude that we're so much more in tune to these things," he said. "We both know the reality of what exists. We've seen a lot and we cannot deny any of it." Jesse placed a comforting hand on Father Larry's shoulder. He gave him an encouraging squeeze, then leaned back in his chair. "Now tell me the whole story," he said.

Father Larry took a deep breath, then told Jesse all the details surrounding his visit to bless Roni's house, and Christian's recent visit to the church. But he mentioned no names. He found that he began to relax as Jesse sat listening, intent on what he had to say. He was less frightened by the conversation, unconcerned as to the way he might come across now that he was in the middle of getting it off his chest. When he was finished with his story, he stared at the table, and sighed.

"What is it, exactly, that has you upset enough to come all the way out here to see me?" Jesse asked.

Father Larry gave Jesse a wide-eyed, incredulous look. How could he not see it? "He's a vampire," Father Larry said. "Aside from that, I don't really know. I can't put my finger on it. I would've thought his vampirism was enough, but now I see that I'm almost used to it. I mean, he's a nice enough man. His inner strength is intense and powerful. That part of him scares me a little, I'll admit. But his love for this woman is as strong as he is. That part of him surprises me."

"Why is that?" Jesse asked.

Father Larry looked quickly at Jesse, then out the window at the surf. "It's not what I would have expected," he said. Father Larry shook his head, then took another sip of his drink. What was it that bothered him? Why did anything about Christian bother him? Could it be that he was prejudiced? Father Larry was ashamed of himself at the very thought that he might actually be so biased. He was a priest.

"Did you believe the stereotype of vampires?" Jesse asked.

Father Larry shook his head in affirmation only partly aware of what he was doing.

"How could you believe the stereotype without believing in them at all?" Jesse asked.

Father Larry looked stunned for a moment. Jesse had a point. Had he believed in them all along without knowing it? What a thought! But it was possible when he considered how easy it could be to believe in something when you never expect to face the reality of it.

"You know, you're right." the priest said. "I think what bothered me all this time is that I kept waiting for him to do some 'Tales of the Crypt' kind of thing, but he didn't. I had a preconceived notion of what he should be like, and I used it to judge him before I'd even gotten to know him." Father Larry rested his head on his hands in shame. "This is the worst," he lamented. "God accepts all of mankind equally and openly. He expects us to do the same, and to teach each other how to accept everyone. Yet, I failed in this."

"Larry," Jesse said. "You're taking this much too hard. Most people wouldn't be able to accept such a person as being a real vampire. But you've seen enough to know the truth."

"But I am prejudiced," Father Larry said.

"It's not that bad," Jesse offered.

"Oh, yes," Father Larry said, looking up. "How can I face either of them?"

Jesse laughed as he reached over to place a hand on Father Larry's arm. "Why don't you simply set the record straight?" he suggested. "Pay them a visit, and explain yourself to them. Don't you know that it's always better to face a situation head on than to try to skirt around it? Go to them, tell them how you feel and why. Then apologize."

Father Larry looked at him. "And how do I advise . . . uh . . . the woman if she asks?" he said. He found it increasingly difficult not to use Roni or Christian's names.

"Obviously, you're too close to her to be objective," Jesse said. "She may never ask for your advice on the matter. Her mind may be so completely made up that she never thinks to ask anyone's opinion."

Father Larry stared out the window and sipped his Hot Toddy. He felt sad because Jesse was right. Roni might never ask for his advice. And Christian might convince her to undergo the change.

"We'd all like to see our loved ones healthy and happy and living forever, but it can't be so," Jesse said. "Without tests from God, and sacrifices for mankind the struggle between good and evil can never be fought fairly or equally." Jesse was silent while he stood up and made fresh drinks for the priest and himself, but Father Larry knew Jesse well enough to know he was thinking about his original question. "Whatever decision this woman makes," Jesse said, "will be the right one as long as she makes it herself, with a clear conscience and for the right reasons." Jesse placed Father Larry's mug in front of him on the table, then leaned against the counter. "All we can do is teach the rules," he said. "We cannot enforce them. This is not a court of law, this world. This is life. It must be lived, not enforced."

Father Larry turned to him and frowned. "We enforce for each other as part of our mission," he argued. "At least, that's what I was taught."

"Yes, we do," Jesse said. "In some ways. But without faith on the side of those who we are enforcing those rules for, we are still fighting a losing battle. Each of us has our own learning to do, and our own destiny to fulfill. There's precious little time as it is. The largest part of our purpose here is not to be the judge or the enforcer for others. The largest part of our purpose here is to perfect ourselves to whatever degree that is possible, and to share the knowledge we gain along the way with those around us to help them do the same."

Father Larry took a deep breath and stared at Jesse. "Good heavens, you do make sense," he said. "I know for myself I've tried to do my best in teaching right from wrong. But every so often I have my own questions on the subject."

"You're not alone," Jesse said, "but you cannot wash your hands of humanity once the rules have been taught. You still must advise and guide. You still have an obligation to do your best in leading those who come to you toward a single, specific end."

"Which is?"

"Righteousness," Jesse said. "To live a life that is morally right, free from guilt or sin, and to do everything with a sincere and honest heart." He paused, then looked away for a moment. "Whatever decision this woman makes must be made by her alone, and it must be made with a true heart." He turned toward Father Larry. "You cannot make the choice for her, Larry. That's forbidden and you know it."

Father Larry nodded.

"But you must try to lead her to make whatever choice is truly right for her."

"And what if she chooses to become a vampire?" Father Larry asked. "How can I condone that?"

Jesse was thoughtfull for a moment. "It's not your place to do anything else." He sat down in his chair, then leaned back. "Larry, remember. We each have free will. You cannot take that away from a person. This woman must make her own choice."

Father Larry nodded. "I understand."

"It doesn't mean you can't ask heaven for a little help," Jesse said, smiling. "Just remember, you cannot decide what's right for her. Only she can do that and you have no choice but to accept her decisions. Don't carry this on your shoulders like a huge weight. It's not yours to carry." Jesse pointed toward the ceiling. "It's His."

Father Larry stood up, one hand on his round belly, and raised his mug toward Jesse. "I know what you mean. I don't like it, but I do understand."

Jesse chuckled softly, then raised his mug in return. "I'm glad to see you smiling."

"Again, you do me justice, my friend," the priest said. "For the life of me I don't know what I'd do without you."

"Oh, if not me," Jesse said, "there'd be someone else along to help you out. The Father does those kinds of things quite often, you know."

"That may be true," Father Larry said, "but I'm glad it's you that He sent to me."

Jesse looked at the floor. "I'm touched." He turned around and began to wipe the counter top. "Will you be staying a day or so," he asked. "Or are you going back to the mainland today?"

"Well, if you'll have me," Father Larry said, "I'd like to head back tomorrow. But I feel that I've already been an imposition by arriving unannounced."

"Nonsense," Jesse said. "My house is always open to good people. You'll stay, of course."

Father Larry was deeply relieved. "Thank you," he said. "I'll stay. Of course."

CHAPTER 7

December 10, 1997

Christian and Roni stood on the dock overlooking Woods Hole harbor at the southern end of Cape Cod. The damp, December air suddenly felt more like early spring than it did late autumn. Only four nights ago Roni's roses had been frozen from the snowfall, yet tonight there was no trace of snow to be found anywhere. That was typical of New England weather.

"Tell me again about this friend of yours," Roni said. "Is he like you? Why haven't I met him before?"

"He lives on Nantucket," Christian said. A touch of anxiety invaded his inner being. Jesse had asked Christian to bring Roni there to meet him. The contact was made telepathically, but when Christian tried to find out why, Jesse did not respond. "He's sort of a recluse."

"Well, I know you've gone to see him before," Roni said. "Not that often though. How come?"

Christian looked out over the water. "Jesse's one of those special kinds of friends that you don't have to see every day just to stay close," he said. "He's the type of friend that stays a friend, no matter what."

Roni hooked an arm through one of Christian's. "Does he know about me?" she asked.

Christian nodded. "Mmm, hmmm."

"Well, I'm glad I'll finally get to meet him," she said. "I hope he's not the handful that Samuel can be."

"No," Christian said, trying to hide his anxiety. "Jesse is quite different than Samuel."

"How so?" Roni asked.

"You'll see."

Roni looked up at the sky, then turned to look at Christian.

"Why do I get the feeling you're upset about meeting him here?" she asked. "What's wrong?"

Christian turned toward her, and looked deep in her eyes. An autumn breeze lifted the ends of her hair and released them to lay across her face. "I'm not sure," he said honestly. He reached toward her and brushed the few strands of hair from her cheek. "All I can tell you is that Jesse asked to meet you."

"Is that why we're here?" Roni asked. "Why didn't he just come to our house? What's the big mystery? It was a long drive to get here just so we can meet each other. If he's a vampire, why didn't he just fly over or something?"

Christian turned his view back toward the ocean waters. The world was nearly black except for the dull light of the moon, but the air was wonderfully invigorating. "Don't you like it out here?" Christian asked. "I would have thought such a beautiful night would appeal to you."

"You know it does," Roni said. She leaned her elbow on the rail and looked at the sky. "But the same stars are shining at home. I'm only questioning this drive because your friend doesn't seem to be making much sense by asking us to come here. That's all."

"Everything Jesse does makes sense," Christian said. "He's very secretive. But what he does, he does for very good reasons."

Roni looked at him. "I didn't think anyone could be more secretive than you," she teased.

Christian looked at her and smiled, trying to hide his growing concern. "Samuel's the same way," he reminded her.

"I suppose that means all vampires are," she said, smiling.

Christian watched the few boats that slowly cruised the harbor. "I suppose so," he said without thinking.

Roni turned to face the water. "Is he taking the ferry?" she asked. "I didn't know they ran this late."

"I really don't know," Christian said. "But I don't suppose it matters, either."

Roni looked at him, then shook her head. "I suppose not."

Christian watched her as she breathed in the cold, clean air. He knew Roni to be a fairly accurate judge of character. He believed that given her deeply spiritual nature, she'd quickly come to understand Jesse Nestarius. And given the fact that she accepted him and Samuel, he guessed she would do the same for Jesse.

"Hello, Christian."

Both Christian and Roni turned toward the quiet, masculine voice at the same time. Christian was relieved that his friend had arrived. He was anxious to discover the purpose of this meeting.

"Jesse," Christian said. He put his arms toward Jesse and embraced him. "It's so good to see you man. Why do we always let so much time pass?"

"Oh, it hasn't been that long," Jesse said. He continued to hold Christian tightly to him. "Time is relative. You know that. What does it really matter?"

"Ah, you're right," Christian agreed as their arms loosened from around each other. "And, as you requested, Jesse, I'd like you to meet Roni." Christian held one arm around Jesse's shoulder and gestured toward Roni with his free hand.

Roni stepped forward into Christian's open arm. She placed her right hand in front of her to shake Jesse's hand. "It's nice to meet you, Jesse," she said, staring briefly into his eyes.

Christian watched her study his friend, starting with the warm handshake he knew would surprise her. He saw her check Jesse's eyes for blood lines, but he knew she'd find none. She inspected the long, black, wool coat he wore with the collar turned up and the buttons left open, the same way Christian wore his. Just when he thought she was finished evaluating his friend, a bewildered look appeared on her face as she stared up into Jesse's eyes once more.

"What's wrong?" Christian asked her.

Roni shook her head and shrugged. "I'm sorry," she said. She looked at Christian, then back at Jesse. "You looked familiar, Jesse. I was trying to figure out where I'd seen you before."

"C'mon, Roni," Christian teased. "I know he's handsome and all, but you could have the decency not to hit on another man while I'm standing right next to you." He squeezed her gently around the waist and laughed, but the look Roni flashed his way told Christian she did not find it to be so amusing.

"I wasn't . . . ," she started, then playfully shoved him aside. "You know better!"

Christian couldn't help but smile. "I was teasing," he said, then turned to Jesse. "Are you sorry now, that you asked us to meet you?"

Jesse chuckled softly. "No, not at all," he said. "I've wanted to meet Roni for some time now."

"Since you mentioned it," Christian began. "Why did you 'summon' us, this evening? I've been concerned since our communication earlier."

Three geese flew overhead squawking loudly as they passed by, while Christian stood anxiously awaiting Jesse's answer. It occurred to him how odd it was to see geese flying at this time of the night. But unusual occurences seemed to signal Jesse's presence more times than not.

"It's getting close to Christmas," Jesse said. "'Tis the season for visiting friends and such."

"You could've come to our house for that, you know," Roni said. "We could've done the egg nog thing and opened presents and all that if you wanted to celebrate Christmas together."

Jesse laughed wholeheartedly. "I have other obligations at Christmas," he said. "I make it a point to visit beforehand so I don't leave anyone out." He turned his full attention to Christian. "Where's Sam? Have you met with your sister yet?"

Jesse's question was an angry reminder of Christian's biggest disappointment in recent days. "No," Christian said. "He's hoarding her. Keeping her all to himself in case she leaves him once she finds out about his five hundred year old charade." Christian turned to face the harbor again and began to sulk. He made no attempt to hide his disappointment.

Roni put her arm around him, then looked at Jesse. "It seems that Samuel is afraid of losing Diana because of this big secret he's kept from her," she said. "I found out when he called the other day."

Jesse nodded in understanding, but did not say a word.

"Typical!" Christian blurted out.

"Well, put yourself in his shoes," Roni said. "How would you feel?"

"She's got a point, you know," Jesse said.

"I know." Christian turned around to face them. "I know."

"Try to be a little more charitable, then," Jesse said. "And thank God you're not in Samuel's shoes."

"In church!" Roni broke in, changing the subject. "That's where I've seen you before. In St. Joseph's church almost two years ago. Maybe less. But that's where it was, all right."

"What?" Christian asked. He had no idea what she was talking about.

"Jesse," she said. "That's where I saw him." She turned toward Jesse. "You were standing in the back of the church near the fonts when I was leaving one morning."

Jesse smiled. "You could be right," he said. "When I'm on the mainland I usually do stop in at some of the churches just to visit with our Creator, say a few prayers, and marvel at the architecture in many of the older ones."

"Do you remember seeing me in one of them?" Roni asked as she studied his face. "We looked right at each other."

He squinted a bit as if trying to recall the event. "I can't really be sure," he said. "I've seen many people walking in and out of the churches while I visit. But I'm sure it's very possible that our paths have crossed at some point or other."

Jesse answered Roni's inquisitive stare with a smile and an

unblinking glance. To Christian's relief, it was enough to cause Roni to drop the subject.

"So, how have you been?" Jesse asked Christian. "What's new in your life? Make any new friends lately?"

Christian looked at his celestial friend, extremely curious about what he might be getting at. He wished he could pick up Jesse's thoughts, but it was impossible. Jesse had full control of his telepathy.

"I believe he did," Roni spoke up, smiling at Christian. "A Catholic priest, as a matter of fact."

Christian was surprised at her sudden answer. He cast a glance her way to tell her as much. He was beginning to feel cornered, but he didn't know why.

"Did you?" Jesse commented. "A Catholic priest, Christian? You are showing better choices these days."

Christian was perturbed. "Don't tease me, Jesse," he said. "I think I scared the heck out of him the other day when I went to see him. But our visit turned out to be very nice."

"I'm surprised the poor man didn't have a heart attack when he walked in the church," Roni said.

Jesse smiled at Christian. "How did you meet?"

"Through Roni," Christian answered. "He's a long time friend of hers."

"I invited Father Larry to bless our house quite a while ago," Roni said. "I've known him my whole life."

"How nice," Jesse said, then turned toward Christian. "So, the two of you hit it off." Christian did his best to maintain his composure, but his uncertainty about this meeting was wearing him down. "Not exactly," he said. "At least, I'm not sure how we hit it off at first. I know I felt sorry for the position he was in at our house. I mean, I saw him watching every move I made. He calculated every word I said very carefully. He studied me."

"Much like Roni studied me a little bit ago," Jesse commented, glancing at her.

Roni blushed. "Sorry."

Jesse let out a short chuckle. "Don't be," he said. "We just met. I wouldn't have expected any different. Let me ask you, Roni. What is it you were looking for?"

Roni hesitated.

"Don't be shy," Jesse said. "We're all friends here."

She glanced at Christian, then turned her attention back to Jesse. "Well, I wanted to see if you're a vampire, too," she said. "When I met Samuel, I knew immediately that he was. But," she shook her head. "I still can't tell about you."

Christian and Jesse looked at each other and smiled.

"I'm not," Jesse said. "That's why you still can't tell."

"Oh," Roni said, shaking her head as if she completely understood. But Christian knew she didn't. She couldn't. Not yet.

"Father Larry is a nice man," Christian said to Jesse. "I was impressed."

The ocean breeze blew Jesse's coat open, but he didn't seem to notice. "Well, it sounds to me like Father Larry took the whole thing quite well, considering."

"He really did," Roni agreed. "But I still feel so bad about the confusion it must have caused him. He's been so wonderful to me all my life that I really should have prepared him for it." She looked down as if she were ashamed.

Christian and Jesse exchanged a quick look and suddenly Christian felt that Roni was the one being cornered. What was going on here?

"Why didn't you then?" Jesse asked her, but she continued to stare at the ground.

He looked at Christian. *He came to see me,* he telepathically told him.

Why, Christian asked in the same fashion.

He, too, carries a guilty conscience sometimes.

Is it my fault? Christian asked.

No, Jesse said. *And it's fine now, anyway. He cares for both of you very much.*

"'Cause I didn't know how," Roni said. "I just didn't know

how. But I knew that, if he was meant to know, he'd figure it out when he came to bless the house. And it must have been meant to be because he did figure it out."

Christian now understood why Jesse felt this meeting was needed, and he was concerned for the priest's welfare.

Is Father Larry alright? he asked.

He's fine, Jesse answered, then turned his attention to Roni.

"So, you left it to God more-or-less," Jesse stated.

"I always do in situations like that," Roni said.

Jesse looked at her as if he'd already known what she was going to say. Neither surprise nor shock registered anywhere about him. He simply continued to look at her even after she was finished speaking. "That's a good habit to keep," he said.

Roni looked at Jesse with a sense of curiousity about her, but did not say a word.

Jesse turned to face the moon reflecting off the water. He leaned his hands on the rail then pushed himself back from it. "I believe I should let you two enjoy whatever is left of this glorious night," he said. "I'm sorry to have called you out like this, but sometimes it's best to meet on neutral ground the first time."

"I'm glad we finally met," Roni said.

Jesse bowed his head toward her. "As well as I."

"You know, the invitation stands for Christmas," Christian said. "No matter how clumsy an invitation it may have been." He glanced at Roni.

"I appreciate it," Jesse said, "and I'll consider it."

Christian smiled. "Please do." He took a step toward him.

Jesse leaned forward to hug his friend. "You know I'm always close by."

"I know," Christian said. He released Jesse, then turned his attention to Roni. "Let's go home."

They waved good-bye to Jesse, then started toward the car.

"We may need him as a referee if Samuel and Diana show up," Roni said, employing her occasional sarcastic tendencies.

Christian cast her a scolding glance, but Roni smiled and shrugged her shoulders.

Behind them Jesse chuckled at Roni's comment. "I doubt it," he said.

Together they turned in response to Jesse's unexpected remark, but he wasn't there.

Roni stopped dead in her tracks. "Where'd he go?"

Christian was still walking toward the car. "He always does that. You get used to it after awhile."

Roni turned to follow him. "If Jesse's not a vampire, then he's just human right?"

Christian looked at her and smiled. "He's human."

"You two are like brothers," she said. "I watched you when you said hello to each other. You have similar gestures and everything. But I know that isn't possible, is it?" She opened her car door, and sat down on the passenger seat.

"Anything's possible," Christian replied as he took his place behind the steering wheel. He caught Roni's sideways glance and knew the conversation was far from over.

"Well, you can't be brothers in the 'blood-is-thicker-than-water' sense," she said. "But you both have that 'wisdom of the ages' look in your eyes. Only his eyes are so much older than yours."

"That's because Jesse is so much older than I am," Christian told her.

"How can he be?"

Christian put the key in the ignition, then sat back in his seat. "He's an angel."

Roni's bottom jaw fell open, leaving her with a stunned expression. "He's what?"

"An angel."

Roni looked out the window, then back at Christian. "For real?"

"For real."

"But how?"

Christian looked at her and shrugged. "God's choice, I guess."

"I don't get it." Roni shook her head and waited for an explanation.

"And you know so much about God," Christian teased her.

"That's not funny," Roni said. "I never met an angel before."

"How do you even know that?" he asked her.

Roni sat silent while Christian started the engine, then pulled out of the parking lot. When they were headed north on route twenty eight, Roni turned to him. "Where are his wings?" she asked.

He laughed a little, then smiled. "The way Jesse explained it to me, there are many different kinds of angels. The ones who reside in this world seldom need wings, but if they were to find a need for them, God would provide."

"Oh."

"It's mainly the angels who reside on the other side, in the realm of the absolute where God is, who have a need for wings when they come here to help someone," Christian explained. "The visits from those angels are so brief that they need the wings for some sort of unearthly propulsion." He shrugged. "I guess it has something to do with the fact that earth has gravity." He smiled. "Heaven doesn't."

"If you knew all this," Roni asked, agitated, "then why was it so hard for you to know about your own soul, and God's presence, and all the things we've discussed that you never understood?"

Christian laughed. "Jesse tried for centuries to make me understand," he said. "It wasn't until I found real love in myself that I finally could understand. Jesse loved and cared about me, but I didn't love or care about anyone."

"Why not?"

"Because I never loved anyone before you," he said, looking directly at her. "I never knew how that felt."

"So learning to love opened the door for you to understand?"

"Guess so," Christian said, changing lanes.

Roni put her arm across his shoulders and gently twisted his hair between her fingers. "Jesse must know Samuel, too" she said. "At least it seemed that way from the conversation."

"He does," Christian said.

"Does he know Diana, too?"

"He knows who she is, but they've never met."

"Did Jesse know about all this mess between you and your sister?" Roni asked.

"Yes, he did."

"So why didn't he tell you about her being alive?" she asked. "Wouldn't that have saved a lot of time and had this whole thing fixed long ago?"

Christian nodded. "Except for one thing."

"What's that?"

"He couldn't do it."

"Well, why not?" Roni sounded angry. "Isn't he your friend?"

Christian smiled. "Yes, he is. But he's also Samuel's friend. And he's an angel. That whole free will thing applies even though he's here as a human being. Besides, he felt it was Samuel's place to take care of it since he's the one who caused the problem. Honestly, I have to agree with him."

"But it meant you had to go that much longer without knowing about her," Roni said. "And the same with Diana."

"I know," Christian said. "And the waiting is hard now that I know about her, but Samuel asked me for time, so I gave it to him. Jesse is not going to make a decision that goes against my will. He would never step in unless he was asked, or unless it was a life-and-death situation which this is not."

Roni nodded in agreement. "I suppose that makes sense." She straightened herself up in her seat and looked around. They were approaching the turn for highway four ninety five. "So, Jesse is an angel," she muttered softly, but Christian heard her.

"Mmm, hmmm."

He turned on the exit to four ninety five and they headed home.

CHAPTER 8

December 13, 1997

Samuel struggled to maintain his composure as he and Diana waited to exit the 6:14PM, British Airways flight from Heathrow to Logan International Airport. "It's so inconvenient to travel this way," Diana complained. "It would have been quicker if we'd flown ourselves."

Samuel smiled and kissed her forehead. "Yes, but who would carry all the luggage?" he said. "By my calculations it would have required five trips for both of us to transport it all."

Diana cast him an angry look.

"You're the one who wanted to go shopping in London."

"And did you argue?" Samuel asked, winking.

Diana smiled back at him, then dropped the subject. She stood to retrieve her carry-on bags from the overhead compartment. "Where did you say we're staying?" she asked. "In Cambridge?"

"No," Samuel said. "I changed hotels. We're staying at the Harbor Hotel."

"Why did you change plans?" Diana asked. "I thought we were staying at the one in Cambridge you always liked."

Samuel did his best to conceal how nervous he felt. He couldn't tell her about Christian yet. And he wasn't ready for Christian and Roni to show up at the hotel unannounced. He had changed plans without informing anyone. "It's a much older hotel," he said. "It appeals to me more than the newer ones do."

Diana paused and cast him an uncertain look. "Since when?"

"You're holding up the line," Samuel said, nodding his head

at the passengers who waited behind her.

Diana turned to them. "Sorry," she said, then quickly glanced at Samuel before starting up the aisle.

Samuel followed her, but all he could think of was Christian. The hardest part was keeping it from Diana's telepathic channels. He knew the meeting between her and her brother was inevitable. Still, he had to buy himself time. The longer it took before he was forced to face Diana with the truth, the more time he would have with her.

"Tell me our bags are being delivered to the hotel," Diana said. "It takes forever to collect them in the airport."

Samuel placed a hand on her arm. "Don't worry," he said. "It's all taken care of. We need only get ourselves there."

"No cabs," Diana said. "Let's fly. My limbs have been dormant too long already. And the traffic here is a nightmare. Let's just get there fast."

Samuel took her hand. "Agreed." He led her through the airport, down the escalator, and out into the freshly plowed parking lot. From there they walked the sidewalk along the front of the terminal, turned the corner and continued along the side of the building until they reached the very back where the baggage was removed from the planes, loaded on to baggage transports, and hauled into the claim areas. The snow had been piled up along the parameters of the paved areas. "No one's watching," Samuel said.

They wasted no time loosening their molecular structures so as to become invisible from those who might wander by. Then they rose together and headed toward the hotel.

"Oh, this feels wonderful!" Diana said as they drifted through the air. "I'm invigorated."

"Glad to hear it," Samuel said. He searched below for the familiar curved roof of the Harbor Hotel. He knew they were only a short flight away.

"There it is," he said. "We'll land, then reappear under the archway where there are no windows."

"I see it," Diana said, then began her descent.

In seconds they were on the ground, Samuel watched her in admiration as they reforged their molecules back to solid visibility. Her beautiful, windblown hair sent his pulse racing. The light in her eyes made his heart pound with love. *How could I spend eternity without her,* he thought to himself.

"You'll never be without me," Diana said. "I'm yours forever."

Samuel felt his heart drop, sadness invaded him. "Promise?" he asked.

"Promise," Diana said, her eyes sparkling.

He paused, staring at her as he took in the words, and soaked up her feelings for him. "Let's check in," he said without looking away.

Diana took his hand in hers and they headed for the front door of the hotel. They checked in, making sure their bags would be delivered to their room. Samuel began to wonder how they could avoid Roni and Christian. Why did he ever agree to bring her here? What was he thinking? He knew that even he could not run forever. "What would you like to do this evening?" he asked. Deep down he knew that before this week was through the dreaded meeting would have occurred.

"First, the Hard Rock Cafe," Diana said.

"How about, first, we dine, then the Hard Rock Cafe?" Samuel asked.

"Neither of us has had nourishment for nearly four nights now. I, for one, am feeling the weakness set in. And you look un-usually pale, my love."

Diana rubbed her stomach. "I guess I am hungry," she said. She plopped down backward on the settee in the middle of the living area of their suite. "I wasn't even thinking about it in all the excitement, but now that you mention it, I think I could drain a herd of cattle."

Samuel laughed outright as he walked over to the telephone and dialed room service. He ordered a bottle of port wine from the Desmonde Estates Winery in South France. He knew the hotel would have it in stock because they had been stocking it for over one hundred twenty years, since Samuel made it clear to the hotel manager that he only stayed at the hotels that carried his favorite wine. Because he and Diana were worth a fortune, the hotel was only too happy to accommodate them, as was every manager thereafter.

Samuel dialed room service, then called housekeeping to have their laundry picked up so it could be washed and ironed.

"I would've called," Diana said. "I usually make those arrangements for us."

Samuel walked over to her and sat on the edge of the settee. "This is a partnership, my love. You look a bit peaked from not dining, so I thought I'd save you the trouble."

Diana smiled with half-closed eyes. "You're a dear," she said.

She looked adorable in her traveling clothes, sweat pants and a sweat shirt. Comfort for comfort's sake. That was his Diana. "We'll be dining shortly, my love," Samuel said. He lifted her up off the settee, and held her tightly in his arms.

"I can't wait to eat, now," she said. "Why did you have to remind me?"

"Because it's my duty to take care of you," he answered, setting her back down on her feet.

Diana stood on her toes and gave Samuel a fleeting kiss on the lips.

He smiled. "What was that for?"

"Because I love you," she answered, then turned and walked into the bedroom to get her things together for housekeeping.

Samuel went over to the window that overlooked the inner harbor and became immersed in the activity along the waterfront. He watched the couples who strolled down the docks, and the passengers who were boarding for the dinner cruise that would be leaving port very shortly. Inevitably, he found himself thinking about Christian. He fantasized the perfect meeting of brother and sister that did not, in any way, involve Diana's wrath. In his brief fantasy, Samuel knew a more grateful Diana. One who was so thankful to him for such a wonderful surprise that she loved him even more. But Samuel knew better. He knew Diana far too well. She would see the whole of her relationship with him as one huge lie, and to her, their's would become a love born of deceit.

The doorbell rang distracting Samuel from his thoughts. He shook his head lightly before going to answer it. "Who is it?" he asked through the door.

"Room service," came the reply.

Samuel opened the door to the waiter who held, in his arms, one bottle of the finest French wine in the world.

"Is this what you ordered, sir?" the waiter asked politely.

"Yes, it is," Samuel answered, gesturing for the man to come in. "Just set it on the table." Samuel gently closed the door, then followed him. When the young man bent to set the bottle down Samuel reached out, grabbed the back of his neck, and pinched off the blood supply to his brain, rendering him unconscious. He caught the waiter in his arms before he could hit the floor, then set him up on the huge, antique, wing-back chair in the next room right by the window. Quickly, he began to drain enough of the waiter's blood to satisfy himself without depleting the man completely. As he did so, housekeeping arrived to pick up the laundry. The hotel had sent up two women for the task as he had expected them to do. Samuel could hear their Boston accents in the other room. He hoped they would be enough to hold Diana over for the time being. Her appetite, even in life, was enormous. She had always been small, yet she could consume the equivalent of two men, sometimes going for second or even third helpings. Yet, she never seemed to gain an ounce. Samuel had never foreseen that this trait would carry over into her vampirism, but when her appetite for blood was equally as large as her appetite for food had been, he realized he had never known a vampire to be any different than they'd been in mortal life, except for the act of survival.

When Samuel was fully sated he left the waiter and went in the living room to wait for Diana to finish her meal. She walked out of the bedroom sooner than he had expected, and was rubbing her stomach. "I'm stuffed," she said. "My stomach must have shrunk from going too long without a meal. I could barely finish the first one." She plopped onto the settee, and looked up at Samuel. "I won't even fit into my jeans, now."

"No one said you had to eat so much," he teased. "C'mon, now. Let's put them back where they belong."

They took the waiter and the two women from housekeeping down to the laundry room, then made a second trip to drop off their laundry. They hung the clothes that needed ironing on the lines across the room, near the row of ironing boards. Diana found a piece of paper and a pen. She placed a label with their room number on the clothes so the housekeeping staff would know where to take their clothes when they were done.

Then they turned their attention to the three mortals who lay unconscious on the floor. They placed them in a compromising position that resembled the beginnings of a menage a' trois. Samuel enjoyed this little game so much when he and Christian did it that he had started doing the same thing with Diana. She was from the same mold and enjoyed it as much as her brother did. Diana had a sadistic streak in her that she seemed to be quite unaware of. It was natural; as natural as her appetite.

"Perfect," Samuel said, surveying the scene on the laundry room floor. "Too bad we won't be here to see them when they wake up." He stared at the pile of dirty laundry on the floor. The younger of the two women from housekeeping lay on her side. Her name tag said, "Alicia." Across her thighs, which were loosely spread and flattened by their contact with the floor, lay the waiter with one arm wrapped around her legs. Behind him lay the second woman from housekeeping in a 'spoon' position with her arm around his waist. Diana guessed that she would awaken first since none of her blood had been lost to the vampire's appetite.

"I'd rather be at the Hard Rock," Diana said. "Don't worry, Sam. We'll hear all about it in no time. The hotel will be buzzing with the gossip when we get back. I just hope they don't get fired."

"We'll cross that bridge when we come to it," Samuel said. He took one last look at the scene on the floor. "We'd better get going if we're going to do anything tonight. Time's a wastin'."

They returned to their suite to change and freshen up before going out. Diana quickly unpacked the rest of their belongings. She neatly placed Samuel's things on the bureau. All that was left she folded and left on top of the waist high dresser.

Samuel was changed and ready to go first. He sat in the spacious living room to wait for Diana. Ten minutes later she walked out of the bedroom wearing her navy blue stretch mini-skirt and one of the tunic style sweaters she'd bought in London. Samuel fell in love with her again.

"Delicious," he said.

Diana smiled flirtatiously. "Now, Sam," she said. "There's a saying among the mortals."

He nodded once and looked at her through half closed eyes. "And that is?"

Diana sat on the settee and began to put on a pair of white ankle socks. "Keep it in your pants," she said, giggling.

Samuel watched her tie her sneakers and felt a pain shoot through him as it crossed his mind that this might be the last time he'd see her perform this simple task. "I'm not so sure a mini-skirt in December makes a whole lot of sense," he said.

Diana stopped tying her sneaker and looked up at him. "I don't recall asking you," she said. "Besides I can't feel the temperatures much anyway so it's not like I'll freeze or anything. I just had to find something comfortable that wouldn't show my huge belly. I ate too much."

Samuel smiled, then went to get their coats. "Well, you've succeeded in hiding your stomach," he said.

He quickly checked the suite to be sure they didn't forget anything. "Ready?"

Diana stood up and took her coat from him. "I'm ready."

They locked the door and headed for the Hard Rock Cafe.

"C'mon, Roni," Christian said nervously. "Hurry up. For all we know they're on their way here. We'll miss each other."

Roni emerged from the bathroom and gently place a finger over Christian's lips. "Sshhhh," she whispered. "Everything will be just fine. Relax."

He put his arms around her, and held her for a moment. He tried to stay calm, but he was anxious to see Diana after all the years of separation. Finally, she was close by. "What if she's someone I don't even recognize?" he asked her. "What if she's someone I don't like?"

Roni caressed his hair while he held her. "Relax, Sweetheart. It's going to go the way it's meant to. All the worrying in the world isn't going to change that. Give it to God and let Him deal with it. All you can do is be yourself and settle down." She held his face in her hands, and looked deep into his eyes.

"I love you," Christian said softly.

"And I, you," she answered. "Now let me finish up here so we can get going."

While Roni finished dressing, Christian checked the cats' food and water supply more so to kill time than anything else. He gave them each a few extra treats as well, then made sure the house was locked up tight.

"Are you ready?" Roni asked.

Christian turned to see her standing by the table. She was wearing a pair of black stirrup pants and a long, bulky sweater in charcoal grey that went down past her thighs. He walked over to her. "You look gorgeous."

Roni smiled, then leaned on him for balance while she put on her black, pumps before going to the closet to get her coat. "All set," she said.

He wrapped his arms around her. "You know you're beautiful."

Roni reached behind her to pat his cheek. "Thank you," she said.

Christian helped her position her arms in the sleeves. "Ready?"

"Ready."

They went outside, and got into Roni's little truck with Christian in the driver's seat. He liked it that Roni preferred him to drive when they were out together. She didn't mind driving rural streets or country roads, but traffic in the city was right up there on her list of 'The Top Ten Things I Hate Most About This Planet'.

Christian turned onto Route One and headed north toward Boston. It was a crystal clear night, but cold. He could see the steam from Roni's breath. "So what's the game plan?" he asked.

"We'll go to the Bostonian and surprise them," Roni said.

"Just like that?"

"Yep, just like that."

Christian drove in silence for a few seconds. "Don't you think that might infringe on Samuel's plans a bit?" he asked. "I mean, what if he isn't ready for this to happen?"

"After talking to him on the phone that day, I'm banking on the fact the he hasn't told Diana a thing yet," Roni said.

Christian glanced over at her, then looked back at the road. "Then why don't we let him handle it in his own time?"

"Because he never will," Roni said. "Samuel said they'd be arriving on the thirteenth. Well, today is December thirteenth and we still haven't had a phone call, or a note or anything letting us know that everything went well, or that they're here. I'm willing to bet that Samuel will put this off as long as he possibly can which, for him, could be eternity."

"You're probably right, Roni," Christian said. They approached the intersection at Route 109 and stopped for the light. "But I don't want to mess anything up for him, you know. He's been a good friend. He kept this secret for me for centuries. That's quite a lot to ask of anyone."

Roni looked at him incredulously. He knew that look; the one that said, 'I can't believe you just said that.' The traffic light changed to green, and Christian turned his attention back to the road, thankful for an excuse not to have to see the look on Roni's face.

"Had he been such a great friend, Christian," Roni began, "he would've done a little more to make sure there still was a friendship between you two. Keeping your secret was easy. By keeping your secret he was able to 'keep' Diana. Don't you think that if he'd told her about you right from the beginning things would've been different? You might have talked her out of being changed. But once she was changed, Sam couldn't tell her because she might have revolted against him. Who knows? She might have spent the last five and a half centuries travelling around with you instead of with him." Roni paused and looked out the window. "Just imagine how different things might have been at any time in the past five hundred eighty-six years, if Sam had told her."

Christian didn't like hearing it, but he knew Roni was right. He was thankful Samuel had kept his secret at first, but five hundred years ago would've been a better time for him and Diana to find out about each other. Samuel could've tried to find him much earlier than he did. If Christian's very life hadn't been at stake a year and a half ago when another vampire tried to kill him, Samuel might still be safe in his secret. But Christian would never know that for sure. "You're right, Roni," he said. "But, as you say, everything happens for a reason."

"That's very true, Honey," she answered with a smile.

They drove for another half hour. They were on Storrow Drive, only minutes from the hotel.

"I'm actually nervous," Christian said. "I think I have butterflies in my stomach."

"I'm excited myself," Roni said. "I think it's wonderful this is finally going to happen. I'm a little worried about Samuel, though."

"Don't be," he said. "As you told me, he did this to himself. All I care about now that we're so close, is seeing my sister again. I only hope she isn't angry at him. I don't want anything to ruin this evening." He turned right into the parking garage of the hotel.

"No matter how this meeting goes, just accept it as God's will and leave it alone for Him to take care of," Roni said.

"I will."

He parked the car and they got out. They entered the lobby,

and approached the reception desk of the beautiful, old hotel that overlooked the Charles River.

"We're looking for Samuel LaFleur and Diana Desmonde," Christian said to the man behind the desk. "They should have checked in earlier today."

"What was the last name?" the man asked.

"Desmonde or LaFleur," Roni answered. "It could be under either or both."

The thirtyish looking man checked the roster once again.

"Here it is," he said. "D. Desmonde and S. LaFleur. Unfortunately, these reservations were cancelled a few days ago. On Thursday, it looks like."

Christian was stunned. He looked at Roni, hoping it wasn't true, then turned back toward the desk clerk. "Did they say why or where they might be staying instead?"

"No, I'm sorry, sir," the man said, shaking his head. "They simply cancelled. I didn't take the call, myself, or I might have been able to help you more."

Christian couldn't believe what he was hearing. All his excitement from moments ago had vanished, and been replaced by yet more disappointment over the meeting with his sister that kept being delayed. "Thank you," he said. He turned around with Roni and walked across the tree-filled lobby back to the garage.

"I knew it!" Roni said. An angry sneer quickly crossed her face. "He couldn't do it! That coward! Wait until I get my hands on him."

Christian couldn't help but chuckle at her conviction. "Calm down," he said. "I don't know who Sam should be more afraid of. You or my sister."

"It isn't funny," Roni said as they reached the car. "He's only making it worse for everyone."

Christian started the engine and headed for the exit to the parking garage in silence. It only took a few seconds, but he didn't want to lose his train of thought while he was rummaging through his wallet for money to pay the parking fee.

"Well, obviously not for Diana," Christian said. He pulled out of the garage and turned right. "She hasn't got a clue what's going on."

"But she will. And for now, three people are sitting on pins and needles because of Sam's cowardice," Roni said. "I'm going to kill him."

Christian chuckled again. "Before you do anything, you might give some thought as to what you'd like to do now that we're here," he said. "I'd prefer not to drive around aimlessly all night."

"Well, it's pretty silly to check every hotel in Boston," Roni said. "Can't you do your telepathy thing and try to track him down?"

"I've tried a few times, but he's blocking me," Christian said. "He's got a protective block around Diana, too, or I'd have picked up her thoughts when we were still in Norfolk. Nope, the ball is definitely in Samuel's court, now." Christian pulled over by the curb, and put the car in park.

"Where to now?" he asked, turning to look at Roni. He propped his hand on the back of her seat, and waited for an answer.

She tapped her finger nails on the dash board. "I don't know," she said. "I'm so angry at him. Let's go somewhere for a drink and relax. I need to settle down."

"Pick the place, then," Christian said. "We don't come up here too often so we might as well make the most of it now that we're here."

"Alright," Roni said. "How about the Hard Rock? It's right across the river. We haven't been there in ages. Why don't we go there for awhile and then work our way home?"

Christian put the car in gear and made an illegal U-turn. "You really are upset with Sam. Now you want to go bar-hopping."

Roni giggled. "I didn't say that. Don't go putting words in my mouth," she warned him playfully.

"Well, what does 'work our way home' mean?" Christian asked, teasing. He had reached the bridge that crossed the Charles River.

"It means we'll work our way back," Roni said. "I didn't hear the words 'bar' or 'hop' in there anywhere."

"Oh, so now we're going to play the semantics game, are we?" Christian said, accepting her challenge.

Roni shook her head. "No, we're not," she said. "Alright, so maybe we can stop at another place or two on the way home. We'll see what happens at The Rock."

"We will, indeed," Christian said. They crossed the Charles River Dam, then made their right onto Charles St.

"This should be an interesting night," he said.

CHAPTER 9

December 13, 1997

Father Larry sat at his desk in the study of the rectory at St. Joseph's writing a letter to his sister in Wisconsin whom he hadn't seen in three years. Since his return from visiting Jesse, he'd been thinking he might need a vacation. The last time he'd taken a substantial amount of time off was five years ago when his arthritis began to get worse.

What was happening to him?

Was he finally getting too old to accept what stood right before his eyes? Or were his eyes just going bad?

He thought he'd had such a revelation while talking with Jesse, but his mind had not been as completely at ease as he'd hoped it would be on the short flight back to the mainland. Did the drinks have something to do with his outlook? He couldn't be sure, but whatever was causing his unrest, he had to find out what it was.

When he returned three days ago he immediately began to research vampires, but found nothing that helped him understand Christian. He discovered hundreds of stories written about vampires, some of which had characters that resembled Christian in many ways, but they were all modern, fictional works. The reference works he found used the original Bram Stoker's vampire as a point of discussion and gave Father Larry no more information than he would have learned from watching the old movies.

After three days of looking for answers he was no closer to understanding Christian than he had been on the day of his unexpected visit. His brief, obsessive search had left him physically exhausted, mentally drained, and more confused than enlightened.

Sitting at his desk now, he was no longer sure exactly what it was he was trying to understand. What was bothering him so much? *Isn't it enough that the man's a vampire?* he thought. That would be enough to bother anyone. So why didn't that feel like the real issue?

He thought about Christian's intense inner strength that frightened him, yet seemed to make Roni feel secure. He considered his own impressions of Christian. He was an honest man. Father Larry could sense that during their visit in the church. He had a likeable personality. His intentions toward Roni were true. There was no denying that.

But, . . . where were the fangs?

Where was the threatening snarl, the angry hiss one would expect? Was that a part of him that Father Larry just hadn't seen yet?

Christian walked into a room like any mortal. He wore ordinary clothes like everyone else. Even the cape Father Larry thought he saw when Christian walked into the church a week ago was nothing more than his overcoat blown open by the wind. Yet the sight of it had scared him because it created an illusion that Father Larry expected from a vampire.

And it was also quite obvious that Christian would not be changing into a bat. Or could he? How much was there about Christian that Father Larry might never see? And how much of the whole picture had Roni seen? But she would have to know all there was about him. They were living together, one point that Father Larry did not approve of.

Then, like a ton of bricks it hit him. There was no denying it, no rationalizing in any way. He thought he had come to terms with the truth during his visit to Jesse, but instead he'd been hiding behind it in order to convince himself he had found what he was looking for. It was true that the prejudice of the ages was alive and well in a supposedly open-minded, jolly, old priest from eastern Massachusetts named Father Larry Donnelly. But that prejudice was quite a convenient shield.

Imagine that!

He had become a contradiction of all he preached about during mass each week.

"Love your neighbor as you love yourself."

"Do unto others as you would have them do unto you."

How had he let those fundamental teachings fly right out the door?

When did it happen?

And why had he wasted three days trying to learn about vampires when there was no reference material of any substance to be found, especially in a case like this? Why hadn't he been content with the idea that it was simply a matter of prejudice that he was dealing with?

The truth upset and embarrassed him. He felt deeply ashamed when he realized that he was jealous.

Jealousy is what first made the old priest look for information about vampires. He was actually trying to dig up some compromising facts about Christian. Father Larry was looking for something that would cause Roni to doubt Christian's love and his intentions in order to separate them. And now that he'd admitted it to himself, he clearly saw why he felt the way he did. It was because of the life he had almost left the priesthood for, and the woman he would always wonder about.

The ultimate sacrifice Larry Donnelly, the man, had made for God, was his entire life. Not the mortal life on earth, but the kind of life that might have been; the life he had wanted so badly at one time, that he yearned for it every day.

When he saw Roni and Christian together it was like looking back in time at the way he had felt about Nora Bratis. He wondered how she was as he had done so many times in his life since he decided to remain in the priesthood. He wondered who she might have married, and if he was the kind of man she always wanted. Thinking of her made Father Larry feel alone. He felt as if he'd been left out and cheated of something that should've been his.

A sudden peace came over him and he thought of God. What a fulfilling life he'd had in service to Him. What he had gained in the joy and satisfaction of his work more than outweighed what he might have lost in his decision to remain a priest. Nora would always be a part of him, but God was everything to him. So how did jealousy find its way into his life?

He hadn't meant to destroy Roni or Christian. It was a sub-conscious thing over which he seemed to have no control.

Until now.

Thank heavens he realized it before it was too late. Oh, the damage he could have done.

Father Larry had only wanted to destroy the memories of the pain that had occurred during a brief period of his life, the pain that had nearly destroyed him. It was a time that Jesse had helped him through. Jesse was the only person who knew about Nora. Father Larry was confident it would remain their secret. No one needed to know.

"How could I do such a thing?" he asked himself out loud. He began to pace back and forth in the study. "How could I be jealous of what Roni has with Christian? How could I be so selfish as to think to destroy it just to be rid of my own painful memories?"

He quickly prayed ten consecutive Acts of Contrition, a prayer that begs God's forgiveness and promises to "sin no more with the help of Thy grace."

When he was done something else occurred to him. Another reason for his relentless search for information. He couldn't find anything on the surface that caused Christian to want to be with Roni. Their relationship made very little sense to him outside of their love. Many people had fallen in love and been married, while other things influenced their lives and destroyed those marriages. Would it happen with Roni and Christian as well? What really bothered Father Larry was that Christian had so much more to offer Roni than she had to offer him, but he stayed with her and looked past all the differences between them. Why?

Christian was a wealthy man. Money destroyed many marriages. Roni wasn't dirt poor, but she wasn't worth millions. She owned her own house, in partnership with the bank, but she was making ends meet even with her own business. Apparently, they had found a balance on that issue.

Christian was immortal, but Roni was mortal. He faced an eternity alone after her years on earth were through and wanted so much to try to keep her with him. Yet he respected her wishes to live naturally, the life she'd been given.

What could Roni possibly give to Christian that he didn't already have?

The very instant the question entered his mind, he knew the answer. In fact, Father Larry had his answer the very moment when he'd walked into Roni's house the evening he blessed it.

He remembered the sparkle in her eyes, and the tender, protective feeling surrounding Christian. His answers were written in the caring, respectful exchanges between them, in the bond that so tightly connected them it seemed easier to cut it with a chain saw than to try to walk between them.

Father Larry's answer was found in a rare and powerful kind of love. The kind of love that pleases God more than anything else in the world. That's why Father Larry hadn't tried to talk to Roni about her relationship with Christian. And that's why Roni hadn't come to see him, either. Because she knew him very well. She knew he'd see it just this way. Maybe she hadn't realized it would take so much time, but she knew none-the-less. And she counted on it.

So that was it. Roni gave Christian her love. It was that love that held him so tightly to her.

"Only love." Father Larry shook his head. "Amazing."

For that, Christian loved her in return more than all the possessions he owned, more than all the places he'd been, and more than all the experiences he'd ever known. It was clear in the way he looked at her, in the way he spoke of her.

But he didn't love her more than God. It was obvious a week ago when Christian had come to visit him. Father Larry could see the love and respect the vampire felt for the Almighty One. That was as it should be, but it was also surprising to see it in a vampire. Christian must have been alone for a long time before meeting Roni. How difficult a solitary life like that must be. God knew what Christian needed and He sent Roni. Or was it the other way around? Would God even do such a thing? Of course He would. All things went back to the Father. *So who am I to question the will of God?* he thought.

Father Larry stopped pacing and looked out the window behind the desk. It was a beautiful night. The snow had all but melted making the world outside a muddy mess. The priest could feel the cool air seeping through the spaces around the window frame. He made a mental note to mention it to Cora so that she would call someone in to seal it up.

He turned around, and picked up the phone on the desk. He dialed Roni's house, but all he got was the answering machine.

"Veronica, this is Father Larry," he said into the receiver. "I thought we might get together over tea soon. Let me know if that's agreeable with you and when it might fit in to your schedule." He left his phone number, as if Roni didn't know it by heart after all these years, then hung up.

A vampire who loves God. A being who must feed from the lives of others to survive, yet who respects and even shows humility to the Creator. How did such a creature ever come to be?

"Father?"

Father Larry turned to see the housekeeper, Cora McCarthy, peeking in through the partially open door. He could see the corner of a silver tray and realized her hands were full. He walked to the door and held it open for her. "Of course, come in," he said. "I was just thinking about you."

"Oh?" Cora asked.

"There's quite a draft coming in through this window," Father Larry said, pointing to the window behind the desk. "Do you think you'll have time to call someone in to seal it up for the winter?"

Cora looked at the window and nodded. "Sure, I will," she said. "First thing tomorrow."

"That'll be fine."

"I brought an evening snack." Cora placed the tray on the little coffee table on the other side of the study. "Tea and a few sweets for that tooth of yours."

Father Larry chuckled, rocking back a few inches with his hands on his belly. "Thank you, thank you, Cora," he said. He looked down at the pastries and felt his mouth begin to water. "Your timing is incredible as always. This is well needed."

Cora stood with her hands on her hips like an old school marm overseeing her students. "Well, good, then," she said. "You get to sleep soon, y'hear?"

"I will," the priest said, pouring himself a cup of tea. He could smell the herbs and mint in the steamy blend. He felt the sedative effects as the first sip worked its way through his body. He sat on the old, wingback chair he'd had reupholstered so long ago, letting the tension in his muscles fade slowly away. He took another sip of tea and stretched his legs out in front of him.

"Oh, 'fore I fergit," Cora said in her natural brogue.

Father Larry sat up and turned around, amused to hear the prim and proper woman with her guard down for a change, but Cora corrected herself instantly.

"Veronica March called earlier," she said. "It was some time after dinner. Father Francis took the call. He says he was tied up and forgot to tell you."

Father Larry thought about the message he had just left for Roni and decided it would suffice as a return call.

"That's fine," he said to Cora.

"Oh, and Jesse called only a half hour ago to see how you were," Cora said, looking at the priest curiously.

"Where was he calling from?"

"He didn't say and I didn't ask," Cora said. "He just wanted you to know you were on his mind."

"Is that what he said or is that what you're surmising?" Father Larry asked.

"Actually," Cora began as she turned to finally exit the room, "that's what he said."

Father Larry smiled. "Thank you, Cora."

"Good-night, Father," she said. She left the room and closed the study door softly behind her.

Father Larry breathed deeply, then sighed as he sat back and stretched his short legs out in front of him once more. The herbal tea Cora had brewed was exactly what he needed. She always seemed to know what was best for him. He chuckled when he thought of her. She tended to have a strict air about her, but her very name was so close to the only woman he'd ever loved, that it put a soft spot in his heart for her.

He reached for a cream puff from Cora's special tray, and thought about the complexities of the world. He marvelled at the surprises that never seemed to stop. *Just when you think you've seen it all,* he thought, biting into the weightless, yet fattening, treat. *What next?*

CHAPTER 10

December 13, 1997

When they walked into the Hard Rock Cafe a group of bikers in their leather and chains nearly blocked the entrance just inside the door, but they moved fast when they saw Christian. He was surprised and wondered if they actually knew, but he shrugged and followed Roni further into the night club. At the farthest end of the bar stood a group of punk rockers with their brightly colored hair and safety pins placed through pierced ears and noses. Roni almost seemed a little out of place in her normal attire and classically layered, long hair, but Christian, on the other hand, felt right at home in a place that brought together the strange and unusual of the world. In five centuries he had seen so much that nothing surprised him. He remained aloof as if he were not part of the surroundings, but watched it all with a curious yet unimpressed eye.

The unique atmosphere at the Hard Rock Cafe had an eerie, other-worldly feeling that emanated from the combination of so many different types of people surrounded by the clouds of cigarette smoke through which everything appeared as if it were a tavern scene from one of the Star Wars movies. Rock and roll collectibles and memorabilia decorated the interior, hanging from the ceiling, and all over the walls. The musical paraphernalia in itself was enough to bring in the tourists and keep the local crowds coming back for more even amidst the incredibly high prices charged at the bar.

Of course, there were always the Hard Rock Cafe fans which

were an entirely unique group on their own. They were the ones who just had to visit every HRC location in the country. Many of them had been all over the world collecting HRC sweatshirts, t-shirts, and anything else that would prove to the masses exactly who had been to more Hard Rock Cafes than anyone else. The locals laughed about it.

"What are you thinking?" Roni shouted into Christian's ear.

He leaned back and deliberately cast her a stern look. "You know I can hear you quite well even if you whisper, don't you?" He could see she was startled at the tone of his voice, but she knew his hearing was more sensitive than that of mere mortals. Still, it was a rare occasion that brought them to a place as noisy as this.

"Sorry," she said without asking her question again.

He nodded and was about to tell her it was alright when he suddenly felt very uncomfortable. He looked around the room trying to see what might have happened to cause such a feeling, but there was nothing out of the ordinary for a place like this.

"What is it?" Roni asked, quieter this time.

Christian shook his head. "I don't know for sure," he said. "Something felt out of place, but I couldn't identify what it was. Now it's gone."

"Do you think it was Sam?" she asked.

Christian shook his head, still looking around the room. "No," he said. "I would've recognized him right away."

Christian shook his head. "Come on. Let's get a drink and relax." He took her hand and led her to an opening at the bar where they could squeeze in among the other patrons. The bartender was there almost immediately. "Glass of port and a Coors Light," Christian told him. He placed a twenty on the bar, then continued to scan the crowd while their order was filled.

"See anything?" Roni asked.

Christian handed her the beer. "No, nothing," he said. "It could have been anything with all the different people around. It's been a few days since I've eaten and I just can't be sure what it was that I felt."

The people around them had moved slightly, giving Roni and Christian the room they needed to stay where they were for the time being rather than have to walk around to find an open area in the crowded bar where they could relax. Christian leaned one elbow on the bar facing Roni and scanned the throngs of people. "It could've been a strong psychic, for all I know," he said. "But it bothers me just the same."

"Well, don't spend the rest of the evening waiting for it to happen again," Roni said. "We have to figure out what to do about Samuel."

Christian nodded. "You're right."

"Hey, Lady," a familiar voice called. Christian looked up while Roni turned around to see her best friend, Chelle Gambert, shoving through the last human obstacle that was in her path as she made her way over to them.

"What are you doing here?" Roni asked, smiling.

"Well, isn't that a nice way to say you're glad to see me?" Chelle said. She looked at Christian, but didn't say anything to him.

Christian nodded. "Hello, Chelle." She was not one of his favorite people. They did not get off to a good start when they'd first met. Mostly because of his own insecurities that were centered on Roni back then. He was jealous at how close the two of them were, and afraid that Chelle was trying to influence Roni against him. Once he realized Roni felt the same for him as he did for her, he was able to see that Chelle was as true a friend as there could ever be, but by then it was too late. Christian had pushed her too far and Chelle was having a hard time trying to forget how cold he was to her. Even now they had only reached a point of relative civility.

Chelle stood with one hand on her hip. "Hello, Christian," she said. "How've you been?"

Christian sipped his wine, then nodded his head in response. He wanted to keep as much peace between them as he could for Roni's sake, but he didn't want to give Chelle a reason to pick at him, either.

Roni leaned toward Chelle to be heard better. "So, who'd you come here with?" she asked.

Chelle looked around the bar, then shrugged. "Jason Hobbs, his brother, Marty, and Paula, Marty's girlfriend," she said.

Roni nodded. "How long has it been for you and Jason?" she asked.

"Oh, five months, I think," Chelle said. "I'm not sure how much longer I'll be seeing him, though."

Roni had to yell over the noise around them. "Why not?"

"Long story," Chelle shouted back. "I'll tell you some time. Do you know Paula?"

Roni nearly spilled her beer when she was accidentally bumped by a woman covered in leather as she walked by. "No, I don't know her," Roni said.

"I just met her tonight, myself," Chelle said. "I don't think she'll be with Marty very long, either. They're not each other's types."

Roni nodded her head without saying a word. Her voice was already growing hoarse from having to shout to communicate.

"I don't know where they went, but . . . ," Chelle said, shrugging her shoulders. She looked around quickly, then abandoned her brief search as if she really didn't care where the rest of her party had gone. "I'll find them eventually." She leaned over the bar between Roni and Christian to order another drink. "What about you?" she asked. "What brings you all the way into the city?" She glanced at Christian out of the corner of her eyes. "Did you drive or fly?"

Christian let out a sardonic chuckle and stared at her with a sinister dare in his eyes.

"We drove," Roni told her.

"I drove," Christian said, his eyes flaring at her.

Roni cringed visibly.

"No way!" Chelle exclaimed, overacting her mock surprise. "Not you, Christian! You drove? I would never have thought you'd waste the gas when self-propulsion is so much cheaper." Chelle paid for her drink, then stepped back to stand beside Roni.

Christian was about to respond to Chelle's remarks when another strange feeling came over him. This time it felt as if someone had just run through his mind, but was too fast to be seen. Again, it was an unfamiliar feeling that unnerved him. He searched the bar and examined his own instincts to get a handle on what was happening, but was unsuccessful. Maybe it was the many distractions around him, though it was rare when he could be distracted at all. Maybe his lack of nourishment made the situation worse. Whatever it was that prevented him from being able to locate the source of his discomfort, it didn't matter. The feeling had passed again as quickly as it started. He gave up searching just in time to catch the tail end of the conversation between Roni and Chelle.

"So, what's he doing?" Chelle asked. "He looks like a mannequin. I don't think he's even breathing."

"Stop it," Roni said. "He's trying to pinpoint the source of the feeling he keeps having. It's no big deal, really. It might be a psychic playing games or something."

"So, what happens once he finds the source?" Chelle asked.

"I don't know," Roni said. "Maybe it's . . . " She was suddenly interrupted by Chelle's boyfriend, Jason.

"Hey! There yooarr," he yelled. They all turned in time to see him stumble into the man wearing a cowboy hat who stood behind Christian. The cowboy caught him before he fell, then sent him on his way. "I'fe bin lookin all o . . . fer fer yoooo," Jason said without excusing himself to the stranger. There was no doubt he'd had too much to drink. "Why'd you take off . . . like 'at?" He continued toward them, but shoved Christian with too much force when he tried to pass. Christian was still a bit dazed from trying to find the source of his unease and Jason's shove forced his anger to rise. Without thinking, Christian reached out and grabbed Jason by the throat, lifted him, and held him suspended a foot above the ground while Jason was gasping for air.

"I guess that answers my question," Chelle said.

Roni turned to her. "Oh Chelle, I'm sorry."

"Don't be," Chelle said. "He deserves it. That's why he won't be around much longer." She glanced at Roni, then turned her attention to Christian. "In more ways than one, apparently."

"Sss . . . oooorr . . . y," Jason managed to stammer in between gasps. He held onto Christian's forearm and tried to push himself free.

Christian looked at Chelle with a deliberate menacing glare in his eyes and strained to keep his anger in check. "I suggest you take him home." He slowly lowered Jason to the ground. "He's a nuisance."

"Screw him!" Chelle said. "I'm embarrassed by his drunkenness. He can drive himself home for all I care. I'll go home with Paula and Marty." Chelle turned her back to Jason as if he wasn't there. She took a sip of her drink and looked around the room, pretending not to know him at all.

Roni went to stand in front of her friend. "Chelle. At least drive him home so he gets there safe."

"If he wanted to get home safe then he shouldn't have gotten drunk," Chelle said, shrugging one shoulder toward Roni. "Don't you think?"

Roni looked at Christian, asking for help with the look in her eyes. He was sure she knew how angry he was with Jason's conduct, but he also knew Roni and how important Jason's safety would be to her.

Christian shook his head. "Don't look at me like that."

"Christian, please," Roni said. "He's better off at home sleeping it off. He's just going to cause a problem here. Besides, you can get him there faster than any of us can."

He looked from her to Jason and smiled. He had an idea. "You're right," he said. "It's best for everyone if I get him out of here." He hoisted Jason over his shoulder while all around him people turned to look briefly at the scene, then went back about their own business.

"I think he passed out," Roni said.

Christian looked sideways at Jason's head, then let out an angry grunt. "An unconscious drunk is better than a rude drunk, and much easier to transport. Besides, I don't really mind." He smiled. "Your wish is my command." He bent down to kiss Roni on the forehead. "I'll be back in a flash." Then he turned to Chelle. "Would you like to tell me where this guy lives?"

"Not especially," Chelle said. "But I suppose that's the only way you'll get him out of here. He lives in Westwood on Fox Meadow Lane." She had that haughty edge to her voice, that irritated Christian. "But you can dump him off on the corner of the street somewhere. Let him sleep under the stars. He'll be fine." She walked up to the bar to order another refill of her vodka and iced tea.

"Terrific," Christian said, nodding, then headed for the door.

The bouncers said nothing when he walked past them and out into the cold night air with a sleeping drunk slung over his shoulder. It wasn't unusual to see someone's friend helping him get home safely once they'd had too much to drink. Especially in this day and age when the penalties are so stiff for those who get caught driving under the influence.

Christian chuckled to himself and shook his head as he headed through the parking lot. He looked behind him to see who was around, but the parking lot was empty of people and the bouncers had stopped watching him once he'd reached the first row of cars.

Christian had his own ulterior motive for agreeing to take Jason home. He swiftly rose into the air, high above the city lights, and headed south to Westwood. His weakened state caused him to feel Jason's full weight over his shoulder. He hoped they'd make it without dropping out of the sky before he could regain his strength. But it didn't take long, and in minutes they had reached their destination.

Christian quickly found a wooded area along Route 1A in which to hide while he took advantage of the situation, feeding on the unconscious Jason's tainted blood until he was sufficiently replenished.

The first bite was still the hardest for him, causing him to go so long between feedings. But after that first bite was made an instinct in him took over and the blood flowed easily, even sweetly down his throat. The alcohol would be sifted from Christian's body within seconds after he ingested the blood that contained it, and Jason would sober up a bit quicker without it in his system.

As he drank, Christian could feel every pore of his body soak up the life-giving energy that came from the blood. He drank until he was fully sated, taking in every last drop that Jason could spare without doing the young man any permanent harm.

Once Christian was back to full strength he carried Jason out of the woods. He made sure the streets were clear when he headed toward the area where Jason lived. He propped him up on top of the mailbox at the corner of Fox Meadow Lane and Greenlodge Street, leaning him against the light pole that stood directly behind it so that Jason would find himself sitting on the property of the United States government when he awoke.

He stood back to admire his work, and thought of Samuel. How clever his friend would think him for posing Jason the way he had. He felt a twinge of longing for Samuel's return and his sister's first embrace in nearly six hundred years, but the thought quickly passed. It was halted by the same strange feeling he'd felt at the bar. This time, however, with his senses at full strength, Christian knew it was coming from the Hard Rock Cafe, and he knew he had to get back there.

He looked at Jason once more before taking flight and heading back to the Hard Rock Cafe. "Poor fool," he said.

The return trip was much quicker without the extra, dead weight that Jason had been.

"That was quick, man," one of the bouncers commented when Christian walked back into the night club.

Christian licked his lips to be sure he left no telltale signs. "He only lives ten minutes away," he said, smiling.

As soon as he entered the bar, Christian did his best to pick up the source of the unease he'd experienced three times already that night, but to no avail. The feeling that had begun when he stood at the corner of Jason's street had ended just as he approached the parking lot outside the bar.

He looked around for Roni, and quickly found her in the same place she was when he'd left less than thirty minutes ago. He was disappointed to see that the rest of Chelle's party had now joined them. He walked over to Roni and put a protective arm around her.

"Hi, Sweetheart," Roni said. "That didn't take you long at all, now, did it?"

"No, as a matter of fact it didn't," Christian said.

"Is everything alright?" Roni asked.

He shifted his gaze to Chelle and her friends. "Everything's fine," he said. "What about here?"

"It looks like I'm going to be walking home," Chelle said, rolling her eyes. "That's Marty." She pointed to the man who stood between her and another woman in the bar. "He's here with Paula." The other woman waved to Christian.

Christian looked at Marty who was falling asleep on his feet with a full glass of beer in one hand and the empty bottle in the other. The only thing holding him up was Paula, his arm slung over her shoulder still holding the empty beer bottle.

"You won't be walking," Christian said. "We'll drive you."

"How gallant of you," Chelle said. "There might be hope for you yet."

Roni turned to Christian and handed him her glass. "Would you get me another," she asked.

Christian winked at her. "Playing referee, again?"

Roni smiled.

"I'd be glad to." He took her glass from her, then turned to Chelle. "What about you?"

"Who me?" Chelle feigned flattery by lightly placing her fingertips to her chest. "First a ride home, then a drink. To what do I owe the attention?"

Christian frowned and shook his head. "Never mind," he said, waving a hand at her. "You can get your own drink. You're right, Chelle. A ride home is more than enough for you."

He turned to the bartender and ordered a glass of port wine for himself, and a refill for Roni's light beer.

What the hell is he doing here? Samuel was careful not to let Diana pick up his thoughts.

He had been watching the familiar group of people across the bar for quite some time. He had noticed Chelle first when she was introducing Christian to a man and woman Samuel did not recognize. He wanted to leave right then, but Diana was nowhere near ready to go. That meant he was stuck in this cat and mouse game from hell with Christian.

"Samuel," Diana said. She turned to face him. "You're no fun tonight. What's wrong with you?"

Samuel grabbed her and turned her back around before she had a chance to look across the bar. He had not expected this, and he certainly wasn't ready for the effect it would have on her to see her brother standing right before her eyes after five hundred eighty-six years, and with no warning.

He had to think.

He had to figure out what to do.

Most of all, he had to keep Diana distracted as long as possible in order to buy himself some time.

Just a little more, he thought desperately.

"Just a little more, what?" Diana asked.

"Just a little more . . . uhhhf you in my arms," he quickly made up.

Diana leaned toward him. "Oh, I'm not going anywhere," she said.

Samuel wrapped his arms around her and did his best to control the panic he felt. He couldn't afford to have Diana read the truth right out of his own mind.

Not now.

Especially, not after all the time he'd kept it so well hidden.

CHAPTER 11

December 13, 1997

What the hell was he doing here? Samuel glanced at Diana to be sure she hadn't picked up his thoughts.

Diana looked at him over her shoulder. "Who, Honey?"

As he feared, her telepathy nearly caught him. "No one, Di," he said. He couldn't let her see how nervous he felt. "I thought I saw someone I knew, but I was wrong." Samuel stood behind her with his back to the bar. He held her around her waist, swaying to the music. The subtle act had the desired effect in keeping Diana's back to her brother while he tried to figure out what he should do next.

He waited until Diana was too preoccupied with the crowd to pay attention to his inadvertent thoughts. He turned around to see what was happening on the other side of the bar. Christian looked right at him, but didn't see him. How was that possible? Samuel was afraid to make eye contact with him, but he found himself staring in disbelief. He shook his head, then turned back around. He tried to watch a couple of punk rockers, instead. They were sporting multi-colored hair, and wearing more chains than a snow plow would have on its tires. But as intriguing as he found them, he had trouble keeping his mind off the situation he was in.

Samuel knew it was inevitable that Diana and Christian would meet. They deserved to see each other after so much time, but he just could not bring himself to accept the fact that these intensely happy, centuries were drawing to an end so quickly. It was too

BISH

soon for this to happen. Where had the time gone? How had he reached this point?

He began to agonize over the thought of losing her, even though she was still physically within his reach. He should be enjoying these last moments with her, but he couldn't control himself enough to appreciate this time. He'd grown so used to having her in his life that he couldn't imagine being alone again. She was part of him. He would never be whole without her. The very thought sickened him.

"Samuel, what the hell is the matter with you?" Diana had turned around to face him and now stood where she could clearly see Christian if her eyes were to move in the right direction.

Samuel grabbed her quickly and turned her away from the bar once again, but he could feel the ire rise in her this time. She tensed, suspicious of him. She had good reason to be. He knew he was doing a terrible job in hiding his feelings. He tried to joke around her anger. "'Tis the season," he said.

"Bullshit!" Diana whipped around again to face him. She stood with her arms crossed in front of her and her foot tapping angrily out to the side. "Either start having fun with me or tell me what's wrong. You're bringing me down, Sam. Don't ruin our good time in this country!"

"I'm sorry," Samuel said. He was losing control faster than he could think. He tried again to turn her out of Christian's line of sight. "I didn't mean to upset you."

Diana yanked herself out of his arms and backed up a step. "Stop turning me around!" she yelled at him. "You're really pissing me off! What's over there that I'm not supposed to see, anyway? An old girlfriend? A current girlfriend, maybe?" She pushed him out of the way, and walked right up to the bar, deliberately look-ing across to the other side. "What if I want to watch those people over there?" she said pointing right at Roni and Christian. "What's the big deal, Sam? I'll watch whoever I damn well please."

Samuel reached across the front of her and put a hand on her arm. "All right, all right," he said. He had to appease her anger, and do some fast thinking at the same time. "I didn't mean anything by it. I just wanted you close to me."

Diana looked sideways at him, and studied his expression for such a long time that Samuel began to wonder if she had figured out what was really going on. Had she seen Christian or hadn't she? Was she still angry or was she calming down? He had no idea what to do next. Finally, he threw his arms up in the air in total frustration, and sat back. "I give up," he said. "Do whatever you want."

If Diana were to see Christian right at that very moment, he would not have cared. Living with the guilt and fear that was slowly consuming him was hard enough, but this game of hide and seek was putting the finishing touches on his demise. He had finally begun to realize the damage his selfish secret had caused. He had now reached the point where he just wanted the whole thing to be over.

Diana curled herself up against him like a kitten. "I'm sorry," she said. "I was being a real witch, and I'm sorry." She lay her head on his shoulder and nuzzled his neck.

Samuel was stunned. He had finally decided to let her find out about Christian, but she hadn't. Instead, she further tortured him without knowing what she'd done. He was back to square one. In another second he'd be playing the same game, again. He put his arms around her and pulled her close to him. "Forget about it," he said. "Let's just forget about it."

On the other side of the bar Christian was growing bored with the level of maturity in the conversations between Paula and Marty-the-drunk, who had turned out to be a carbon copy of his brother. Christian had no intention of taking another Hobbs brother home, though he could think of a number of interesting positions for the two brothers to share on the mailbox. He looked around the room at the variety of people hoping to get a sense of where his strange feelings had come from now that he was stronger because of his recent meal. Nothing. He would try again in a few minutes.

He turned his attention back to the group he was with and saw that Paula had given up trying to have a sensible talk with Marty and had left him standing alone. He was a quieter drunk than his brother, Jason. He seemed just fine where he stood outside the rest of the group swaying back and forth with his eyes half closed. Christian almost couldn't resist the temptation to give him an encouraging nudge in one direction or the other, but he knew that sooner or later someone would walk by and do it for him. It was just a matter of time.

Roni leaned toward Christian. "What's the matter?" she asked. "You seem so far away."

Christian put his arm around her and smiled. "No, I'm right here. I'm just waiting for our friend Marty to topple over."

Roni looked at Marty and laughed.

"Ten bucks says he doesn't last another five minutes on his feet," Christian said.

"I think you're being too generous," Roni said. "Ten bucks says he's down in less than three."

They shook hands. "You're on," Christian said.

"What's going on over here?" Chelle asked. "Share the joke."

Roni pointed at Marty just in time for them to see him fall face forward into a small group of young men who caught him as he headed for the floor. Paula looked disgusted, but started to laugh when Chelle broke out in hysterics.

Roni put her hand out toward Christian. "Pay up."

'Wonderful Tonight' by Eric Clapton had just come on over the sound system. "I'll pay up, alright," Christian said. He swept her into his arms and turned her toward the dance floor on the other side of the room. "They're playing our song. Would a dance do for now?"

Roni took his hand. "Fine, but don't think you're getting away without paying me in cold, hard cash."

They moved through the crowd quickly. In no time at all, Christian's arms were around her waist, their bodies moving in time with the music. "I'll pay you, alright," Christian said, squeezing her.

"Mmmmm," Roni moaned, laying her head on his shoulder. "Now that's better than cash any day."

Christian smiled. "I thought you'd see it my way."

Diana watched all the couples who stepped on to the dance floor. Samuel was relieved that her attention was somewhere else besides the other side of the bar.

"Look at that." She pointed to the same punk rockers they'd been watching most of the night. They were now snuggled close in a slow dance.

"What about them?" he asked.

"They look funny."

"It's just the way they dress," Samuel said.

"No, I mean dancing all lovey-dovey like that."

"Well, how did you expect them to dance?"

Diana shrugged her shoulders. "I thought they'd be slamming into each other or something," she said. "Isn't that what punkers usually do?"

Samuel looked at her, then shook his head in disbelief. He couldn't help but laugh.

Diana turned to him, her eyebrows raised in question. "What?"

"Diana, you never cease to amaze me." He looked toward the dance floor once more, but instantly picked up an unexpected emotion from Diana's aura. The sad expression on her face confirmed what he'd felt. "What's wrong?" he asked her.

Diana shook her head slowly. "Nothing really," she said. She glanced toward the dance floor then looked away. "I saw a man dancing over there that reminded me of Christian, that's all. It happens all the time. Something starts me thinking about that last day at the Spring Festival, and how much fun we had. Then I get sick inside thinking how awful it must have been when he was dragged away into the woods by those wild animals."

Samuel's insides rolled over. He felt selfish. Even worse, he felt guilty. "I know, Sweetheart." He put an arm around her more to comfort himself, than to comfort her. He looked around for signs of Christian, but could not find him. Hopefully, he had left, but Samuel couldn't be sure. "Would you like to dance?" he asked Diana.

"Not really," she said. "I'd rather sit here and watch."

Samuel was worried. "Are you sure?"

"Oh, yes." She nodded. "I'm sure."

Samuel looked around the room. *Where is he?* he thought. Paranoia grew quickly now that he'd lost sight of him. He couldn't pick up his thoughts, it confused him. Why would Christian block him? Did he know they were there? Part of him was hoping they'd left, but another part of him wanted to be on the other side of this dilemma once and for all. He had become so uncomfortable that he couldn't decide if he should sit or stand. His mind was becoming a blur. He leaned toward Diana and rubbed her shoulders. "Je t'aime," he said to her, using the language of their homeland.

She placed her hand over his. "I love you too, Sam." Diana looked backward at him, and he bent down to kiss her. She warmly answered his kiss with hers, then turned back toward the dancing crowd.

"There he is again," she said.

Samuel's nerves felt like they were going to snap. "Where? How can you remember what your brother looks like after all these years?" He knew he'd said the wrong thing, but he couldn't think clear enough to stop himself.

Diana looked hurt. "I miss him. That's how I remember what he looks like. He meant everything to me." She stretched sideways to look around the crowd. "Oh, I can't see him now."

Samuel breathed a sigh of relief, but he knew it was for the moment only. *It must be him,* he thought. But he still couldn't find him.

"Can you imagine how wonderful it would have been all these years if you had reached him before he died?" Diana said. "If only you had been there to save his life."

Samuel squeezed her shoulder and felt the melancholy flow through her into him. He didn't know what to say. He was afraid he'd give it all away if he didn't keep his thoughts in check.

"What do you think he'd wear today?" she asked him. "What would his style be? Do you think he would have enjoyed being a vampire as much as I have?"

Samuel was beside himself. To make matters worse, he now felt Christian's presence. He was still in the bar with them, but where? "I'm sure he'd be quite dapper," Samuel said, trying hard to smile.

Diana shook her head, then leaned into him. "Oh, I have to stop this," she said. "I was angry at you for spoiling the evening and now look at what I'm doing. Forgive me. I haven't been to the States in well over two years. I'm not going to ruin it for us by dredging up the past. And I don't want you feeling guilty over getting to Christian too late to save him. Do you hear me?"

Samuel wanted to crawl under the floor. The charade had gone too far, but he just couldn't let go of it. He should tell her right now while it was fresh on her mind. But he couldn't do it. Even though he knew it was time, he still couldn't bring himself to tell her the truth.

Diana turned back toward the dance floor. She had only watched the people for half a minute when Samuel felt her body tense. She was staring at the dance floor with a most incredulous look on her face. He looked at all of them, but still could not see if Christian was among them. To his relief, Diana turned away from the dance floor and started to laugh.

"Now what?" he asked.

"There's a man on the other side of the bar who just fell down," Diana said. "The bouncers are carrying him to the door."

Samuel turned to see what she was referring to. He saw Chelle and another woman, but no sign of Roni or Christian. That was not good. When he turned back toward Diana, her eyes were drawn back to the dance floor. He followed her line of vision as best he could. "That one couple keeps looking over here," Diana said.

"Look, Sam. That's the man who reminded me . . . Wait a minute." Diana froze and so did Samuel.

Indeed, it was Christian, and he had seen her.

"Oh my God!" Christian swore emphatically into Roni's ear.

"What?"

Christian stopped moving and stood, frozen on the dance floor with Roni still in his arms. His heart was pounding as if he had just flown around the world. "Diana is here," he said. He knew Samuel very well. There was no mistaking who was with him.

"Are you sure?" Roni asked.

"Look for Samuel," Christian said. "You'll know."

She turned around to look in the same direction as Christian. "You're right. I see him." She looked at Christian. "Sam doesn't look too good. He looks scared and guilty. What should we do?"

"I don't know," Christian said.

"Do you think we should just ignore them and give Sam the chance to bring her to us?"

"I don't know," Christian said, again. He was totally bewildered. That was his sister only twenty feet away. He hadn't seen her in centuries. He wanted to run to her and give her the biggest hug she'd ever had, but his loyalty to Samuel played tug-o-war from the other side of his heart. He didn't know what to do. "I think it's up to Samuel."

Roni didn't say anything.

Christian stared at Samuel and locked minds with him. *Tell me, buddy,* he thought to Samuel. *Tell me what to do.*

Samuel fixed his gaze on Christian and held it before he spoke. *She's your sister, mon ami,* he told him. *Blood is thicker than water, after all.* Samuel nodded his head one time, a tear rolled down his cheek.

In an instant, Christian began to move with Roni following right behind him as he headed toward his sister. When he reached her, he stopped. "Diana," he said.

"Christian?" She reached out to him, her arms shaking. "Really, Christian?"

"Yes, really!" Christian said. He grabbed her shaking hands and pulled her to him. He picked her up and hugged her for the first time in nearly six hundred years.

"Oh, my God, Christian!" Diana said, holding him as if he'd just saved her life. Tears poured down her face as she kissed every inch of Christian's head over and over, again. When she was through kissing her brother repeatedly she hugged him so tight Christian thought they'd be joined at the neck forever.

When he felt Roni touch his arm he put Diana down. They both took a moment to get a hold of themselves while the reality of their situation set in. A crowd had gathered around them wondering at the reunion, trying to get an idea what all the commotion was really about. Very quickly they gave up and went about their own business.

Christian looked at his sister. "Diana," he said, "I'd like you to meet the love of my life."

Roni who'd been standing behind him stepped forward, smiling, but Diana cut the familial introduction short.

"Wait a minute," she said. "You're a vampire." She turned to look at Samuel with an accusatory glare in her eyes.

Christian glanced at Samuel. "Yes, Diana," he said. "Like you."

Diana flew into a rage as if he wasn't there at all. "You lied to me!" she said to Samuel.

He stood motionless with obvious guilt written all over his face.

"He really didn't, though," Christian said.

Diana spun around, glaring. "Sure he did," she said. "He told me you were dead. He told me you were dragged off by wild animals. I should've known better. He even felt guilty for years because he didn't get to you in time to save you. He lied over and over, again." She turned to face Samuel. "He lied about everything."

"No, Diana." Christian put his hands on her shoulders to make her look at him. "He only told you what I asked him to tell you. I didn't want you to find out what I'd become. I was ashamed. I swore him to secrecy, Diana. It wasn't his fault."

Diana listened to her brother without saying a word, but when he stopped talking she let her wrath fly. "What about after I'd become the same as you, Christian? Why didn't he tell me then?" She turned toward Samuel once more. "I'll tell you why, you cowardly bastard!" she flared. "You didn't tell me about my brother because you didn't want me to know that you had lied to me at all. You let a little lie turn into a colossal one without any respect or concern for me. What were you afraid of, Sam?!" Diana emphasized his name as if it were a repulsive word. "Where you afraid I'd choose my brother over you, Sam? What the hell were you thinking?"

"I didn't want to lose you for any reason, Diana," he said. "I just didn't want to lose you." He stared at the floor, then raised his head to look her in the eyes, pleading with her to forgive him.

"So you held me by a lie?! Forget it, Sam," she said. "Five hundred eighty-six years of lies is over!!!"

And Diana was gone.

Before anyone had a clue that she was going to disappear she had already done so leaving them all speechless.

"And so," Samuel said, obviously stunned, "that is that."

Christian had no idea what to do to help Samuel face the situation he had avoided for so many years. He felt his pain, but could do nothing to save him the way Samuel had rescued him so many years ago.

Roni reached out and put her hand on Samuel's arm. "Come stay with us, Sam," she said. "We'll all figure out what to do to make her see that it wasn't your fault. Not the way she thinks, anyway."

"That's a great idea," Christian said. "She's going to need time to cool off. If I remember my sister correctly, it's quite likely she'll be gone for awhile."

"That's exactly what I was afraid of," Samuel said, fidgeting with his hands.

"Then it's best for you to stay with us for the time being," Roni said. "You shouldn't be alone. Not when we can all think this through together." She gently shook Samuel's arm.

"No," Samuel said softly. "I think it's best for me to go back to the hotel room and wait for her return."

Christian felt terrible. He knew Samuel had to be left alone for the moment in order to accept what had just happened. There was very little his friend could do to hurt himself, after all, so there wasn't much to worry about. "If you need us, you know where to reach us. At least we're in the same time zone now."

Samuel didn't smile. "Thanks," he said, then stood up and shook hands with Christian before heading for the exit alone.

"Why did you let him go like that?" Roni asked. "He shouldn't be alone right now."

"Stop thinking like a mortal," Christian said. He was only half joking. "What can happen to him? He'll sulk for awhile, then wait for a while, then sulk a little more. He might go out to look for Diana here and there and he might forget to feed. But in the long run he'll be ringing our doorbell or going out to see Jesse."

"Are you sure?" Roni asked. "I'm worried about him."

"I'm positive." Christian put his arms around her and pulled her close to him. "That doesn't mean we can't try to find my sister first, though," he said. "But for now, I think we've had enough excitement for one night. Let's go home."

"Just like that?"

"Just like that," he said.

"Aren't you at all concerned? Don't you want to try to fix it right now?"

"Sure I do," Christian said. "But I can't?"

"I'm sure you can send out your little telepathic feelers or whatever it is you use to find me when you want to," Roni suggested. "Why don't you go find Diana right now and talk some sense into her?"

"Because I still know her well enough to leave her alone," Christian said. "After seeing her old, familiar temper I feel much better in knowing that even after nearly six centuries some things will stay the same."

Roni looked at Christian for a second before shrugging her shoulders.

"Alright," she said. "If you say so."

"Don't worry," Christian said. "Tomorrow night we'll think about it more and see what we come up with."

Roni walked around the bar to where Chelle and Paula stood. She picked up their coats and handed Christian his.

"Leaving all ready?" Paula asked.

"We've had enough for the night," Christian said, helping Roni put her coat on. "Do you girls want a ride home?"

"No, thanks," Paula answered. "I snagged the car keys out of Marty's pocket and had the bouncers put him in the back seat of the car. He's sleeping peacefully. I'll be driving when we finally leave."

"Call me tomorrow," Chelle said to Roni. "I know I saw a familiar face over there, but you can tell me all about it another time."

"I will," Roni said. "Promise."

Christian led Roni out of the Hard Rock Cafe and they headed home. Regardless of what he told her, he was doing his best to pick up Diana's whereabouts by trying to track her anger. But Diana was strong. She blocked him from finding any trace of her emotions and that had begun to unnerve him. This was worse than he thought. In the old days she ran to him with every problem she had. This time she was running away.

PART II

"Since nothing we intend is ever faultless, and nothing we attempt ever without error, and nothing we achieve without some measure of finitude and fallibility we call humanness, we are saved by forgiveness."

—David Augsburger

CHAPTER 1

December 14, 1997

Diana disappeared at the Hard Rock Cafe and flew straight to the suite she and Samuel had taken at the Harbor Hotel.

"Five hundred years!" she screamed into the night air. "I loved him! I trusted him!" Tears streamed down her face, the wind tore them from her cheeks. She searched for the curved roof of the hotel, but could hardly see a thing through her stinging eyes. How could he have kept this secret for so long? How could he have done such a thing, separating her from her own brother, her best friend.

Diana found the hotel through her blurred vision. She landed under the archway, then quickly made her way to her room. The clock on the night stand showed exactly twelve midnight on the nose. That figured. She unloaded her things from the drawers and closet, all the while trying to make sense of what Samuel had done to her and why. She couldn't stop thinking of the part she and Christian could have had in each others lives if Samuel had told her the truth years ago.

Samuel had been there throughout her mourning over Christian's 'supposed' death. He had seen her pain. He had wiped the tears from her cheeks time and time again for weeks on end, and still he had said nothing. It had been Samuel who had eased the pain and made her smile again. It had been Samuel who had filled the void in her life that Christian's passing had left.

Diana packed up the bulk of her belongings, unconcerned with the laundry they had left in housekeeping. The anger inside her was so fierce she didn't care. She had been betrayed! The man she had chosen eternity and immortality for, had lied to her. Love was not supposed to include lies of this magnitude. It was supposed to be truth, honesty. Not this.

She carried the larger bags to the door, then wrote down her address in France on a piece of paper. She rang for the porter, then went back in the bedroom to throw a few choice items together in a smaller duffle bag that she intended to keep with her. She had decided to remain in the States for awhile, but incognito, if that were possible. Sending her bags home to France would throw Samuel off in his search for her, though temporarily at best.

"I need time alone," she muttered, pacing back and forth. "I need time to think. I need to be where no one will find me, especially not a vampire like Samuel."

The doorbell to the suite rang. Diana answered it.

"Did you summon a porter, ma'am?" a male voice politely asked.

"Yes, I did," she said. She stepped away from the door so the young man could enter. "I'd like these trunks picked up and sent to my home in France as soon as possible."

"No problem, ma'am," the porter replied. "Is the correct address on them?"

"No," Diana said. She handed him the piece of paper. "I wrote it on this. All three trunks must be sent there."

"We can do that for you." The porter began to place the trunks on the dolly he'd brought with him. When he was finished he rolled them to the door, then turned to face Diana. "Will you be following me down to pay for them now?"

"Yes," Diana said. She held the door open while he rolled the dolly into the hall, then locked the door to the suite behind her. "Then I'll be checking myself out."

"Very well," the young man said. He proceeded to the elevator. Diana followed.

When they were in the lobby Diana made the necessary arrangements for the shipment of her belongings back to France, then checked herself out of the hotel.

"And your companion?" the concierge inquired, raising his left eyebrow suspiciously.

"I don't have a clue," Diana snapped back. She recognized the look on the man's face which showed how clearly he understood what was hidden between the lines, but she didn't care. She was thankful he didn't ask any more questions. All that was left to do was get as far away from this place as she could. Telepathy knew no distance, no boundaries, but how far was far enough so Samuel couldn't find her? It didn't matter. If he found her, she'd run again. The hurt ran far too deep for her to be able to see him now. She could travel a few hundred miles at least. Her telepathic powers were strong enough to block him for quite awhile.

She walked out into the dark night and looked around. Niagara Falls was the first place that came to mind. It would be safe enough for starters. It was at least five hundred miles away and she knew her way around the area fairly well from having spent a considerable amount of time there in the past.

She quickly rose into the snappy, midnight air, and headed west toward Lake Erie where its northeastern shores touched the southernmost beaches of Ontario, Canada, and Western New York State before reaching the point where its waters dumped thunderously into the Niagara River to continue on its way up to the St. Lawrence Seaway.

Because of its great tourist appeal, the giant waterfall was surrounded on all sides by hundreds of hotels and motels both on the Canadian side as well as on the American side. Diana knew she could easily get lost in that area for awhile before she would be forced to move on. And she might even enjoy the many plazas and shopping malls as she had done in the past. It would be a lot of fun to see how much the area had changed since she and Samuel had gone there.

Diana flew inconspicuously with her travel bag slung over her shoulder as the intermittent breezes tugged at her hair, and the stars winked continuously overhead.

Oh, how she loved to fly like this. The feeling was indescribable. As far back as she could remember she'd always felt the exhilaration of each flight as if it were the first time she'd done this. She felt so free being this high up in the air with no barriers or constrictions around her. It was thrilling to look out over the world as if she were not even a part of it, but merely watching it like she would watch a gnat in a terrarium like the ones her mother used to make.

She winced in disdain when she thought of the airplanes she hated to ride with all the effects of the wind resistance and atmospheric changes. Airplanes unnerved her tremendously. If she were ever unlucky enough to be aboard a plane that went down, she would perish just like the other passengers unless she could think quickly enough to transport herself outside of the long metal tube.

She did not want to ever find out if she could.

As she made her way west, the air became sharper. Though she rarely felt the effects of temperature changes, she did feel the difference in the way the air responded as she pushed through it. Colder, drier air gave way easier than did warmer, humid air. She remembered well the kinds of winters that occurred around the Great Lakes and she found herself looking forward to experiencing three feet of snow piling up in a single night, assuming she were fortunate enough to be in that area at the right time.

Diana's mind wandered as she flew free and open in mid-air. She thought about the mortal days when Christian was still home. She thought about how close they were back then. They had been more important to each other than anyone else in their lives. They had shared all of their secrets, trusting no one else. Christian had been her protector and her guardian as well as her friend.

Diana thought back to a particular time when she was seventeen, or so. There had been a nice, young man named Robert Moliere whom she had met in passing on the road into town, one afternoon. He was handsome beyond compare to anyone else she'd known. Just looking at him made her knees weak and took her breath away.

Shortly after their meeting he started to call on her. In no time at all she had become completely smitten by him, even to the point where she found herself constantly listening for the sound of hoof beats that might signal his arrival.

Christian and Robert seemed to get along well enough, though Christian always held a part of himself in reserve. Diana believed Christian's attitude would disappear once he knew that Robert's intentions were truly honorable.

One night Christian was visiting a neighboring town on business when he discovered through a casual conversation that Robert had been courting a few different young women from other towns around theirs. Christian was boiling mad when he got back home that day, but he would not tell anyone what had made him that way, not even Diana.

Later that evening, it started to rain. But the rain did not stop Christian from going out in search of Robert Moliere. It wasn't until the next day that Diana had learned what happened. Christian was out with a few of his friends when they found Robert right in their own town. After confronting Robert with what he had learned, Christian proceeded to beat the young man to within an inch of his life.

"How dare you!" Diana stormed at her brother.

Christian's face was frozen in an angry scowl. "One day you will thank me for ridding you of that trash," he said.

"I will not!" Diana turned her back to him, but she could still see him clearly in the mirror on the dining room wall. "Nor will I forgive you for what you've done, nor even speak to you again." She still remembered the hurt look that had quickly crossed Christian's face, but he'd held his ground.

"So be it," he had said, then left the room.

Diana had kept her distance for weeks, until she found out for herself that Christian had been right all along. So much so, in fact, that Christian was barely surprised when Robert was arrested and jailed for violating the daughter of a very wealthy landowner.

Diana smiled as she remembered Christian's loving protection, and how angry she was over something she didn't understand. She sighed. "Oh Christian," she said aloud. "The fun we could have had together all these years. But Samuel robbed us of that. And he will pay for it. He'll pay!"

Diana had been in the air for just over an hour and a half when she noticed the huge, plume of spray rising up from the massive waterfall far off in the distance. It distracted her momentarily from her anger. How beautiful it was. It resembled a cloud, alone and alive reaching down to touch the earth. It was thick and white and looked more like confectioners sugar than water. She wanted to fly right through it and feel the soaking wetness while the falling water roared beneath her. But she knew she didn't have time for that. She was still too far from her destination and she knew it was better to be on solid ground when the sun came up.

Diana knew exactly which hotel she wanted to stay at. She remembered it from the time when she and Samuel had spent a month at Niagara Falls to celebrate four hundred fifty years together.

Or was it four hundred sixty?

No matter.

It was one of the many special times they'd shared during which Samuel had continued to keep that secret. That lousy, stinking secret. Just thinking about it started the fire burning in her again and her anger rose. "How could someone I loved so much do something so cruel to me?" she asked herself. "Did he really think I'd never find out about Christian?"

"Samuel LaFleur I hate you forever!" Diana shouted to the open air. "Forever!"

With that out of her system, Diana began her search for the hotel that she remembered from days gone by. It was on the American side of the falls less than a mile from the edge of it, and overlooking the river.

Within twenty minutes she found it, and quickly descended behind the hotel where a mass of trees hid her from view. The Rivers Edge Hotel, as she remembered it, was now a Days Inn. But she knew it was the right one because it stood right where she remembered it, overlooking the developing rapids that would soon pass Goat Island on both sides before plummeting over the edge to the continuing river below.

It was an older hotel, but beautiful, nonetheless, for its rich history and old world feeling. It was fairly new when she and Samuel stayed there, but now, as she floated slowly down to earth, she could see that it showed the signs of its age in the weathered brick finish and the slight cracks in the cement foundation. But Diana loved it for the memories it held for her.

The sun's rays were just beginning to push their way through the December air, shining early signs of pink and orange through the floating mist that billowed in the distance. Diana almost wished she could feel the cold just for this moment, but all thoughts and fantasies had to rest for now. She'd had a long night and knew that she'd have to sleep very soon. The flight and her anger had taken more out of her than she'd realized until this moment. Nourishment would be foremost on her mind when she awoke.

She entered the hotel and crossed the lobby.

"Good morning."

Diana looked up to see a young girl behind the front desk smiling at her. The name on her pin said "Deborah". She walked up to the counter, and set her bag on the floor. "I'd like a room for a few days," she said.

"I'll need to see a major credit card," the desk clerk said, still smiling.

Diana dug in her wallet and produced a wad of one hundred dollar bills that made Deborah's eyes grow huge.

"Will cash do?" Diana asked.

"I'm sure that will be fine." The desk clerk checked the computer to see what they had available. "Smoking or non-smoking?"

"Non," Diana said.

"Single?"

"Unless you've got a better idea," Diana said.

The desk clerk's eyebrows rose when she looked up at Diana. She wasn't smiling, now.

"I'm sorry," Diana said. "Just tired." She smoothed her wind-blown hair with her hands and attempted a smile herself.

"I understand," the desk clerk said. "I'll get you checked in as quickly as I can so you can get some rest. You must have been travelling all night."

"I was," Diana said. She signed the folio card and pushed it across the counter.

The desk clerk handed her the keys. "Room 501," she said. "The elevators are right down this hall. Take it to the fifth floor and you'll see the signs directing you when you get off. Have a nice stay."

Diana picked up her bag. "Thank you," she said. She walked through the lobby to the elevators. She pressed the button for the fifth floor, then leaned back against the elevator wall. Sheer exhaustion had begun to take hold of her body and her mind. She was famished and weak. Her stomach rumbled, her limbs were drained of energy. She doubted whether she'd make it until morning without sustenance, but she didn't care. She decided to sleep until the hunger pains woke her, and she was forced to find food.

The elevator doors opened. Diana began looking for the signs directing her to room 501 the minute she stepped out of the elevator car. She saw them almost immediately.

The first thing she did once she was inside her room, was hang the "Do Not Disturb" sign on the door knob outside. She locked the door, closed the drapes as tightly as she could, and plopped down exhausted on the bed. The first serious pains of hunger were just beginning.

"Oh, I have to fall fast asleep before I'm too hungry to rest," she told herself. "I won't have the energy to feed if I don't."

Sunset would be too early for her to awaken at this point.

But moonrise would call her.

It always did.

CHAPTER 2

December 14, 1997

Samuel waited alone in the empty suite. He knew Diana was really gone from the absence of her belongings when he had arrived a little after one. Memories ran through his mind non-stop, one on top of the other, like raindrops pouring from the sky. His thoughts were a loosely woven mesh of events that confused the centuries, intermingling the very threads of day and night, weeks and months, as if there had never been any such divisions in time. Samuel remembered well all the chances he had and all the times he should have told Diana the truth. His secret had grown stronger with each passing decade. Time gave it strength and fear gave it anonymity. But Samuel had given it life in the first place, and he nurtured it as if it were his child by staying silent so his lie could live. That is what Diana saw him anguish over for nearly six centuries. His guilt had never been the result of him reaching Christian too late to save him as Diana had always believed. It stemmed from the hard fact that Samuel had saved Christian's life, thus separating him from everyone he knew and loved in the process. He would've had nothing to feel guilty about if he hadn't fallen in love with Diana, then changed her as well. After that, the older the secret grew, the harder it was to tell until it finally became as much a part of him as his own name.

By the time Samuel met the angel, Jesse Nestarius, and learned that he was a friend of Christian's, he had buried the secret so deep within him it simply did not seem likely that it would ever be more than just a secret. In time, Samuel had even separated Christian from the deception, discarding the fact that a simple promise to his friend had helped give birth to the complicated mess. However, separating Christian from the situation made the secret something that existed outside both of them, like a rumor one is aware of, but not part of.

Samuel lay on the bed while thoughts and memories continued to clutter his mind. Some were so strong they reminded him of an event as if he were reliving it. One of his fondest memories was from a trip he and Diana had made to Italy in 1504 when they went to witness the installation of the statue of David at the Palazzo della Signoria in Florence. One of Samuel's very good friends in those days had been Michelangelo Buonarroti whom he had met while on a trip to Italy in 1498, shortly after Michelangelo had begun his work on the Pieta. In 1499, when the work was finished and ready to be placed at St. Peter's Basilica in Rome, Samuel had taken Diana with him to view the event and to introduce her to the artist. From that day on they became an integral part, in the way of friendship and support, of everything Michelangelo did. Samuel had even done his best to convince Michelangelo that immortality was the best thing for an artist of his caliber.

"You should be one of us," Samuel told him.

"No," Michelangelo replied. "Impossible! When my time is done, my time will be done."

"But the world will never be given enough of your talents, my friend," Samuel argued.

Michelangelo smiled. "There will be others," he said. "I will be outdated in time. Better to be gone before that occurs."

Samuel shook his head, then smiled at his friend. "It is your choice, mon ami," he said. "I will be here if you change your mind."

"I know you will."

In early sixteenth century Italy, when physical beauty was believed to be the manifestation of a virtuous spirit, Samuel and Diana had many terrifically romantic trips all over Europe. However, the trip to Italy in 1504 was a very special one during which

Samuel had almost confessed his secret to her for the first time. He had many reasons for wanting to do this, the biggest one being his mounting sense of guilt. Deep inside Samuel knew the promise he had made to Christian was of no consequence since Diana had become a vampire. He decided he would tell her. But as they stood together admiring Michelangelo's masterpiece of the naked young boy, Diana had been so spiritually aroused that Samuel kept quiet for fear of losing her. The moment had been wrong for the disclosing of secrets. Samuel had been hesitant to destroy one of the many romantically passionate moments of a trip that was full to brimming with many such intense snippets of time. Hence, Samuel and Diana had returned home after a full month in Italy with Samuel's secret still neatly tucked away while the gnawing guilt grew stronger.

Samuel sighed at the memory, but his mind continued to wander until sleep overtook him. Even then the memories did not stop, but continued to weave their way in and out of his dreams. Each dream replayed a different time when Samuel had almost told Diana his well-kept secret and the reasons why he ultimately had not. Each dream reminded Samuel of the guilt and how fast it grew within him. Though Samuel's psyche tossed and turned in an emotional struggle throughout the daylight hours in the hotel suite in Boston, his body remained frozen and still in its hotel bed. In his dreams, Samuel asked himself time and time again, "Why didn't I tell her?" Each time the same answer came from deep within the recesses of his mind. "Because you'll lose her," he told himself. "It's been too long."

And as day turned to night, his dreams turned to nightmares. They rattled through his mind giving birth to a new torment, whose name was Regret, and whom Samuel would carry with him as his companion long after the guilt had subsided. Of all the things he regretted, the worst was that he had not trusted enough in Diana's love for him to tell her the truth, but had closed his eyes to his own irrational fear of losing her love to her brother. Instead, he told himself over and over that he could not betray the trust of his friend. He'd relive the desperation in Christian's eyes at the moment he begged Samuel to keep quiet about the truth, and decided he couldn't break the promise he'd made. He understood Christian's shame, his fear of allowing the single most important person in his life to ever learn the truth. The fear of seeing his sister back away from him in terror. *I'm nothing if not a man of my word,* Samuel rationalized. But he also knew that in remaining a man of his word, he became a fiendish sneak as well.

"The choice was clear from the very beginning," a voice suddenly spoke to him in his dream.

Samuel looked up to see where it came from. In the distance, he saw a dark speck in the center of a bright light. The speck grew larger as it drew near. Samuel was soon able to recognize the man that had taken shape. Jesse stood on a cloud that floated silently toward him. He stared at Jesse as the cloud came to a gentle stop right in front of him. Jesse's face was gentle and loving, but it held a premonition of the judgement Samuel had imposed on himself. He was unsure if he should be afraid or relieved. There was an element of comfort in the familiar regardless of its intention.

Waves of power emanated from within and around him; colors in cool hues of blues and greens seemed to pour themselves out of his very core as if they had minds of their own. Even Jesse himself seemed ethereal, without substance, yet real as he floated on a cloud of white surrounded by the calming, peaceful colors.

"What do you mean?" Samuel asked, panic-stricken. "There was no choice to be made."

The cloud rose a foot as if it were angry, then settled back down. "Wasn't there?" Jesse asked.

"I made a promise," Samuel argued. "I had no choice but to keep it." He bent over, cowering in fear, though the vision before him did not frighten him. He realized it was himself he feared the most.

"You have always had a choice, Samuel," Jesse said. "But you made the wrong one."

"How was it wrong?" Samuel nearly yelled in defense. "I kept my promise for five hundred years!! Who else could have done such a thing?"

"Possibly no one could have," Jesse answered in a consoling manner. "But you kept it for selfish reasons, not honorable ones."

Samuel stood motionless with his mouth agape while Jesse's words registered in the thought patterns of his dream. There was no argument against the truth. There were no fancy rationalizations for what Samuel had done, but he gave it one last valiant attempt anyway.

"I protected Christian from shame and Diana from being terrorized by her own flesh and blood!" he proudly argued.

Jesse frowned. "Love protects us from fear of any kind," he said, disappointment evident in his voice. "You protected Christian in the beginning, Samuel. But that was no longer a valid argument when Diana had chosen you over loneliness."

"I didn't trick her," Samuel said. "I loved her with my whole heart and soul."

"That you did," Jesse said. "No one can take that much away from you. But you did both brother and sister a grave injustice by trying to keep them apart. They shared a brighter love that would have deeply enriched all of your lives, but you chose to keep her love all to yourself rather than risk losing any of it to her brother. Didn't you know that her love for Christian would always be her love for Christian? Her love for her brother never belonged to you. Love exists so far beyond this life, Samuel, that nothing can change it." Jesse shook his head in disappointment as the cloud began to retreat.

"Wait!" Samuel yelled as the cloud drifted away. "Don't go."

But the cloud that carried Jesse continued to grow smaller as the distance widened between it and Samuel.

"Where was your faith?" Jesse asked sadly before disappearing completely.

When the vision of Jesse on the cloud had gone, the space in front of Samuel was replaced by a familiar landscape from another time. It was the Desmonde vineyard in 1410 A.D. and all operations in the fields had stopped as a result of Christian's death.

Diana stood alone under a willow tree staring out across the countryside. Her eyes were red and swollen from crying, her face was drawn from the spent expressions of misery the awful news had caused.

It was sundown when Samuel approached her, realizing as he did so, that he had quickly fallen in love with the sister of the man whom he had changed into a vampire and to whom he had promised never to reveal the truth of that change.

It was too perfect!

He could woo Diana in her misery without ever having to tell her what he had done. He could use the sad situation to reveal the truth of his own existence to her without shedding a poor light on himself. He could make Diana his for the duration of her lifetime. If he never knew love again, it would be worth it.

It was a good plan for a vampire who constantly faces aborted relationships and a lonely, empty eternity. He believed that it would have worked perfectly for the fifty or sixty years that Diana might have lived, except for the heartache of watching her age. But for one unforeseen flaw, Samuel could have had a mortal lifetime of memories to carry him through the rest of his existence.

The scenery shifted to a time two years later when he and Diana stood at the same spot in the vineyard having a different conversation. Diana was arguing with him in his dream just as she'd done in life.

"But, Samuel," she said, "I'll be with you anyway. Even in the afterlife I'll stay by your side. Wouldn't it be better to see me and touch me rather than to simply wonder if I'm really there as I said I would be?"

"Your arguments make sense, mon Cheri," Samuel said to her. "I must admit, if I could choose to touch you for all of eternity I would most definitely make that choice." He looked out into the darkness in silence.

"How unsettling it will be for me," Diana said, "to float all around you and through you, but to never be able to feel you again. I would be no more than a puppy dog following you around, but never receiving any notice from its master. Can you imagine how you would feel if it were you in such a position?"

Samuel turned to her. "No I can't," he said. "Nor do I want to imagine such a thing. And I don't want to imagine it for you either my beloved, Diana." He touched her cheek, and shuddered from the enormous amount of love he felt for her. "I will give you what you ask."

"That was the time when you should have told her, Samuel."

There was that voice again.

Samuel looked around in his dream, but he could see no one. Once again, he stood behind Diana, watching her mourn the loss of her brother.

"There was no better time, Samuel."

Where was it coming from?

Samuel quickly whirled himself around in his dream. When he stopped, Christian was there. "You!" he said. "Are you going to pass judgement on me, too?"

"No one can pass judgement on you, mon ami," Christian said. "You've actually done quite well at that yourself."

"Why are you here, then?"

Christian looked at Diana first, then back at Samuel. "Why did you summon me?" he asked.

Samuel was speechless.

Christian walked over to Diana, then stood beside her. "Is that how it really was?" he asked. "Did she really convince you to change her?"

"Yes," Samuel said.

Christian shook his head, then walked back toward Samuel. "I had no idea."

Somehow the tables seemed to have turned and Samuel did not feel on the defensive now. Instead, he tried to comfort his friend. "How could you have known? I kept that secret as well as I'd kept yours."

Christian looked behind him at Diana. "Who would have ever thought that she would choose, actually choose, to be like us?" Christian asked. "Had I known I would have come forth myself."

"I love her," Samuel said.

Christian turned to his friend and placed his hand on Samuel's shoulder. "I know you do, Sam. And she loves you."

Samuel fell to his knees with his face buried in his hands. "What do I do now? I've lost her because of my lack of foresight. I carried the lie too long, kept the promise too long, even when I knew how outdated the promise had become. I became selfish out of fear of losing her. And now I've lost her anyway."

Christian lowered himself to one knee before his friend. "We've both lost her, Sam," he said. "You because of your ultimate selfishness; I because of my shame, my pride. Two cardinal sins for two grown men who should have known better."

Samuel looked up. The surroundings of his dream dissipated leaving him alone in a void with no ground beneath him and nothing around him. It was dark. So dark that when he opened his eyes in his hotel room nothing changed . . . except the bed. He could feel the bed beneath his body. He knew his dreams had ended. He was awake and alone in the huge empty suite. All the events of the previous evening came rushing at him in full force. He knew he had to get out of there or go crazy from the loneliness. He sat up in bed and immediately felt the weakness in his body take him and spin him around.

He had to eat.

He had to get strong.

He had to get out of this place.

Then, he had to find Diana.

CHAPTER 3

December 14, 1997

Diana awoke with a start. The anger and disappointment came flooding back to her as soon as she inhaled the hotel smell of her room and remembered her early morning flight to the tourist town of Niagara Falls. In the distance, she could hear the hundreds of thousands of gallons of fresh water as it rushed to clear the edge of the magnificent cliff on its way to the river below. It was two miles away, but to her sensitive ears its angry roar was as loud as a jet engine.

Pain!

Diana doubled over as the claws of hunger ripped through her insides. How long had it been? It made no difference. She had to feed now. There was no time to waste before the pain would paralyze her. It had been like this from the beginning. Even Samuel could never figure out why 'the hunger' grabbed her the way it did. Samuel was able to go for days without sustenance until he felt weak and realized it was time to feed. But Diana had not been so fortunate. For her there were no warning signs of weakness or disorientation. Whenever she let too much time pass without the red elixir, there was only pain, intense and debilitating. It came in waves with brief respites in between. She could only wait for the pain to subside enough for her to move around. She thought hard to come up with a plan that would allow her to feed as inconspicuously as possible before she lost her wits to the animal instincts of survival. Once that were to happen she would be out of control. But she knew from experience that as long as she had a pre-formulated plan locked in her mind she would follow it to the letter without a second thought, no matter what happened. It didn't take her long to decide on one.

As soon as she was able, Diana rose from the bed and dressed quickly. She could feel her self-control slipping away. She fought to hold on to it as long as she could, but she knew the harder she fought against her own instincts, the quicker the pain would start again. She picked up the phone.

"Room service," the bubbly, female voice said from the other end of the line.

"I'd like a bottle of Moet brought to my room, please," Diana said.

"I'll send someone right up."

"Thank you." Diana hung up. She sat in the little chair near the dirty, hotel window that overlooked the swiftly moving Niagara River, and did her utmost to keep her emotions in control until the time when the door to her room would be firmly closed with her prey safely inside. She could hear the footsteps of the other guests as they walked down the carpeted hallway past the door to her room. If they only knew there was a vampire on the same floor there would be a mad dash of people running to the front desk in a panic to check out. But Diana was no threat to anyone yet.

Her head snapped to attention when the buzzer sounded. Her muscles had begun to tighten and the quick movement sent a shot like an arrow down her spine.

"Room Service," a man's voice said cheerily through the door.

Diana did her best to keep from pouncing right through the metal door. "Just a minute," she said. It only took a moment for her to transport her body from the far side of the room to the door. Her hand was on the knob before her body had completed its momentary trek through space.

Her hunger was growing out of control.

Slowly she opened the door a crack and peered out into the hallway to see what sumptuous meal the hotel staff had sent her.

He was dark skinned and muscular. Hispanic from the looks of him. A young and healthy meal just in time.

"Did you call for Room Service?" the man asked.

Calmly, Diana opened the door all the way and took a step back motioning for him to enter the room. She could taste him as she caught a whiff of the blood beating through his veins while he waited for her to confirm the order.

"Yes, I did," she said, forcing a smile.

"Well, here you are." He entered the room. "This is my last call for tonight. I'm off the clock in five minutes."

Diana nodded and watched him walk by without taking her eyes off the movements of every muscle that carried him past her. She began to salivate when she caught the human scent that drifted through the air behind him.

Slowly and without a sound, Diana pushed the door closed, then waited for him to place the ice bucket and bottle of Moet on the table across the room.

"Will there be anything else tonight?" he asked.

Diana did not miss his roving eyes as they studied every part of her. Nor did she miss the appreciative nod of his head when his visual inspection of her was through. And she especially did not miss the obvious bulge in his pants that she knew he wanted her to see. Slowly, she walked toward him. "As a matter of fact," she said, "there is something else you can do for me before you go."

Diana stood directly in front of the young man and stared into his line of vision. There was no way he could miss the bloody veins that filled her eyes from the need to satisfy her hunger. But it didn't matter what he saw. By the time the young, Hispanic waiter from Niagara Falls realized what Diana was, he had nearly lost all control to her and he did not care.

Put your arms around me, Diana directed him with her thoughts.

The man did as he was told.

Now kiss me, Diana ordered him. She knew she did not have total command of him yet. If she made her move too quickly, he could easily overpower her and call for help. She was physically weak, too weak to stop him. She knew she had to have a solid hold on his mind.

Kiss me, she told him again.

This time the waiter did not hesitate. He belonged to Diana the minute their lips touched. By the time she broke their kiss and bit into the warm, male-scented flesh at the base of his neck, the young man had grown so anxious with the desire to feel her teeth cut through his skin that he exploded in his pants from the most forceful orgasm of his young, adult life. Diana would make sure he never remembered the experience when the night was over.

She feasted insatiably, as always. Her body soaked up the nourishment like a house plant soaks up water after having been left dry too long. She could feel her pulse race as her body was replenished. She felt the strength in her muscles return, and was soon able to stop draining the man's blood before she killed him. She laid him on the bed and sat down at the little table by the window. Then she opened her bottle of Moet, filled one of the two wine glasses the waiter had brought with him, and took a sip. The cold, effervescence chased the remaining blood down her throat and further on through to the pit of her stomach. It felt good to mix the chilled fermented grapes with the warmth of the living blood. So good, in fact, that Diana sat through two glasses of the champagne and relaxed while she waited for the full rejuvenation of her body to complete itself.

Finally, her strength and sanity renewed, Diana started to consider the event that had brought her to this tourist town in the first place, the lies of a man she had loved and trusted without question throughout her entire life, and the years with her brother those lies had cost her.

Christian!

"Oh my," Diana said out loud in anguish. "What did I do?" When she left Samuel in her fury she had also left the company of her brother without allowing so much as a moment for catching up. She could only imagine what Christian must be thinking about her now. No sooner did they see each other after centuries, but she had disappeared in an angry huff. "Good job, Di," she said to herself. She stood, shook her head, then walked into the bathroom to wash up. "Now what?" She didn't want to see Samuel whom she suspected was probably crying on Christian's shoulder at that very moment. But she did want to see her brother. She wanted to know what he had been doing all this time. And she wanted to know about the woman who had stood so patiently and quietly beside him while he came to meet her.

"It's going to have to wait until I'm calmed down," she said to herself.

For the time being, Diana only wanted to get away from the betrayal and disgust that she still felt over Samuel's secret. She had to allow her outrage a chance to cool. Once again, she had been too head strong and she knew it. But it was too late to change what she had done.

Diana freshened herself up. It was a little before seven in the evening. She decided to go out for awhile, simply forget about the whole thing, maybe have some fun. She knew the young man on her bed would sleep at least until dawn. She left him lying there and grabbed her coat, keys to the room, and some money. She locked up on the way out, hanging the 'Do Not Disturb' sign on her door to keep from having him discovered in the room of a guest. She certainly did not want him to be in any trouble because of her.

When she was in the lobby she went right to the front desk. "Would you please call me a cab?" Diana asked the girl behind the desk. She was different than the one who had checked Diana in the night before.

"Certainly," the girl replied. "Where are you going?"

"I'm not sure, yet," Diana replied. "Any suggestions?"

"What are you looking for?"

Diana thought for a moment before answering. "Someplace dark," she said. "Someplace different where the music is loud and the people are young and . . . you know what I mean."

The girl blushed, then smiled. "I know just the place," she

said. "Just a little further into the city is a place called The Factory. It's really different. I think it might be just what you're looking for."

"I'll give it a try," Diana said. "Thanks."

"No problem," the girl said. She dialed the number for the cab company and made the arrangements. "All set," she said, hanging up the phone. "The cab will be right outside in a minute."

"Thank you," Diana said. She started toward the front doors to wait for the cab's arrival, all the while trying to keep thoughts of Samuel and the hurt he had caused her at bay. In less than a minute the cab pulled up directly in front of her. She got in the back seat and rode in silence most of the way. She found it nearly impossible to keep her emotions under control. So many questions ran through her mind.

Had Christian known all along that she had crossed over? He couldn't have. He would've come to her and shared his own existence with her if he'd known of hers. She knew her brother well enough to know that for sure.

It had been Samuel all along. Samuel had kept the truth from her because he was selfish and self-serving and . . .

An unsettling thought occurred to her. Why hadn't Christian been as angry with Samuel as she was? Didn't he love her? Didn't he want to see her? Maybe the woman in his life had taken her place in his heart. Diana looked out the window of the taxi cab and tried to shake off her doubtful thoughts about her brother.

"Impossible!" she said out loud.

"What was that?" the cab driver asked.

Diana was caught by surprise. She hesitated, then realized she had spoken aloud. "I'm sorry," she said. "Nothing."

The driver shook his head in acknowledgement as he looked at her in the rear view mirror, then turned his attention back to the road.

Samuel had not taken Christian's place in her heart. He was her brother. She couldn't believe for one minute that it would be any different for Christian.

Still, it didn't make sense. She would've thought her brother would want to beat the traitor to a pulp and feed him to the crows.

But he hadn't.

In fact, Christian seemed to understand the situation Samuel was in. Even at the very moment when Diana and Christian had recognized each other Christian didn't seem to be surprised. It was almost as if he already knew.

But then, that would make him a traitor to his own sister and Diana simply could not, and would not, accept that of her own flesh and blood. But how else could his reaction be explained? The very thought made her anxious.

The taxi pulled up outside The Factory to let Diana out. The music inside the night club was so loud it pulsated through the cab. Diana paid the driver, then joined the short line of people who stood out in the cold waiting to show their proof of age in order to be allowed in. But the line went quick and within minutes, Diana was inside. She hadn't needed to show any identification. Her telepathic persuasiveness had been enough to get her in the door without any questions.

Surrounded by the heavy drum beat and heart stopping bass guitar that echoed from the sound system, Diana walked deeper into the throngs of people and clouds of smoke. Above each table she saw a series of three digit numbers hanging from a wire that was anchored in the ceiling above. Directly beneath the numbers was a telephone on each table, many of which were in use. She looked toward the bar as she made her way to find an opening where she could sit. She noticed there was a telephone for every two barstools set along the top of the bar. In fact, there were telephones everywhere!

Diana settled in on the last barstool near the wall. The bartender was there in seconds.

"Lite beer, please," she said without looking at him.

"Comin' right up."

For a moment Diana was reminded again of Samuel who could

drink nothing but port wine and even that did not sit well with him at times. She, on-the-other-hand, seemed to be able to drink almost anything without a problem.

"Here you go," he said, placing the bottle and glass in front of her.

Diana gave him a fifty dollar bill. "Start a tab," she said.

"Aren't you going to answer it?" he asked her.

"What?" Diana asked. She had no idea what he was talking about.

"The phone," he said, pointing to the telephone on the bar right next to her. "Someone's calling you."

Diana looked at the phone for a few seconds as if she had never seen one before. She listened while it continued to ring, barely audible beneath the pounding beat of the loud music. "Why would someone be calling me?" she asked without thinking.

"Because someone here wants to meet you." His voice was loaded with sarcasm. He shook his head and walked away to tend to the other patrons who were sitting at the bar.

Diana scanned the room to see if anyone was looking in her direction, but no one was that obvious.

The phone continued to ring.

What the hell? She reached for the handset. "Hello?" she said tentatively.

"Hello, Diana." The voice was deep, male, and leisurely. Something about it made her naturally suspicious.

"How do you know me?"

"I know you."

Diana had never liked insolent men. "Well, now you can forget me," she said, then slammed the phone back into its cradle. Immediately her senses perked up. From behind and to the left of her she could feel the thoughts of another vampire. For a brief moment she thought it was Samuel, but it wasn't. There was nothing soft in the energy level she felt from this one. Samuel always had a lovingness about him. Whoever this was in the bar had a dark intensity that permeated the air.

The phone rang again. This time she picked it up right away. "What do you want?"

"I want to meet you," he said. "It's very rare that I get to meet one of our kind. I saw you walk in, but I felt you in the air all around me as soon as you entered the city."

Diana crossed her legs and turned her back to the crowded room. "Did it occur to you that I might not be interested in meeting you?" She deliberately tried to sound bored.

"Yes, but it doesn't matter to me if you want to meet me or not," he said. "The point is that I want to meet you."

"Oh, you're one of those," she said.

"One of what?" His manner suggested he already knew what she meant, but dared her to say it anyway.

"Always get what you want so you think you always will."

There was a pause on the other end. "Something like that."

"Well, I'm not interested." Diana hung up on her caller for the second time. She did not look around the room to see if anyone was watching her. She really didn't care one way or the other. Neither did the phone ring again like it had before. Something inside of her was slightly annoyed that her caller had given up so easily, but it was just as well. Vampire or not, she'd had enough of men for awhile, especially after what she had just learned about the one she had trusted for the majority of her life.

And her own brother!

She still didn't know what to think about Christian. Had he known about her this whole time or hadn't he? If not, then why wasn't he angry with Samuel? So there's the answer. He must have known she was still alive.

But if that were so, why did he pick now to make himself known to her? Why did he wait so long? Didn't he want to know his own sister, anymore? Maybe he was ashamed of her because she had chosen to cross over. She frowned as she signaled the bartender for another beer. She needed to forget about everything for awhile, but drinking any form of alcohol was not going to do it. It took far too long for a vampire to feel the effects of it.

"You still love him?" the bartender asked.

"What?" Diana was caught off guard by the question.

"Look," he said. "I'm not prying, but I see a lot of faces in my line of work. Yours is the face of a woman who just left her boyfriend or whoever. It's a face I've seen before."

"I don't think that's any of your business," she said.

"Suit yourself." The bartender turned to wait on another customer.

In her heart there was a gaping hole that Samuel could have filled just by speaking her name. The truth of the matter was she still loved him and she knew she always would. But she couldn't trust him anymore and what was love without trust? She couldn't allow Samuel to mean anything to her. She would not allow it. There was no room in a vampire's life for someone who could not be trusted. That included her own brother, Christian, whom she was now forced to question as well.

She needed time to figure it all out somehow. Until she did that, she wanted nothing to do with either of them. She poured the last of her bottle of beer into the glass.

"Need another one?" the bartender asked.

Diana placed the empty bottle at the edge of the bar and waited for him to bring her another.

"I'd like to buy that for you."

It was that voice from the phone. And it was right behind her. She whirled around to face her romantic predator with an angry glare in her eyes, but there was no one there.

"Is something wrong, Miss?" the bartender asked.

Diana was embarrassed and not sure what to say. She and Samuel could talk to each other with their minds, but to speak out loud without their voices was another matter. *What kind of vampire is this?* she thought.

"No," she stammered. "Nothing's wrong."

The bartender looked at her inquisitively, hesitated, then turned around and headed for the farthest end of the bar to fill another order.

Diana sat staring into her glass of beer trying to think what to do. She was getting angry, now. She didn't want to be bothered and she hated these kinds of head games. But she was also nervous at the unusual talent this mystery man had displayed.

"I'm not far."

There he was again!

Diana looked up slowly and began to pan the crowds from face to face within the room determined that this time she would find her pest.

Suddenly, she felt a mental tug at her from the same direction where the voice had originated. She snapped her view directly into the midnight black eyes of the oldest vampire she had ever encountered.

He stood as erect as a palm tree with the same breezy aspect as the topmost branches have when they sway in the wind. He had black, wavy hair that was almost shoulder length and tied in back as a ponytail. His attire consisted of a black dress shirt tucked into a simple pair of black jeans.

But it was his eyes that caught hers as if they were magnets from which she could not pull away. They were locked together in a battle of wills that Diana was too young and inexperienced to win.

In a matter of moments as brief as the twinkle of a single star, he revealed to her his age and his unquestionable strength. She knew that even as old as Samuel was, he would never be a match for this one.

Suddenly, Diana was frightened.

CHAPTER 4

December 14, 1997

Christian lay in bed thinking about Diana. Sunset had only just begun, but he was too preoccupied to sleep easy. He kept mulling over all the years that separated them and they only had an instant together, before she was gone. He understood her anger and he'd grown up with her self-assured temper, but he had never expected her to disappear from him like this. Samuel, maybe. He really did deserve it, but Christian was her brother. He'd been so excited at the thought of seeing her. She was the best of his past brought into the best of his entire life. It seemed too perfect which was probably why it didn't work out the way he'd expected. What if he had known about her all these years, but stayed away? That would make her feel totally betrayed and angry with him as well. He hoped that wasn't the case. Maybe she didn't understand what he'd tried to tell her just before she left the night club. She was so busy yelling at Samuel, she probably didn't hear most of what Christian had to say.

He got out of bed and went to the living room to watch the rest of the sunset and wait for Roni to join him. He felt empty. He had never realized how much a part of him Diana still was, but the brief moment he had to see her brought it all back to him. How good a friend she was. How much they could trust each other. How much she'd meant to him. Now what was going to happen? All he knew for sure was that he had to stay calm and not alarm Roni. She always wanted to fix things for people so he expected she'd feel that way for Diana and Samuel. He didn't need to add his own concerns to that pile of worries.

He sat down in his favorite chair near the fireplace and watched the world turn dark. It wasn't long before he saw Roni coming down the hall toward him. He stood up and went to her. He needed her arms around him just then to fill the void his sister's disappearance had created. "Good evening," he said. He leaned forward to kiss her on the cheek. "How did you sleep?"

"Terrific, actually." She sat down at the kitchen table. "But I'm really worried about your sister and Samuel."

As he'd expected. Christian walked around to the other side of the table and leaned on the back of the chair. "Ah, yes," he said. "My sister. Is she everything I told you she would be?"

"You're awfully casual about the whole thing," Roni said. "Aren't you even the least bit concerned?"

Christian sat down next to her and thought for a moment. He didn't want her to know how torn up he really felt inside. She'd only worry about him, too. "I'm more concerned about Samuel than I am about Diana," he said. "Diana has the upper hand. You see, Samuel is not only heartbroken, but he's at her mercy as well."

Roni nodded. "Well, you have a point. But don't you think she was a little unreasonable? I mean, you'd think she would've been so happy to see you. It shouldn't have mattered that Samuel had kept it from her for so long. She should've been glad she finally knew. After all, if it wasn't for him, you wouldn't be alive."

Christian smiled and nodded his head in agreement as he reached down and picked up the white cat that was winding herself in and out of his ankles. "That's true," he said. "But think about it, Roni. If I were in her shoes I might be wondering how big this secret really was."

"What do you mean?" Roni stood up and went to put a cup of water in the microwave. "Weren't five centuries long enough?"

"I didn't say how long it was," Christian corrected her. "I said how big it was. In other words, how many people really knew she and I were both still alive?"

Roni turned around to look at him, her head tilted to one side. She shrugged and shook her head. "What difference would that make?"

Christian leaned back in his chair. "Let's see," he said. "Suppose I knew all this time that Diana had crossed over, but I didn't do a thing to contact her or force Samuel to tell her. Don't you think she might be upset about that?"

Roni's eyes opened wide. She stared at him in disbelief. "Oh no. What if that's exactly what she's thinking? I mean, does Diana think that way?"

"Indeed she does," Christian said. "She tends to be quite the suspicious one when she's been wronged. After all these years I can only imagine that her nature is stronger than I remember."

"Isn't there some way to contact her so we can make her see it's not true?" Roni's face was a mask of alarm. "Oh my God," she said. "She's out there pissed off at Sam for not telling her about you and probably pissed off at you for not contacting her, and thinking that neither of you loved her as much as she believed you both did. If I was in her shoes I'd be devastated."

Christian leaned forward and nodded. "Exactly."

Roni shook her head. "This is frustrating." She took her cup out of the microwave, grabbed a tea bag, and went to sit back down at the table. "She's feeling betrayed, hurt, and outraged by both of you. What can we do? Can't you find her?"

"I'm not sure where to look after all these years," Christian said. "She could be anywhere on the planet."

Roni frowned. "This is your sister," she said, tapping her fingers on the table. "Shouldn't you at least try?"

Christian didn't like her tone of voice. "I intend to as soon as I hear from Samuel," he said. "If he doesn't locate her at home in France or anywhere else in Europe, then we can both start looking elsewhere." He stood up, letting Sammi jump to the floor, and walked to the window that looked out over the back yard. This was hard. If Diana didn't want to be found she wouldn't be, but as a mortal, Roni had trouble understanding how that was possible.

That made it more difficult for Christian to stay calm. The explanations alone drained him. "There's no sense running around blind. Samuel is going to have to fill me in on a lot of background before I'll have a clue as to what I can do to help or where I should look for her."

"I understand what you're saying," Roni said. "But that doesn't change my need to do something to help them. I can't just sit around and wait to see what happens. What about your telepathy? Can't you try to 'feel' where she is?"

Christian turned to look at her and tried to stay calm. She was pushing his patience to its limit. "These are not mortals you're dealing with. They're vampires like me. They can disappear at will, they can fly, and they can mask their thoughts and feelings even from each other. Do you really think I haven't tried that already?" he asked. "She is my sister."

Roni gave him a startled look. "I'm sorry," she said. "Of course you would've done that first." She looked down at the table, and was silent.

Christian turned to the window again. He'd done exactly what he hadn't wanted to do, take his distress out on her. Already he felt even worse than he did a few minutes ago. "Actually, I didn't try it until we were already headed home last night. But it was too late by then." He continued to watch outside.

Roni didn't say anything.

"At the very least, I might've been able to pick up the direction in which she was headed, but as I said, I thought of it too late." He stared straight ahead. He was upset with Diana and angry at himself for the way he'd spoken to the one person who made him feel whole.

Roni sat quietly sipping her tea.

"There's very little that can be done until we hear from Samuel," Christian said, thinking out loud. "Until then we have to sit tight and wait."

Just then the phone rang. He turned to Roni and they stared at each other for a few seconds. "Samuel?" she asked. She reached for the handset, obviously excited. "Hello?" She looked at Christian and shook her head. "Hi, Father."

Christian's heart sank as he watched her walk to the sofa. She sat down, curled her legs beneath her, and looked at him, but he turned around and tried to feel out either Diana's or Samuel's location. But he got nowhere and his efforts were exhausting. He heard Roni's voice, but did not catch anything in particular about her conversation until he heard his own name mentioned.

"Well, Father Larry. Christian finally met his sister last night," Roni said.

Christian turned around and listened to her tell Father Larry about the previous evening. Was it any of his concern? What would he think?

Roni smiled at something the priest had said. "Maybe just pray," she said. At that moment Christian felt better though he wasn't sure why.

"Actually, no." Roni said. "I wanted to let you know how glad I was to hear you and Christian had such a pleasant visit the other day."

There was a brief hesitation then Roni handed the phone to Christian and smiled. "He wants to talk to you."

Christian took the phone from her hand. "Hello, Father."

"I'm glad you told her," the priest said.

"So am I."

"As for the other matter," Father Larry said, changing the subject, "let me know if there is anything at all I can do to help."

"Thank you, but I think prayers will be fine for now."

"Then prayers it will be."

Instead of saying good-bye as it seemed he was about to, Father Larry was suddenly silent.

"What's the matter?" Christian asked. "Are you alright?"

Father Larry cleared his throat, then took a deep breath that Christian could clearly hear. "I suppose I should've asked this before," he said.

"What's that?"

"Well, it just occurred to me," he said. "This is your sister you met last night?"

"That's right." He knew what was coming next.

"As in, blood relation sister?" the priest asked.

"Yes."

"So. Just how many vampires are there in this little family of yours?"

"One that's family and one that's an old friend," Christian said.

"Three," Father Larry said. "'Three vampires."

"Are you alright, Father?"

"I'll be fine. New things always take some getting used to."

"We did discuss this," Christian reminded him.

"I remember," Father Larry said. "I guess it seemed more . . . hypothetical at that time."

"And now?"

Again Father Larry breathed deeply. "And now I have to accept the truth."

Christian smiled and looked at Roni.

She held her arms out to her sides and mouthed, "What?"

He shook his head to reassure her that nothing was wrong, then turned around to finish his conversation. "When the other two decide to call a truce and show up I'll let you know. You can drop by and say, 'Hello', if you'd like."

"I'll let you know," Father Larry said. "In the meantime, I'll keep those prayers going. They'll need all the help they can get. And if you need me, don't hesitate to call."

"Thanks." Christian hung up, then turned to Roni. "He's quite a man."

"I hope he gets used to all this," she said.

"He will." Christian leaned against the wall and watched the cats play hide-and-seek beneath the table. "I really do like him, you know."

"But?"

Christian cast her a questioning look, then smiled. "You know," he said. "Sometimes I wonder which one of us is the vampire. You seem to know what's on my mind more than I know what's on yours."

"Women's intuition," Roni said. "Now tell me the rest."

"Of what?"

Roni raised her eyebrows at him, and he laughed.

"Alright," he said. "I guess I'm a bit intimidated by him."

"Why?"

"Because of his relationship to God," Christian said. "I don't know if that threatening feeling will ever go away."

"What are you threatened by?" Roni asked. "God still?"

Christian nodded. "Irrational, huh?"

Roni repositioned herself on the sofa. "Yes, but you're doing better than you used to be."

Christian chuckled. "What made him call you, anyway?"

Roni sipped her tea slowly. "He was just returning my call from yesterday."

Christian nodded then turned to stare out the window. Suddenly, all he could think of was how he'd know where Diana was if he'd kept his thoughts sharp enough to follow her trail the night before. He looked down and saw the cats crawl behind the curtains as if they instinctively knew it was best to stay out of the way for the time being. Roni walked over to him and placed her arm loosely around his back. She leaned her head against his shoulder and sighed.

He put his arm around her waist and pulled her to him gently. "How're you feeling?"

"I'm feeling pretty good this evening," Roni answered. "Except for being worried about this whole situation." She looked at him. "And about you."

He had done his best to hide what was on his mind, how he really felt, but he couldn't hold it in anymore. "I should've waited," he said. "There must have been a better way to handle telling her."

"How could we have expected this to happen?" she asked. "We didn't even know for sure if they were in town or not."

Christian looked away again. "I know, but I forced the issue."

"It isn't your fault."

"Mmmm, hmmmm."

"Christian." Roni pulled away from him.

Slowly, he turned around and looked at her.

"It's not your fault, Christian," she said. "Sam should've told her a long time ago."

"But I pushed him into bringing her here so I could hear it from her own lips that she chose to cross over," he said. His eyes bore into Roni's soul begging her to understand.

"If it hadn't happened now, it would've happened later. It was inevitable," Roni said. "You're intelligent enough to know that."

"I do know that."

"Then what else is eating at you?"

He didn't answer. Instead, he moved the curtain out of the way and bent down to pick up Sammi whose happy, white tail swishing back and forth beneath the curtain had been the only clue to her whereabouts. The unusually loud purring began immediately as Christian flipped her onto her back and carried her to the sofa to sit with him.

"Nothing," he said. He looked up at her. "Stop worrying. I'm fine."

Roni continued to watch him, but said nothing.

He smiled. "Really."

"Alright then." She started toward the hall. "I'm going to shower. Do you want anything?"

He shook his head to indicate that he did not.

"OK. Well, I've got an appointment with the Brandison's."

Christian nodded, then watched her turn and walk away. He remained on the sofa after she'd left the room and he stroked Sammi who purred contentedly in his lap. He thought about Diana. He thought about their childhood years. He thought about the past five centuries and the time they had lost together as brother and sister and he wondered how much different the years might have been if they'd each known the other was still out there.

"I feel responsible for what happened," he said to the cat in his lap. He stroked her under the chin, then lifted her head to look at him. "I swore him to secrecy about me. I refused to take his word for how my sister became immortal. I was stubborn when I started pushing him to bring her here. I couldn't imagine any human being would actually choose to live as a vampire. The loneliness, the incessant changes, the losses." A single tear fell to Sammi's fur leaving a tiny, pink spot where it landed.

Sammi nuzzled him and purred louder as if she understood his thoughts. Christian rubbed her belly, kissed her on the nose, then put her on the floor. He would be glad when Samuel turned up so he might learn something, anything, about Diana's where-abouts.

"Did I hear you talking?" Roni asked.

Christian looked up in time to see her still wiping her hair with the damp towel. She looked beautiful. "I was talking to the cat," he said.

Roni removed the towel from her head and stood looking at him. "About what?"

"My sister," he said, lowering his eyes to the floor.

Roni walked toward him. "Did Sammi have any answers for you?"

Christian looked up at her, his eyes filled with sadness. "I'm concerned about her," he said. "Not only for her state of mind, but because of all the nasty characters that walk this earth. Even a vampire is not immune to the sludge of society. There's always someone strange enough or sick enough out there, somewhere, who would be able to harm even one such as her. If not physically, then emotionally. My sister is very vulnerable right now. There's no telling how far she might go to mend her wounds."

"I know," Roni said. "Maybe it will help you feel better if you said a prayer for Diana."

Christian flashed her an angry look. "I don't think I'll push my luck that far," he said. "I'm not fully convinced God loves me the way you are."

"There's always confession with Father Larry," Roni said.

"Now you're pushing your luck with me." Christian stood and headed for the hallway. He wanted to be alone, but Roni followed him to the bedroom.

"I'm sorry," she said. "I know how you feel about that. I just thought maybe . . ."

Christian stopped walking and ran a hand through his hair. "I know what you thought." He turned quickly, wrapped his arms around Roni's waist, and let out a deep breath.

"It seems you're feeling better," she said as he held her close.

"Not really," he said. "But I thought you might have the cure for this man's poor self esteem." He lifted her, then carried her to the bed.

"I might." She placed her hands behind his neck and pulled him down to kiss her. "You never know."

He looked deep into her eyes. "You'll be late for your appointment."

Roni brushed her fingers along his cheek. "You come first."

CHAPTER 5

December 14, 1997

The man in black gave Diana the creeps. Not the "ooooo spooky" kind of creeps, but the too-awful-to-be-believed kind of creeps. He was the thing that made a person afraid to get out of bed at night for fear of something sinister lying beneath it waiting to grab the first pair of ankles that appeared. He was the footsteps one might hear following behind, even though no one was there. He was the unexplainable "bump in the night."

He was suspense personified.

He was anguish untameable.

He was fear.

With his thoughts, he told Diana more about himself than she would ever have wanted to know about anyone. In his mind he showed her horrors and passions; anger and passivity; reality and delusions. Things he had done and things he had only thought of passed through her mind like a motion picture.

His soul was blackened by time unforgivable and his heart was scarred by wounds unhealable. But his mind was strong. His powers were incredible.

And Diana was as intimidated as he intended her to be.

She wanted to run. But she couldn't make her legs move.

She wanted to hide. But she knew he would find her.

She wanted to be with Samuel and Christian; safe and protected. But her vampire's forethought showed her that she would be risking their lives if she got them involved with this . . . this . . . this thing.

Diana sat on her barstool as still as a statue while he over-whelmed her with his powers, and his secrets, and his evil, black-ened soul. When he took his first step toward her, from his place across the room, something in Diana cried out for him to come quicker while part of her feared for her very life.

She was a vampire. She had lived for five centuries, yet this man showed her how fragile she truly was next to his enormous strengths. He could crush her like an ant without a second thought, or he could nourish and pamper her with the same amount of effort.

Nothing meant anything to him.

Until now.

The solitude of a vampire's life was enough to harden its heart against the world. But this stranger had been more than just lonely. He had seen Moses part the Red Sea. He had seen the birth of Jesus Christ. He had seen nearly everything that had happened on the planet Earth since the days before the Great Pyramid was ever built.

He had seen far too much change and far too much pain. His heart had grown harder and his soul had turned blacker with each day of loneliness and each disappointment. Nothing stayed the same for long. Even the truth today would be a different truth tomorrow as new realities evolved. There was nothing to rely on but oneself. And even the self was known to change from time to time.

That, in itself, could be an ugly truth.

Diana tried to remain calm as he moved closer and closer. She tried to vaporize, but somehow, he would not allow it. She had no idea how he was able to stop her, but he did, and that frightened her even more. It had never even crossed her mind that stopping a vampire from becoming vapor would be a skill she might need to master someday. But this one apparently had a need for such tal-ents and that only added to her fear.

And he knew it.

Everything that passed through her thoughts since she had

stepped through the doorway, he knew. Every emotion she had experienced, he knew. By the time he had stopped walking toward her and stood before her like a sentry there was nothing about Diana that he did not know.

Diana felt naked before him. He had stripped her mind of all that she knew. He had raped her heart of all that she felt, leaving her disheveled and confused as he stood before her soaking in her very essence.

"I am Gaetano Minotti," he said to her, bowing slightly in greeting. "I believe I have waited a long time for you."

"I don't even know you," Diana replied in the haughtiest tone of voice she could muster. "And I don't care to, either." Her words came out sounding more like a spoiled child who was trying to exercise an imaginary amount of power, knowing all too well that she would not get her way.

Minotti simply laughed.

"I'm so pleased to make your acquaintance." He signaled the bartender for another round of drinks.

Diana sat on her barstool like a first grader being made to sit in the corner for violating the teacher's rules. What was left of her emotions had gone into hiding and she felt very little. What had he done to her? "Why do you have to pick on me?" she asked.

"My dear, Diana," he said, smiling as he handed her, her drink, "I am not picking on you, as you so colorfully put it. I've chosen you. It's that simple."

"But I don't want to be chosen," she said in a whiny voice that was totally uncharacteristic of her. "I want to be left alone."

"To sulk?" he asked. Remnants of an old world Italian accent snuck into his voice. "What good does that do you?"

Diana sat looking at him, but said nothing. Instead, she took a few gulps of her beer and looked around the nightclub in a futile attempt to ignore the man. But he would not be ignored.

"Diana," he began. "I do not want to control you. I'd much rather have you come to me willingly. But I knew the emotional state you were in when you arrived, and I knew there was no other way to approach you." Minotti stopped for a moment and sipped his drink without taking his eyes off her. He seemed to be waiting for a response, though he did nothing to force the response he wanted from her. He'd been able to control her almost entirely except for what she might say or feel. It seemed to be the only lack of power he had.

Diana caught on to this handicap of Minotti's rather quickly. As a result, she chose to neither say nor do a thing. In fact, her fears had subsided somewhat with the onslaught of this realization. Whatever weakness he might have only gave her room, however small, to gain the advantage.

"If I were to release my hold on you, what would you do?" he asked, appearing to know the answer before she spoke it.

She looked him right in the eyes this time. "I'd leave."

"Now, see," he said, "that's the problem. I'm not through talking to you yet, and it would be rude of you to simply walk out of here, leaving me to look the fool."

Diana said nothing.

He took another drink from his glass before placing it on the bar. "In that case," he said, "I believe the best thing for me to do is to leave this place." He looked at her with his chest puffed out like a peacock. "Gaetano Minotti cannot be publicly rebuked without some form of retaliation." He reached toward her and cupped her chin in his hand. "And I would hate so much to have to retaliate against you, Diana." He let go of her chin and took a step back to look at her almost fondly. "We will meet again, Diana," he said. "That is for certain." He bowed slightly in parting, then turned around and started toward the door.

With each step he took away from her the hold he had on her movements lessened and she could feel the anger in her begin to rise rapidly to boiling "Why that. . . . ," she said. She was finally able to stand again and wanted to fight back. When Minotti was halfway to the door, Diana raised her nearly full glass of beer and cocked her arm back to throw it at him right across the room. She felt a hand on her wrist and turned to see the bartender who had reached across the bar and grabbed her just as she was about to launch the liquid missile at her target, unconcerned for those who might be hit in the process.

At the same moment her assault on Minotti was stopped, Diana saw two huge, men step out of the crowd directly behind him. They stood at attention and faced her squarely.

"I would've hit those two instead anyway," she said angrily to the bartender.

Minotti stopped walking, but he did not turn around to see what had caused his bodyguards to be alarmed. Diana heard him as he chuckled to himself when she hurled her anger at him through telepathic airwaves, but he continued his walk to the exit as if he had not noticed a thing.

The two men fell in on either side of Minotti while two others fell in behind them. Together the four men created a wall of muscle behind the evil vampire.

Mortals for protection, Minotti? she threw at him mockingly in her mind.

Why not? he answered her in kind before shutting her out completely.

When he was gone the bartender released his grip on her wrist and apologized to her. "I just couldn't let you do it," he said.

Diana lowered her arm and nodded. "I know. I understand," she said. "The rest of the place didn't need to get in the middle of a trail of beer flying over their heads, I'm sure."

"Well, it wasn't really because of that," the bartender said. "That man was Gaetano Minotti!"

Diana looked at the him and saw an expression on his face that told her Gaetano Minotti was someone very important. However, she had never heard of him before so she was not as impressed as the mortal behind the bar seemed to be. "So what?" she said.

"Gaetano Minotti is the head of the crime family here and in a few other cities as well," he told her. "I've even heard that he's the number one man, not only in the good ol' U.S. of A., but in a few other countries, too."

The scope of his words shocked and bemused her. It was such an awful thought. A vampire as the head of the largest crime organization in the world. The MAFIA! It couldn't be true. Who would have ever thought? He would be unstoppable. No one could ever kill him. He could never be held in jail nor would the death sentence be effective against him. He would always come back some how or other. Maybe as himself, maybe pretending to be one of his relatives.

But he would always come back.

Diana slowly sat down on her barstool. "Oh," she said. "I didn't know."

"I figured as much," the bartender said. He took two shot glasses out from a shelf on the wall and placed them on the bar in front of Diana.

"Have one with me?" he asked after he'd poured a shot for himself.

Diana shook off her shock and looked up at him, wondering just how much he really knew about Minotti. Did he know Minotti's a vampire? She quickly searched his mind, but found only fear of a mortal man and nothing more.

"What is it?" Diana asked. "Some types of alcohol bother me more than others."

"Captain Morgan," the bartender said.

"Ah, rum," she said. "The sweet elixir of the gods. And one of my favorite tension tamers. Ya, go ahead." Diana glanced back at the door, half expecting to see Minotti still standing there. "I believe I need it."

Outside, Gaetano Minotti stood at the entrance to the night club with two of his bodyguards and waited for his limousine to pull around. When the burgundy vehicle pulled to a halt at the curb he turned to the two men. "She's staying at the Days Inn by the river," he said. "Wait for her to return, but do not let her leave."

"Right, Mr. Minotti," they said in unison as he got into the back of the limousine. He rolled down the window and peered out menacingly at the two men who remained in place waiting for the limousine to pull away. "Don't fuck this up!" he said with a growl in his voice. "I want her!"

"We're on our way, Boss," one of the men said.. "She's as good as yours."

A smirk grew on Minotti's face as he looked in the man's eyes and leaned a little further toward the window.

"Take extra care with her, Vincent," he warned. "She's like no one else you've ever known." He hesitated as if he were waiting for the weight of his words to sink in. "Except for me."

With that, Minotti rolled the limousine window back up and signaled the driver to move on, leaving the two, huge men standing on the sidewalk in confusion over the meaning of his words.

"He's a strange one, Howie," Vincent said. "'She's like no else you've ever known,'" he mimicked Minotti as he pulled a set of car keys from his jacket pocket. "C'mon, let's go stake out the lady's hotel for the boss."

"Be careful, Vinnie," Howie warned. "He scares me worse than anyone else I've ever met. He's probably got us bugged or somethin'."

Vincent looked at him as if the man were nuts. "Be real, Howie," he said. "He's flesh and blood just like you and me."

"I don't know," Howie said as he turned to look behind him. "I'm not so sure."

CHAPTER 6

December 15, 1997

The sun had just begun to peek out above the horizon through the reflections of orange and pink that bounced off the sparkling snow. Diana stepped into the hotel lobby after her eventful night out in the American side of Niagara Falls. She flew back from The Factory rather than take a cab, but after a full night out in Western New York where the bars are open until four o'clock in the morning, she was ready to sleep simply from exhaustion.

She walked through the spacious lobby and noticed the same clerks on duty now were there the previous morning when she first arrived. She waved as she passed the front desk and headed for the elevator. Her mind was busy replaying all the things the bartender had told her about Gaetano Minotti, stories that made her skin crawl. And that was not easy to do to a vampire who had just about seen it all in the span of five hundred years. Still she replayed the conversation in her mind.

"Was he ever married?" she asked the bartender.

"I heard a story that said he was, but somewhere along the line his wife had pissed him off and he got rid of her."

"What do you mean?"

The bartender looked around as if to see who might be listening. "What I heard was that he gave her to his body guards. He gave them instructions to torture her to death. As it turned out though, they raped her . . ." At that point the bartender hesitated and looked around once more. He leaned closer to her over the bar. "Until she died," he finished.

Diana did not believe him and she laughed at the mere thought. "That's impossible," she said.

"Yeah?" He looked cocky and sure of himself. "Did you notice the size of his body guards?"

She had indeed, but they were only human, after all. Surely Minotti would've been married to one of his own kind. "I saw them. But I still can't see them capable of doing something like that."

"They sure did." He shrugged his shoulders. "So, the story goes, at least."

"Holy shit!" Diana shook her head in disbelief. "How did he get away with it?"

The bartender stopped what he was doing and looked at her. "He's **GAETANO MINOTTI**," he said. "He gets away with everything!"

Diana shook off the recent memory as she took the elevator up to the fifth floor. She turned the corner that led to her door, but she did not notice the two men who stood guard outside her room until she looked up at the last minute. She nearly bumped into them, then jumped back in surprise. "What do you think you're doing?" She looked at each of them in turn.

"Mr. Minotti sent us to keep an eye on you."

Diana looked at the man whose jacket had the name Howie embroidered on one side. She shifted her eyes back to him. "Isn't that nice?" she said, wondering if they might have been the ones who raped Minotti's wife to death. She pushed her way between them so she could unlock the door to her room. She felt both men watch her as she worked the key, then turned the door knob. Before she entered the room she turned back around. They stood with their arms folded, obviously determined to stay put until their master told them otherwise. "Just what is it you're supposed to be watching me for?" she asked.

Howie and Vinnie looked at each other, then back at her. "Don't know for sure. Just doing what we're told," Vinnie said, sticking his chest out as if to dare her to move him.

"Where is 'the Boss'?"

"Don't know."

"Sleeping, maybe?" Diana said in a playful manner.

They both shrugged, again.

"He must be," she said, playing dumb. "He's been out all night. What time can I expect him to come calling?"

The two men looked at each other once more, then turned toward her with menacing glares on both their faces, but neither said a word.

"Hmmm." Diana turned and went into her room. She closed the door behind her and immediately began to think of a way to get out of Niagara Falls before sunset when she expected Minotti to come looking for her. The very thought of his interest in her made her shudder. His nearness gave her the creeps. The more she thought about him, the more desperate she was to get as far away as she could, as fast as possible.

But where could she go? She walked across the room to the bed. Would she be risking her life if she tried to leave now with the sun coming up in such a short time?

She had never spent an entire day out in the sun, only a few hours after sunrise. Even that happened only once in a great while. When it did, it was because of Samuel.

"Oh Samuel," she said out loud. "Your lie doesn't look quite as bad compared to this vampire who's head of the M.A.F.I.A."

Diana finally decided she would be risking her life for sure if she stayed where she was. She figured she had nothing to lose by trying to get away while she had the opportunity. She stuffed everything she had brought with her the night before back into her duffle bag, zipped it up, and placed it over her shoulder. Then she slid open her window, and stepped out onto the ledge. She rose into the air as high as she could, and headed west in order to avoid the rising sun as long as possible. She was tired and had no idea how long her body would hold up until she found a safe place to hide.

How far would he really go to find her? Maybe he'd give up and move on once he found out she made a quick escape. After all, he didn't know her well enough to be that taken with her. It's not as if they had shared anything memorable. He'd simply move on to the next female that crossed his path like every other male and forget all about her by the time the next sunset rolled around.

Samuel had told her of a vampire who had flown from one time zone to the next, always staying in darkness until he got tired. He would let the sun come up around him while he slept. Then he would wake up and do it again. *It'll work,* she thought to herself. *It has to.*

"Maybe I'll fly all the way home to France," Diana said out loud to the wind. "The long way." She giggled, then shook her head when she realized that the beer and the shots had gotten to her a little more than she would've thought possible. And she realized she'd make even less distance because of it.

She flew for almost two hours without a clue as to where she would actually end up. The longer she was in the air the more tired she grew and it wasn't long before she knew she was fighting with herself to stay afloat. She had to come down to rest and feed before she would be able to go much further, but she hadn't a clue where she was. In the long run it wouldn't matter, though. She could land by choice or she could land by gravity's pull on her exhausted body. The latter had little appeal to her at all so she began a slow, careful descent while looking for landmarks that might give away her location.

The first thing Diana recognized was the Black Hills and she knew right away where she was. South Dakota. *What the hell am I doing in South Dakota?* she thought. She could hardly remember getting there.

At least it hadn't taken her long. She must have been much higher up than she had thought, but that was alright with her.

South Dakota had to be far enough away to prevent Minotti from finding her, assuming he would even try.

She landed near a huge barn in a wide, open pasture and wasted no time heading straight toward shelter and shuteye. Her presence in the barn made the cows uneasy. A few of them began to 'moo' seemingly aggravated, but they settled down when she was safely out of sight, way up in the loft behind a pile of old riding gear and horse blankets. The dust was piled so thick on top of it all that Diana was certain no one had been up there in years. She crawled all the way to the farthest corner of the loft under the pile of old saddle bags and other things she'd found. She curled up in a ball even as she was giving herself over to the manic call of exhaustion.

It seemed like mere minutes when she was awake, again. From her place under the pile of leather and wool, the sun felt the same as it had when she had crawled into her corner, but something was different in the sounds around her and the feelings that were in the air.

Diana listened carefully. She could hear cows being led back into the barn. She heard the voices of men talking about supper being on the table, and the herding being almost done for the day. She waited until the barn doors were shut and the voices were fading away before she looked out.

The sun was setting in the west which meant that it was probably eight o'clock in the evening back in Niagara Falls. Minotti would be wide awake by this time and probably very angry that Diana had managed to disappear.

She smiled to herself, and crawled out from her hiding place. She went down into the barn to look around. She was no more rested than when she'd arrived and she knew that malnourishment had a lot to do with.

The thought of feeding off the cattle made Diana's stomach churn, but the reality of her weakness told her she clearly had no choice. It was imperative that she rebuild every last ounce of her strength in order to continue the journey across the Pacific. The following night she would try to continue all the way through to Europe, if she could make it. She was determined to get home to France where she'd be safe.

Diana walked next to a big, brown cow and began to pet her gently while she attempted to crouch down next to the animal's front legs. The cow gave her very little trouble having eaten its own fill of grass and tiring itself out from a full day grazing in the winter sun. The cow flinched just a bit as Diana bit into its upper leg, but it settled right down when it felt its blood begin to rush out of its body. The cow's blood was not as sweet as that of a human, but Diana was desperate to maintain her strength rather than put her life in peril.

"How sad that you would have to stoop to this level just to stay away from me."

From the corner of her eyes, she saw the form of Gaetano Minotti walking toward her. She turned to look directly at him and noticed two bodyguards at the barn door. She had not seen these two men the night before, but she was reasonably sure they did not get to South Dakota with Minotti so quickly by walking.

Diana looked up embarrassed and frightened. The cow's blood was smeared across the lower part of her face as she started to rise, but she was too frightened to think clear enough to wipe it clean.

"Didn't think I'd find you?" Minotti reached over and wiped the blood from Diana's chin. "Didn't think I'd try, either." He took a step toward her, and wrapped his arm tightly around her waist. Diana froze, too frightened to say a word. "Foolish little vampire girl," he mocked her. "Did you really think my influence was limited to one little part of the world?" Minotti sneered as he walked behind her, then to her side where he softly whispered to her. "I have a vast army of followers all over the world," he bragged. "There's nowhere you could have gone without one of my mortal or immortal watchdogs seeing you."

The evil in his eyes burned clearer in the barn than it had in the smoke filled night club. Diana wished she had attempted to fly all the way home to France even if she had died trying. It would've been better than facing the monster who now held her locked in a vice grip of fear.

"I am not controlling you now, love," Minotti crooned menacingly into her ear, "yet you make no move to release yourself from my embrace. Can it be that you're already in love with me? Or have I frightened you to death?"

Minotti began to release the most awful laugh she had ever heard. It was a laugh that was born in the depths of hell where nothing was funny and nothing would ever be. It was a life threatening laugh, a laugh that found the destruction of everything good to be entertaining. It was the laugh of the devil himself.

Diana stared at him. She wished more than anything else that she hadn't been born as stubborn as she was. She wanted to be with Samuel. She wanted to be with Christian. She wanted to be at home in France. She wanted to be anywhere except in that barn in South Dakota, but it was too late. She had not traveled far enough to escape discovery and she had underestimated his desire for her. "How did you find me?" she finally asked.

Minotti did not answer her right away. He continued his awful laugh while Diana held her tongue until he was through.

"You know who I am," he said to her. "And you know what I am. There could be no secrets from you in the long run, anyway. It's better that you know me right from the start." He released her, and took a step away. "Unfortunately, now that you know, I can't possibly let you go."

Minotti looked at her, daring her to ask another silly question, but Diana was beginning to feel less intimidated and more angry at being treated in such a belittling manner. She could feel the fresh, strengthening blood beginning to blend with the little that had been left of her own, but she did her best to camouflage her replenishment from the enemy who stood only a few steps away. "Why did you even bother to come looking for me?" she asked. "The world is full of women. You could pick any one you wanted and they'd be yours. Why do you have to bother me?"

"Ah, Diana," Minotti purred condescendingly. "There are so

few women like you." He began to pace slowly away from her as he seemed to be thinking. But he stopped quickly after a few steps and turned to face her before he spoke. "I made the mistake of marrying a mortal woman once in my life," he said. "But you already know about that, don't you?"

Diana did not answer, but stood her ground next to the brown cow and returned Minotti's stare.

"No matter," he said. "The fact is that there are not so many of our kind as you might think. I need an eternal companion, Diana." He began to walk back to her. "I need a soul mate."

"Just because we're of the same kind does not make us soul mates," Diana said. "You're nothing like me. You are everything I abhor."

Minotti stood only inches away from her by the time she finished speaking, but his closeness did not threaten her the same way this time.

"You have a very strong will, Diana," he said. "It makes you appeal to me even more. You could almost be my equal."

"Don't insult me, Minotti," Diana nearly spat at him. "I would never consider you to be my equal. We're complete opposites, you and I, and I'm proud to be better than you."

The fire in Minotti's eyes blazed with Diana's last remark. She knew she had pushed him too far. But the truth was the truth and she wouldn't change a word of it if she were given the chance to say it again.

"You will regret that!" Minotti roared. He sounded more like a crazed lion than a man.

"I doubt it." Diana tried to sound menacing. The cow's blood had fully revitalized her tired body, and replenished most of her strength. But she was certain that even when compared to her best, Minotti was still the stronger. His time on this planet far outweighed her own. So did his experience and knowledge. She had already seen an example of his powers at the night club in Niagara Falls. That experience had been enough to show her what she was dealing with now. She decided to hold her temper before she ended up like his wife or worse.

"We'll see." Minotti grabbed her roughly by the arm. Before she knew what was happening, Diana felt herself being dragged upward through the air, out the barn window, and up into the ever darkening sky. He pulled her along at a speed faster than anything Diana had ever dreamed possible. Her body was aching and she had no choice but to use her own powers of flight in order to take the intense pressure off her arm, which was beginning to throb.

Even though Diana had started to fly under her own power, Minotti never loosened his grip on her arm. She was forced to fly alongside what was comparable to a roller coaster ride in an amusement park. Minotti's aeronautic technique mirrored his evil fury.

They flew for what seemed to be hours in this manner until Diana was finally able to make out a huge, billowing cloud of vapor in the distance and she knew Niagara Falls was only minutes away. Sunrise couldn't be that far off either. They had just cut three hours off the night's darkness and Diana hoped she'd be in a position to make another escape once Minotti fell asleep.

As the cloud from the great waterfall grew larger, Diana's apprehension grew as well. Minotti seemed to be in more of a hurry the closer they got to their destination. That made her worry more about what he had planned for her. But once they reached the falls, he began to slow his pace and lead them down the river.

"Today you will spend with me so that I'll know where to find you when I wake up," he said to her.

"I don't want to spend the day with you," Diana said.

Minotti looked at her as if he found her amusing. "I don't care," he said. "You will learn to love me no matter what. I'll see to that."

They descended from the clouds and landed in front of a huge, old colonial with grounds that seemed to have no end. Minotti stood and looked at the mansion for a few moments, still holding Diana's arm. Then he led her toward the house.

Once they passed through the double, front doors they entered a very large foyer with a staircase on each side that curved around to meet at the top as they ascended to the balcony above. Directly in front of her Diana could see into a great room with windows that lined the wall on the other side.

Minotti led her into that room and left her for a moment. "I won't be long." He slowly retreated down the hallway to the right.

Diana looked around to get a feel for the layout of the expansive house. She wanted to have her escape carefully planned when the opportunity arose. She had already decided that she would go right back to Massachusetts and try to find her brother as soon as she was free. She needed help to keep Minotti away from her and she didn't have a clue where else to find it. Her only concern was whether or not Christian would want to help her after the way she had disappeared on him. Five hundred years of missing him, thinking he was dead, and what did she do the minute she found him to be alive? She threw a temper tantrum and took off. Brilliant.

Diana walked toward the windows that made up the far wall of the great room. She was truly touched by the magnificent view of Niagara Falls and the gorge below that seemed to wrap around the cliff on which the house was built. She stared out the window wondering how someone so evil could possibly deserve to have something so beautiful as the view from those windows. She noticed there was only a three foot ledge behind the house before the straight drop hundreds of feet to the bottom of the gorge, yet there was a sliding glass door leading outside. That bothered her tremendously. She could only imagine the number of human beings who'd met their deaths at Minotti's hands through that door. She could feel the residue of terror from the souls who had passed through here on the way to their obvious doom. Suddenly self-conscious, Diana looked behind her, but no one was there. She walked to the opposite side of the room where Minotti had exited, but was only able to go so far. When she tried to step out of the room it felt as if she were walking into a wall. It was at that moment she knew that she was trapped. It explained why Minotti had left her so easily without a second thought.

She walked back toward the foyer. Again, she encountered an invisible barrier. She was trapped in a plush room with enough open area to play basketball, and a view that could occupy a person for days without getting bored. But trapped was still trapped and she didn't like it at all.

"It's only temporary." Minotti strolled back into the room. "I can't allow you to leave until you've had a chance to get to know me."

"Does it matter to you that I might not want to get to know you?" Diana asked. "I came here to get away from everyone. I want to be alone!"

"I know, I know," Minotti said, waving his hand at her as if her desires made no difference to him. "Mad at your boyfriend and brother, I know."

"I'm not mad at them," Diana said. "I was disappointed, that's all."

Minotti stood looking out the window at the falls and said nothing for a long time. Diana waited in the hopes that he was reconsidering his desire to keep her with him and that, maybe, he'd simply let her go.

"I have some things to take care of tonight," he finally said, turning around to face her. "If you're in need of more nourishment I can have one of the servants come in for you to feed on."

Diana gaped at him in astonishment.

"Or you can ring for one yourself." He brushed a finger gently on a tapestry bellpull that hung in the corner near the hallway. Then, he turned and walked across the room. He grabbed her roughly around the waist and nudged her affectionately. "I'll be home sooner than you think," he said. "In the meantime, make yourself comfortable." He turned and walked out into the foyer. Diana tried to follow him, but again she ran into the unseen barrier.

"I'm sorry," Minotti said, laughing. "I'll extend the force to give you a little more room to move around. But don't try to get past it. It's lethal to vampires."

In a soft cloud of wispy smoke, Gaetano Minotti was gone, leaving Diana captive in one of the most beautiful mansions she had ever seen. But it was the last place on earth she wanted to be.

CHAPTER 7

December 15, 1997

Father Larry stood at the window of his study, and watched the snow fall in buckets. It piled up faster than it could be removed by the city plows, but that was the least of his concerns. For the past twenty-four hours he had been deeply bothered by his conversation with Roni in which she had described for him the events that occurred at the Hard Rock Cafe. The argument between Diana and Samuel was a simple enough matter to understand. People hurt each other every day in one way or another. They got mad, they made up, then went on as if nothing had ever happened.

What really bothered Father Larry was the fact that there were actually two more vampires roaming the earth that he was now vividly aware of. Two more vampires living normal, human lives except for their immortality, except for their diet of human blood.

Father Larry rubbed his forehead when the image crossed his mind, as if the act of rubbing his head would wipe the horrific vision away. But it didn't. It was still there just like so many other images the priest carried with him. He thought he should be used to all the strange things his ministry had shown him, but he wasn't. The supernatural occurrences that so many priests find themselves faced with, normally involve the destruction or banishment of an evil presence. Most times it required a simple exorcism, not that any exorcism is actually a simple matter.

The situation surrounding Roni and Christian was different. There was a moral issue involved with the relationship between a mortal woman such as Roni, and Christian, a vampire. Father Larry shook his head. "It's absurd," he said aloud. Just thinking about it made him wonder if he should be committed to a loony bin. Realistically, though, if he looked at it from a racial standpoint, then he saw things more clearly. He considered the traditional vampire genre. The reality of Christian's situation hit him hard. Because Christian was immortal, Father Larry felt a rush to judge him as being something born of evil due to the infamous stereotype. It was no wonder Christian was so secretive about his identity. Father Larry knew such a viewpoint was unacceptable in these modern times, but that point of view made Christian more likeable than many of the mortals Father Larry had known in his lifetime. He was able to see him in more human terms. Christian had been born as all human beings are born. What happened to him later in his adult life was a matter of circumstances. We've all been victims of circumstance at some time. It's God's hand that guides us all. It must have been God's hand that led Christian to his transformation. But for what reason, only God could know.

Father Larry noticed how Christian was conscientious and polite, strong and caring. It made him wonder if the age old belief in vampires as blood-sucking killers was nothing more than an extreme extension of racism. He had to admit the likelihood of such a thing seemed possible. He had seen Christian's devotion to Veronica. It was so much deeper than most of the husbands he knew in his own parish had toward their wives. And when had he ever seen a woman rearrange her entire life to accommodate for the differences between herself and the man she married the way Roni has done for Christian? These days two people marry and continue on with their lives as if they were not married at all. They start out their marriages with stars in their eyes, but it never seems to last more than a year. They live as they did before they had taken their vows. More times than not, they refuse to adjust or make changes to anything they had grown accustomed to. The next thing you know, they're divorcing each other without even making the attempt to reach a compromise or make sacrifices for the sake of the love they had once shared. As a result, they push God right out of their lives and further out of this world. By rejecting the gift of love He gave them they fail to ever recognize that God's gift of love was actually the gift of Himself. This creates a compound loss experience that most of them aren't even fully aware of.

Father Larry shook his head sadly as he watched the snow continue to pile high on the sill outside. It covered the window pane until he could hardly see through it.

Then there's Christian, he thought. He wondered how much an immortal like Christian could accomplish as a result of his years and experiences. The endless possibilities were almost too much for Father Larry to digest.

He had seen so much that main stream America will not acknowledge as truth, but it all paled in comparison to the experiences of those like Christian Desmonde. The truths a vampire must know, for all those things mankind is still searching. It must be astonishing. He rubbed his cheek, then fiddled with the wooden cross that hung from the chain around his neck.

"The things Christian might be able to teach me," Father Larry said out loud. He thought back to his visit with Christian in the church. That night Christian had asked him if he wanted to be a vampire. The question echoed in Father Larry's head, bouncing back and forth between the opposing ends of his conscience. Would he? But the truth evaded him. Maybe he was afraid to face it. For a moment he felt sacrilegious in his thinking. Who wouldn't consider it? He shook his head in self denial. "But I couldn't," he whispered.

He turned from the window and went to sit down in his chair by the fireplace. The gout in his legs bothered him badly from the cold, damp weather, and he suddenly felt the need to rest. He was getting old. The thought used to bother him, but lately, he had come to accept it. Even to look forward to it as the next, natural step in his mission for the Lord. Had he been given the chance for immortality when he was younger he might have jumped at it. But now, at this point in his life he wondered how useful a tired, old priest could be with his limited knowledge compared to a gentle vampire whose incredible amount of time on earth amassed more knowledge than Father Larry could ever hope to have.

That must be part of God's master plan. He rubbed his belly and sighed. Maybe, but how could we ever hope to know for sure unless He came down from heaven and told us Himself? Father Larry chuckled. "He probably has and we weren't even listening," he said softly to himself.

"Listening to who?" he heard Cora ask.

Father Larry turned around with a grunt from the pain that had suddenly shot through his leg. His body was twisted so he could see Cora before he yelled at her for not knocking, but he stopped himself when Roni and Christian entered the room. He was surprised to see the very people he'd had on his mind all evening and he stood up without a single thought for his discomfort. He took a step toward them, but his legs gave out. Before he knew what happened, Father Larry was in Christian's arms, not on the floor as he had expected. He was stunned. It took Christian mere seconds to travel from the doorway to his side, a distance of fourteen feet. All he could do was stare, speechless, as the vampire carried him back to his chair.

"How?" Cora stammered, then shook her head in an attempt to forget what she had just seen. "Enjoy your visit." She meekly backed out of the room, closing the door behind her.

"Poor woman," Father Larry said. "She sees a lot, but says very little." He repositioned himself in the chair in order to be more comfortable, taking as much weight off his aching legs as he could. He looked toward his visitors almost as if it had just occurred to him that they were there. "Thank you, Christian," he said. "That fall might have broken my leg."

Christian nodded. "You're quite welcome."

Father Larry looked around the study and motioned with his arm for them to sit with him. "Pull up another chair," he said. "Don't be bashful about moving my furniture around."

Christian carried both of the chairs that were normally set in front of the desk over to the hearth, and placed them across from the priest.

Father Larry leaned back, placed his hands on his big, round belly, and chuckled to himself. "What a nice surprise it is to see you both," he said. "What brings you this way?"

Roni smiled. "A long overdue visit."

"Oh, don't worry about it," Father Larry said, waving his hand toward her. "I told you I understood."

Roni looked down as if she were embarrassed. "I know you did," she said. "But I still felt bad." She raised her head and looked at him. "It was pretty cowardly of me not to face up to things and make sure you were alright with . . . everything." She looked at Christian, then back at the priest.

"All's forgotten," Father Larry said. He turned to Christian. "Any word?" Christian shook his head. "We still haven't heard from either of them." The worry in his voice was evident.

Father Larry felt sorry for him. But thinking about it made him wonder if he was ready to acknowledge the other two vampires as easily as he'd been able to get to know Christian. "I'm sorry to hear that," he said. "Isn't there some way you can contact either of them? I mean, I've been reading about your special talents and what-have-you."

Roni and Christian looked at each other briefly. The looks on their faces showed an inexplicable frustration that Father Larry hoped was not a reflection of something he said wrong.

"You see, Father," Roni said. "There's really very little you can do to find a vampire if he or she doesn't want to be found."

Father Larry smiled. "There's very little any of us can do to find a mortal who doesn't want to be found as well," he said.

Roni nodded. "That's true."

"What has been done so far?" the priest asked.

Roni leaned forward, resting her elbows on her knees. "Well," she began, "Christian has searched telepathically as much as he could. But it seems that Samuel is too distraught to pick up his thoughts. And Diana, we're guessing, has chosen to close him out."

"Telepathy, huh?" Father Larry asked. He was very interested in the subject. "I had a little experience with that during my visit with Christian, if I recall correctly. It seems to me that it must be awfully difficult to shut a person out of your mind." The priest looked at Christian and waited for an answer.

"For a mortal, it would be," Christian said. "But for a vampire, it's easy."

"I see." Father Larry nodded his head. "So, does that mean you at least know where your friend, Samuel, is, but he won't answer you?"

"In a nutshell," Christian said, "yes."

"And where might that be?"

"Right now he's in Italy," Christian said. "He's been to Diana's and my childhood home in France, already." He sounded sad. "I tried to reach him again this morning just to tell him to come back, but once again, he didn't acknowledge my attempt to contact him."

"Why don't you go to him?" Father Larry asked.

"We thought of that," Roni said. "But Christian is torn between going to Samuel and being available in case Diana returns."

"Does she know where you live?"

"It doesn't matter," Christian said. "If she starts to look for me I'll be able to pick up her thoughts right away." Christian looked away for a moment and Roni placed a hand over his. "She's my sister," Christian said. "I didn't even know she was alive for five centuries. Then, once I found out I couldn't wait to see her. When I finally did, she disappeared after just a few minutes together."

Father Larry felt his sorrow. "How hard it must be after believing for so long that someone you love is dead only to find out the loved one is really alive."

"We're afraid she might think Christian didn't really want to see her during all those years and that's why she hasn't tried to contact him yet," Roni said. "She doesn't know Christian knew as little about her as she did about him. For all we know, Diana could be out there trying to deal with the belief that the brother she thought had been her best friend when they were younger really didn't care much about her after all."

Father Larry pressed a hand to his cheek and nodded his head. "Oh my," he said.

"Based on what Christian and Samuel have both told me about her," Roni said, "she might be hurt enough, and stubborn enough to stay away for a long time."

Father Larry could only imagine what Christian must feel, and he didn't know what to say. In his mind he was no longer trying to come to terms with the additional vampires as much as he was trying to find a way to comfort his two friends and give them hope. "I'm not sure what I can do to help," he said.

Christian stood up without a word and walked to the window. Roni and Father Larry watched him for a few seconds, then Roni turned to the priest. "Pray?"

"Of course!" he said. "The power of prayer is amazing."

Christian turned to face them both. "Is that possible?"

Father Larry looked at him, not sure what he meant. "Is what possible?"

"To pray for . . . ," Christian turned back toward the window without completing his thought.

"To pray for a vampire," Roni finished for him. "Is it possible to pray for a vampire?"

Father Larry pushed himself up on the chair and chuckled. "It's possible to pray for anyone or for anything," he said. "What did you think would happen?"

Roni tapped her nails on the arm of her chair. "I feel pretty stupid right about now."

"It's understandable, Child." Father Larry leaned over to pat her hand comfortingly. "I've been asking myself some very similar questions since our conversation on the phone the other night."

"Why is that?" Christian asked, turning from the window. He began to walk slowly back to the hearth where Roni and Father Larry sat.

Father Larry suddenly felt ashamed. "Well," he began, "I guess it's because I never gave it any thought as to how many of you . . ." He looked away. "How many of you there might actually be."

"Vampires!" Christian shouted. "That's what my sister and Samuel and I are."

"I know." Father Larry nervously waved his arms in the air to calm Christian down. "It's just taking me a little while to get used to the idea that you really exist. I'm not sure how I should feel about it."

"Why do you have to feel any way at all about it?" Christian stormed back to his empty chair and sat down.

Father Larry and Roni sat quietly watching him for some time. They glanced once at each other while Christian stared into the slowly dying fire.

"I'll pray for them," Father Larry said. "As well as for both of you."

Christian sank against the cushioned arm of the empty chair as if all the energy had been suddenly drained from his body. "I'm sorry," he said. "It's just . . ."

"No need," the priest interrupted him. "She's your sister, after all." Father Larry leaned forward and took one of Christian's hands in both of his own. He felt the cold skin, but did his best to ignore it. "And you're my friend," he said.

Christian looked toward the priest from under his slumped head, raised his eyebrows, then placed his free hand over the priest's. "And you are mine," he said, looking directly into Father Larry's eyes.

The two men stared at each other in silence. Father Larry could feel Christian's sincerity flow directly into his own soul. He felt closer to him than he'd thought possible. Finally, he broke the silent exchange by sitting back to relieve the pressure on his ailing legs.

"Thank you." Roni leaned over and gave Father Larry a big hug.

"For what?" he asked. "A few prayers? It's nothing."

"It means everything," Christian said.

Father Larry looked at Christian for a few moments. "Your faith is stronger than many of the mortals I've known," he said. "You know, it might do your sister and your friend more good if you did some praying yourself."

"I don't know about that," Christian said, shaking his head. "It's been a long time. I'd just as soon leave that job to the ones who are trained for it."

Father Larry laughed. "Memorizing prayers isn't all there is to praying," he said. "Sometimes it's what's in your heart the Lord hears the loudest."

Christian appeared thoughtful while he looked at the priest, then shook his head again. "Even so," he said. "I think I'll feel a whole lot better knowing you're on our side as well."

"I'm always on the side of what's good," Father Larry said. He tried to stand so he could see his guests to the door, but his legs shook ever so slightly.

"Sit, Father," Roni said. She placed her hand on his arm to stop him. "We know our way out."

Father Larry huffed and tried to catch his breath from the energy it took to ignore the painful gout, but he ended up falling backward into his chair. "Thanks," he said, waving to them both. "Let me know as soon as you hear something."

"We will," Christian said. He opened the door for Roni, then followed her through.

When they were gone Father Larry breathed a huge sigh. "Lord," he said, looking up at the ceiling. "I hope I'm doing the right think by asking you to watch out for those two. But I need to ask you to take care of the other two that are missing as well."

The priest grunted and groaned a bit while he changed positions and tried to prop his legs up on the chair that Roni had been sitting in. When he was comfortable, he started to think about Diana and Samuel, but soon felt himself drifting off to sleep.

CHAPTER 8

December 15, 1997

Jesse had been on the mainland visiting friends nearly all day. At any other time of the year he would know if something were wrong with one of them, but at Christmastime all the turmoils of humanity overlapped each other making it difficult to feel the needs of those around him.

It was close to ten o'clock at night and he was almost ready to head home, but there was one more thing he needed to do. He had to see Father Larry who had been on his mind since his visit. Father Larry had an open heart that accepted whatever was thrown in his path, but he had found it difficult to accept Christian's existence. That was understandable, but it caused Jesse much concern.

He was only half an hour from St. Joseph's church so he turned the car around and headed for Dedham. Ten minutes into the short distance he began to hear Father Larry's voice in his mind. The priest was praying for Diana and Samuel! But why? And how on earth did he know them?

Jesse was alarmed. Father Larry hadn't been able to deal with knowing about Christian's vampirism. What caused him to accept the existence of two other vampires enough to pray for them? He directed his thoughts to Christian in order to get a better idea of what happened. Christian was praying for Diana and Samuel, too! He'd never prayed before. What was going on? Even Roni's prayers had begun to enter his mind, weaving through those of Christian and Larry. He was able to pick up thoughts of the evening at the

Hard Rock Cafe from the visions that flashed through Christian's mind. He saw Diana disappear. Now no one seemed to know where she was. And Samuel was believed to be in Europe.

Jesse shook his head to clear it. Once more he tried to read the feelings of Christian, Roni, and Father Larry, but they were just as confusing. He caught snippets of Christian's remorse over not having followed Diana immediately, Father Larry's concern over whether or not he should be praying for vampires, and Roni's helplessness because she didn't have any special powers to offer to fix the situation.

Jesse was overwhelmed by the amount of turmoil Diana's disappearance had stirred up. He had to find her. It was the only way to help all of them. He had the most important piece of evidence, the point where the whole thing started. There would be a residue of thoughts and feelings left that he could follow. He had to go there to read what Diana did after she left.

He was too far from the Hard Rock Cafe to drive, especially with the traffic in the city, so he parked the car a friend had loaned him and set out the quickest way possible. In an angel's instant, he was there tracing the trail of anger, hatred, and betrayal Diana had left behind. He experienced the turmoil of the moment when she and Christian recognized each other, and Samuel knew he could no longer put off telling her the truth. *Ah Samuel,* Jesse sighed. *I tried to tell you.* Now that he had picked up the feelings of Diana's soul he knew he'd be able to follow her path more easily.

Diana's negative emotions created a path to the east, where the Harbor Hotel sat on the edge of the Boston Harbor. Then the trail of emotions headed back the way they had come, passed the Hard Rock Cafe, and continued west. West?

Jesse transported himself to the place where Diana's emotions were the strongest. Niagara Falls. He hadn't been there in years. He stood by the rushing waters that gracefully plummeted one hundred fifty-eight feet down. The vision sent shivers of pride in the Creator's work running through every nerve in Jesse's body. There was nothing quite like it anywhere else in the world.

Jesse took a moment to track Diana's emotions through the area. Watching the magnificent waterfall in all her midnight glory, hearing the roar of her current, was like a meditation that cleared his mind. He knew Diana was on the American side of Niagara Falls, but something was different. There was an element of her that changed from the time she left Massachusetts until now. She was still angry, but the feelings of betrayal had turned to feelings of fear. It gave Jesse great concern and a sense of urgency in finding her. What had frightened her? Or who?

Jesse studied the air for clues. She had left something of a double image. Two distinct paths of emotion. The feelings Jesse picked up were similar in nature, but the traces of her presence had occurred at different times. He knew Diana had left suddenly, then quickly returned. Judging by the strength of the feelings she left that still throbbed with life her return was quite recent.

Jesse's instinctive sense of foreboding told him that putting this matter to rest was not going to be quite as easy as simply finding her. There was something else at work here, but first things first.

He followed the strongest trail of fear Diana had left behind, but there was something unsettling about it. It wasn't just her fear. It was the other presence that caused the fear. It was more like thoughts, nasty, evil, and sinister. Only someone with no conscience, morals, or remorse could think such dark thoughts. Only one without a soul. Suddenly, he knew exactly what he was dealing with. He recognized him by the hellish personality, that awful mind, the frightening power. They'd met a long time ago, and battled over a very similar situation. Neither had won any true victory over the other.

Jesse felt his senses peak. "I always knew you'd surface eventually my old adversary," he said to the air. "It was just a matter of time."

Jesse knew what Gaetano Minotti could do to a person, even a vampire. There was no way he could leave Diana in his presence. Minotti was strong, powerful, and very dangerous.

He followed the path of Diana's fear to the mansion on the cliff's edge overlooking the Niagara Gorge. When he stood outside the huge house he sensed the danger that lay ahead, but he knew it did not come directly from Minotti. He was not at home.

Jesse walked in the front doors. He felt the force field that surrounded the perimeters of the outside walls just inside the mansion. Straight ahead of him, through the foyer and the entrance to the Great Room, Jesse saw Diana. He watched briefly as she reached for the bell pull that hung near the entrance to a hallway. He tested the force field to determine what trick Minotti was using this time. It was one that had a life of its own because it was part of its Creator. If another vampire tried to pass through this barrier, the wall would squeeze until the vampire's energy was drained, trapping it inside until its heart finally blew apart. But Minotti had underestimated who Diana's friends were.

Jesse wasted no time. He quickly began to fuse his molecular structure with that of the invisible wall until he was able to move each molecule past the barrier and deeper into the foyer. It was a slow process. Jesse's essence could be reduced to a form of energy that even a vampire could not reproduce. Jesse could become as ethereal as the air when he had to. And right now, he had no other choice. It was uncomfortable. He could feel the evil that was the wall mesh with his own energy as he forced his physical form to pass through. His presence fought a battle of wills in order to be successful, but with the celestial powers that were always at his disposal, Jesse was successful.

Once he was on the other side of the dangerous force field, he proceeded with caution into the Great Room where Diana stood looking out the wall of windows.

"Diana," he said.

She turned toward him slowly while he stood still and waited. He knew she was famished. He could feel the drain on her system and the weakness in her body. She'd never make it to Christian's in that state. In an instant he knew everything she'd been through in the past forty eight hours.

"Who are you?" she asked. Her voice was calm, but uncertain.

"I'm a friend of your brother, Christian, and of your companion, Samuel," Jesse said. He started to walk toward her while she appeared to study him as he approached.

"Are you here to help me get out?" she asked, a tremor in her voice.

"Yes, I am," he said. "I'm going to take you to your brother's house. You'll be safe there, but only for a very short time, I'm afraid." Jesse paused before he said too much. Honesty was good, but too much at a time like this might be more than a frightened soul like Diana could handle. "But we'll take care of one thing at a time."

Diana leaned against the windowed wall and slumped over, visibly relieved that help had arrived. She began to sink to the floor very slowly as the last crumbs of energy left her, and the feeling of defeat invaded her soul. "I can't travel," she said. It was almost a whisper. "He drained me. He did it on purpose. Now I see why he flew the way he did. He drained me so I wouldn't have the strength to escape." Diana raised her head and looked pleadingly at Jesse. "It worked."

One of the housekeepers, an older woman, appeared at the entrance to the hallway. "You rang?" She stood in place like a robot awaiting her instructions.

Diana looked at her. "I did," she said, then turned toward Jesse.

"I've taken care of it," Jesse said softly to the housekeeper. "It was nothing important."

The woman looked at him for a few moments, then huffed. "Very well," she said. She turned and left the room, mumbling to herself about being taken away from her work for no reason.

"She was going to be my sustenance," Diana said, looking out the window.

Jesse crouched down in front of her. "I know," he said. "It's likely Minotti has tainted her blood with that of his own to make her more subservient. Had you ingested that woman's blood, it might have poisoned you so that you would become like her. You may have given in to him without question afterward."

He straightened his arm out in front of him, then raised his wrist to Diana's lips. "Drink mine," he said. "It's pure."

Without a moment's hesitation, Diana grabbed his forearm. Jesse could see the saliva run onto her lips. She leaned over his arm and bit into his wrist almost gently. Then she began to drink his blood in a state of rapture. Jesse held steady without flinching. He knew the structure of his blood was such that Diana would feel herself being replenished and restored quicker than she ever had before. The energy it would give her would get her home to her brother.

After only one minute, he began to caress her hair as a signal to stop. "We're running short on time."

She released his arm and looked at him as if she were embarrassed. "I know," she said. She brushed her hand across her mouth to wipe away the traces of blood that remained. "Thank you."

Jesse smiled. "We have to go."

Diana cast him a frightened look. "How do I get past the wall he's left around the place?"

Jesse stood up. "I can make an opening in the force field that you'll be able to move through. Now come with me." Jesse reached over, took Diana's hand, and pulled her to her feet. Together they approached the barrier that divided the foyer in two. When they stood before it Jesse pushed one hand into the wall. Diana watched while it disappeared as if his arm had been cut off. Jesse then forced his other hand in alongside it. When both arms were completely lost in the wall, he moved them away from each, creating a visible hole in the mysterious barrier that could be seen as if it hung in midair.

"The wall is that thick?" Diana asked.

"Vaporize and go through," Jesse said to her. "Be careful to go straight through the center. Do **NOT** touch the barrier itself. Then wait for me on the other side."

Diana hesitated.

"Do it," Jesse said gently. "Trust me."

Diana smiled. "I do trust you," she said. "It's just that he told me the wall is lethal to my kind."

"It is," Jesse said. "But you have to go through it if you want to get out of this place safely."

"What about you?"

"I'm strong enough," he said. "Don't worry about me. Just get yourself through."

Diana took a deep breath. "Alright," she said. She began to turn herself to a thick mist, each part of her moving through the wall as it was changed.

Jesse watched until she was completely through the barrier before he pulled his arms out, letting the hole he had created close instantly.

Diana waited on the other side of the barrier. She began to panic when it seemed as if Jesse was taking too long to appear. What if Minotti were to come home right now? She wondered if she should just run out the door and head for Massachusetts, but she trusted that Jesse had a good reason for telling her to wait for him. What if he couldn't get to this side himself? What if she had drained his strength by drinking some of his blood and now he can't make it? Diana waited. *No, I won't panic,* she told herself.

For ten minutes she watched the front door for Minotti and the barrier for Jesse. Finally, she saw Jesse's form pass slowly through the invisible wall. It appeared as a ghostly apparition at first, then solidified as more and more of him came through.

"Are you alright?" she asked. She was relieved that she was no longer alone. "What took so long?"

"It's a long story," Jesse said. "Suffice it to say that one molecule at a time is a lot of molecules to maneuver."

"Oh," Diana said.

Jesse put his hands on her shoulders and stared at her, commanding her attention. "Listen to me," he said. "And do exactly as I tell you."

Diana nodded her head in consent.

"You're going to fly back to Massachusetts as fast as you can," he said. "Your brother and Roni live in a town called Norfolk to the southwest of Boston."

"Is that her name?" Diana asked, realizing she didn't know anything about her brother's life.

"Yes," Jesse said. "She's a good person and she'll do everything she can to help. When you get close to Norfolk send out a signal to Christian and he'll guide you right to him."

"How do you know this?" Diana asked.

"He's been waiting for your signal, Di." Jesse used the familiar nickname Christian had given her when they were younger. It sent a melancholy pain through her heart. "Listen."

She looked at him.

"He didn't know about you, either."

"I didn't really think so," she said.

Jesse smiled. "Now get going."

"What about you?" she asked. "What are you doing?"

"I'm going to prepare for Minotti's appearance in eastern Massachusetts," he said. "He'll be looking for you simply because you escaped again and he'll be very angry. He'll find you the same way I did, but he'll know that I had a hand in it. Trust me, Diana, he's going to be in a very bad mood."

Diana let out a nervous giggle as she stood on her tiptoes to give Jesse a thank-you kiss on the cheek.

"Tell Christian everything that has happened and tell him I'll contact him," Jesse said. "Now get going." He opened the front door.

Diana walked through, then turned around. "Is she one of us?" Diana asked Jesse. "Roni, I mean. Is she one of us?"

Jesse's face softened. "If you mean 'does she have a good heart' like you, then the answer is yes, she is one of you."

"You know what I mean," Diana said. "Is she a vampire?"

"Does it matter?"

Diana looked at him strangely, then thought a moment. Before she could answer him, however, he closed the door that separated them leaving her on the outside of captivity, and himself inside Minotti's mansion.

Diana waited a moment, but instinctively knew Jesse would not be coming out.

"Thank you," she whispered, then rose in the air and headed straight for safety with her brother. "Thank you so very much."

She flew quickly over the city of Niagara Falls and headed east, but she heard Jesse's voice in the wind from miles away.

"You're welcome, Diana."

PART III

"Tell the truth. It only hurts for a little while."

—Christopher A. Bishop

CHAPTER 1

December 16, 1997

"Relax, Honey," Roni said. "I know one day soon Diana and Samuel will be enjoying a moonlight stroll through the woods with us."

Christian put his arm around her shoulder and kissed her hair. The soft, midnight breeze rustled through the trees and sent clumps of snow plummeting to the ground. "I hope you're right," he said. "I'm worried about both of them. I'm considering going after Samuel to get him back here so I can look for Diana in the States. I don't think she's anywhere in Europe."

Roni looked at him, her head slanted. "Why not just start looking for your sister where you think she is? With Samuel in Europe and you here, don't you think your chances of finding her would be better?"

Christian was silent. He listened to the deer that were headed toward them. Tonight they were safe. Christian had no appetite. "I thought about that, too," he said. "And you're right. But I wouldn't feel comfortable leaving you alone for any length of time. There's no telling how long I might have to be gone."

"I'm a big girl," Roni said. "I can take care of myself."

"I know you can," he said.

"Then what's the problem?"

Christian hesitated before answering her. "How can I leave you alone not knowing how long I'll be gone? What if something were to happen and you needed me?"

"I could always have Chelle come stay with me for a few days, maybe a week, if necessary," Roni said. "I'm sure she'd love it."

Christian smiled. "I'm sure she would, too."

"Chelle's a good friend," Roni said.

"And a bit of a character."

"She'd be great company for me."

"That's true," he agreed.

"She'd even be a great help."

"Maybe."

"Then what's the problem?"

"You still come first," Christian said. "It's my heart and my conscience that won't allow me to leave you alone indefinitely. As I said, there's no telling how long the search for Diana might take. I won't do it." He sighed. "Not yet, anyway. Besides, Diana or Samuel could show up here and I'd be off looking for them somewhere else."

They walked on through the wintery night. The only sound was the crunch of snow beneath their feet and the occasional breeze that forced the bare branches to touch. "I hope Father Larry didn't think we were too insane to ask for his prayers earlier," Christian said.

Roni kissed his hand that rested on her shoulder. "I'm sure he didn't," she said. "He seemed a little bit uncomfortable at first, that's for sure. But I think he's more upset with the reality of vampires than he is with the idea of praying for one."

"How's that?" Christian asked. "You'd think he'd be used to our existence by now." They started to make the familiar turn that led through the woods and back to their house.

"Well," Roni said, "Praying is easy. Father Larry has always said that anyone can ask God for whatever they want. That doesn't mean God will give it to them, but there's no harm in trying."

Christian couldn't help but laugh. "Good point," he said. "The worst He can do is say, 'No.'"

"Exactly! But to look a vampire straight in the eyes and have to admit he's real because he's right there in front of you," Roni said, "now that's another thing."

"And now the poor man had to find out there's more of us

than just me." He let out a quick chuckle.

"I almost feel sorry for him," Roni said. "But then I think about how Chelle was when I first told her the whole story about you. She might as well have heard me say what time it was, for all the reaction I got out of her."

They were almost out of the woods when they came upon a huge tree stump that Christian had cut into the shape of a chair so Roni could sit comfortably when she was out here without having to carry a chair from the house. They stopped there to rest.

"How did you and Diana become so close?" Roni asked. "You never really told me. With the large family you had, why her?"

Christian thought about it a minute. He looked deep passed the trees and watched a small, brown rabbit hop across their path. He could see Diana as a young girl in his mind, standing in the vineyard, sweated and dirty from showing the workers the proper way to harvest grapes. She'd look at him and motion in such a way that he knew she had something to tell him. "I really don't know," he said. "I think it was a matter of conscience with us."

"What do you mean?"

"Well, we had more scruples than most people we knew," he said. "I could never lie to her and she could never lie to me. We kept each other's secrets to ourselves."

"But that's supposed to be normal," Roni said.

"Not where we came from," Christian said. "In those days, and in that part of France." A strange feeling came over him without warning and he lost his train of thought. He tried to identify it, but it quickly passed, leaving him confused.

"What is it?" Roni asked.

Christian shook his head. "Nothing," he said. "Just a feeling."

Roni smiled. "A good one I hope."

"I'm not sure." He looked around and tried to reach out with his mind to find what had distracted him, but it was gone. "Anyway," he continued. "We weren't always wealthy, you know. Everyone has to start somewhere and we started at the bottom just like most people did in those days."

"These days, too," Roni said.

Christian hardly heard her. That feeling crept through him again, making him feel disjointed, then disappeared as fast as it came. He shook off the distraction for the second time and went on with his story. "I was changed into what I am now when my family was just starting to make a name for themselves," he said. "I never experienced the great wealth they had amassed over the years. I never knew the respect for the reputation that came with it. I took my earnings as soon as I made the decision to leave the area for good. It was small by today's standards, but it was quite a fortune in the thirteenth century."

"You must have felt like a king," Roni said.

Christian looked around thoughtfully. He rested his hand on the back of the tree stump chair and leaned on it. He sighed. "Not really," he said. "I was angry and confused. I was disappointed in everything around me." He looked at Roni and laid his arm across the back of her shoulders. He bent down to kiss the top of her head. "I wasn't happy again until I met you."

Roni turned her head toward him. She kissed him lightly on the lips, then leaned against him. "It's beautiful here," she said.

Christian looked at her. "Yes, it is."

Diana was still one hundred miles from Norfolk, moving as fast as she could. Since she'd left Western New York State she'd been wondering about the man who had saved her and why he had stayed behind. She wondered how long it would be before Minotti came looking for her.

But most of all, she wondered what she was going to tell Christian.

She was still angry with Samuel for not telling her about her brother, but she was sure there had to be a reasonable explanation for the whole thing. It was amazing how a bad situation helps a person see things more clearly. If only she'd kept her cool and stayed put instead of running off in a tantrum she never would have ended up in this predicament.

She remembered Jesse's instructions, and decided to try to contact her brother before she had gone too far in the wrong direction. She said his name in her mind and did her best to push the thought as far through the atmosphere as she could.

Christian, help me. It's Diana.

She felt no response. Maybe she wasn't close enough yet.

She thought of the times Samuel had been able to get her attention from another country. Maybe it was easy for him because she and Samuel were so much in tune to each other every second of the day and night. But she and Christian hardly knew each other anymore. Diana used to know what he was going to say before he said it. Christian used to know what she was going to do before she did it. Could that kind of kinship change with time? She hoped not and she couldn't think about it now. She was growing weaker by the minute. She forced her tired body to keep moving and tried again to contact him. *Christian.*

Nothing.

Please, Christian, she thought. *You've got to hear me.*

Again, nothing.

Diana didn't have a clue where Norfolk was, but she tried to move faster. Her body was aching and her limbs were beginning to go numb. Even her mind wasn't too clear. She was afraid she wouldn't have the strength to hold out at this speed for long, but she had to try. Maybe she was too weak to get her message to Christian and that was why she'd received no response. She decided to wait until she got a little farther before trying again.

Christian felt Roni shiver from the cold. "Time to go in," he said. He softly kissed her temple, then took her hand and gently pulled her to her feet.

"I guess." She sounded disappointed.

"You're freezing," Christian said. "Why would you want to stay outside when you're so cold?"

"I know," Roni said, looking around. "But it's so quiet and safe out here."

He looked out among the dark trees, and the starlight reflected in the snow. "I know what you mean," he said. "I feel the same way sometimes." He thought of all the creatures that passed through their wooded backyard in the middle of the night. She had no idea how often he'd had to dine out there. Christian stood up. "Let's go inside." He started to walk back toward the house with Roni's hand in his.

When they approached the deck that spanned the back of the house, Christian felt it again. He stopped dead in his tracks. This time the feeling was strong.

"What's the matter?" Roni asked, sounding alarmed.

He put a finger to his lips. "Sssshhh." He was thankful for her silence. This time he knew he was close.

Diana had travelled only five more minutes, but she knew she had to be closer to her brother than she was before. Maybe even close enough to get a message to him this time. She tried again.

Christian.

No response. Her efforts had grown feeble. She was so weak it was hard to think. She did her best not to panic and tried again.

Christian.

Nothing.

She felt alone and afraid. What would she do if Christian didn't answer her? *I'll have to find Samuel,* she thought. But, would he come to her after the temper tantrum she threw? She began to cry and with her tears came a feeling of intense desperation.

"Christian!" she yelled, frantic. She could see the ocean ahead, but still hadn't heard from him. She began to sob uncontrollably. "Christian, help me."

Roni stood by Christian waiting for some idea of what was going on. A huge smile widened across his face, and his eyes shifted happily toward her.

"It's Diana," he said. "She's looking for me. She's not far from here."

"Well, go get her," Roni said. "What are you waiting for? Get her and bring her back here. I'll have the spare room ready."

Christian hugged her and held her close to him for a few seconds. Then he gave her a passionate, joyful kiss.

"I love you so much," Roni said to him. "Be careful."

"I'm always careful," he said. He stepped away from her and turned to go. "I'll be back very soon. I love you."

Roni smiled at him, then turned and entered the house through the back door before he disappeared into thin air, as she knew he would.

CHAPTER 2

December 16, 1997

Father Larry had fallen asleep in his chair by the fireplace after Roni and Christian left. He didn't know what time it was when he awoke, but he guessed it was the middle of the night, judging by the stars that twinkled outside the study window. His right arm was asleep. He waited a few minutes for the pins and needles sensation to subside, then pushed himself up out of his chair. The tray Cora had brought to him earlier was still on the little table by his chair. He picked it up, carried it into the kitchen, and placed it on the counter next to the sink. He put the unused tea bags back in the box they came from, and returned the cookies to the jar where Cora kept them. Then he turned out the lights and left the kitchen.

Father Larry headed for the church to take a quick look around before going to bed. He'd had a dream that upset him terribly, but he couldn't remember most of it. The fact that he couldn't remember it bothered him more than the dream itself. His father used to tell him, dreams that could leave such unsettled feelings were dreams that needed to be dealt with. It made sense when he was a boy, but thinking about it now he realized his father had never told him how to deal with a dream he'd forgotten.

Father Larry shivered as he entered the church. The candles in St. Joseph's still burned with life, lending a warm eeriness to the inside. Cora always complained that it was dangerous to leave them lit all night with no one to attend them, but Father Larry believed they were lit with prayers, and should burn until they could burn no longer in order to keep the prayers of the faithful alive.

The priest strolled casually down one side of the church and stopped at each station of the cross for a few seconds. He genuflected when he passed the altar, then did the same up the other side. With each short, careful step the aging priest allowed himself to look back through his own life at the sacrifices and joys of his vocation as well as the heartaches and triumphs of his life. There was so much to think about, so much he had seen and done in his seventy-eight years, so much he knew, and so much he still had not learned. He had no regrets. Wonders maybe, but no regrets.

He finished his walk around the church, then sat down in the front pew and tried to clear his mind before heading off to bed. He could hear the snap and crackle of the candle wicks as they burned down into the pools of wax that ultimately form at their bases. He could hear the creaks of the church and he could almost feel it shift ever so slightly as it, too, settled for the night. He breathed in the musty odor of old wood, age, and incense and tried to settle his soul enough to be able to sleep peacefully for the remainder of the dark hours.

Father Larry looked up at the crucifix that hung on the altar and sighed. "Ah, Lord," he said. "Why did you send the vampires to me to deal with? Isn't there a younger priest out there somewhere who has the energy for this?"

But of course, the figure on the crucifix did not answer his questions.

Father Larry sat for fifteen minutes before deciding it was time to finish his sleep. He rose stiffly from the front pew, genuflected once again before crossing in front of the altar, and started to head out the side door that lead back to the rectory.

When he approached the side entrance he heard a soft noise. It sounded like the door at the back entrance to the church when it was opened, but that couldn't be. Those doors were locked after the final mass each evening. Who had left them open? He resolved to find out first thing in the morning.

He looked around the pillar that blocked his view of the main entrance and was surprised to see a figure walking very slowly up the center aisle. He took a few cautious steps back into the church.

The stranger dragged himself up the aisle as if he had just finished a ten mile race and was ready to collapse. He stooped over as he walked, leaning on every second pew for support. Father Larry hoped this shadowy figure just wanted a place to sit and rest.

He continued to watch as the man came closer until something about the visitor's long hair and overcoat looked familiar. "Jesse?" he asked.

The man stopped walking for a moment and looked up at Father Larry. "Hello, Larry," Jesse said. His voice sounded raspy, his face was a mask of exhaustion.

Father Larry went to him and put his arm out toward his friend for support. "What are you doing here at this hour?" Father Larry took Jesse's arm and started to lead him to a pew so he could sit down.

"I came to see you," Jesse said, bowing his head at the altar.

"How on earth did you know I'd be awake at this hour of the night?" the priest asked.

Jesse cleared his throat. "I had a feeling." He sat down in the front pew and motioned for Father Larry to sit next to him, but the priest shook his head. "I'm too stiff to get up, again."

The two men looked at each other solemnly for a few moments, but it was more than enough time for the old priest to realize that Jesse might need to have him close. He decided to sit next to his friend after all, sore bones or not. "What's the matter, Jesse?" he asked. "What on earth has happened to you? You look awful."

Jesse looked toward the altar. "I need to ask a favor of you."

Father Larry spread his arms open in front of himself. "Ask," he said. "Ask whatever you want from me."

Jesse looked at the ground, then up again. "I would like you to keep the church open for the next few nights."

Father Larry stammered at first because leaving the church open at night was not safe. Too many valuable items had been stolen from this place in recent years. Since the thefts began they had changed their policy on keeping the church doors unlocked after hours.

But then Father Larry realized that Jesse had seldom asked him for anything. Yet he'd always been there for him. Jesse had been a part of every important chapter in Father Larry's life, especially the sadder ones, and he had bailed the priest out on more than one occasion. How could he not do this for such a devoted friend? Were a few artifacts worth more than a friendship of this depth? Even the sacrimentals had to be left to God's protection this time. When it came right down to it, Father Larry knew it was more important to him to have his friends and loved ones close by than it did to have the 'things' around him that did nothing more than look good and collect dust. "If that's what you need from me," Father Larry said. "Then that's what I'll do."

Jesse let out a satisfied sigh and stood up. He put his hand on the priests shoulder, and looked down at him. "Thank you, Larry," he said.

Father Larry met Jesse's severe look with one of his own, but said nothing. Instead, he went through the ordeal of standing up again, then took a deep breath once he was on his feet. "You look like hell," he said, smiling. "Why don't you let me put you up for the night. Get some rest. Cora can fix a nice breakfast for us in the morning." He looked at the clock in back of the church. "Or lunch," he said. He couldn't believe it was four in the morning. He didn't think he could have been in the church for more than an hour, but he was.

"I'd like that," Jesse said.

The priest studied Jesse's face. He saw the lines across his friends forehead, and the sagging skin beneath his eyes and on his cheeks. "Would you like to tell me about it?" he asked him.

Jesse shook his head. "Not at the moment."

Father Larry looked at him and sighed. "Fair enough." He led

Jesse out the side door and down the hall to the rectory. Once they were inside, they continued on through the foyer and straight down a short hallway that appeared immediately to their right. There were four doors off this branch of the hall. Father Larry led Jesse to the last door on their left. "These are our guest rooms that we use for visiting clergy members," he said. "I sleep down here now because it's too much for me to walk the stairs anymore." He chuckled gaily as if his gout and arthritis really didn't bother him. "There's a bathroom right around this corner." He pointed to a turn in the hall they had not entered, yet.

Jesse nodded his head. "Again, thank you," he said.

"My pleasure." Father Larry patted Jesse on the back. "It's nice to be able to do something to help you for a change."

Jesse smiled. "It's nice to have a friend like you to come to in a time of need," he said. "I rarely find myself in this position."

"We all find ourselves in a state of need at sometime or other," Father Larry said. "You taught me that. Now get some rest. Sleep as long as you like. I'll just jot down a quick note for Cora to see in the morning so she knows you're here." Father Larry reached through the doorway of the room and turned on the light for his friend. The room was small and very plainly decorated with only a single bed made up with pure white linens and a yellow blanket. There was a night stand with a small lamp on it and a single dresser against the adjacent wall. A crucifix hung above the bed.

"I feel right at home," Jesse said.

"Good, then. I'll see you in the morning." Father Larry turned and headed back down the hall.

"Larry," Jesse called after him.

Father Larry stopped walking and turned around.

"The doors were locked tonight," Jesse said.

Father Larry thought for a moment, then realized what Jesse meant. This wasn't the first time his friend had done some remarkable act. He smiled. "I figured as much when I saw it was you." He turned around and headed back down the hall.

Before he turned the corner to enter the kitchen he looked

back at Jesse to say 'goodnight', but his friend had already entered the guest room and closed the door. "Ah, well," he sighed. "Goodnight, anyway, my friend." He grabbed the pen and a sheet of paper from the little note shelves Cora had hung on the wall. He wrote a note for her, then turned out the light and went to bed.

A little more than five hundred miles away Gaetano Minotti had just returned to his castle on the cliff overlooking the Niagara Gorge. He knew Jesse Nestarius had been there before he even opened the front door. Jesse had been sure to leave the residue of his aura everywhere until the air was saturated with it and there could be no mistake who it was that had come to call.

And if Jesse had been there, that meant Diana was gone.

"Aaaaarrrrrgggghhhhhhhhhhh!!!"

Minotti let out an insanely furious roar that sent the house servants running for the safety of their rooms and his mortal body guards trembling from fear. Life in the mansion literally froze while he threw off his coat and began to pace angrily throughout the entire house. Down the halls, up the halls, through the Great Room, into the foyer, back down the hall, into the kitchen, up the stairs, down the stairs and on and on he continued for well over an hour, mumbling to himself the whole time. His thoughts were governed by anger and hatred. His mind ran the gamut of everything from wanting to tear the limbs off both Jesse and Diana to letting them go and forgetting about them.

But he could not forget about them. And he certainly would not let them get away with it.

Finally, when the first rays of the sun were just reaching the horizon, turning the midnight sky to a mere navy blue, Minotti was silent and still. He could hear everyone in the house let out the breaths they had been holding inside ever since his arrival home.

He had worked out a plan.

It was a smart plan that would require some patience, which

Gaetano Minotti had never known the need for. Until now. He was going to let Jesse get away with his little invasion, but only for two or three days until Jesse's guard was down and he thought he was safe. "Then I will show up when he least expects it," Minotti said to himself, smiling. "And get rid of that busybody, do-gooder, Nestarius once and for all."

He walked to the wall of windows that scanned the back of the house, and thought about Diana. "As for her," he mumbled in a sinister tone, "where on the planet could she possibly go that I would not be able to find her?" He moved back a few steps to get away from the rising sun. He chuckled to himself. "Absolutely nowhere." He had plans to make her captivity much harder the next time because of this little game in which she had joined Nestarius. "She will belong to me and she will do so willingly or see her beloved Samuel and her precious brother die, for good this time!" he said aloud.

Gaetano was well satisfied with his simple, but seemingly effective plan. He was ready to retire for the day and sleep quite peacefully now that he had cleared the confusion and anger out of his head. He was on a clear path, and he would not waver until he had what he wanted.

And what he wanted was Diana Desmonde.

CHAPTER 3

December 16, 1997

Christian found Diana on the beach in Falmouth, crying uncontrollably. He sat on the snow speckled ground beside her and took her in his arms. Her face lay buried against his shoulder as he stroked her hair. He gently rocked her back and forth while her sobs continued. What could have happened to upset her like this? She was a vampire. That made her virtually infallible. "It's OK, baby," Christian said. "C'mon." He lifted her to her feet. "I'm taking you home with me until I can contact Sam. You can tell me all about it later."

Diana stood up slowly using Christian for support until she could stand on her own. Her body felt weak, and her legs seemed about to give out beneath her. "I can't fly," she said between sniffles. "I just can't." Her arms flopped to her sides, her head leaned forward like a rag doll.

Christian felt the air around her move as she began to fall. He caught her in his arms and lifted her up off her feet. It took great effort, but he was able to raise them both up into the air. "Hang on," he said. "We're going home." He held her close and headed for Norfolk where he intended to let her rest until she was strong enough to tell him what happened. "I swear," he vowed, "whoever did this to you will die." But even as he spoke those words, he felt an uneasiness rise in the pit of his soul. Anyone who could do this to a vampire must surely be a person to be wary of.

Christian was furious, but it gave him additional strength to get them home safe. He flew them to the woods behind the house where he and Roni lived. He knew the first and most important thing Diana needed even before rest was nourishment. Besides, Roni's safety might be in jeopardy if Diana were to see her while she was still in this depleted condition.

He set his sister down to rest against a fallen log that lay under the tall, blue spruce whose bottom branches Christian had cut off the previous Spring. She awoke when her body touched the soft, wet ground. "Wait here," he told her. "I'll be right back."

In a panic, Diana grabbed for her brother's arms and looked as if she would begin to cry all over, again. "Don't leave me alone." Terror beamed intense from her eyes.

Christian took her hands in his. He could see the thirsty veins in her eyes. "Relax, Di," he said. "This is where Roni and I live. This is our back yard. It's alright." He leaned forward and kissed her on the forehead.

Diana looked around, fear in her eyes. She looked at him then settled down in the bed of wet pine needles and leaned against the base of the tree. "Please hurry." She curled her knees up to her chest as a soft wintery breeze floated by.

"I will." Christian inched away slowly so Diana would have a chance to adjust to his absence, but once he was out of her sight he hurried to search for a deer, a fox or, if he was lucky, a lone hiker out for a midnight walk. But he knew he was hard pressed to find human nourishment at this time of the night.

It only took a few minutes before Christian saw a couple of deer far in back of his yard where the neighbor's property met their own. The deer were eating from a frozen berry bush, fully engrossed in their meal. He used his thoughts to make them walk toward Diana. They both raised their heads and began to move almost immediately with him following close behind. He floated in the air so as not to scare them with the sound of his footsteps.

When they approached the tree where Diana rested, Christian withdrew his thoughts and allowed them to stop and resume their digging for anything edible they could find beneath the fallen leaves and snow.

While the deer ate Christian sent his thoughts to them, again. This time the messages were soothing ones designed to put the deer at ease and, eventually, to sleep. It took just short of ten minutes to convince them it was safe to lay down and rest. When they were asleep, Christian carried them to Diana one at a time. "Here," he said to her, "drink as much as you need, but don't kill either one."

Diana wrinkled her nose at him and frowned. "I've never killed a living thing in all my years!" she said.

Christian laughed at her remark, thrilled to see the familiar show of his sister's Taurean attitude. "Glad to hear it," he said. "Now, go ahead." He turned his back to make her feel more comfortable. "I'll sit right here 'til you're done."

"Thank you," she said.

Christian sat on a large rock and looked through the woods all around him, conscious of the animals scampering back and forth. He could hear Diana behind him sucking and slurping the life sustaining blood from the sleeping deer. He tried to imagine the kind of demon that could send a vampire running for life the way something obviously had done to his sister. What would it take to destroy such a being? The more he thought about it the more he realized it was not something he should attempt alone. He'd never run into anything like this before. He'd need Samuel's help. Maybe Jesse's, too.

But Samuel hadn't acknowledged any of Christian's attempts to contact him, and he hadn't tried to let them know how he was. Christian was merely guessing at his friend's frantic state of mind, assuming all he could think of was finding Diana by himself. He would never consider that Diana might actually come back on her own. Christian knew he'd have to try to get a hold of him again as soon as Diana was taken care of. He was going to need him back in the States as soon as possible.

"How are you doing?" he asked without turning around.

Diana didn't answer right away, but Christian could feel her behind him. She was done feeding. He could hear her petting one of the deer, and cooing softly to it. He heard the other one walking around nearby. Christian turned and looked at her. He couldn't help but smile. "What are you doing?" he asked.

"Relaxing," Diana said. She moved only her eyes to look at him from under drowsy eyelids. "Thank you."

Christian stared at his sister in awe. "I never thought of that," he said.

"Never thought of what?"

"Making friends with the wild animals I feed on," he said. "I always let them wake up on their own some time after I'm gone."

Diana said nothing. She continued to pet the deer still laying on her lap while the other stood close by nudging her every so often for a little attention of his own.

"Amazing," Christian said. "I wish Roni was here to see this."

"It's not really amazing," Diana said. "They're both vulnerable already because they're weak. They know they could never run from either one of us so what other choice do they have?"

Christian shook his head and smiled. "As I said, I never thought of that."

Diana raised her eyebrows at him. "You're a man," she teased. "That's why."

"That's not fair," Christian said.

She laughed, then turned her attention back to the deer. "They're just babies, you know."

"Oh yeah," Christian said. "They look like babies, alright. Two ninety pound babies."

"But they are." She continued to stroke and coddle each deer.

"Feel better?" he asked.

"Much."

They sat in the woods for awhile, Christian on his rock and Diana on the fallen log under the spruce tree. Christian was at a loss for words. He wanted to know what had happened to her, what had brought her to him in such a desperate state, but she was so much calmer now that he was afraid to dredge up the bad experience.

"I met a friend of yours earlier this evening," Diana said out of the blue.

"And who might that be?" Christian asked.

"I don't know his name." The standing deer nuzzled her cheek, "but he got me out of an awful situation. I was trapped."

"How do you know he was a friend of mine?"

"Because he told me he was your friend, and Sam's too," she said.

Christian's curiosity was peaked. "What did he look like?"

"He had long, straight, sort of dirty blonde hair," Diana said. "Maybe it was brown. I'm not sure, now. I don't really remember what he was wearing, either, but I do remember that he had some strange kind of powers."

"Where is he now?" Christian asked. He was certain it was Jesse. But where did Jesse fit into this? How did he know where Diana was?

Diana looked straight at her brother for the first time since the subject of her disappearance had begun. "He stayed behind," she said. Diana had slowed down petting the deer, and both of them were suddenly on the alert.

"Stayed behind where?"

"Niagara Falls." She was beginning to tense up and Christian knew it. Even the demeanor of the deer was not quite as relaxed as it had been until now. Diana turned to each one and gently steered them away. "Go on," she said to them. "Go now." Quickly, they obeyed, stopping only once to look back at her for a few short seconds before darting into the woods. "I don't know why he stayed behind," Diana said after the deer were gone. "He just told me to head east toward Norfolk and to try to reach you when I got close. He said I'd only be safe with you for a short time, but to tell you what happened."

"Well, then," Christian said, "what did happen?"

Diana hesitated.

"You know you're going to have to tell me sooner or later."

"I know," she said. "It's just . . . hard."

"But you're back with me now and we haven't seen each other in ages. Literally." He smiled. "We've got a lot of catching up to do."

But Diana quickly changed the subject. "Where's Sam?"

Christian was startled. He expected her to tell him about her experience in Niagara Falls, not to inquire about Sam.

"Where is he?" she asked again.

"In Europe looking for you."

She frowned. "Oh, he's such an ass!"

Christian wasn't sure what she meant by that. "Why, because he's in Europe?" he asked. "Or because he's looking for you at all?"

"Both." She waved a hand at him. "Oh, neither."

"Or are you referring to the centuries old secret he kept from you?"

"You mean the secret that caused this whole mess?" she asked.

"Mmmhmmm."

"Yeah, that too." She looked away. "What's wrong with him, Christian?" Christian shook his head and shrugged. "Samuel is just Samuel."

Diana pushed her bangs out of her eyes, then started to draw in the snow with her finger. "You know, as strong as he can be for others in tough situations," Diana said, "he's equally as mindless where his own concerns are at stake."

Christian let out a short laugh. "Well, no one's perfect."

Diana shook her head in half-hearted agreement.

"So, tell me everything, Sis," Christian said. "What happened in Niagara Falls? It must be important if Jesse wants me to know."

"Is that his name?"

"I'm sure that's who went to your rescue," Christian said, looking around. He noticed the stars seemed to be fading already. "Now, out with it. When you're done telling me the whole story I'm going to take you to the house to get some rest. The sun will be coming up soon."

Diana started from the beginning. She stopped every so often at a particularly difficult point before going on. She left nothing out including her own reactions, her own thoughts, and her own fears.

"My God," Christian said, growing angrier with each word. "To think there's someone so powerfully evil sharing the planet with us and yet, we never knew of him until now."

"Yeah," Diana said. "That's what makes him so dangerous."

"There doesn't seem to be any way to stop someone like this Gaetano Minotti," he said. "And it's very clear that he will be coming for you Diana, simply because you managed to get away a second time. It's the principle of the thing with someone like him. A man like Gaetano Minotti refuses to acknowledge his own failures. He'd rather destroy the source of his failure than have to admit it happened at all."

"Does that mean he might also come looking for your friend, Jesse?"

"Unless Jesse stayed behind in order to face him head on," Christian said. "And that's my second biggest concern at the moment."

"Don't you think Jesse can handle him?"

"I don't know," Christian said. "I don't know who this man is."

"Then why do you think Jesse stayed behind?"

Christian shook his head. "I'm not sure."

"Is he one of us?"

"Not exactly."

"Then what?"

"It's another story." Christian stood up. "I'll tell you later. For now let's head up to the house. You have to get some rest."

The early morning sky had already begun to brighten leaving a pink glitter on the patches of snow that lay on the ground between the trees. Christian put his hand out to help Diana up, then he led her through the woods and headed for the house.

"Is your girlfriend home?" Diana asked.

Christian smiled. "Her name is Veronica," he said, "but everyone calls her Roni. And yes, she's home."

"How long have you known her?"

"A few years."

"She's not one of us, is she?"

Christian flinched inwardly at the question. His sister had hit a sore spot with him. "Does it matter?"

"Not to me it doesn't," Diana said. "Does it matter to you?"

"It matters to me only because I can't imagine life without her," Christian said. "Time is short for mortals, but for us it drags when we're alone." They crossed the snow that covered the back lawn and walked up the stairs to the deck. "I don't want to be without her." He opened the back door for her and stopped. "Not ever." He stared at her knowing she would understand how intense his feelings for Roni were.

When they entered the house Roni was awake and waiting for them. "What happened?" She took a step toward Christian then stopped dead in her tracks. "It's uncanny," she said. "You could almost be twins."

Diana smiled. "So we were told."

"That was many years ago when we were kids," Christian said. He walked toward Roni. "I'll tell you what happened later." He put his arm around her and kissed her. "Right now, I'd like to introduce you to my sister before she disappears again." Christian put his free hand on Diana's shoulder and loosened his grip on Roni so the two women could face each other. "Roni, this is Diana," he said. "Diana, Roni."

Roni extended her right hand toward the vampire that almost qualified as her sister-in-law. "I'm so glad to meet you, finally," she said, smiling. "I turned the bed down in one of the spare rooms for you. I hope you'll stay with us for awhile."

Diana looked at Christian, an obvious question in her eyes. He knew her concerns because of what Jesse had told her, but he didn't give her any indication as to what she should say because he didn't know what to expect.

"I'll stay as long as I can," Diana said, shaking Roni's hand.

"Well, you're more than welcome here."

"I think you should get some rest," Christian said to his sister. "You've been through quite a bit in the last few days and I don't think you should be caught off guard . . ."

Diana held up her hand to silence him, and laughed. "I agree," she said. "No more advice. Please!" She turned to Roni. "Where do you want me?"

"Right down that hall," Roni said. "C'mon, I'll show you." She led Diana to her room, and turned on the light.

Diana looked in at the brass bed and the deep, green carpet. "Cozy," she said.

Roni smiled. "Get some rest."

"I will," Diana said. "And thanks."

"No problem." Roni left Diana to herself and went back to Christian who waited for her as he looked out the back window. "The tension in you is incredible, Christian."

"I'm sorry," he said.

Roni tapped her nails on the nearby table. "Don't be sorry," she said. "I just can't tell if you're angry or worried."

Christian was silent.

She walked up next to him and slipped her arm through his. "We should talk?" she asked.

Christian did not look at her, but stared out the window as if it were important for him to do so. "We should talk." he said.

CHAPTER 4

December 17, 1997

Normally, Father Larry awoke every morning at seven o'clock. After his bout of insomnia and Jesse's unexpected visit last night, he wasn't surprised to see that it was almost ten o'clock when he first opened his eyes.

He showered, shaved, and prepared to greet his guest in the kitchen. He made it a point to remember to ask for more details regarding Jesse's unusual request to keep the church doors unlocked for the next three or four nights. Father Larry had agreed to do as he was asked, but he was still uncomfortable and concerned about it.

He donned his vestments, then knelt beside his bed facing the crucifix that hung on the wall above the headboard, and started his morning prayers. He prayed for Roni and Christian as he was becoming accustomed to do in the mornings. Every day he tried not to think of Christian as a vampire, so he would not be unfairly prejudicial toward someone as good-hearted as he was.

Father Larry finished his prayers, then headed for the kitchen. He was surprised to see that Cora was the only one present when he entered the room. The table was set beautifully as it was most every morning, with an array of munchables, as Cora liked to call them, and all the trimmings needed for pancakes, but there was only one place setting. He poured himself a cup of coffee and sat down at the table. "Where's our guest?" he asked.

"He left early," Cora said. "Are you hungry?"

Father Larry patted his belly. "I'm starved."

Cora spooned batter on the griddle. "What else is new?" she mumbled.

Father Larry heard her, but only smiled. "Oh, Cora," he said. "If you ever left St. Joseph's I'd really miss your cheery smile at the breakfast table." He began to spoon marmalade on a slice of toast that had already been buttered.

Cora flashed him a quick scowl, but Father Larry saw her cheeks push out in a huge smile as she turned back toward the stove to check on the griddle. "Did Jesse have anything to eat?" he asked.

Cora turned around and leaned against the cupboard next to the stove. "A cup of tea and a slice of toast and he was gone."

"What time was that?"

"Around seven this mornin'," Cora replied, reaching up into the cupboard to get a plate.

"Did he seem rested to you?" Father Larry nibbled on his toast while he waited for an answer.

Cora placed the full plate of pancakes on the table in front of him, then stood with one hand on her hip. "I don't make it a habit to study every person who stays here at St. Joseph's."

The priest gave her a look that told her he knew her much better than that.

"Alright," she said with a shrug. "He looked just fine. A little sleepy around the eyes, but otherwise, just fine. He said to thank you again."

"How does he do it?" the priest wondered aloud.

"I haven't a clue," Cora said. "But whatever it is he ought to bottle it and share it with us all." She walked across the kitchen to the door opposite the hall. "I have other things to attend to," she said. "So you can eat in peace."

Father Larry smiled. "You always know what's best," he teased.

Jesse had arrived home on the island around ten o'clock that morning and had immediately begun to plan his meditation exercises that would empower and renew his inner strength. He regretted having to leave the rectory without seeing his friend to thank him once more in person, but Larry needed his sleep and Jesse decided it was best to leave him alone to rest as long as possible. Larry was getting on in age. He was ailing more than he probably should be, but he rarely discussed his pains. It was because of Father Larry's condition that Jesse hated to ask for the priest's help in keeping the church open, but there wasn't much choice in the matter. The odds for defeating a power such as Gaetano Minotti were much better if all the parties involved in the struggle were bound by heart strings. Jesse already knew Christian and Samuel would be involved. That was inevitable. It was also the reason he wanted Diana to tell Christian what he was up against. He couldn't allow Christian to be taken by surprise the way he had been. But even with all these precautions, Jesse knew their best chance to end up victorious against Minotti would be in a sanctified place. St. Joseph's was perfect.

Jesse made a cup of the herbal tea he blended himself during the previous summer, from the herb garden on the side of the house. Then he went outside to sit on the porch in the crisp December air and use the ocean before him as the backdrop for his meditation. The tea would help him relax quickly and enable him to open his mind and release the negative stirrings that the reappearance of Gaetano Minotti had brought to his soul. He'd exhausted himself when he saturated Minotti's living space with his essence. But he had to make sure Minotti came after him first. After what he'd seen him do in England in 1253 to the village witch, Serella Stone, he couldn't afford to let Diana suffer the same way. So much of what had been happening with Diana was the same as had happened to Serella. She was a wonderful, powerful woman who Minotti had decided he wanted to own. She was a good person who was in tune to the feminine side of God, the true Mother Earth, and everything that existed. Just like Diana, Serella had escaped from Minotti. But she'd done it on her own. Jesse didn't know of Gaetano Minotti in those days, but he had met him shortly after Serella escaped. But nothing could have prepared Jesse for someone such as Minotti. As a result, Minotti managed to capture Serella and torture her unmercifully in retribution for what he considered her disrespect of him.

Fortunately, Diana had not been put in that position, yet. Jesse had to make sure she wasn't. This time he knew better how to handle the evil. When Serella's life was at stake, he did not. He fought Minotti then, but he didn't know that brawling was not the way to beat someone like Minotti. While Jesse fought a physical battle, Minotti attacked their souls, both his and Serella's. By the time Jesse realized what had happened, all he could do was run home and take Serella's soul with him. By then it was too late to save her life on earth.

He still felt great remorse over that memory. Now he was faced with the same problem. He had lost Serella's battle for life here, but he had saved her soul. Minotti had lost Serella's presence, but saved his life on earth. Jesse could not let that happen again. This time he needed all the strength and power he could muster, both to save Diana, and to destroy Gaetano Minotti so this would be the last time. He only hoped he could handle it better now. He didn't like the odds, but there was no choice. He would do whatever was necessary.

It will be over soon, he told himself. He sipped his tea and waited for the tranquil effects of it to overtake his body. *It will be over soon.*

Samuel had been everywhere from the Musee de Cluny in Paris, in which many of Diana's favorite tapestries hung, to the glorious hills of Austria. He searched relentlessly, all the while calling upon every memory that might lead him to where Diana might be hiding. But she was nowhere to be found.

His heart was broken, he was physically drained. Even his mind was exhausted from the thoughts that were in contradiction with each other. One minute he believed he deserved to go through these horrors as punishment for his secrecy with her. But the next minute he felt it was unfair since he had been a trustworthy friend to Christian by keeping his promise all this time. Who else had ever lived who could say they were trusted to keep such a secret? But that wasn't the point and he knew it. He had used his promise to Christian as an excuse to justify his selfishness and for that he deserved to suffer. It was time to face himself so he could face Diana. The truth was that he had deliberately kept her from her brother so he would be most important to her. He knew how close they were in their mortal years. But he was insecure enough to believe he would mean nothing to her if they were reunited. Samuel wasn't willing to play second fiddle to anyone in Diana's heart, not even to her own brother. He had wanted Diana solely and completely to himself every second of every day for five hundred years. Mortals don't see that kind of luxury in their short life spans, yet Samuel had managed to enjoy such an arrangement for six times that long. He would have gone for longer if circumstances had not reunited him with Christian. *I'm only in this position because I got caught,* he admitted to himself. Fate had decided on her own to set the record straight.

He looked down and saw a familiar site. Wedged into the side of a huge mountain slope was part of an old, wooden sea vessel. He knew it was Mount Ararat. That meant he was over Turkey. He started his descent when he heard Diana's voice. She wasn't calling to him, though, she was calling to Christian. No matter. He knew where she was. Telepathy knew no barrier, and now that Diana had opened hers, she could be found. He started immediately to travel the time zones heading west, and keeping the sun behind him. He knew he needed to rest, but there was no time now. He hadn't stopped to eat in the three nights since he'd left Massachusetts, and he hadn't slept much either. In fact his body had gone numb hours ago, but he had to keep pushing himself forward. Although Diana had sent her cries for help to her brother, Samuel knew he had to be there for her, too. *She'll forgive me,* he thought. *She just has to forgive me.* At least he hoped she would. *Oh Diana,* Samuel cried out as another piece of his heart snapped in two.

Faster. He must travel faster. He must get there as quickly as possible. He looked down to see where he was, but nothing looked familiar to him. Samuel thought about landing to get his bearings, but he doubted whether he'd have the strength left to raise himself into the air one more time. In the long run he realized he couldn't afford to take the chance. He had to keep going in order to cover as much ground as he could, as fast as he could. If he dropped out of the sky it would be worth the pain as long as he was able to make it back to Diana's side before that happened.

Just then a huge mass of clouds surrounded him. He was momentarily caught off balance and took some time to steady himself. He thought if he just flew straight he'd still be heading west and would end up out of the cloud mass, eventually. But it didn't happen that way. Samuel had flown into a huge storm with lightening flashing close enough to nearly blind him, and thunder booming in the very cloud masses he occupied. He had to get out of there before he was burned alive or made deaf. He flew higher until he was over the storm clouds. It was beautiful, surrounding him with mountains of white fluff so huge they cast shadows on the clouds at their bases. *I must be hallucinating,* Samuel thought. He couldn't feel his muscles and his thoughts were all over the place. Maybe he'd been hit by lightening. Maybe burned.

But he heard it again. Diana's voice calling to Christian a second time. It sounded frantic. Samuel's heart flipped, his senses perked, and he knew he was alive. There was only one problem. Land had been out of sight for too long and he was sure he'd gone off course. He had to get below the storm in order to see where he was going. He let his body drop down, out of the silent beauty, through the atmospheric war zone. Further he descended until he could see where he was. The rain continued to fall, but it didn't matter. He could see water in the distance and he knew it was the Atlantic Ocean. He didn't have much farther to go. He was on the last leg of his long and terrible journey to find Diana, but he knew he was going to make it. A few hours at the most and he'd be there.

He was going to take the bull by the horns for a change and do the right thing. He must face Diana and Christian together and admit his mistake. Whatever happened after that, well, he deserved it.

CHAPTER 5

December 17, 1997

Christian finished his shower, then went to the kitchen to see Roni who was sitting at the table drinking a cup of rose hip tea. The aroma was sweet, almost soothing. "Good evening," he said. He walked around the table and gave her a kiss. "Didn't sleep well?"

Roni shrugged. "Not really. I was probably overtired or something."

Christian sat down across from her and studied her face. He reached his arm over to her and took her hand in his. "Or something, would be my guess," he said softly.

Roni looked up at him. He could see the effect of her restless night written all over her face. Her eyes were red and puffy with little bags hanging beneath them. The skin on her cheeks was drawn and slightly swollen and there were worry lines across her forehead. Christian regretted ever telling her about Minotti, but he had no choice.

"I'll be alright," Roni said. "I'm just . . ."

"Scared?" Christian asked, finishing her sentence.

"Yeah," she said. "Scared is a good word."

She smiled, but Christian knew she was just trying to be strong. The very idea that someone like Minotti could exist even frightened him.

"I've been up for a couple hours already just trying to think what we could do about this whole thing, how we could protect Diana, but I don't have a clue," Roni said. She ran her hand through her hair, then started to tap her nails on the table. "That Minotti thing would step on a mortal like a mortal steps on a bug. I'm useless in this situation and I know it."

"Don't say that." Christian squeezed her hand. "You're never useless. You give me the strength I need and that may be all you have to do to help Diana."

Christian didn't have any idea how to handle Diana's evil suitor, but he knew Roni would have to be strong if he was going to be able to do anything at all. "You know what they say about every successful man," he said, smiling.

"Yeah, I know." Roni smiled back at him, then changed the subject. "How long do you think Diana will sleep?"

"As long as she needs to, I suppose," Christian said. "She never was one to get up at the crack of dawn."

"Well, I've got an appointment with the Brandisons in an hour," Roni said. "So I'm going to get ready to go. I shouldn't be too long tonight, but it'll give you a chance to really sit and talk with your sister."

Roni drank her last sip of tea, then pushed herself up from the table. She walked to the kitchen very slow. Christian wondered if she was simply tired or if Minotti's existence bothered her more than she wanted to let on. He stood up. "Let me help you."

Roni shook her head and smiled. "I'm fine. My leg fell asleep while I was sitting there, that's all."

Christian hesitated a second, then pushed his chair in place under the table. He stood behind it watching Roni as she walked back toward him and right into his arms.

"I love you so much, Veronica," he said, holding her tight.

"I love you so much too, Christian." She nestled up under his chin, and sighed deeply.

He rubbed her back and kissed the top of her head. "Why don't you cancel with the Brandison's and stay home?"

Roni leaned back and looked at him. Then she started to laugh. "Because they finally agreed on everything and I think I'd better finalize this agreement before they start fighting, again," she joked.

"Alright." Christian released her. "Just be careful and come home, soon."

"I will," Roni said. She kissed him on the cheek, then went to get ready.

When she was out of the room Christian began to wonder about Minotti and Jesse. He wondered what happened after Diana left Niagara Falls. Nothing Jesse did ever really surprised him. But Christian had never known about anyone like Gaetano Minotti and he didn't think Minotti sounded like someone who could be dealt with single handedly. He hoped Jesse would give them a clue as to what he was up to, but he also realized the chances of that happening were slim.

Jesse does everything in silence, he thought. *He does everything alone.*

Maybe he would learn more tonight when he had a chance to talk to Diana. If nothing else could be accomplished, though, he needed to set the record straight with her about the secret he had asked Samuel to keep for him. Christian never thought for one minute that Diana would ever have to know about his vampirism. In a way, this whole situation was his own fault as much as it was Samuel's. But she definitely had to know the truth before she made any rash decisions regarding her future with him.

Roni emerged from the bedroom fully dressed. "I'm going," she said.

"That was mighty quick."

"Yeah, well, I just washed up, brushed my teeth, combed my hair, and threw some make-up on," Roni said. "I'm good to go."

Christian stared at her and was amazed at how good she looked even when she 'threw herself together' like this. "You look terrific."

"Put your eyes back in your head," she said, smiling. "I'll be back in no time." She kissed him warmly on the lips, then grabbed her car keys and jacket, and was out the door.

Christian waited until Roni had pulled out of the driveway and was headed up the street. Then he looked in on his sister. She was still sleeping, but Christian could tell it wasn't a sound sleep. She'd be awake soon and realize where she was.

Christian closed the door to her room and went into the living room to watch television while he waited for his sister. He kept wondering about Jesse. Christian was certain one person alone would be helpless against Minotti. Angel or no angel, Jesse was still stuck with human flesh and blood just like Christian. But who else could they possibly turn to for help?

Samuel! he thought. *Where the hell is he?* All of a sudden Christian realized he hadn't tried to contact Samuel in a day and a half. Regardless of whether or not Diana stayed angry with him, Christian knew he was going to need Samuel's help when Minotti showed up. He had to get Samuel back here now that Diana was safe.

He walked over to the big window off the kitchen and looked out into the backyard. The snow had started to melt during the day while they slept and now there was very little left to reflect the starlight. But Christian could still make out the movement of wild animals among the distant trees.

Samuel, Christian thought. *Samuel, it's me Christian. Answer me, dammit!*

Samuel did not answer, but Christian knew where he was none-the-less. He was on his way. He must have found out Diana was here. Now he had to tell Diana about the secret and fast. He had to do it before Samuel arrived.

"Anything happening out there?" Diana asked.

Christian turned to see her come out of the hallway and into the kitchen. "Yes and no," he said, trying to remain calm.

"What's the matter, Chrissy?" Diana asked.

"I hate that." he said, frowning. "Don't call me that."

"I'm sorry." She smiled. "I was just kidding. You know, sort of for old times sake. I didn't know you'd get so pissed."

Christian realized he had let his growing panic escape and he couldn't allow it to happen again. From this point on he had to keep a clear head and stay under control until Minotti was dealt with and this whole mess with Diana and Samuel was resolved once and for all. "I'm sorry, Di," he said. "It wasn't the nickname." Christian walked back into the living room and turned to his sister. "We have to talk and we don't have a lot of time."

"Is Minotti on his way, already?" she asked.

"No," Christian said. He sat down on the sofa and ran his hands through his hair. "Sit down, Di."

Diana walked into the room behind her brother and sat down on the opposite end of the sofa, but Christian quickly stood up and began to pace.

"About the secret," he began.

"Forget the secret," Diana snapped. "I don't want to talk about it anymore."

Christian wheeled around to face her. "Well, I do!" he said. "That stupid secret got so far out of control it was sickening and it was my fault to begin with."

"What do you mean, it was your fault?"

Christian changed to a softer tone of voice. "Just what I said. I tried to tell you at the bar the other night, but you weren't listening."

Diana appeared dumbfounded as she stared at her brother. "When I was running from Minotti I finally realized there had to be a reasonable explanation why Samuel kept your existence from me for so long," she said. "But I never expected it would end up to be your fault." She had a suspicious look in her eyes. "How is it your fault, Christian?"

"Look," he said. "Do you remember the night when I was, supposedly, carried off by wild animals?"

"Sure I do," Diana said. "It was the night of the Spring Festival in our dinky, little town."

"Well, the truth is that I got into a brawl at the tavern," he said. "I was beaten up pretty badly, nearly dead."

The expression on her face changed to anger as she listened to him. "What the hell were you fighting over that was important enough to get yourself killed?"

Christian looked up at his sister very slowly before he answered her question. "You," he said. "I was fighting over you."

Diana froze. "Why?"

"Because, little sister." Christian walked over to her and pinched her chin. "I didn't like the way the men were hanging out the windows and doors yelling at you and your friend, Barbara."

Diana's mouth fell wide open as she watched Christian pace by her like a preacher who delivers his sermons by acting them out on stage. "Do you mean to tell me you almost got yourself killed because a bunch of drunks were yelling obscenities at me?" she asked. "Are you nuts?"

"Correction," Christian said. He held up his index finger and leaned against the archway into the kitchen. "I did get myself killed because a bunch of drunks were yelling obscenities at you. Samuel brought me back to life." Christian saw the dawn of understanding begin to appear on her face.

"He made you a vampire to save your life," she said.

Christian nodded once. "Exactly," he said. "But when I realized what he had turned me into I was too ashamed to face you, Mother, or anyone so I made him promise to keep it from everyone. He was the one who made up the story about the wild animals right from the beginning just to buy me time. I could have straightened it all out whenever I chose. But I chose to let everyone think I was dead." Christian hung his head ever so slightly, unable to hide his intense feeling of regret for having made that fateful decision so long ago.

"Why?" she nearly whispered.

He looked directly at her. "Because I was embarrassed and ashamed."

"So, how did I get involved in all this?" she asked. "Why didn't Samuel tell me about you after I was changed?"

Christian raised his head and looked at his sister. "I hung around our village for a long time," he said. "And I watched you and Samuel getting closer and closer. I watched how he began to take my place in your life." Christian walked quickly over to the sofa and sat down next to her, imploring her with his telepathic emotions to understand. "And I was jealous because I had lost my life and everything I ever knew and loved," he said. "But most of all because I had lost my best friend."

"Oh, Christian." Diana leaned over to hug her brother. "I'm so sorry I did this to you."

Christian sat back and held her shoulders firmly. "You didn't do anything," he said. "Do you understand me? You didn't do anything. It was me!" He stood up and began to pace the floor, again. "You see," he said, "I kept fighting with Samuel, accusing him of misleading you by trying to fill my shoes. I warned him against changing you and I accused him of tricking you into wanting to be changed. Finally, after two years of living in the shadows watching my old life end before my very eyes, I left. But I made Samuel promise never to tell you or anyone else about me."

"And he did," Diana said as if she were guessing.

"He did." Christian nodded. "And he did one hell of a good job at keeping his promise." He chuckled at the irony of the whole thing. "Right before I left, Samuel and I had one last, nasty argument over you," Christian said. "We did not part company on the best of terms."

Diana shook her head and shrugged. "Well, he kept your promise, anyway."

"That's my point," Christian said. "He didn't tell you about me because I made him promise not to."

At that moment there was a loud rap repeated four times on the front door. Diana and Christian looked at each other quickly, but Christian already knew who was out there.

"That's the other thing," he said as he headed for the door.

"What is?"

Christian looked at her as his hand touched the door knob. "That's Samuel. Don't ask me how he knew you were here, but he did." He opened the door with Diana beside him. They saw Samuel sitting outside on the porch, leaning against the door. He was as white as the snow that had finished melting a short time ago and his flesh hung very loosely on his bones. It was obvious he was in great pain and fully drained of all energy. If he were mortal, he would be dead by now.

"Oh, my God, Samuel," Diana nearly screamed. She ran to his side before Christian could think to do anything. She knelt down beside him, cradled his head against her shoulder, and rocked him back and forth. "Oh, Samuel! You silly bastard, Samuel," she said, laughing and crying at the same time.

"Now you know how I felt when I found you last night," Christian told her.

"I know," she said. "I'm so sorry. I won't ever do anything like that again."

"Good," he said. "Now let's get him some nourishment fast." Christian crouched down in front of Samuel and put his hand on his shoulder. Samuel tried to raise his head, but his entire body quivered with the effort. "Stay here," Christian said to him. "I'll be right back."

Christian started to leave, but Samuel grabbed at his pant leg. When Christian looked down at his friend, who didn't even have the strength to lift his eyelids, he knew Samuel wanted him to take Diana as well. Even she wasn't safe in Samuel's company right now. *I'll kill her,* Samuel thought to Christian. *It's draining me to hear the blood . . .*

On that single word, Christian saw the faintest hint of the sinister side of this existence, and he snatched Diana away. He knew she understood by the sad look she gave him.

"Quickly," Christian said, then disappeared.

Diana followed right behind her brother and they were back in the woods behind the house in only seconds. "I'm glad he's back," she said. "But he's frightening to be near."

"I know, Di," Christian said, sensing for wildlife. "He won't be for long, though. We recuperate fast, you know. Samuel will be fine in no time at all just like you were."

"He could feed from us just as well," Diana said.

"The minute he tasted our blood he wouldn't be able to stop.

He'd kill us right now and you know it," he said. "Better he should kill an animal than one of us."

Diana shook her head in understanding and turned away from him. "That's what he looks like," she said. "An animal."

"I know."

"That's how Minotti always looks."

Christian turned directly to her. He was surprised that she had brought up the subject of Minotti.

"I feel much safer with both of you here, now," she said. "Jesse was right when he told me to come to you."

"That reminds me," Christian said. "I still have no idea what that one is up to."

Just then a huge buck with an incredibly large, ten point rack crossed their path unaware that another presence lurked close by. Both Diana and Christian played the mind control on him and led the animal straight to the front door for Samuel to feed.

"I can't watch," Diana said, turning her view from Samuel. "He's savage. I've never seen him like this before."

Christian stood facing her. "I know." He looked passed her to where Samuel sat and watched his eating frenzy.

"It's scary," Diana said. "It makes me feel terrible."

Christian looked at her. "Why's that?"

"He got this way because of me. He hasn't eaten in days because of me." She turned her head away.

"He's been out looking for you," Christian said. "But it was his choice to starve himself in the process. No one told him to be so self-sacrificing. If he'd been thinking clearly, he would have realized that he would only make it harder to find you if he was too weak to move."

"So, the two men I love the most in the world I also hurt the most." Diana started to cry.

"Don't put me in that category," Christian scolded her. "I left centuries ago out of pride, not because of anything you ever did. But I don't think either one of us can say the same for Samuel. If he could've died trying to find you he would've gone that far."

Diana looked back at the savage, famished beast that sat on the front porch with a vise-like grip on the defenseless animal that lay in his lap. She watched as this man who had loved her so devotedly drained the blood from the dying buck while he glared at both her and her brother as if they were intruders who had come to take his food.

"Let's go inside." Christian nudged her to walk beside him. "We'll use the back door."

"What about Sam?"

"Leave him be for now," Christian said. "When he comes to his senses he'll knock again and we'll let him in to rest just like Roni and I did for you."

"Where is Roni?" Diana asked.

"Working," Christian said. "Let's go in."

Together, they vaporized and wafted under the back door, re-forming themselves once they were inside the house.

Diana sat down at the table and stared into space. "How long do you think it will be before he's sociable?" she asked.

"I don't know for sure," Christian said, "but I think the buck's blood will be enough to get him on his feet so he can find the rest for himself."

"I had no idea how sick we can get," Diana said, still staring at the door.

Suddenly there was a loud and frantic banging.

"What the hell?" Christian said. He and Diana ran toward the front of the house at the same time. Christian ripped the front door open.

"My God!" Diana exclaimed.

What they saw immediately caused Christian's eyes to flare, his anger to burn out of control, and his sister to jump back from fear of her own brother.

Roni had apparently come home just as he and Diana walked around to the back of the house. Samuel had abandoned the deer and now had Roni's body bent over backward, both arms flailing to her sides, waiving frantically, his fangs locked into the side of her throat.

In an instant Christian reached out and grabbed Samuel by the back of his neck. He squeezed until he had pinched off the blood supply to Samuel's brain, causing him to pass out and release Roni who fell to the porch floor. "I should kill you," he hissed, then threw Samuel's limp body over the railing onto the lawn below. Christian lifted Roni and carried her into the house. He shut the door behind them with his foot, leaving Samuel outside. "He can rot for all I care now," he sneered.

Diana followed him. "He didn't know what he was doing."

Christian said nothing. He carried Roni into the bedroom and laid her gently down on the bed.

"Christian," Diana begged. "He wasn't himself. You said so yourself."

Christian was caressing Roni's hair when he turned his head slowly toward his sister. He purposely allowed the look in his eyes to hold the threat of death so Diana would know it was better not to mention Samuel's name again.

"Will she be alright?" Diana asked.

"Yes," Christian said. "She'll be fine." He moved her head to the side so he could get a good look at the wounds Samuel had made in her neck. "I don't think he had enough strength, yet, to do much damage," Christian said. "There's hardly any blood smeared. She probably passed out from fear."

"Thank heavens."

"I'm going to let her rest a bit," Christian said, but he continued to sit on the side of the bed and hold Roni's hand.

"I'm sorry." Diana stood up to leave.

Christian kissed Roni's lips before he followed his sister out into the hall and down to the kitchen.

"Are you better, now?" Diana asked him.

Christian looked at her, glaring, before a slight smile showed on his face. "I'm better," he said. "As long as she's alright, I'm better."

"What are you going to do about Samuel?" Diana asked.

"I don't know yet." Christian deliberately used a tone of voice that made it clear the subject was not up for discussion.

He knew Diana was smart enough to let it be.

CHAPTER 6

December 17, 1997

Samuel came to his senses and saw that he was lying on Roni and Christian's front lawn. He could tell from the stars in the sky that it was after midnight and he suddenly remembered everything that had happened, including Christian's harsh words. He knew he wouldn't be welcome here now, and he had no where else to go except home to France. Or to Jesse's. He chose Jesse's since it was closer to where Diana was now.

He wasted no time. He brushed himself off, then headed for the island as fast as he could. It only took twenty minutes to reach Jesse's doorstep. Samuel wasn't surprised to see his friend waiting for him.

"You knew," he said.

Jesse opened the door and walked out into the December night. "Yes, I did."

Samuel turned around and stormed across the beach. "I really screwed up, Jesse." He paced back and forth near the water's edge. The tide was beginning to rise, causing Samuel's feet to get wet every so often. But he hardly noticed. He told Jesse everything that happened right up to the moment he had begun to drink from Roni. He felt almost relieved to get it all out.

"Under the circumstances it's really quite understandable," Jesse said.

Samuel reached up with his hands and grabbed both sides of his hair. "Oh, but I can't believe I did that," he said. "I didn't even know who I was at the time."

Jesse took Samuel's hands down from his head. "Christian is a reasonable man, Sam. He'll understand once he settles down."

Samuel cast Jesse a doubtful look.

"I'm not saying it won't take awhile," Jesse said, "but I'm sure it'll be all right once he realizes there's really no harm done."

"But there could've been!" Samuel wailed. "I know. I'm being punished aren't I?"

"For what?"

"For not telling Diana that Christian was still alive," he said. "That's what this is all about, isn't it?"

"Calm down, Samuel." Jesse placed a hand on Samuel's shoulder. "Stand still and calm down."

Samuel stopped walking and looked Jesse straight in the eye. "I always knew this would happen," he said. "I always knew she'd turn on me once Christian was back in her life."

Jesse smiled. "I'm sure she hasn't turned on you, Samuel."

"She's there right now with him and Roni," Samuel said. "I don't see her here by my side. Do you Jesse? Do you see her standing next to me?"

Jesse shook his head and looked out across the frozen edge of the ocean. He said nothing.

"Maybe if I had told her five centuries ago, then none of this would've happened," Samuel said. "But, on-the-other-hand, maybe this would've happened back then and been done with sooner." Samuel picked up a seashell and skipped it across an open patch of water that thawed slightly. "But then I might have missed out on all the memories we've made." He picked up another shell and skipped it across the water. "I suppose it'll be light years this time before Christian and I are back on speaking terms."

"I hope not," Jesse said. "We don't have that much time."

Samuel picked up a third shell, but he held on to it this time. "What do you mean?"

"I think you better know what happened to Diana in the two nights that she was gone."

Jesse's tone of voice was unnerving. Up to that point Samuel was only concerned about what he'd almost done to Roni, and relieved that Diana was back. He never considered where Diana had been all that time. He dropped the seashell and stood staring at Jesse, mouth agape.

"Walk with me," Jesse said. He put his arm across Samuel's shoulders. "And try to stay calm. I know Christian is angry with you at the moment, but he's going to need your help again, and soon."

Samuel did as Jesse instructed and listened to the story of Gaetano Minotti and what he had put Diana through. As Jesse talked, Samuel grew angrier by the moment and the anger began to make him sick inside. But he did his best to stay calm and hold his temper under control until he heard it all.

When Jesse had told Samuel all he could it was nearing dawn.

"How old is this vampire?" Samuel growled.

"As old as time."

Samuel looked at him and frowned. "That's awfully cryptic."

"It's also true."

"Then he is the devil, himself."

"Could be," Jesse said.

Samuel sneered and clenched his fists at his sides. "Then he should die."

"Not possible, I'm afraid," Jesse said.

"What do you mean, 'Not possible'?!" Samuel stormed. "Everything's possible! Isn't that what you taught me?"

"Yes," Jesse said. "It is what I taught you. I guess, what I should've said is that it's not possible for us."

Samuel stopped walking and faced Jesse, putting a hand on his shoulder to lock him in place while he waved the forefinger from his other hand wildly in the air. "Do you mean to tell me we can't do a damned thing to this guy?" Samuel asked. "Is that what you're telling me, Jess. Cause if it is, I want a second opinion. I want to hear it from God Himself that this is the truth you're telling me!"

Jesse stared through Samuel's eyes. "God doesn't make too

many personal appearances these days."

"I've noticed." Samuel let his hand drop from Jesse's shoulder. "I've noticed."

"Look, Sam," Jesse said. "The blackness inside you churns from the hatred Minotti has caused." Jesse looked past him toward the ocean. "But remember. Evil always destroys itself by its own actions." He turned back to Samuel. "I'm counting on that."

"Then so am I." Samuel started to walk back toward the house. "When do you think he'll show up for Diana?"

"For certain?" Jesse hesitated a few seconds. "Within the next forty eight hours."

"How do you know?"

Jesse looked straight ahead. "Because I do."

"Where will he look for her?"

"Where ever she happens to be at the time he decides to take her back." They walked up the front stairs on to the porch, then stopped.

"So, how do we protect her?" Samuel asked. "There must be something we can do?"

"There is," Jesse said. "When was the last time you went to church?"

Christian was on edge until Roni awoke a short time after her run in with Samuel. She could not remember a thing, so she didn't understand his concern or Diana's repeated apologies on Samuel's behalf. They explained it as best they could without frightening her. Diana did most of the talking since Christian was about to explode if he thought about it any more. Roni sat on the edge of the bed and listened. When they were done, Christian sat back and let out a huge breath.

"Christian, relax," Roni said. "There's no harm done. Besides, Samuel would never have hurt me or anyone else intentionally. You know it and I know it."

"And I know it," Diana said.

Christian turned around, his eyebrows raised at her.

"Well, I do," she said.

Roni walked over to Christian and put both of her hands on his back, then around his waist and leaned against him. "Samuel has come to your rescue more than once, if I recall correctly," she said. "In fact, if it weren't for him I wouldn't be fortunate enough to have you in my life right now, if you think about it."

"That's right," Diana said.

Christian turned and put an arm around Roni.

"And if it weren't for Samuel," Diana went on, "then you and I wouldn't have the chance to be around this long and still have each other."

"I get the point," Christian said. "Enough about Samuel. We'll cross that bridge when we come to it. But right now we've got another situation to face."

"Let's go in the kitchen," Roni said. "I'd like to get something to drink."

Christian motioned for the girls to leave the bedroom first. He followed right behind them into the kitchen and sat down at the table. "All joking aside," he said. "It's nice to see that you two can get along well enough to gang up on me, but we really have got to face this new problem with Minotti."

"What can we do?" Roni asked.

"At the moment, nothing," Christian said. "But I've got to get in touch with Jesse to find out what he knows."

"Are you sure that's who saved me?" Diana asked.

"Positive," Christian said.

Diana leaned back in her chair. "Well, where is he?" she asked. "Why don't you try to reach him right now?"

"Oh, right," Christian said. "And while I'm gone Mr. Minotti shows up and whisks you away to Never-Never Land. That's just perfect."

"What about telepathy?" Roni asked.

"No good," Christian said. "Once my mind is open Minotti could pick up everything. I'm sure he already knows exactly where Diana is just from her calling to me."

"Well, how are you going to be able to talk to him otherwise?" Diana asked him.

"Wait a minute!" Roni said. "I think I have an idea."

"Uh oh." Christian smiled, trying to be playful, but it didn't help ease the tension in him at all.

"No, really," Roni said. "Look, I know that you have no trouble entering a church or anything like that, but you're a good-hearted person. Maybe it really is true that pure evil cannot enter any sanctified place. It sounds to me like this Minotti character fits that description. Maybe we'd be safe at St. Joseph's until you're finished talking to Jesse."

"And maybe you won't be safe anywhere," Christian said.

"It's worth a shot," Diana said. "With any luck at all he won't be around at the same time you're with Jesse, anyway."

"I don't know," Christian said. "I have a feeling, from what you told me, that somehow he knows, and he waits for the perfect moment."

"OK, so when do we do this?" Roni asked. "When do you want to try to reach Jesse?"

Christian looked at the clock on the wall across the room, then at both Roni and Diana.

"It's up to you," Diana said. "I'm in no hurry at all to see that jamoke's ugly face again."

"Tomorrow night," Christian said.

Diana rolled her eyes and through her hands up. "What about right now?"

Christian ignored her sarcasm. "No," he said. "I want to make sure Roni is alright and that you're back to normal."

"I'm fine," Diana said. "You worry too much."

Christian just looked at her.

"That's alright," Roni said. "We couldn't get in the church now anyway."

"Do we have to do something special?" Christian asked. "Aren't the churches open all the time?"

"Not anymore," Roni said. "Too many robberies. I'll call Father Larry tomorrow evening and ask him to let us in at, say, seven?"

"That'll do just fine," Christian said. "That should give me more than enough time to reach Jesse and find out what I can about Gaetano Minotti's weaknesses."

"If he has any," Diana said.

Christian raised his eyebrows and nodded. "Exactly."

"What do you mean, 'When was the last time I went to church?'?" Samuel asked. "How the heck do I know!"

Jesse laughed at Samuel's confusion as he sat down on the porch railing and watched the scattered snowflakes drift slowly down to the sandy beach below.

"I may be wrong," Jesse began, "but I think Minotti might lose a bit of his strength in a sanctified place."

"That's bullshit!" Samuel said. "You and I both know it's a bunch of crap."

"For those who are essentially good, it is," Jesse agreed. "But not for pure evil. I don't think it is."

"Even that's a pile of rubbish," Samuel said. "I've seen murderers walk into a church, sit there for Mass and the church was still standing when they left."

"Don't argue semantics with me," Jesse said. "Even a murderer can be fully repentant. I've seen that with my own eyes." Jesse leaned back against the post that held up the gable above the porch. "What we're talking about here is pure, unaltered evil," he said. "Evil that enjoys evil simply for evil's sake."

"What we're talking about," Samuel said, "is a real sick mind."

Jesse shook his head slightly in agreement. "A real sick soul." He looked at Samuel. "I don't believe he has a mind left."

"He couldn't have a soul either," Samuel said. "What kind of a thing is he?"

Jesse looked at him, tilting his head slightly. "What are you saying?"

"I can't even imagine it." Samuel shook his head. "A man-sized eternal being made of everything bad and wrong and backward and sick." Samuel started to walk down the few steps to the sandy beach that was Jesse's front yard.

"He's not worth thinking about so much," Jesse said. "Better to hold it in until you're face-to-face with him. You'll be revolted enough then."

Samuel stopped walking and turned around "Why? Is he that ugly to look at?"

"No," Jesse answered. "It's the way his aura feels when you're too close to it. It makes you feel physically ill."

Samuel stood for a moment, then he turned, went down the last step and onto the hard sand. The sky had turned black with clouds. Not even the moon could be seen. He walked toward the water a few steps then turned and headed back to sit on the porch stairs.

"So what's the plan?" Samuel asked.

"To wait," Jesse said. "That's all we can do for now."

CHAPTER 7

December 18, 1997

While Father Larry waited anxiously for Roni and Christian, he was plagued with apprehension over meeting Diana. Another vampire. What would she look like? What kind of personality would she have? He hoped she'd be like her brother.

He heard the door open, and his heart began to pound as he turned around to see who was there. As he expected, it was them. He stood up, did his best to hide his nervousness, and went to greet them. "I'm glad you called," he said, glancing at Diana. It was amazing. Same upturned nose, same olive skin, and round eyes.

Christian shook his hand, then put his other arm around Diana. "Father," he said. "This is Diana, my sister."

Father Larry slowly reached his right hand toward her and tried to control the shaking. "I'm so happy to meet you," he said. "Christian has told me so much about you."

Diana took his hand, but glanced sideways at her brother. "Has he?"

"I'm sorry to impose on you like this," Christian said. "I appreciate you opening the church for us."

Father Larry smiled. "I was almost expecting it."

Roni glanced at him, her eyebrows raised. "Oh?"

Father Larry shook his head and waved his hands in the air. "It's a long story," he said, smiling. "I'll tell you about it some other time."

"I don't expect to be long," Christian told him. "But I do feel much better knowing they're here with you."

"Everyone is in good hands in the Lord's house," Father Larry said. "Especially when the faith is strong." He patted Christian on the back and wondered if there was some way he could have seen this friendship coming. He decided it was impossible. "You take as much time as you need."

"Thank you," Christian said. He hugged Diana first, then Roni, kissing her tenderly. "I love you," he said to her. "Be careful."

Roni ruffled his hair. "We'll be fine," she said. "I love you, too. Now get going so we can get this over with."

"Thanks again," Christian said to Father Larry. He leaned closer toward him. "I never thought I'd be friends with a priest either," he whispered.

Father Larry smiled at him. "I feel much better now," he said, half-teasing.

"I thought you might." Christian turned and quickly left the church.

When he was gone Roni and Diana followed the hobbling priest up the center aisle toward the altar. They took a seat in one of the pews ten rows back from the front of the church and sat for a few moments before either of them spoke.

"So," Father Larry said, "what's this all about?"

The two women looked at each other. "Well," Roni said, "I'll tell you what I can, but I hope you're not sorry after you hear the whole story."

Father Larry let out a short, sardonic laugh. "I hope not either," he said. "But something tells me I'm going to need to know. So, shoot."

Diana turned to her and put her hand on Roni's arm. "I'll help you if you get stuck," she said.

Roni smiled at her, nodded, and began to introduce Father Larry to, yet, another vampire.

"Christian is on his way," Jesse said to Samuel. "This might be as good a time as any to make amends with him. Did you sleep well?"

"Well enough."

"Good," he said. "You're going to need as much strength as you can muster, later. For now, try to make peace."

"I'll try," Samuel said. "But I doubt he's gotten over it yet. He's a stubborn one."

Jesse said nothing. Samuel's effort would be enough for the time being.

"Where's Diana and Roni if Christian's on his way here?" Samuel asked. "I hope he didn't leave them alone."

"Chances are he had to."

"Well, that leaves the door wide open for Minotti, then, doesn't it?" Samuel said, frowning.

"It would seem so."

"You're awfully calm about it, Jess."

"Not really, Sam," Jesse said. "Let's go watch the snowfall outside. It might help you stay calm."

They went out to sit on the front porch while they waited for Christian to arrive. Huge, gentle snowflakes that seemed to float to the ground like feathers, were falling all around.

"You know," Samuel said. "There are times I wish I could feel the cold just once more. I almost never miss the extremes I experienced as a mortal. But at times like this there's a constant, obvious something missing that would complete the experience of a simple snowfall." Samuel held out his hand to catch a snowflake and watch it sit there, still frozen in his palm. "It might sound stupid, but I've always found it fascinating the way they won't melt in my hand. I can clearly see every crystalline element right down to the detailed symmetry of the six arms. It's one of the most beautiful things I've ever seen."

"That it is," Jesse said. "Now relax. Christian is here."

Samuel looked up, alarmed. "Where?"

Jesse nodded toward the beach and Samuel turned to see Christian walking toward them.

"I didn't expect him to be here," Christian said to Jesse. He walked to the porch, then stopped in front of the steps. He stood there and stared at Samuel. "I would like you to leave," he said. "I'm not ready to see you."

Samuel rose to his feet and went to the top of the stairs where he stood in place like a stone sentinel. The two men just stared at each other. Jesse knew they had to get passed this now. It was best to leave them alone and hope they would handle it sensibly.

"Christian," Samuel said.

Christian quickly held up his hand indicating to Samuel to stop talking. "I should've killed you."

Samuel lean forward, holding one hand out to Christian in a gesture of peace. "I'm sorry."

But Christian didn't wait to hear it. He lunged at him. Samuel saw him coming and disappeared, leaving Christian grasping at the empty air.

"Now was that very smart?" Jesse asked. He was sitting on the porch railing when Christian turned to him.

"Do you know what he did?" Christian asked.

"I know what he almost did," Jesse said.

Christian walked quickly up the stairs. "If I hadn't been there at just the right moment he would've gone through with it."

Jesse nodded. "Then it's a good thing you were there at just the right moment."

"What?" Christian yelled.

Jesse stood up and walked toward him. "What did you think you were you doing leaving him alone on your front porch like that, anyway?" he asked. "Don't be angry at Samuel. Be angry at yourself. You should've known better."

Christian stood his ground and glared at Jesse.

"You're mad at yourself because you let Roni down and it could've been disastrous," Jesse said.

Christian stood silent for a moment, then turned to face the ocean. "I came here to talk about something else and you turned the tables on me."

"I didn't do anything but watch," Jesse said. "Now forgive yourself and let's get on with the reason you're here. You frightened Samuel away and you're going to need his help. He's one of the best allies you'll ever have in this world."

"Besides you?"

Jesse shook his head and smiled.

"Fine," he said. "Let him know I'll do my best not to ring his neck the next time I see him. Right now I need to know about Gaetano Minotti. Roni and Diana are alone. I need to get back to them as soon as possible."

Jesse looked at Christian, then shifted his gaze away. Out of the corner of his eye he saw that Samuel had returned and stood on the far side of the porch. He was glad to see him. "What do you want to know?"

"What did you do in Niagara Falls after you got my sister out of his house?" Christian asked.

Jesse turned toward Christian, surprised. "Of all the questions I expected you to ask, that one is of least importance," Jesse said. "But you want to know so I'll tell you." He sat down on the top stair and looked out at the icy ocean. "When you wake up," he said, "do you know whether or not Roni is at home, assuming, of course, she's already awake and out of bed?"

"What has that got to do with it?"

Jesse didn't answer him. He sat and waited for Christian's response.

"Yes," Christian finally said.

"How do you know?"

Christian frowned. "I just do," he said. "I can hear her thoughts sometimes. Other times I can feel her there. Why?"

"You feel her essence," Jesse said.

"Yes."

"What I did in Niagara Falls was to simply leave enough of my own essence in Minotti's house so he would know without a doubt that it was me who freed Diana," Jesse said. "Nothing more."

Christian spun around, swirling his coat. "Why would you do

that?" he asked, flailing his arms. "Why not just stay there and ask him to follow you right to her?" He shook his head and looked away.

"In the hope that he might back off and leave her alone if he knew he had to deal with me the next time he tried anything," Jesse said.

Christian stared at him for moment, then stormed back down the stairs and headed toward the water. He stood at the edge of the beach and watched the surf roll in for a few minutes. He was silent. Then he turned around and faced Jesse. "Who is he?"

Jesse looked up at the clouds that continued to drop the unusually large snowflakes. He deeply wished none of them would have to deal with Minotti, but he knew that was impossible now. "Everything that is evil," he said. "Without a doubt."

Christian headed back to the porch. He stood in front of Jesse, snowflakes resting on his hair and shoulders. "Satan?" he asked.

"No," Jesse said, "but very close."

Samuel came forward. "What's the difference?"

Christian cast him an angry look, but said nothing.

"Gaetano Minotti is a vampire," Jesse said. "Satan has no such limitations. But Satan is, most definitely, a very large part of who Minotti is."

"OK," Christian said. "I guess I need to know, then, if he can be destroyed."

Jesse looked at each of them, then shook his head. "Honestly, I don't know."

"What do you mean 'you don't know'?" Christian asked.

Samuel took a few steps closer then stopped. "My reaction, exactly."

Christian turned to look at him. "You knew about this, too?"

"Only after Jesse told me."

Christian sat down on the top step of the porch next to Jesse and dropped his head onto his hands. "I left the girls with Father Larry at the church," he told them. "Roni thought it might keep them safe from him until I returned."

"She might be right," Jesse said. "But I don't honestly think so. Minotti won't be afraid of the church. He's not afraid of anything. It might be wiser if both of you went back to them."

Christian stood up.

"I'm going with you," Samuel said.

Christian glared at him, his eyes glowing red, but he relaxed and nodded his head. "One more thing," Christian said to Jesse. "How did you know Diana was in trouble? And how did you know where she was."

Jesse smiled. "Telepathy," he said. "I heard all the prayers that were being said for her. Especially yours, Christian."

"But how did you know where she was?" Christian asked.

"The same way," Jesse said. "Everyone leaves their essence wherever they go. Her pain was strong. It led me right to her. Now get going."

"Wait a minute, Jess," Christian said. "We'll need your help too if this guy is everything you say he is."

"I'll be along shortly," Jesse said. "I wouldn't leave you stranded, you know."

Christian hesitated, then smiled. "I know," he said, then turned to Samuel. "Let's go."

By the time Roni realized Father Larry had heard enough she was too far into her explanation to turn back. She continued to tell the story right down to the phone call she made to him earlier that evening asking to be let into the church.

Father Larry let out a huge breath, leaned back, and rested his hands on his belly. "Well," he said. "I certainly understand Christian's concern, now. And a few other things as well."

"What other things?" Roni asked.

"Oh, personal things," he said. "Nothing important."

Roni shrugged her shoulders and nodded.

"I'm really sorry to dump all this on you," Diana said. "This is all my fault for taking off the way I did. I just wanted to get away to cool off and think. I didn't expect it to back fire like this."

"We seldom see the effects of our actions beforehand," Father Larry said. "But 'hind sight is the best foresight,' as they say. Maybe you'll learn from this once it's all over."

"I already have," she said. "I'm surprised something like this hasn't happened to me sooner."

Roni looked at her. "So am I."

Just then the doors to the church swung wide open letting in a blast of ice cold air that filled the church so quickly both Roni and Father Larry began to shiver.

"Oh no," Diana said.

Together they turned toward the doors. Coming toward them was a mass of black movement in the solemnly lit church.

"It's him," Diana said.

Roni gasped, Father Larry began to pray.

"Ah, Diana." Minotti floated the words eerily around the three of them. "How I've missed you."

Father Larry stood up and walked out into the center aisle, standing directly in front of Gaetano Minotti and halted his progress. "How is it that you're able to enter here?" he asked.

"SILENCE!" Minotti yelled. He jerked his arm forward at the brave priest.

The girls watched as Minotti's evil strength slowly lifted the priest ten feet into the air. In the blink of an eye he was propelled backwards and landed before the altar. Roni saw his head strike the marble rail that cordoned it off from the seats. He fell to the floor, unconscious.

Roni stood up and screamed. "Father Larry!!" She spun furiously to face his assailant. "Just who in the name of God do you think you are?"

Minotti looked at her and laughed while he strolled menacingly toward her. "Oh, let me assure you, gorgeous one," he said, looking her up and down with lust in his eyes. "You will not find me in the company of THAT one."

Diana jumped in front of Roni, her arms out as if to shield

her. "Get out of here, Minotti!" Diana yelled. "You're not welcome here. Leave us alone!"

Minotti laughed a raucous, amused laugh that bellowed and echoed throughout the entire church making the girls cringe in fear. "It was very clever of you to think you could hide safely from me in this place." He cupped Diana's chin in his hand. "But you were wrong, weren't you?"

Diana jerked her head backwards, forcing his hand from her. "Don't touch me!" she said.

"No?" Minotti asked. "NO?!" he roared, leaning toward her.

Roni began to shake outwardly from fear, her audible prayers, coming in gasps. She saw Diana defiantly bare her fangs, hissing at Minotti like a wildcat. But the offensive act that was intended to protect Roni frightened her nearly to death.

Minotti laughed at Diana. "Is that the way it's going to be?" he asked. "Oh, that's precious. You can't honestly hope to threaten me and live?" He pushed his left hand at Diana and froze her in place. From his palm a long, oily, black object began to ooze its way straight toward Diana's heart. Just as the snakish slime struck out with its lashing tongue, Roni jumped to Diana's side and pushed her out of the way. The first attack caught Roni square in the left shoulder. It burned like fire and immediately caused her knees to go weak. She looked at her shoulder, but all she could see was the inside of the church as it began to spin around. She turned and started to fall. The last thing she saw before she hit the floor was the crucifix on the altar hung sideways in an eerie, other-worldly joke. She accepted that she was already dead.

CHAPTER 8

The first thing Christian saw when he entered the church, was Roni laying face down in the middle of the center aisle. Her head was twisted in a strange, unnatural position. Her eyes were toward the altar and her arms lay straight down along her sides. She looked broken and dead.

Gaetano Minotti stood directly behind her, a mad man in black, older than the hills and angrier than a rabid dog. He held Diana above him in one hand. Her face clearly showed her fear. Christian didn't know who to go to first, but Samuel wasted no time in attacking the ageless monster. That left Christian free to rush to Roni's side.

In the blink of an eye Samuel reached Minotti and bit clear through the veins in his wrist, forcing him to open the hand that held Diana captive.

"Agghhh!!" Minotti yelled.

Diana tumbled out of his grasp, quickly righted herself, then raced to Roni's side where Christian was already trying to bring her to consciousness. "Is she alright?" Diana asked.

"She's alive." He turned Roni onto her back, placing her body in a more natural position, then he looked up at Diana. "What about you?"

"I'm alright." She glanced back to where Minotti and Samuel were fighting.

Christian turned to look and saw Minotti angrily holding his bitten, bleeding hand. Samuel had not stopped his attack, but was unable to get a blow in as crucial as his first. Christian turned back to Roni and saw Father Larry where he lay at the foot of the marble rail. "Di," he said. "Over there." He gave a quick nod in the priest's direction. "See how he is."

Diana rose to do as Christian asked, but they heard Samuel yell out in pain. They turned in time to see him being hoisted to the cathedral ceiling by a giant fish hook Minotti had created out of thin air and jammed through Samuel's back.

"Chris, he needs you." Diana dashed towards Minotti without giving Christian any warning.

Christian left Roni where she was and rose to the ceiling alongside Samuel as quickly as he could. He did his best to remove the man size hook from Samuel's back, but Minotti's telepathy was stronger than all of theirs put together. Christian couldn't budge it. "Hold on, Sam," he said.

"It was Minotti," Samuel said.

Christian looked down in time to see Diana's mindless charge at Minotti. She ran into him and knocked him off his feet. When he was on the floor the hook through Samuel's back disappeared. Christian reached out and grabbed Samuel by the shoulder of his jacket just moments before he began the straight fall to the seats below. Slowly, he eased Samuel down, and laid him across one of the pews. "How're you feeling, Sam?"

"I've been better," Samuel said, intense pain evident in his voice.

Christian looked at his stomach where the hook had exited his body. He could see the wound already beginning to heal as Samuel's immortal blood began to repair the damage done by Minotti's sorcery.

"Chriiistiaaaan!" It was Diana. Christian looked down the aisle toward the entrance to the church in time to see Minotti with Diana slung under his arm like a newspaper. They were headed towards the door followed by Minotti's three henchmen.

"Heal quickly, old man," Christian said to Samuel. "I need your help." In the blink of an eye, Christian was at the exit before the evil entourage could reach it. "Too much extra baggage?" he asked Minotti. It bought him enough time to create a force field across the doorway, similar in nature to the one Minotti had created at his home to imprison Diana.

"You can't possibly hope to win against me," Minotti sneered.

Christian saw Samuel stand up and begin to charge down the aisle. "But I do," he said.

Samuel wrapped his arms around all three of Minotti's mortal cohorts and knocked their heads together. They fell forward onto Minotti's back.

"Wha??" Minotti gasped. His fall pushed him into the force field, slamming him hard enough to loosen his grip around Diana's waist. She fell to the floor, but was on her feet in a split second. She joined Christian and Samuel in their barrage against him.

Minotti looked up in time to see them coming. He rose above them and headed back into the church.

"What's he doing?" Diana asked.

"More room," Christian said.

They followed him.

"The odds outweigh you," Samuel yelled. "Leave us alone and go back to whatever hell hole you climbed out of."

"Not until I get what I came for," Minotti said.

"I don't belong to you or anyone else!" Diana yelled at him. "Get out of here and leave us alone!"

Minotti landed on the floor in front of the altar and stood facing them. "Such spirit," he said, laughing. He stood like a statue, staring down the aisle. Behind him, Father Larry had begun to stir.

They approached slowly, determined to beat him, with nothing to block their progress but air. When they were only twenty feet away they began to slow down.

"He's doing it again," Diana said.

Samuel nodded. "I feel it. He's trying to make me lose my drive to fight him."

"I don't know if we can fight him."

"If we pool our strengths we can," Christian said. "We've got to try. I need both of your powers."

Samuel put a hand on Christian's shoulder. "I'm with you."

Christian immediately felt his friend's damaged strength merge with his own, while Minotti laughed at their efforts.

"It's no use," Samuel said. "I don't have the energy."

"Diana?" Christian looked at his sister. "What about you? How are you doing?" He saw the glazed look on her face and knew their battle was lost. Without her he was finished.

Minotti began to laugh wildly as he watched the three before him succumb to his powers. "Come to me Diana!" he commanded. She slid across the floor without moving her legs, and stood beside him. "We will be leaving together." Together, they began to walk to the back of the church.

"You evil bastard!" Samuel yelled.

"Away with you." Minotti waved a hand and Samuel was pushed aside to let him and Diana pass.

"You'll never win." Christian said in a growl.

"I already have." Minotti laughed victoriously with every step he and Diana took together.

"M-I-NO-O-OTTI-I-!!"

The name reverberated throughout the entire church. It echoed off the domed ceilings, rattled the stained glass windows, and shook the huge fans that hung suspended from the main beams.

Gaetano Minotti turned to look behind him toward the source of the voice that called his name. The look on his face showed fear and gave Christian and Samuel new hope.

"Samuel," Christian said.

"I see him."

"You won't win." Minotti turned back around and did his best to maintain control over his three mental hostages. "I've almost got what I came for and I won't let you win now."

Jesse stood on the altar dressed all in white. "You don't really have much choice," he said. He walked over to Father Larry and bent down to check on him.

Minotti turned towards Jesse. "He's dead. He was the first one to go."

Jesse looked at Minotti, then at Christian. He nodded once to let Christian know the priest was alive.

"Let them all go," Jesse said to Minotti.

"I'll bring this whole place down before I'll take an order from you." Minotti looked down the aisle to where Diana was still walking towards the back of the church.

Jesse walked down the stairs from the altar and stood by Minotti's right side. He stared at his profile for a few seconds. Then he lifted his right hand and moved it slowly across Minotti's line of vision.

Diana instantly stopped walking and turned around. Samuel and Christian relaxed from the release of Minotti's mental hold. They shook off the cloudiness and met Diana half way.

"Is that who rescued you?" Christian asked her.

"That's him." She nodded. "Is that Jesse?."

"It sure is," Samuel said, smiling.

"Good," Diana said. "Now what?"

"He doesn't need our help," Christian told her. "But stay close."

They stood in the aisle and watched to see what was going to happen.

"Destroy yourself," Jesse said to Minotti. "Give up this foolishness and leave this house."

Minotti faced Jesse and glared at him. "I told you," he said. "I do not take my orders from you." He raised his left hand toward Jesse. An electrical flash like a thin lightening bolt seared straight from Minotti's hand to Jesse, but Jesse raised his right hand again, and the lightening bolt fizzled out.

"Haven't you learned anything, yet?" Jesse asked him. He looked sad. "I don't want to do this to you."

"What are you talking about?" Minotti asked. "What could you possibly do to me?" The slight quiver in his voice was unmistakable.

Diana nudged Christian. "He sounds scared."

"I hope he is," Christian said. "Let's check on Roni. I want to try to move toward her as soon as Minotti has his back turned."

"I'll follow you," she said.

Jesse gazed briefly at Christian to let him know he heard the conversation. Then he turned away from Minotti and walked back up to the altar. "Let's not do this, again," he said.

Minotti's sight was glued to Jesse's every move and his body turned to keep Jesse directly in front of him. He appeared to be on his guard.

Christian, Diana, and Samuel all took advantage of Minotti's diversion and went to Roni's side. They did their best to bring her around while the verbal battle continued in the front of the church.

"Oh, no you don't!" Minotti screamed at them. He stretched out his arm toward Diana and Christian.

"Oh, no YOU don't," Jesse said to Minotti.

Diana and Christian looked up from Roni just in time to see Jesse deflect a streak of blue light that began with Minotti and traveled straight at them. It appeared to stop mid-air, turn completely around, and aim itself right back at its source. Minotti jumped and let out an angry yelp, as he received a taste of his own medicine. He turned his full attention back to Jesse and stormed at him like a soldier on the march, his ankle-length coattails flaring menacingly behind him. "You have no right!" he yelled.

Jesse said nothing.

"You're always interfering!" Minotti said.

Still, Jesse said nothing. He shifted his gaze toward Christian. *Tend to her.*

Christian nodded, then turned to Roni.

"Look at her shoulder," Diana said. "It looks like she was stabbed or bitten. It's terribly swollen. The thing that did it was directed at me. It looked like a snake."

Christian touched the blood on Roni's shoulder, then put it to his lips.

"Poison," he said.

"What?"

"Poison," he repeated. "We have to get the poison out of her blood."

"How can we do that?"

Christian looked at her. "You're kidding, right." He took a small knife from his back pocket and sliced across the puncture wound. Then he leaned over and began to suck the poisonous blood from Roni's body.

"Don't swallow it," Diana warned.

Christian stopped and looked at her. He did his best to be as gentle as the tension in his soul would allow. "Our blood detoxifies," he said. "If I don't have to spit it out, it won't take as long to get the poison out of her."

She gave him a sheepish look and nodded. "Oh, right."

Samuel stood behind them. "I think it's been in there too long," he said.

Christian ignored him and continued to work on Roni.

"Christian," Diana said. She placed her hand on his arm. "There might not be anything we can do."

"There is!" he shouted. "There has to be."

"Samuel," she said. "Help him."

"I don't know what else to do," he said. "He adores her."

"I can't stand to watch this anymore," Diana said.

Christian stopped and looked at her, but she had turned towards Jesse who was still on the altar with Minotti. After a few seconds, she faced Christian. "Change her," she said. "I can't stand the agony on your face, Christian. Change her and be done with it."

Christian saw Minotti's head turn sharply in their direction when he heard Diana speak. "Yes," Minotti said. "Change her. Make one more of us. Go ahead. Change her." He started to float towards the makeshift rescue team leaving Jesse and the unconscious priest behind. "I'm hungry for a glorious transformation," he sneered.

Christian ignored him and spoke to Diana. "I can't," he said. "She doesn't want to be one of us."

"What's wrong with us?" Diana asked, sounding insulted.

"Nothing," Christian said. "It's just her . . ." He looked at Jesse and pleaded in his heart for help.

"Change her," Minotti said. He grabbed Samuel from behind and pushed him out of the way. "Change her or I will."

Diana looked at him sideways. "You make me sick!" she snarled at him.

Samuel grabbed Minotti and dragged him to the center of the aisle and started to push him towards the altar. "Leave us alone!" he said.

Minotti continued to look around Samuel apparently more interested in seeing the transformation than he was in fighting back.

"You're sick!" Samuel said.

When they were too far away to see what was happening with Roni, Minotti became enraged. He attacked Samuel, lifted him high above his head, and threw him with all his strength towards the far right side of the church. Samuel crashed into the wall and fell to the ground in a heap.

"Work on her," Christian told Diana.

Diana looked at him with wild, startled eyes. "Christian."

"Please," he said.

She leaned over and began trying to remove the poison from Roni's blood as Christian had shown her.

He looked up to see what Minotti was going to do. He saw him start to walk past the altar all the while looking in their direction, and he saw Father Larry's eyes flutter open. When Minotti was close enough, Father Larry moved his leg just enough to cross his path. Minotti tripped, but the impact jarred the priest's whole body. His head shook and hit the step. Father Larry was unconscious once more.

Minotti fell forward and landed flat on his face. He rose cursing and swearing, then floated upwards until he stood on his feet. "You'll be sorry you did that, old man," he said. He reached down and grabbed the priest by the labels of his jacket. He lifted Father

Larry high over his head and threw him up in the air like a rag doll. When Father Larry came back down Minotti caught him by his throat.

"That's enough!" Jesse said. He sent a flood of hot, white light to circle around the wicked one.

Minotti tossed the priest up in the air one more time, then screamed when the white light reached him. The shock induced by Jesse knocked him off balance and he crumbled to the ground creating a safe cushion for the priest to land on.

"That's enough," Jesse said again. He approached Minotti who was rolling himself out from beneath the robust priest.

"I've had quite enough myself," Minotti said. He sent a red electric bolt hurling in Jesse's direction, but his attack was stopped again. This time the detour sent his effort towards the marble railing near the altar. It chipped a four inch chunk out of the solid structure.

Jesse did not fire back, and he didn't say a word. He looked around the church at each person there. Father Larry was still unconscious, but Samuel was already back on his feet.

Christian turned his attention back to Roni. "How's she doing," he asked Diana.

Diana looked up at him, then shook her head.

CHAPTER 9

Christian was relieved to see Samuel back on his feet. *Are you alright?* he thought to him.

Samuel nodded.

Christian looked at Roni to see if there was any change. There wasn't. He caressed her hair and glanced up at Jesse. *Will she be alright?* he thought.

Jesse's face wore a serious expression that worried Christian. *The poison has been in her body too long,* Jesse told him.

What can we do?

Jesse turned toward Samuel. *Take them water from the fonts.*

In seconds, Samuel was by the side entrance. He lifted one entire marble container that held the holy water right out of its base and transported it straight to where Roni lay. He sat down on the pew behind Christian and held the font on his lap.

Christian looked to Jesse for instructions, but his back was toward them. "Is she supposed to drink it?" he asked Samuel.

Samuel shrugged. "Jesse told me to bring it. He wasn't clear what to do with it."

"Put some on the wound," Diana said. "Wash her shoulder with it. If that doesn't work, then we can try to get her to drink some of it."

Christian nodded, then opened the sleeve of her shirt. He began to dip his hands in the water and spoon it onto Roni's shoulder, waiting for an instant healing to occur, but it did not. He looked up at Jesse to see if that was what they were expected to do, but Jesse still wasn't watching them. His attention was on Minotti who was back on his feet and poised to kill.

"Your mistake," Jesse said to Minotti, "was thinking you could walk into this place and remain safe. Your own companions are mortal men. Why is that? I give your evil comrades credit for knowing better than to insult the Lord by entering His house without a soul." Jesse approached him and stood in silence. They looked at each other with a melancholy, soulfulness. It seemed to hold a deeply buried secret, a mournful regret that caught Christian off guard. It looked as if they shared a common pain, but that didn't seem possible.

He turned back to see how Roni was doing. Water had dripped all over the floor.

"Wet your shirt with the water," Samuel said to Christian. "Hold it on the wound. You won't lose so much of it that way."

Christian took off his coat and shirt, then dipped his shirt in the font. He placed the wet fabric on Roni's shoulder and looked at Samuel. "I hope this is over soon," he said.

Samuel nodded, then turned toward the altar. "I wish we could help Jesse."

"I don't think he needs us," Christian said. "Roni needs us more right now."

They watched the altar while Christian held the wet shirt to Roni's wound and waited to see what effect the water would have.

"Why won't you leave them alone?" Jesse said to Minotti. "I don't want to fight you."

Minotti hesitated. For a split second it looked as if he was about to agree, but he took a few steps away from Jesse, then whirled around. "Then let me have what I want," he said to Jesse, "and we'll have no need to fight."

Jesse looked at him with sadness in his eyes. "You know that's not possible."

Minotti extended his arm and pointed at him. "Then destroy me if you can," he dared. "I'm not leaving unless I take with me what I came for."

"Then you're not leaving," Jesse said. His head leaned forward as if he were disappointed, then he turned around placing his back to his adversary.

"Bad move," Samuel whispered.

Christian nodded, quickly rinsed the shirt in fresh water, then held it to Roni's shoulder again while he looked up to watch the confrontation on the altar.

Minotti wasted no time taking advantage of what seemed to be Jesse's biggest mistake. Suddenly, the roof of the church began to pitch and creak, the sound of splintering wood rang loud off the marble pillars and stained glass windows. A shower of small, sharp, wooden splinters began to fall from the ceiling. They increased in speed until they were dropping as fast as bullets fired from a gun. They fell all around Jesse, but never touched him. Father Larry and Roni, however, were vulnerable and right in Minotti's line of fire.

Christian jumped to cover Roni and took the brunt of the wooden attack into his own body while Diana scurried under the nearest pew. He glanced at Samuel and nodded to reassure him that Diana was safe, then watched as Samuel rushed to protect Father Larry. He picked him up and carried him to the rectory door, but it slammed shut and wouldn't budge. Samuel turned around and looked for somewhere else to take the priest, but saw Minotti laughing at him. Samuel laid Father Larry on the floor against the adjacent wall and used his own body to shelter him. Christian turned his attention to Jesse in case he was able to stop Minotti and buy them time to get out of the church. It took his mind off the pain in his back and hoped it was doing the same for Samuel who looked at him and nodded. They both turned their attention back to the altar.

Jesse closed his eyes and tilted his head forward for a few seconds. Slowly, he lifted his head and arms together toward the dome where the wooden frames of the stained glass windows were breaking apart. A light breeze could be felt throughout the church when Jesse opened his eyes to look up, and the torrential attack stopped.

Christian sat up and looked around to see if everyone else was alright. Diana was already by his side pulling the wooden needles and daggers from his back. "Samuel's next," Christian said. "I'm alright."

Diana nodded and they both went to Samuel's aide to do the same for him. Christian turned to see if the battle was over, but it was not.

Jesse climbed the few stairs to the marble rail. Behind him Minotti began to form a fiery tube encircling Jesse that seemed to hinder his movements as it shrunk around him. But Jesse raised both arms over his head, lowered them straight out at his sides and down through the ring of fire. His arms touched the fire like buckets of water as they sliced through the tube and extinguished the flames. He continued to walk up the stairs while Minotti hurled arrows of flame at him, but each was deflected before they reached their target. They hit various parts of the altar instead, chipping marble and plaster. Two of the wall sconces were destroyed and a ceramic angel was shattered.

Samuel checked Father Larry's pulse, then laid his coat to cover him. "Probably a concussion," he said to Christian.

"He'll live," Diana said. "It's Roni I'm worried about."

Christian turned toward the pews. "I'm going back to her."

"I'm going with you," Diana said.

Christian turned toward her, already on his way to Roni, and saw that both she and Samuel were beside him in no time.

"Any better?" Samuel asked.

Diana cast him a doubtful look, then turned to Christian. "Try putting some water on her lips," she said.

"We have to get her and the priest out of here," Samuel said. "Minotti is tearing the place apart."

Diana frowned. "And take them where?" she asked. "He wouldn't let you out of here with the priest. What makes you think he'll let us leave at all?"

Samuel shook his head, then turned toward the altar. "Oh no," he said.

Christian looked up in time to see one of the fiery spears pierce the huge crucifix that hung from the ceiling.

Jesse turned toward Minotti. "That's enough."

Minotti looked at him, his eyes burning red. "I don't think so," he said. He hurled another fire spear in Jesse's direction, but it went through Jesse's body and hit the statue of the Blessed Mother that stood beside the image of her son near the back of the altar. The noise it made commanded everyone's attention and brought Jesse around full force with danger in his eyes, and fear for Minotti written on his face.

"Oh no," Samuel said.

Minotti's face was suddenly cloaked in fear. He stepped back, his vision glued to something at Jesse's left. "It can't . . . ," he stammered, but seemed unable to finish speaking. His mouthed moved, but nothing came out.

Just then Roni began to cough. Christian lifted her so she could sit against him. "How do you feel?" he asked, rubbing her back.

"My head," she said. "My shoulder, too."

"Look," Samuel said to them.

They looked at Jesse and saw what Minotti was so afraid of. Jesse took a few steps backward. "I can't help you," he said. "This fight belongs to someone much higher now." He turned toward the crucifix and bowed. "I concede this victory to you," he said.

Christian was glued to the scene on the altar. "Do you see it?" he asked, but no one answered him. He didn't care. He stared in awe and watched the eyes in the statue of Jesus that hung on the cross above the altar, flutter, then open wide. His head moved from where it hung on His right side, lifted straight up, and shifted its entire attention on the persona of evil that had cared so little as to inadvertently and irresponsibly attack His mother.

"I don't believe it," Diana said as if to herself.

Jesus was sad. It was unquestionable, so huge was the expression on His face. But His sadness turned to anger as He focused on the form cowering before Him.

"Do you feel it?" Christian whispered to Samuel.

"Yes."

Minotti knew everything in that instant. His entire existence had boiled down to this single moment. Everything he had ever done was done to reach this time when he would face the Great One head on and lose. There was nothing he could do now, but accept his fate.

The eyes of Jesus bore into Minotti as they began to glow a brilliant mix of yellow, orange, and red. In the speed of light, the colors of anger and retribution were sent straight out from the statue in pulsating beams that pierced the core of Gaetano Minotti's purely evil heart.

There was no sound, except the thud when Minotti's body fell to the floor. It lay there for a few seconds, then disintegrated back into the dust from which it had come.

As if on cue, the first rays of the early morning sun shone brilliant through the stained glass windows. The light cast colorful shadows throughout the church while Roni, Christian, Diana, and Samuel sat in speechless awe. They stared at the altar in silence long after the statue of Jesus had returned to normal.

CHAPTER 10

Roni put her hand to her head and moaned. "I think I need a hospital."

"You're right," Christian said. "How do you feel? Can you move?"

"A little," Roni said, pointing at the altar. "But I'm hallucinating. That's never happened to me before."

Christian put his arms around her and smiled. "You're not hallucinating. None of us have ever seen that before."

Roni turned to look at him, then jumped when her shoulder touched the back of the pew.

"Take it easy," Christian said. "You're not out of the woods yet."

"You mean that really happened?" she asked. "The statue really . . ."

Samuel nodded. "It really happened," he said. "Here comes Jesse, ask him yourself."

Jesse approached them and put his hand out to Roni. "That was quite a heroic thing you did for Diana," he said. "It nearly cost you your life."

Roni took his hand, and shrugged. "I wasn't thinking about that."

"I know you weren't," Jesse said. "That makes your action even more special." He squeezed her hand. "Come here. Let's see your shoulder."

Roni stood slowly using the back of the pew to support herself. Her body shook, but she managed to make her way to Jesse. He placed one hand on her shoulder and the other on her forehead. He closed his eyes and whispered to himself. Roni felt an intense warmth go through her and she stopped shaking. When Jesse removed his hands and opened his eyes, Roni looked at her shoulder. The wound and the pain were both gone. She turned to him and smiled. "Thank you," she said.

Jesse smiled back at her, then walked over to Diana.

"Who are you?" she asked him.

"I'm sorry." He put his hand toward her and she took it. "We didn't meet properly, did we? I'm Jesse Nestarius."

"That's not what I meant," she said. "Who are you that you could do what you just did?"

Jesse released her hand and looked at Samuel, then at Christian. "I didn't have a chance to tell her," Christian said.

Jesse nodded, turned back to Diana, and smiled. "I'm an angel."

Diana stood up. "But you're flesh and blood."

"So are you."

"But all three of us together couldn't do to Minotti what you did," she said. "We don't have that kind of power."

"I fought him," Jesse said. "But I didn't destroy him."

Diana looked at the altar and nodded. "You mean . . ."

"You saw it yourself."

Diana nodded, looked toward the altar again, then sat down without saying another word.

"What about Father Larry?" Christian said. "We didn't check on him."

"I did," Jesse said. "He's fine. But he was unconscious during the whole episode. It's best that he doesn't know the details of what happened here tonight."

Samuel flung his arms in the air and looked around. "Look at this place," he said. "How can we not tell him what happened?"

Jesse leaned on the side arm of the pew and looked at each of them. "Larry is a very good friend of mine," he said. "But he doesn't know me as you do."

"You mean he doesn't know you're an angel?" Roni asked him. "How can you keep that from him if he's your friend?"

Jesse looked at her, then put his hand on her shoulder. "It's not part of the plan."

She stared at him, hesitated, then nodded. "Well, where is he?"

"Sleeping," Jesse said. "I carried him to his room. I'll check on him tomorrow. You might all want to do the same."

"Absolutely," Samuel said. "After all, he let us in to use the church and look what we did to it."

"I'm sure he'll care more about all of you being safe," Jesse said. "The church can be repaired. Now go home and get some sleep."

"Wait." Samuel stood up and walked over to Diana. "First, I have something to take care of." He took both her hands and kissed them. He looked into her eyes and took a deep breath. "Diana," he said. "I'm sorry for keeping you and Christian apart all these years. I wasn't willing to share your love. I was selfish. I didn't want to lose you, but in truth I never deserved you." He looked down. "No matter how much I've loved you." He held her hands against his chest. "And still do."

Tears began to flow down Diana's cheeks. She turned to Christian. He nodded once. She looked at Samuel, then pulled her hands from him and gave him an angry look. "What you cost us can never be replaced."

"I know," he said.

"I chose immortality to be with you."

"I know."

Diana looked away and was silent.

"I'm not asking you to forgive me," Samuel said. "I don't hold a false hope that it's even possible. I'm just deeply sorry for what I've done."

Christian stood up and went to Samuel's side. "Wait a minute," he said. "Diana knows I made you promise not to tell her about me."

Samuel hung his head. "It doesn't matter."

"Sure it does," Christian said. "I started the whole thing." He looked at Diana, but she remained silent.

Jesse stepped between Christian and Samuel. "Listen to me," he said. "What all of you need to think about is this. Although we may learn from our mistakes and plan ahead, the bottom line is that the past does not exist. Neither does the future. The only truth is here and now."

Diana cast him an angry look. "What I feel in my heart is real and it hurts because of the past."

"No," Jesse said. "Your past with Samuel was happy. The hurt started a few days ago."

"And now I have it," she said. "I feel the lost time I could have had with Christian. I have a thousand questions running through my head."

"And they will all be answered in due time."

"I'm not sure I want any more time." Diana looked down at her lap. "I haven't hurt like this since I heard Christian was dead."

"But I wasn't," Christian said.

Diana looked at him and frowned. "So how long will it be until I find out that this secret isn't true like your death wasn't true?"

Jesse held his arms away from his body, his palms toward them. "There are truths and there are lies," he said. "Right now you can see for yourself what is true."

Diana looked at Christian and sighed. "But I can never trust Samuel again," she said. "That's what hurts."

Christian put his hand on Samuel's shoulder. "I can trust him."

"He didn't hurt you," Diana said.

"Hold on there." Christian leaned toward her, one hand on the back of her pew, the other on the pew in front of her. "It was both you and I who were separated," he said. "I've missed you for nearly six hundred years. I've been sick over leaving the whole family. Besides that, you were there when Roni came home the other night. Do you think that didn't hurt too?"

Diana stared at him, so angry she seemed ready to attack.

"You know," Roni said from where she sat behind Diana. "I've listened to all of you. I know how you all must feel." She put a hand on Diana's shoulder. "I agree with Jesse, Diana. I heard you play mediator between Christian and Samuel the other night. Christian told me how you cradled Samuel on our front porch. Samuel made a huge error in judgement and it was for terrible reasons. But just like you have learned what can happen when you throw tantrums and play games disappearing, he has learned how damaging what he did can be." Roni stood up, walked to Christian, then faced Diana directly. "Besides everything that has happened, Diana, you and Samuel are still in love. Nothing is going to change that."

"I can't trust him," Diana said. She looked directly at Samuel. He turned and started to walk down the center aisle toward the door.

Roni stepped into Diana's line of vision and smiled. "Do you love him enough to try?"

Diana stared at her as if she didn't understand a word she said. She wiped her eyes and looked away.

"He's leaving," Roni said.

Diana looked at her again and shrugged.

"It's your choice." Roni went to Christian and put her arms around him. "Let's go home," she said. "Enough is enough."

Diana watched them, then jumped up, and turned around. "Samuel, wait." She stepped out of the pew and ran toward him. "I'll try," she said. "I'll try to trust you. I'll do my best."

Samuel swept her up in his arms and spun her around. "I'm sorry, I'm sorry," he said over and over. "There are no more secrets. I promise. I love you." He kissed her forehead, her nose, then her lips, and they embraced in the center aisle of the church.

Jesse nudged Roni. "Nice job."

Roni looked at him, her head tilted. "I only said what was true."

He winked at her, then smiled. "Exactly."

CHAPTER 11

December 20, 1997

Roni entered the kitchen, poured herself a cup of tea, then sat down at the table across from Diana. "Christmas is only a few days away," she said. "So much has happened I haven't even thought about it."

Diana was petting one of the cats. "Me neither." She looked at Roni. "I'm glad Father Larry went to the hospital. That really bothered me."

"What do you mean?"

"I only saw him briefly when all that chaos was going on in the church," she said. "I was with you the whole time because of. . ."

Roni nodded. "Your brother. I know."

Diana hesitated while she stroked the cat. "Father Larry had a concussion, so I'm glad he was checked out."

"Me too," Roni said. "But I don't understand why Jesse didn't heal him. He fixed my shoulder. It seems to me he should've taken care of Father Larry first."

Diana felt her stomach quiver, but she kept her composure. Christian made her swear not to tell Roni why Jesse healed her. Another secret. But she promised. "Father Larry wasn't going to die," she said.

Roni tilted her head and frowned.

"You were going to die, Roni." At least that part was true.

Roni nodded and tapped her forefinger on the table. "Christian told me the same thing," she said. "I guess I was so out of it, I had no idea. If I had died, I never would've known."

"Oh, you'd have known," Diana said. "You just would not have seen it coming."

Roni turned to look out the back window at the woods. "Can I ask you something kind of personal?"

"Sure." Diana snuggled the fluffy, white cat up under her chin.

"Did you really want to be changed?"

Diana looked at her and smiled. "Yes," she said. "I really did."

"Why?"

"Because I loved Samuel so much I thought it was worth preserving for all time," Diana said. "Love is a good thing, right?"

"Sure it is," Roni said. "But what about the way you were raised and your family's religious beliefs?"

Diana focused all her attention on the cat for a few seconds, then she put her down, and looked at Roni. "Times were different when I was mortal," she said. "People still believed in all kinds of things. What I did wouldn't have been looked at the same way it would be today if people knew we exist. But if I were in the same position today as I was in back then my decision wouldn't change. I know that for sure."

"Didn't you feel guilty?" Roni asked. "Weren't you afraid you'd be punished somehow later on?"

Diana raised her eyebrows and smiled. "Why would I?" she said. "It wasn't a bad thing that I did." She saw Roni twitch, but resolved to stay out of her mind. "Christian told me how you helped him get reacquainted with God."

Roni turned and nodded.

"Then you know how important love is," Diana said. "How often have you seen bumper stickers and posters that say 'God Is Love'? Well, if that's true, then how can it be wrong to make Him stronger by preserving the love around us?"

Roni tapped her fingers on the table, then turned to face Diana. "I guess I can't argue with that logic. But was that really what you thought when it happened or did you decide on that later?"

Diana leaned forward with her elbows on the table. "Don't think my transformation happened in a moment of passion or without any thought," she said. "I thought about it for a long time. Sam and I talked about it quite a bit. But he never tried to talk me in or out if it. The decision was all mine."

"But what about your theory on preserving the love?" Roni asked.

"I felt that way long before I made the decision to be immortal," she said. "But honestly, I didn't understand how important it was until after my change was complete."

Roni was quiet.

"Now," Diana said. "I have a personal question I'd like to ask you."

"That's fair," Roni said. "Shoot."

Diana patted the table with her hands, then looked at Roni. "Why don't you want to be changed?"

"I think that's fairly obvious," Roni said.

"Not to me," Diana said. "Our blood would make you immortal. You'd never be sick."

"I know," Roni said. "To me, though, that's too much like cheating when there are so many sick people wishing for a miracle they'll never get."

"Some do, though," Diana said. "And some day, you might."

"I know." Roni nodded. "But if that should ever arise and God intended for me to see a miracle cure, then He'd take care of it Himself and grant it to me."

She couldn't tell her. She promised. "Maybe, he already has," Diana smiled. "Maybe, that's why He sent Christian to you in the first place."

Roni sat back in her chair and took a deep breath. "I suppose it could be possible, but I think God would find a way to let me know it was all right."

"Maybe not," Diana said. "Maybe, He'd expect a decision from you."

Roni smiled. "My decision has been to remain as I am."

If you only knew, Diana thought. "I don't think you've made a decision at all," she said. "I think you're still weighing both sides of it."

Roni smiled. "OK," she said. "I suppose I do weigh the pros and cons occasionally. But I always come back to the same thing."

"Why do you think that is?" Diana asked.

"Because I'm afraid to say what I'd really like to do," Roni said. "I need God, Himself, to come down here and tell me it's all right."

"We both know He's not going to do that," Diana said.

Roni nodded. "So, there's my problem."

Diana studied Roni's face a moment, then relaxed in her chair. "The bottom line is whether or not you have a clear conscience no matter what you do," Diana said. "If you can look yourself in the eye and know you did the right thing regardless of anything else, then God will see it, too."

"Come on, Di," Roni said. "God gave us certain rules, you know."

"I know," Diana said. "But one of the things he told us is that we all have to answer for our actions eventually. If you can do that with a clear conscience and an honest heart, I'm sure God is OK with it."

"What about the insane or the sick minded murderers?" Roni asked. "Many of them have no problem at all with what they've done, but I don't see how God can accept their clear consciences."

"I don't think he does, Roni," Diana said. "I think he looks at them in a different light altogether."

"What do you mean?"

"I don't think there are many murderers out there who have honest hearts to begin with," Diana said. "And the ones who do are insane so I think we're talking about a single group of people when you really look at it. And I don't see how God could hold them responsible for their actions at all when they didn't have a reference point to begin with. They're insane, for heaven's sake."

Roni started to laugh. "So, what's your point?"

Diana shook her head. "No, really, Roni. Do you see what I mean?"

"I do see what you mean," Roni said. "But it doesn't change my mind."

Diana shrugged. "It's your choice." She wanted to tell her how close she came to joining the immortal when Christian sucked the poison out of her body, but she couldn't. She wanted to tell her the damage the poison may have already done, but she didn't. "Maybe you can help me understand something else."

"What's that?"

"Why do you think Minotti was so hell bent on owning me?"

Roni shook her head. "I'm not sure, but what you said a little bit ago does give me some idea."

"Tell me," Diana said. "I really need to know."

"Well," Roni said. "Consider someone like Minotti who was so terrible and nasty. I'm certain his vampirism had nothing to do with it. Not after knowing you, Christian, and Samuel. I think Minotti was influenced by evil itself somewhere along the line. The same thing has happened to countless mortals."

"So?"

"The way I see it," Roni said. "is that, if Minotti truly was evil personified, then he would see you as one helluva threat to his existence."

"How do you mean?"

Roni leaned forward and looked directly into Diana's eyes. "If you really have strengthened God by preserving a genuine love the way you have, then what would happen if more people lived for hundreds of years preserving their own experiences of pure love? How much stronger does God need to be than He is right now?"

Diana looked dazed for a moment. "That's an incredible idea. We'd be strong enough to get rid of evil completely. Just imagine what this world would be like."

"Exactly," Roni said. "I heard once that our souls are actually parts of God that He gives us when we're born. That makes every one of us who is good a part of God. Now, take all the truly good people in the world, put them together and you have God right there before your very eyes. So, the more of these people there are, the stronger God is on earth."

"But that makes the opposite true of people like Minotti," Diana said.

Roni nodded. "Yeah. And when you have evil ones killing good ones and turning more and more people to their side, then the evil forces seem to be winning. But take someone who is good, pure, and immortal and you see how evil can't win because it can never destroy what's immortal."

Diana perked up. "Wow," she said. "That's the scariest thing I think I've ever heard. When you look at it that way you almost have to change over."

Roni stared at her, speechless.

"Am I right?" Diana asked.

Roni slowly nodded.

"Well, then," Diana said. "Now, what do you think is the right thing for you to do?"

Roni shrugged her shoulders heavily and shook her head. "I don't know," she said. "I really don't know. I've always thought of the transformation itself as a form of suicide and a way to cheat my way out of life's trials and tests. Now I have to rethink my whole outlook on everything."

Diana reached across the table and put her hand on Roni's arm. "Whatever you decide will be what's right."

Roni nodded. At that moment Christian and Samuel materialized before them.

"How's Jesse?" Roni asked.

Christian bent down to kiss her. "He's fine just as we thought," he said, "but he appreciated your concern." He turned toward Diana and Samuel. "So, how about Christmas? Are you two planning to stay with us till January?"

"We talked about it," Samuel said. "I think we need time to relax together and put some things behind us."

"I agree with that," Diana said.

Samuel looked at her. "Christian and I discussed the idea of buying a house around here," he said. "That way we could be closer to each other for longer periods of time without having to impose on their hospitality."

"That's a terrific idea!" Diana said. She jumped up and hugged Samuel. "I'd love that! Let's do it!"

"When do you want to start looking?" Roni asked.

"Right now," Diana said. "Right now. Let's go get a newspaper. Oh, I'm so excited about this!"

"That's pretty obvious," Christian teased. He went to get Roni's coat. "Let's go out for a little while and celebrate the idea. We can start looking tomorrow."

"No," Diana said, pouting. "Tonight! I want to start tonight."

"Alright," Samuel said. "We'll get you a newspaper first. Then we're going out to celebrate."

"Deal!" Diana agreed. She looked at Christian.

Does she know? he asked her.

Diana continued to smile, but she winked at him. *She never will, unless you tell her.* Roni rubbed her shoulder just then. Diana and Christian looked at each other. *I think you should,* Diana thought to Christian.

He looked at her and nodded. *Soon.*

EPILOGUE

January 2, 1998

Christian sat with Roni on the living room floor by a warm, winter fire he had started an hour earlier. He was bothered by his conversation with Diana just before she and Samuel left for France. His sister was right, of course. Roni should know the truths of what happened at the church when she was poisoned by Minotti, then healed by Jesse. In his heart, Christian wanted her to know, but he was afraid of how she'd react. Diana told him repeatedly not to start keeping secrets like Samuel had done in case Roni needed his help, but he didn't know how to explain it without her taking it wrong. Still he had to try.

"This was a wonderful holiday," Roni said, laying her head on his shoulder.

Christian heard her, but his mind was so filled with thoughts of what Minotti's poison might still do to her that he didn't answer.

She sat up and looked at him, her eyes squinted in question. "What's the matter? You're so quiet this evening. Is something wrong?"

Christian shook his head, knowing he was already lying.

"Is it your sister already?" she asked. "They're coming back in a few weeks to close the deal on the house in Westwood. You'll be able to visit for a long time once they move in."

Christian looked at her, studied her face, then looked away. "It's not that."

Roni turned around and crossed her legs in front of her, then leaned forward. "I knew something was wrong. Tell me."

He was moved by the concern in her voice. "Not really wrong," he said. "There are just some things I felt should be explained to you about what happened in the church a few weeks ago."

"Like what?" Roni asked. "I was there. I was hurt, now I'm better. What is there to be upset about? What else happened?"

Christian turned to her and took her hands in his. He looked in her eyes and stared deep for a few seconds. *Here goes,* he thought. "That poison you got from Minotti."

Roni smiled. "What about it? It's all gone."

Christian shook his head and looked down. "We don't know that for sure. Jesse didn't even know what it was, exactly."

Roni looked at him as if she had just been hit by a rock, her lower lip trembled. "He healed me. How could he not know what it was?"

Christian looked up at her and tried to figure out how to say this in just the right way. "He healed you according to what he knew," Christian told her. "He knew you were bleeding from your shoulder and he knew you were in pain. He did not know what the poison may have done to you by that time. He did what he could."

Roni looked to the side, tears had begun to well up in her eyes. "So what are you telling me? I'm going to die from something we don't know what it is?"

"No," Christian said, reaching to touch her cheek. He smiled. "I'm telling you what I think you should know. That's all. Diana is the one who told me not to start keeping secrets from you in case something should come of all this. Jesse agreed. So I'm doing what is right." He took a deep breath and caressed her chin. He couldn't bare to see the fear in her eyes. "I expect everything to be fine, but if something were to happen in the future, I'd want you to come to me right away." How could he tell her the rest? "If there is a complication from all that has happened, no doctor will be able to save you." He hesitated, then turned her face to him. "But I could."

The look in her eyes told him she understood what he was saying, but it also gave away her anger. "That's what you want," she said. "Go ahead. Do it now and get it over with." She pulled away from him, her eyes flashing daggers that could've killed him if she'd been immortal. "I'm tired of talking about it. You've wanted me to make the change since we met. Your sister even tried to talk to me about it. Was that for you?"

Her words sent the pain her eyes had only threatened. Christian sat back, stung by her reaction. This was exactly what he didn't want to happen. "No," he said. "That was for you."

Roni stuck her neck out toward him. "Go ahead, Christian."

The daggers pierced his heart. He reached over and took her hand. He kissed it, shook his head, then stood up. "No. I don't want to change you. If I did, it would've happened in the church, but I respect your wishes too much for that. I just want you to know I'm here for you if it ever comes to that, and if you decide it's what you want."

Roni stared at him, her face still masked with anger. Her mouth hung open as if she were about to say something, then she closed it in slow motion. Her whole body seemed heavy as it relaxed in place. "I'm sorry."

"Don't be." Christian turned around and headed for the back door. "I'm going for a walk. Do you want to come? It looks like a beautiful night."

Roni stood up slow, pushing herself with her hands. She looked at him as if she hadn't wanted him to see her effort, but he did. "I'll get my coat," she said.

Christian watched her walk to the closet. When she came back, he put his arm around her. "Happy New Year, again," he said, kissing her forehead.

She looked at him and smiled. "Happy New Year, again, Christian."